Johann David Wyss

Willis the Pilot

A Sequel to The Swiss Family Robinson...

Johann David Wyss

Willis the Pilot
A Sequel to The Swiss Family Robinson...

ISBN/EAN: 9783337023317

Printed in Europe, USA, Canada, Australia, Japan

Cover: Foto ©Andreas Hilbeck / pixelio.de

More available books at **www.hansebooks.com**

WILLIS THE PILOT,

A Sequel to the Swiss Family Robinson;

OR,

ADVENTURES OF AN EMIGRANT FAMILY

WRECKED ON AN UNKNOWN COAST OF THE PACIFIC OCEAN.

INTERSPERSED WITH

TALES, INCIDENTS OF TRAVEL, AND ILLUSTRATIONS OF NATURAL HISTORY.

BOSTON:
LEE AND SHEPARD.
SUCCESSORS TO
PHILLIPS, SAMPSON AND COMPANY.

PREFACE.

The love of adventure that characterises the youth of the present day, and the growing tendency of the surplus European population to seek abroad the comforts that are often denied at home, gives absorbing interest to the narratives of old colonists and settlers in the wonderful regions of the New World. Accordingly, the work known as the *Swiss Family Robinson* has long enjoyed a well-merited popularity, and has been perused by a multitude of readers, young and old, with profit as well as pleasure.

A Swiss clergyman resolved to better his fortune by emigration. In furtherance of this resolution, he embarked with his wife and four sons — the latter ranging from eight to fifteen years of age — for one of the newly-discovered islands in the Pacific Ocean. As far as the coast of New Guinea the voyage had been favorable, but here a violent storm arose, which drove the ill-fated vessel out of its course, and finally cast it a wreck upon an unknown coast. The family succeeded in extricating themselves from the stranded ship, and landed safely on shore; but the remaining passengers and crew all perished. For many years these six individuals struggled alone against a variety of trials and privations, till at length another storm brought the English despatch-boat *Nelson* within reach of their signals. Such is a brief outline of the events recorded in the *Swiss Family Robinson.*

The present volume is virtually a continuation of this narrative. The careers of the four sons — Frank, Ernest, Fritz, and Jack — are taken up where the preceding chronicler left them off. The subsequent adventures of these four young men, by flood and field, are faithfully detailed. With these particulars are mingled the experiences of another interesting family that afterwards became dwellers in the same territory; as are also the sayings and doings of a weather-beaten sailor — Willis the Pilot.

The scene is laid chiefly in the South Seas, and the narrative illustrates the geography and ethnology of that section of the Far-West. The difficulties, dangers, and hardships to be encountered in founding a new colony are truthfully set forth, whilst it is shown how readily these are overcome by perseverance and intelligent labor. It will be seen that a liberal education has its uses, even under circumstances the least likely to foster the social amenities, and that, too, not only as regards the mental well-being of its possessors, but also as regards augmenting their material comforts.

In the *Swiss Family Robinson* the resources of Natural History have been largely, and perhaps somewhat freely, drawn upon. This branch of knowledge has, therefore, been left throughout the present volume comparatively untouched. Nevertheless, as it is the aim of the narrator to combine instruction with amusement, the more elementary phenomena of the Physical Sciences have been blended with the current of the story — thus garnishing, as it were, the dry, hard facts of Owen, Liebig, and Arago, with the more attractive groupings of life and action.

The reader has, consequently, in hand a *mélange* of the useful and agreeable — a little for the grave and a little for the gay — so that, should our endeavors to impart instruction prove unavailing, *en revanche* we may, perhaps, be more successful in our efforts to amuse.

1*

CONTENTS.

CHAPTER VII.

CHAPTER VIII.

CHAPTER IX.

CHAPTER X.

CHAPTER XI.

CHAPTER XII.

CHAPTER XIII.

CHAPTER XIV.

CHAPTER XV.

CHAPTER XVI.

CHAPTER XVII.

CHAPTER XVIII.

CHAPTER XXIV.

CHAPTER XXV.

CHAPTER XXVI.

CHAPTER XXVII.

CHAPTER XXVIII.

WILLIS THE PILOT.

CHAPTER I.

THE COLONY — REFLECTIONS ON THE PAST — IDEAS OF WILLIS
THE PILOT — SOPHIA WOLSTON.

THE early adventures of the Swiss family, who were wrecked on an unknown coast in the Pacific Ocean, have already been given to the world. There are, however, many interesting details in their subsequent career which have not been made public. These, and the conversations with which they enlivened the long, dreary days of the rainy season, we are now about to lay before our readers.

Becker, his wife, and their four sons had been fifteen years on this uninhabited coast, when a storm drove the English despatch sloop *Nelson* to the same spot. Before this event occurred, the family had cleared and enclosed a large extent of country; but, whether the territory was part of an island or part of a continent, they had not yet ascertained. The land was naturally fertile ; and, amongst other things that had been obtained from the wreck of their ship, were sundry packages of European seeds : the produce of these, together with that of two or three heads of cattle they had likewise rescued from the wreck, supplied them abundantly with the necessaries of life. They had erected dwellings here and there, but chiefly lived in a cave near the shore, over the entrance to which they had built a sort of gallery. This structure, conjointly with the cave, formed a commodious habitation, to which they had given the name of *Rockhouse*. In the vicinity, a stream flowed tranquilly into the sea ; this stream they were accustomed to call *Jackal River*, because, a few days after their landing, they had encountered some of these animals on its banks. Fronting Rockhouse the coast curved inwards, the headlands on either side enclosing a portion of the ocean; to this inlet they had given the name of *Safety Bay*, because it was here they first felt themselves secure after having escaped the dangers of the storm. In the centre of the bay there was a small island which they called *Shark's Island*, to commemorate the capture of one of those monsters of the deep. Safety Bay, had, a second time, acquired a legitimate title to its name, for in it Providence had brought the *Nelson* safely to anchor.

By unwearying perseverance, indefatigable industry, and an untiring reliance on the goodness of God, Becker and his family had surrounded themselves with abundance. There was only one thing left for them to desire, and that was the means of communicating with their kindred; and now this one wish of their hearts was gratified by the unexpected appearance of the *Nelson* on their shore. The fifteen years of exile they had so patiently endured was at once forgotten. Every bosom was filled with boundless joy; so true it is, that man only requires a ray of sunshine to change his most poignant griefs into smiles and gladness.

The first impressions of their deliverance awakened in the minds of the young people a flood of projects. The mute whisperings that murmured within them had divulged to their understandings that they were created for a wider sphere than that in which they had hitherto been confined. Europe and its wonders — society, with its endearing interchanges of affection — that vast panorama of the arts and of civilization, of the trivial and the sublime, of the beautiful and terrible, that is called the world — came vividly into their thoughts. They felt as a man would feel when dazzled all at once by a spectacle, the splendor of which the eyes and the mind can only withstand by degrees. They had spelt life in the horn-book of true and simple nature — they were now about to read it fluently in the gilded volume of a nature false and vitiated, perhaps to regret their former tranquil ignorance.

Becker himself had, for an instant, given way to the general enthusiasm, but reflection soon regained her sway;

he asked himself whether he had solid reasons for wishing to return to Europe, whether it would be advisable to relinquish a certain livelihood, and abandon a spot that God appeared to bless beyond all others, to run after the doubtful advantages of civilized society.

His wife desired nothing better than to end her days there, under the beautiful sky, where, from the bosom of the tempest, they had been guided by the merciful will of Him who is the source of all things. Still the solitude frightened her for her children. "Might it not," she asked herself, "be egotism to imprison their young lives in the narrow limits of maternal affection?" It occurred to her that the dangers to which they were constantly exposed might remove them from her; to-day this one, to-morrow another; what, then, would be her own desolation, when there remained to her no bosom on which to rest her head — no heart to beat in unison with her own — no kindly hand to grasp — and no friendly voice to pray at her pillow, when she was called away in her turn!

At length, after mature deliberation, it was resolved that Becker himself, his wife, Fritz and Jack, two of their sons, should remain where they were, whilst the two other young men should return to Europe with a cargo of cochineal, pearls, coral, nutmegs, and other articles that the country produced of value in a commercial point of view. It was, however, understood that one of the two should return again as soon as possible, and bring back with him any of his countrymen who might be induced to become settlers in this land of promise, Becker hoping, by this means, to found a new colony which might afterwards flourish under the name of *New Switzerland.* The mission to Europe was formally confided to Frank and Ernest, the two most sedate of the family.

Besides the captain and crew, there was on board the ship now riding at anchor in the bay a passenger, named Wolston, with his wife and two daughters. This gentle-man was on his way to join his son at the Cape of Good Hope, but had been taken seriously ill previous to the *Nelson's* arrival on the coast. He and his family were invited on shore by Becker, and had taken up their quarters at Rockhouse. Wolston was an engineer by profession, but his wife belonged to a highly aristocratic family of the West of England; she had been brought up in a state of ease and refinement, was possessed of all the accomplishments required in fashionable society, but she was at the same time gifted with strong good sense, and could readily accommodate herself to the circumstances in which she was now placed. Her two daughters, Sophia the youngest, a lively child of thirteen, and Mary the eldest, a demure girl of sixteen, had been likewise carefully, but somewhat elaborately, educated. Attracted no less by the hearty and warm reception of the Swiss family, than determined by the state of his health and the pure air of the country, Wolston resolved to await there the return of the sloop, the official destination of which was the Cape of Good Hope, where it had to land despatches from Sidney.

Captain Littlestone, of H.B.M.'s sloop *Nelson*, had kindly consented to all these arrangements; he agreed to convey Ernest and Frank Becker and their cargo to the Cape, to aid them there with his experience, and, finally, to recommend them to some trustworthy correspondents he had at Liverpool. He likewise promised to bring back young Wolston with him on his return voyage.

Everything being prepared, the departure was fixed for the next day: the sloop, with the blue Peter at the fore, was ready, as soon as the anchor was weighed, to continue her voyage. The cargo had been stowed under hatches. Becker had just given the farewell dinner to Captain Littlestone and Lieutenant Dunsley, his second in command. These two gentlemen had discreetly taken their leave, not to interrupt by their presence the final embraces of the family, the ties of which, after so many long years of labor and hardship, were for the first time to be broken asunder.

During the voyage, Wolston had formed an intimacy with the boatswain of the *Nelson*, named Willis, and he, on his side, held Wolston and his family in high esteem. Willis was likewise a great favorite with his captain — they had served in the same ship together when boys;

Willis was known to be a first-rate seaman; so great, indeed, was his skill in steering amongst reefs and shoals, that he was familiarly styled the " Pilot," by which cognomen he was better known on board than any other. At the particular request of Wolston, who had some communications to make to him respecting his son, Willis remained on shore, the captain promising to send his gig for him and his two passengers the following morning.

Whilst Wolston was busy charging the pilot with a multitude of messages for his son, Mrs. Becker was invoking the blessings of Heaven upon the heads of her two boys; praying that the hour might be deferred that was to separate her from these idols of her soul. Becker himself, upon whom his position, as head of the family, imposed the obligation of exhibiting, at least outwardly, more courage, instilled into their minds such principles of truth and rules of conduct as the solemnity of the moment was calculated to engrave on their hearts.

The dial now marked three o'clock, tropical time. Willis, wiping, with the cuff of his jacket, a drop that trickled from the corner of his eye, laid hold of his sealskin sou'-wester as a signal of immediate departure. Ernest and Frank were bending their heads to receive the parting benediction of their parents, when suddenly a fierce torrent of wind shock the gallery of Rockhouse to its foundation, and uprooted some of the bamboo columns by which it was supported.

" Only a squall," said Willis quietly.

" A squall!" exclaimed Becker, "what do you call a hurricane then?"

" Oh, a hurricane, I mean a downright reefer, all square and close-hauled, that is a very different affair; but, after all, this begins to look very like the real article.".

Now came a succession of gusts, each succeeding one more powerful than its predecessor, till every beam of the gallery bent and quivered; dense copper-colored clouds appeared in the atmosphere, rolling against each other, and disengaging by their shock, the thunder and lightnings. Then fell, not the slender needles of water we call rain, but veritable floods, that were to our heaviest

European showers what the cataracts of the Rhine, at Staubach, or the falls of Niagara, are to the gushings of a sylvan rivulet. In a few minutes the Jackal river had converted the valley into a lake, in which the plantations and buildings appeared to be afloat, and rendering egress from Rockhouse nearly impossible.

However much of a colorist Willis might be, he could not have painted a storm with the eloquence of the elements that had cut short his observation.

" You will not attempt to embark in weather like this?" inquired Mrs. Becker anxiously.

" My duty it is to be on board," replied the Pilot.

" The craft that ventures to take you there will get swamped twenty times on the way," observed Becker.

" The worst of it is, the wind is from the east, and evidently carries waterspouts with it. These waterspouts strike a ship without the slightest warning, play amongst the rigging, whirl the sails about like feathers — sometimes carry them off bodily, or, if they do not do that, tear them to shreds and shiver the masts. In either case, the consequences are disagreeable."

" A reason for you to be thankful you are safe on shore with us!" remarked Mrs. Wolston.

" It is all very well for you, Mrs. Wolston, and you, Mrs. Becker, to talk in that way ; your business in life is that of wives and mothers. But what will the Lords of the Admiralty say, when they hear that the sloop *Nelson* was wrecked whilst Master Willis, the boatswain, was skulking on shore like a land-rat ? "

" Oh, they would only say there was one useful man more, and a victim the less," replied Fritz.

" Why, not exactly, Master Fritz ; they would say that Willis was a poltroon or a deserter, whichever he likes ; they would very likely condemn him to the yard-arm by default, and carry out the operation when they get hold of him. But I will not endanger any one else ; all I want is the use of your canoe."

" What ! brave this storm in a wretched seal-skin cockle-shell like that ? "

" Would it not be offending Providence," hazarded

Mary Wolston, "for one of God's creatures to abandon himself to certain death?"

"It would, indeed," added Mrs. Wolston; "true courage consists in facing danger when it is inevitable, but not in uselessly imperiling one's life; there stops courage, and temerity begins."

"If it is not pride or folly. I do not mean that with reference to you, Willis," hastily added Wolston; "I know that you are open as day, and that all your impulses arise from the heart."

"That is all very fine — but I must act; let me have the canoe. I want the canoe: that is my idea."

"Having lived fifteen years cut off from society," gravely observed Becker, "it may be that I have forgotten some of the laws it imposes; nevertheless, I declare upon my honor and conscience —— "

"Let me have the canoe, otherwise I must swim to the ship."

"I declare," continued Becker, "that Willis exaggerates the requirements of his duty. There are stronger forces to which the human will must yield. It is one thing to desert one's post in the hour of danger, and another to have come on shore at the express desire of a superior officer, when the weather was fine, and nothing presaged a storm."

"If there is danger," continued the obstinate sailor, whom the united strength of the four men could scarcely restrain, "I ought to share it; that is my duty and I must."

"But," said Wolston, "all the boatswains and pilots in the world can do nothing against hurricanes and water-spouts; their duty consists in steering the ship clear of reefs and quicksands, and not in fighting with the elements."

"There is one thing you forget, Mr. Wolston."

"And what is that, Willis?"

"It is to be side by side with your comrades in the hour of calamity, to aid them if you can, and to perish with them if such be the will of Fate. At this moment, poor Littlestone may be on the point of taking up his winter quarters in the body of a shark.   But there, if the sloop is lost while I am here on shore, I will not survive her; all that you can say or do will not prevent me doing myself justice."

At this moment Jack, who had disappeared during this discussion, unobserved, came in saturated to the skin with water, and in a state difficult to describe.   Like the boots of Panurge, his feet were floating in the water that flowed from the rim of his cap.

"What is this?" exclaimed his mother.   "You wilful boy, may I ask where, in all the world, you have been?"

"I have just come from the bay.   O father and mother! O Mr. and Mrs. Wolston!   O Master Willis! if you had only seen!   The sea is furious; sometimes the waves rise to the skies and mingle with the clouds, so that it is impossible to say where the one begins and the other ends. It is frightful, but it is magnificent!"

"And the sloop?" demanded Willis.

"She is not to be seen; she is no longer at anchor in the bay."

"Gone to the open sea, to avoid being driven ashore," said Wolston.   "Captain Littlestone is not the man to remain in a perilous position whilst there remained a means of escape; besides, nothing that science, united with courage and presence of mind, could do, would have been neglected by him to save his ship."

"In addition to which," observed Becker, "if he had found himself in positive danger, he would have fired a gun; and in that case, though we are not pilots, every one of us would have hastened to his assistance."

"You see, Willis," said Mrs. Wolston, "God comes to ease your mind; were we to allow you to go to the sloop now, the thing is simply impossible."

"I have my own idea about that," insisted Willis, whilst he kept beating a tatoo on the isinglass window panes.

Whilst thus chafing like a caged lion, Wolston's youngest daughter went towards him, and gently putting her hand in his, said, "Sweetheart" (for so she had been accustomed to address him), "do you remember when, during the voyage, you used to look at me very closely, and that one evening I went boldly up to you and asked you why you did so?"

"Yes, Miss Sophia, I recollect."

"Do you remember the answer you gave me?"

"Yes, I told you that I had left in England, on her mother's bosom, a little girl who would now be about your own age, and that I could not observe the wind play amongst the curls of your fair hair without thinking of her, and that it sometimes made my breast swell like the mizen-top-sail before the breeze."

"Yes, and when I promised to keep out of your sight, not to reawaken your grief, you told me it was a kind of grief that did you more good than harm, and that the more it made you grieve, the happier you would be."

"All true:" replied the sailor, whose excitement was melting away before the soft tones of the child like hoar frost in the sunshine.

"Then I promised to come and talk to you about your Susan every day; and did I not keep my word?"

"Certainly, Miss Sophia; and it is only bare justice to say that you gracefully yielded to all my fatherly whims, and even went so far as to wear a brown dress oftener than another, because I said that my little Susan wore that color the last time I kissed her."

"Oh, but that is a secret, Willis."

"Yes, but I am going to tell all our secrets — that is an idea of mine. You then went and learned Susan's mother's favorite song, with which you would sometimes sing me to sleep, like a great baby that I am, and make me fancy that I was surrounded by my wife and daughter, and was comfortably smoking my pipe in my own cottage, with a glass of grog at my elbow."

Willis said this so earnestly, that the smile called forth by the oddness of the remark scarcely dared to show itself on the lips of the listeners.

"Very well," resumed the little damsel, "if you are not more reasonable, and if you keep talking of throwing your life away, I will never again place my hand in yours as now; I shall not love you any more, and shall find means of letting Susan's mother know that you went away and killed yourself, and **made** her a widow."

Men **can** only speak coldly and appeal **to** reason—logic is their panacea in argument. Women alone possess those inspirations, those simple words without emphasis, that find their way directly to the heart, and for which purpose **God** has doubtless **endowed** them with those soft, mild **tones,** whose melodies **cause** our most cherished resolutions **to** vanish in the air; like those massive stone gates we **have** seen **in** some of the old castles in Germany, that resist **the** most powerful effort to push them open, but which a spring of the simplest construction causes to move gently on their formidable hinges.

Willis was silent; **but** no openly-expressed submission could have **been more eloquent** than this mute **acqui-**escence.

In the meantime the tempest raged with increased fury, the winds howled, and the water splashed; it appeared **at** each shock as if the elements had reached the utmost limit of **the** terrific; that the sea, as the poet says, had lashed itself **into** exhaustion! But, anon, there came another outburst more **terrible** still, to declare that, in his **anger as** in his blessings, the All-Powerful has no other limit **than** the infinite.

"If **it is not in** the power **of human** beings to aid the crew **of the** *Nelson*," said Mrs. Becker kneeling, "there are other means more efficacious which **we** are guilty **in** not having sought before."

Every one followed this example, and it was a touching scene to behold the rough sailor yield submissively to the gentle violence of the child's hand, and bend his bronzed and swarthy visage humbly beside her cherub head.

CHAPTER II.

THE storm continued to rage without intermission for
three entire days. During this interval, not only was it
impossible to send the canoe or pinnace to sea, but even
to venture a step beyond the threshold, so completely had
the tempest broken up the burning soil, the thirst of which
the great Disposer of all things had proportioned to the
deluges that were destined to assuage it.

All had at length yielded to bodily fatigue and mental
anxiety, for the seeming eternity of these three days and
three nights had been passed in prayer, and in the most
fearful apprehensions as to the fate of the *Nelson* and her
crew.

Nothing in the horizon as yet indicated that the
thunders were tired of roaring, the clouds of rending
themselves asunder, the winds of howling, or the waves
of frantically beating on the cliffs.

Towards evening the ladies had retired to the sick-room
with a view of seeking some repose. Becker, Willis, and
the young men bivouacked in the hall, where some mattresses and bear-skins had been laid down. Here it was
arranged that, for the common safety, each during the
night should watch in turn. But about two in the morning, Ernest had no sooner relieved Fritz than, fatigue
overcoming his sense of duty, the poor fellow fell comfortably asleep, and he was soon perfectly unconscious of
all that was passing around him.

Becker awoke first — it was broad daylight. " Where
is Willis ? " he cried, on getting up.

"Holloa!" exclaimed Fritz, running **towards** the magazine, "the canoe has disappeared!"

In an instant all were on their feet.

"Some **one of you** has fallen asleep then," said Becker to his children; "for when the pilot watched **I** watched with him, and never lost sight of him for a moment."

"I am the culprit," said Ernest; "and if any mischief arises out of this imprudence, I shall never forgive myself. But who could have dreamt of any one being foolhardy enough to attempt the rescue of a ship in a nutshell that scarcely holds two persons?"

"I pray Heaven that your sleepy-headedness **may not** result in the loss of human life! You see, my son, that there is no amount of duty, be it ever so trifling in importance, that can be neglected with impunity. It is the concurrent devotion of each, and the sacrifices of one for another, that constitutes and secures the mutual security. Society on a small, as on a large scale, is a chain of which each individual is a link, and when one fails the whole is broken."

"I will go after him," said Ernest.

"Fritz and I will go with you," added Frank.

"No," said Ernest; "I alone am guilty, and I wish alone to remedy my fault — that is, as far as possible."

"I could not hide the canoe," observed Fritz," "but I hid the oars, and I find them in their place."

"That, perhaps, will have prevented him embarking," remarked one of the boys.

"A man like Willis," replied Becker, "is not prevented carrying out his intentions by such obstacles: he will have taken the first thing that came to hand; but let us go."

"What, father, am I not then to go alone, and so bear the penalty of my own fault?"

"No, Ernest, that would be to inflict two evils upon us instead of one; it is sufficient that you have shown your willingness to do so. Besides, three will not be over many *to convince* Willis, even if yet in time."

"And mother? and the ladies?" inquired Fritz.

"I shall **leave** Frank and Jack to see to them — a mere

obstinate freak, or a catastrophe, it will be time enough, when over, to inform them of this new idea of the Pilot's."

"It is something more than an idea this time," remarked Jack.

Just as Becker and his two sons were issuing from the grotto, the report of a cannon-shot resounded through the air.

Awoke and startled by the explosion, Becker's wife and Mrs. Wolston came running towards them. As for the girls, their guardian angel had too closely enveloped them in its wings to admit of their sleep being disturbed.

"The sloop on the coast!" said Frank; "for the sound is too distinct to come from a distance."

"Unless Willis has got upon Shark's Island," objected Fritz, running towards the terrace, armed with a telescope. "Just so; he is there, I see him distinctly; he is recharging our four-pounder."

"God be praised! you relieve my conscience of a great burden," said Ernest, placing his hand on his breast.

"He is going to discharge it," cried Fritz -- boom. Then a second shot reverberated in the air.

"If Captain Littlestone be within hearing of that signal, he will be sure to reply to it," said Becker. "Listen!"

They hushed themselves in silence, each retaining his respiration, as if their object had been to hear the sound of a fly's wing rather than the report of a cannon.

"Nothing!" said Becker sadly, at the expiration of a few minutes.

"Nothing!" reiterated successively all the voices.

"How in all the world did Willis contrive to get transported to Shark's Island?" inquired Mrs. Becker.

"Simply, wife, by watching when asleep, whilst one of our gentlemen slept when he watched."

"Yes, mother," said Ernest," and if you would not have me blush before Mrs. Wolston, you will not insist upon an explanation of the mystery."

"Mrs. Wolston," she replied, "is not so exacting as you seem to think, Master Ernest — the only difference that her presence here should make amongst you is that you have two mothers instead of one."

"That is," said Mrs. Wolston smiling, "if Mrs. Becker has no objections to dividing the office with me."

"Shall I not have compensation in your daughters?" said Mrs. Becker, taking her by the hand.

"Still," interrupted Fritz, "I cannot yet conceive how Willis managed to reach Shark's Island in a wretched canoe, without oars, through waves that ought to have swallowed him up over and over again."

"Bah!" exclaimed Jack; "what use has a pilot for oars?"

"There is a question! You, who modestly call yourself the best horseman on the island, how would you do, if you had nothing to ride upon?"

"I could at least fall back upon broomsticks," retorted the imperturbable Jack. "Besides, in Willis's case, the canoe was the steed, the oars the saddle — nothing more."

"We shall not stay here to solve the riddle," said Becker; "the storm seems disposed to abate; and the more that it was unreasonable to face certain destruction in a vain endeavor to assist a problematical shipwreck, the more it is incumbent upon us now to go in quest of the *Nelson*."

"But the sea will still be very terrible!" quickly added Mrs. Becker.

"If all danger were over, wife, the enterprise would do us little credit. It is our duty to do the best we can, according to the strength and means at our command. Fritz, Ernest, and Jack, go and put on your life-preservers — we shall take up Willis in passing."

"I must not insist," said Mrs. Becker; "the sacrifice would, indeed, be no sacrifice, if it could be easily borne; and yet ——"

"Remember the time, wife, when I was obliged, in order to secure the precious remains of our ship, to venture with our eldest sons on a float of tubs, leaving you exposed, alone with a child of seven, to the chance of eternal isolation!"

"That is very true, husband: I am unjust towards Providence, which has never ceased blessing us; but I am only a weak woman, and my heart often gets the better of my head."

"To-day I leave Frank with you; but, instead of your being his protector, as was the case fifteen years ago, he will be yours. Then there is Mrs. Wolston, her daughters, and husband, quite a new world of sympathies and consolations, by which our island has been so miraculously peopled."

"Go then, husband, and may God bring back in safety both the pinnace and the *Nelson !*"

"By the way, Mrs. Wolston, how does our worthy invalid get on? We live in such a turmoil of events and consternations, that I must beg a thousand pardons for not having asked after him before."

"His sleep appears untroubled; and, notwithstanding all the terrors of the last few days, I entertain sanguine hopes of his immediate recovery."

"You will at least return before night?" said Mrs. Becker to her husband.

"Rely upon my not prolonging my stay beyond what the exigencies of the expedition imperiously require."

"Good gracious! what are these?" exclaimed Mrs. Wolston as the three brothers entered, equipped in seal-gut trowsers, floating stays of the same material, and Greenland caps.

"The Knights of the Ocean," replied Jack gravely, "who, like the heroes of Cervantes, go forth to redress the wrongs done by the tempest, and to break lances — oars, I mean — in favor of persecuted sloops."

Mrs. Becker herself could scarcely refrain from smiling.

Such is the power of the smile that, in season or out of season, it often finds its way to the most pallid lips, in the midst of the greatest disasters and the deepest grief. It appears as if always listening at the door ready to take its place on the slightest notice. This diversion had the good effect of mixing a little honey with — if the expression may be used — the bitterness of the parting adieus. Becker took the lead in hiding his sorrow; the three young Greenlanders tore themselves from the maternal embrace, and affectionately kissed the hand held out to them by Mrs. Wolston.

Then, between those that departed and those that remained behind, there was nothing more than the ties of recollection, the common sadness, and the endless links of mutual affection.

CHAPTER III.

WHEN they had come within a short distance of the bay, Jack thought he saw a large black creature moving in the bushes that lined the shore.

" A sea monster!" he cried, levelling his musket; "I discovered it, and have the right to the first shot."

" No, sir," said Fritz, whose keen eye was a sort of locomotive telescope, " I object to that, for I do not want you to kill or wound my canoe."

" Nonsense, it moves."

" Whether it moves or not, we shall all see by and by; but do you not observe this monster's young ones gambolling by its side?"

" Which proves I am right, unless you mean to say your canoe has been hatching," and Jack again levelled his rifle.

" Don't fire, it is the hat and jacket of Willis!"

" What!" exclaimed Ernest, "is the Pilot a triton then, that he could dispense with the canoe?"

" Well, yes, unless the canoe has found its way back ot its own accord, which would indeed make it an intelligent creature."

" The Pilot has evidently reached Shark's Island by swimming, in spite of surf and breakers — a feat almost without a parallel."

" Bah!" said Ernest, parodying Jack's witticism about the oars, " what does a pilot care about surf and breakers?"

Strongly moored in a creek of the Jackal River, and

protected by a bluff, forming a screen between it and the sea, the pinnace had in no way suffered from the storm.

The swell was so violent, that they had a world of trouble in making the island; as they approached, Willis, who had made a speaking-trumpet by joining his hands round his mouth, was roaring out alternately, "starboard," "larboard," "hard-a-port," just as if these terms had **not** been Hebrew to the impromptu mariners.

At last, tired of holloaing, "Stop a bit," he said, " I shall find a quicker way;" with that he threw himself directly into the sea, and cut through the waves towards them as if his arms had been driven by a steam engine.

Arrived on board, he gave a vigorous turn to the tiller, laid hold of the sheet, let out a reef here, took in another there; the pinnace was soon completely at his command, and behaved admirably; true, she pitched furiously, and the gunwale was under water at every plunge. He headed along the coast till the point beyond which Fritz had first observed the *Nelson* was fairly doubled; some days before this point was called Cape Deliverance, it was now, perhaps, about to acquire the term of Cape Disappointment, but for the moment its future designation was in embryo.

Leaping on the poop, Willis carefully scanned the horizon as the boat rose upon the summit of the waves; but seeing nothing, he at last leapt down again with an expression of rage that, under other circumstances, would have been irresistibly comic. Abandoning the direction of the pinnace, he went and sat down on a bulk-head, and covered his face with his hands, in an attitude of profound desolation.

" Willis! Willis!" cried Jack, " I shall tell Sophia."

But there was neither the soft voice there, the caressing hand, nor the sweet fascination of the young girl's presence, and Willis continued immovable.

Becker saw that his was one of those minds that grew less calm the more they were urged, and the excitement of which must be permitted to wear itself out; he therefore beckoned his sons to leave him to his own reflections.

The wind still blew a gale, and the pinnace pitched heavily; but the sun was now beginning to break through the masses of lurid cloud, and the air was becoming less and less charged with vapor.

"I can descry nothing either," said Becker; "and yet this is the direction the storm must have driven the sloop."

"The sea is very capricious," suggested Fritz.

"True, but not to the extent of carrying a ship against the wind."

"Unfortunately," said Jack, "it is not on sea as on land, where the slightest indications of an object lost may lead to its discovery; a word dropped in the ear of a passer-by might put you on the track, but here it is no use saying, 'Sir, did you not see the *Nelson* pass this way?'"

"Fire a shot," said Ernest; "it may perhaps be heard, now that the air is less humid."

The two-pounder was ready charged; Fritz struck a light and set fire to a strip of mimosa bark, with which he touched the piece, and the report boomed across the waters.

Willis raised his head and listened anxiously, but soon dropped it again, and resumed his former attitude of hopeless despair.

"It may be," said Ernest, "that the *Nelson* hears our signal, though we do not hear hers."

"How can that be?" inquired Jack.

"Why, very easily. Sound increases or diminishes in intensity according as the wind carries it on or retards it."

"What, then, is sound, that the wind can blow it about, most learned brother?"

"It is a result of the compression of the air, that from its elasticity extends and expands, and which causes a sort of trembling or undulation, similar to that which is observed in water when a stone is thrown into it."

"And you may add," said Becker, "that bodies striking the air excite sonorous vibrations in this fluid; thus it rings under the lash that strikes it with violence, and whistles under the rapid impulsion of a switch: it likewise becomes sonorous when it strikes itself with force against any solid body, as the wind when it blows against the cordage of ships, houses, trees, and generally every object with which it comes in contact."

"I can understand," replied Jack, "how this sonorous effect is produced on the particles of air in immediate contact with the object struck; but how this sound is propagated, I do not see."

"Very likely; but still it travels from particle to particle, in a circle, at the rate of three hundred and forty yards in a second."

"Three hundred and forty yards in a second!" said Willis, who was beginning by degrees to recover his self-possession. "Well, that is what I should call going a-head."

"And by what sort of compasses has this speed been measured, Master Ernest?"

"The first accurate measurement, Master Jack, was made at Paris in 1738. There are there two tolerably elevated points, namely, Montmartre and Montlhéry — the distance between these, in a direct line, is 14,636 *toises*. Cannons were fired during the night, and the engineers on one of the elevations observed that an interval of eighty-six seconds and a half elapsed between the flash and the report of a cannon fired on the other."

"That half-second is very amusing," said Jack laughing; "if there had been only eighty or eighty-six net, one might still be permitted to entertain some doubts; but eighty-six and a half admits nothing of the kind. But why not three-quarters or six-eighths, they would do as well?"

"What is more natural than to reckon the fraction, if we are desirous of obtaining absolute precision? Is six months of your time of no value? Are thirty minutes more or less on the dial of your watch of no signification to you?"

"Your brother is perfectly right, Jack; you are not always successful in your jokes."

"Other experiments have been made since then," continued Ernest, "and the results have always been the same, making allowances for the wind, and a slight variation that is ascribed to temperature."

"To confirm the accuracy of this statement, the speed of light would have to be taken into consideration."

"True; but the velocity of light is so great, that the instant a cannon is fired the flash is seen."

" Whatever the distance ?"

" Yes, whatever the distance. Bear in mind that the rays of the sun only require eight minutes to traverse the thirty-four millions of leagues that extend between us and that body. Hence it follows that the time light takes to travel from one point to another on the earth may be regarded as *nil.*"

"That is something like distance and speed," remarked Willis, "and may be all right as regards the sun, but I should not be disposed to admit that there are any other instances of the same kind."

"Very good, Master Willis; and yet the sun is only a step from us in comparison to the distance of some stars that we see very distinctly, but which are, nevertheless, so remote, that their rays, travelling at the same rate as those of the sun, are several years in reaching us."

Willis rose abruptly, whistling "the Mariner's March," and went to join Fritz, who was steering the pinnace.

At this *naïve* mark of disapprobation on the part of the Pilot, Becker, Ernest, and Jack burst involuntarily into a violent peal of laughter.

"Laugh away, laugh away," said Willis; "I will not admit your calculations for all that."

The sky had now assumed an opal or azure tint, the wind had gradually died away into a gentle breeze, the waves were now swelling gently and regularly, like the movements of the infant's cradle that is being rocked asleep. Never had a day, opening in the convulsions of a tempest, more suddenly lapsed into sunshine and smiles: it was like the fairies of Perrault's Tales, who, at first wrapped in sorry rags, begging and borne down with age, throw off their chrysalis and appear sparkling with youth, gaiety, and beauty, their wallet converted into a basket of flowers, and their crutch to a magic wand.

"Father" inquired Fritz, "shall we go any farther?"

Since the weather had calmed down, and there was no longer any necessity for exertion, the expedition had lost its charm for the young man.

" I think it is useless; what say you, Willis ?"

" Ah," said the latter, taking Becker by the hand, " in consideration of the eight days' friendship that connects you even more intimately with Captain Littlestone than my affection for him of twenty years' standing, keep still a few miles to the east."

"If the sloop has been driven to a distance by the storm, and is returning towards us, which is very likely, I do not see that we **can** be of much **use**."

" But if dismasted and leaky ?"

" That would alter the case, only I am afraid the ladies will be uneasy about us."

" But they w**ere half** prepared, father."

" Jack is right," added Fritz, whose energies **were** again called into play by the thought of the *Nelson* in distress; " let us go on."

" Besides, on the word of a pilot, the sea will be **very calm** and gentle for some time to come: there is not the slightest **danger**."

" And what if there were ?" replied Fritz.

" Well, Willis, I shall give up the pinnace to you till dark," said Becker, " and may God guide us; we shall return **to-night, so as** to **arrive at** Rockhouse early in the morning."

" Hurrah **for the** captain !" cried Willis, throwing a cap into the air.

The evolutions of a cap, thrown up towards the sky or down upon the ground, were very usual modes with Willis of expressing his joy or sorrow.

This homage rendered to Becker, he hastened to let **a** reef out of the sheet, and the pinnace, for a moment **at** rest, redoubled its speed, like post-horses starting from the inn-door under the combined influence of a cheer from the postillion and a flourish of the whip.

" There is a cockle-shell that skips along pretty fairly," said Willis; " but it **wants two** very important things."

" What things ?"

" A caboose and a nigger."

" A caboose and a nigger ?"

" Yes, I **mean a pantry** and a cook; a gale for breakfast

is all very well, one gets used to it, it is light and easily digested; but the same for dinner is rather too much of a good thing in one day."

"I observed your thoughtful mother hang a sack on one of your shoulders, which appeared tolerably well filled — where is it?"

"Here it is," said Jack, issuing from the hatchway; "here are our stores: a ham, two Dutch cheeses, two callabashes full of Rockhouse malaga, and there is plenty of fresh water in the gourds; with these, we have wherewithal to defy hunger till to-morrow."

"Capital!" said Willis.

This time, however, a cap did not appear in the air, as the last one had not been seen since the former ovation.

"Let us lay the table," said Jack, arranging the coils of rope that crowded the deck. "Well, you see, Willis, we want for nothing on board the pinnace, not even a what-do-you-call-it?"

"A caboose, Master Jack."

"Well, not even a caboose."

"Quite true; and if the *Nelson* were in the offing, I would not exchange my pilot's badge for the epaulettes of a commodore; but, alas! she is not there."

"Cheer up, Willis, cheer up; one is either a man or one is not. What is the good of useless regrets?"

"Very little, but it is hard to be yard-armed while absent at my time of life — and afterwards — your health, Mr. Becker."

"That would be hard at any age, Willis; but I rather think it has not come to that yet."

"When it has come to it, there will be very little time left to talk it over."

"Did you not say, brother, that the *Nelson* might hear our signals without our hearing hers? If so, there is a chance for Willis yet."

"Certainly, Jack, because she has the wind in her favor to act as a speaking-trumpet, whilst we had it against us acting as a deafener."

"Is there any other influence that affects sound besides the wind?"

"Yes, I have already mentioned that temperature has something to do with it. Sound varies in intensity according to the state of the atmosphere. If, for example, we ring a small bell in a closed vessel filled with air, it has been observed that, as the air is withdrawn by the pump, the sound gradually grows less and less distinct."

"And if a vacuum be formed?"

"Then the sound is totally extinguished."

"So, then," objected Willis, "if two persons were to talk in what you call a vacuum, they would not hear each other?"

"Two persons could not talk in a vacuum," replied Ernest.

"Why not?"

"Because they would die as soon as they opened their mouths."

"Ah, that alters the case."

"If, on the contrary, a quantity of air or gas were compressed into a space beyond what it habitually held, then the sound," continued Ernest, "would be more intense than if the air were free."

"In that case a whisper would be equal to a howl!"

"You think I am joking, Willis; but on the tops of high mountains, such as the Himalaya and Mont Blanc, where the air is much rarified, voices are not heard at the distance of two paces."

"Awkward for deaf people!"

"Whilst, on the icy plains of the frozen regions, where the air is condensed by the severe cold, a conversation, held in the ordinary tone, may be easily carried on at the distance of half a league."

"Awkward for secrets!"

"And how does sound operate with regard to solid bodies?" inquired Jack.

"According to the degree of elasticity possessed by their veins or fibres."

"Explain yourself."

"That is, solid bodies, whose structure is such that the vibration communicated to some of their atoms circulates through the mass, are susceptible of conveying sound."

"Give us an instance."

"Apply your ear to one end of a long beam, and you will hear distinctly the stroke of a pin's head on the other; whilst the same stroke will scarcely be heard through the breadth of the wood."

"So that, in the first case, the sound runs along the longitudinal fibres where the contiguity of parts is closer, than when the body is taken transversely?"

"Just so."

"And across water?"

"It is heard, but more feebly."

For some time Fritz had been closely observing with the telescope a particular part of the horizon, when all at once he cried, "This time I see him distinctly; he is bearing down upon us."

"Who? the sloop?" cried Willis, starting up and letting fall the glass he had in his hand.

"What an extraordinary pace! he bounds into the air, then plumps into the water, then leaps up again, just like an India-rubber ball, that touches the ground only to take a fresh spring!"

"Impossible, Master Fritz; the *Nelson* tops the waves honestly and gallantly; but as to leaping into the air, she is a little too bulky for that."

"Ah, poor Willis, it is not the *Nelson* that is under my glass at present, but an enormous fish, ten or twelve feet in length."

"Oh, how you startled me!"

"Father! Ernest! prepare to fire! Jack, the harpoon! he is coming this way."

Fritz stood at the stern of the pinnace, his rifle levelled, following with his eyes the movements of the monster; when within reach, he fired with so much success and address that he hit the creature on the head. It then changed its course, leaving behind a train of blood.

"Let us after him, Willis; quick!"

The Pilot turned the head of the pinnace, and Jack immediately threw his harpoon.

"Struck!" cried he joyfully.

By the hissing of the line, and then the rapid impulsion
4

of the pinnace, it was felt that the monster had more strength than the craft and its crew together.

Ernest and his father fired at the same time; the ball of the former was lost in the animal's flesh, that of the latter rebounded off a horny protuberance that armed the monster's upper lip.

Fritz had time to recharge his rifle; he levelled it a second time, and the ball went to join the former; but, for all that, the pinnace continued to cleave the water at a furious rate.

Becker seized an axe and cut the rope.

"Oh, father, what a pity! such a splendid capture for our museum of natural history!"

"It is a sword-fish, children; a monster of a dangerous species, and of extreme voracity. If, by way of reciprocity, the fish have a museum at the bottom of the sea, they will have some fine specimens of the human race that have become the prey of this creature; and it may be that we were on the way to join the collection."

"Did you observe the formidable dentilated horn?"

"It is by means of this horn or sword, from which it takes its name, that it wages a continual war with the whale, whose only mode of escape is by flourishing its enormous tail; but the sword-fish, being very agile, easily avoids this, bounds into the air as Fritz saw it doing just now, then, falling down upon its huge adversary, pierces him with its sword."

"By the way, talking about the whale," said Jack, "all naturalists seem agreed, and we ourselves are convinced from our own observation, that its throat is very narrow, and that it can only swallow molluscs, or very small fishes —what, in that case, becomes of the history of Jonah?"

"It is rather unfortunate," replied Becker, "that the whale has been associated with this miracle. There is now no possibility of separating the whale from Jonah, or Jonah from the whale; yet, in the Greek translation of the Chaldean text, there is *Ketos*—in the Latin, there is *Cete* —and both these words were understood by the ancients to signify a fish of enormous size, but not the whale in particular. The shark, for example, can swallow a man, and even a horse, without mangling it."

" I have heard," said Jack, "of navigators who have landed on the back of a whale, and walked about on it, supposing it a small island."

"There is nothing impossible about that," observed Willis.

" One thing is certain, that we had just now within reach a sea monster who has carried off four leaden bullets in his body without seeming to be in the least inconvenienced by them; on the contrary, he seemed to move all the quicker for the dose."

" Life is a very different thing with those fellows than with us. The carp is said to live two hundred years, and it is supposed that a whale might live for ten centuries if the harpoon did not come in the way to shorten the period."

" Ah !" exclaimed Willis, with a sigh that might have moved a train of waggons, " these fellows have no cares."

" And the ephemeride, that dies an instant after its birth, do you suppose that it dies of grief?"

" Who knows, Master Jack ?"

" The ephemeride does not die so quickly as you think," said Becker; " it commences by living three years under water in the form of a maggot. It afterwards becomes amphibious, when it has a horny covering, on which the rudiments of wings may be observed. Then, four or five months after this first metamorphosis, generally in the month of August, it issues from its skin, almost as rapidly as we throw off a jacket; attached to the rejected skin are the teeth, lips, horns, and all the apparatus that the creature required as a water insect; then it is no sooner winged, gay, and beautiful, than, as you observe, it dies— hence it is called the day-fly, its existence being terminated by the shades of night."

" I was certain of it," said Willis.

" Certain of what ?"

" That it died of grief at being on land. When one has been accustomed to the water, you see, under such circumstances life is not worth the having."

" The day-fly," continued Becker, " is an epitome of

those men who spend a life-time hunting after wealth and glory, and who perish themselves at the moment they reach the pinnacle of their ambitious desires. Whence I conclude, my dear children, that there are nothing but beginnings and endings of unhappiness in this wor'd, and that true felicity is only to be hoped for in another sphere."

" What a curious series of transformations ! First an aquatic insect, next amphibious, then throwing away the organs for which it has no further use, and becoming provided with those suited to its new state ! "

" Yes, my dear Fritz; and yet those complicated and beautiful operations of **Nature** have not prevented philosophers from asserting that the world resulted from *floating atoms*, which, by force of combination, and after an infinity of blind movements, conglomerate into plants, animals, men, heaven, and earth."

" I am only a plain sailor," said Willis " yet the eye of a worm teaches me more than these philosophers seem to have imagined in their philosophy."

" Such a system could only have originated in Bedlam or Charenton."

" No, Ernest, it is the system of Epicurus and Lucretius. Without going so far back, there are a thousand others quite as ridiculous, with which it is unnecessary to charge your young heads."

" All madmen are not in confinement, and it may be that Epicurus and Lucretius had arrived at those limits of human reason, where genius begins in some and folly in others."

" It is not that, Fritz ; but if men, says Malebranche somewhere,* are interested in having the sides of an equilateral triangle unequal, and that false geometry was as agreeable to them as false philosophy, they would make the problems equally false in geometry as in morality, for this simple reason, that their errors afford them gratification, whilst truth would only hurt and annoy them."

" Very good," observed Willis ; " this Malebranche, as you call him, must have been an admiral ? "

---

* " Search after Truth," book ix.

" No, Willis, nothing more than a simple philosopher, but one of good faith, like Socrates, who admitted that what he knew best was, that he knew nothing."

The sun had gradually disappeared in the midst of purple tinged clouds, leaving along the horizon at first a fringe of gold, then a simple thread, and finally nothing but the reflection of his rays, sent to the earth by the layers of atmosphere,* like the adieu we receive at the turning of a road from a friend who is leaving us.

There was a festival in the sky that night; the firmament brought out, one by one, her circlet of diamonds, till the whole were sparkling like a blaze of light; the pinnace also left a fiery train in her wake, caused partly by electricity and partly by the phosphorescent animalculæ that people the ocean.

" Willis," said Becker, " I leave it entirely to you to decide the instant of our return."

The Pilot changed at once the course of the boat, without attempting to utter a word, so heavy was his heart at this unsuccessful termination of the expedition.

" It will be curious," observed Fritz, " if we find the *Nelson,* on our return, snugly at anchor in Safety Bay."

" I have a presentiment," said Jack ; " and you will see that we have been playing at hide-and-seek with the *Nelson.*"

Willis shook his head.

" Are there not a thousand accidents to cause a ship to deviate from her route ? "

" Yes, Master Ernest, there are typhoons, and the waterspouts of which I spoke to you before. In such cases, ships often deviate from their route, but generally by going to the bottom."

Willis concluded this sentence with a gesture that defies description, implying annihilation.

" Remember Admiral Socrates, Willis," said Jack ; "*what I know best is, that I know nothing,* and avow that God has other means of accomplishing his decrees besides typhoons and waterspouts."

---

* The twilight is entirely owing to this.

"My excellent young friends, I know you want to in-spire me with hope, as they give a toy to a child to keep it from crying, and I thank you for your good intentions. Now, for three days you have, so to speak, had no rest, and I insist on your profiting by this night to take some repose; and you also, Mr. Becker; I am quite able to manage the pinnace alone."

"Yes providing you do not play us some trick, like that of this morning, for instance."

"All stratagems are justifiable in war. Master Ernest had fair warning that I had an idea to work out. Besides, a prisoner, when under hatches, has the right to escape if he can : under parole, the case is quite different."

"Well, Willis, if you give me your simple promise to steer straight for New Switzerland, and awake me in two hours to take the bearings —— "

"I give it, Mr. Becker."

The three Greenlanders then descended into the hold, for tropical nights are as chilly as the days are hot, and Becker, rolling himself up in a sail, lay on deck.

In less than five minutes they were all fast asleep, and Willis paced the deck, his arms crossed, and mechanically gazing upon a star that was mirrored in the water.

"Several years to come to us, and that at the rate of seventy thousand leagues a second — that is *a little* too much."

Then he went to the rudder, his head leaning upon his breast, and glancing now and then with distracted eye at the course of the boat, buried in a world of thought, sad and confused, doubtless beholding in succession visions of the *Nelson*, of Susan, and of Scotland.

CHAPTER IV.

TOWARDS five o'clock next morning everything about
Rockhouse was beginning to assume life and motion —
within, all its inhabitants were already astir — without,
little remained of the recent storm and inundation except
that refreshing coolness, which, conjointly with the purified
air, infuses fresh vigor, not only into men, but also into
every living thing. The citrons, the aloes, and the Spanish
jasmines perfumed the landscape. The flexible palms,
the tall bananas, with their umbrageous canopy, the broad,
pendant-leaved mangoes, and all the rank but luxuriant
vegetation that clothed the land to the water's edge, waved
majestically under the gentle breeze that blew from the
sea. The Jackal River unfolded its silvery band through
the roses, bamboos, and cactii that lined its banks. The
sun — for that luminary plays an important part in all
Nature's festivals — darted its rays on the soil still charged
with vapor. Diamond drops sparkled in the cups of the
flowers and on the points of the leaves. In the distance,
pines, cedars, and richly-laden cocoa-nut trees filled up the
background with their dark foliage. The swans displayed
their brilliant plumage on the lake, the boughs of the trees
were alive with parroquets and other winged creatures of
the tropics. Add to the charms of this scene, Mrs. Becker
returning from the prairie with a jar of warm, frothy milk
— Mrs. Wolston and Mary busied in a multiplicity of
household occupations, to which their white hands and
ringing voices gave elegance and grace — Sophia tying a
rose to the neck of a blue antelope which she had adopted

as a companion — Frank distributing food to the ostriches and large animals, and admit, if there is a paradise on earth, it was this spot.

Compare this scene with that presented by any of our large cities at the same hour in the morning. In London or Paris, our dominion rarely extends over two or three dreary-looking rooms — a geranium, perhaps, at one of the windows to represent the fields and green lanes of the country; above, a forest of smoking chimneys vary the monotony of the zig-zag roofs; below, a thousand confused noises of waggons, cabs, and the hoarse voices of the street criers; probably the lamps are just being extinguished, and the dust heaps carted away, filling our rooms, and perhaps our eyes, with ashes; the chalk-milk, the air, and the odors are scarcely required to fill up the picture.

Breakfast was spread a few paces from Mr. Wolston's bed, whom the two young girls were tending with anxious solicitude, and whose sickness was almost enviable, so many were the cares lavished upon him.

"You are wrong, Mrs. Becker," said Mrs. Wolston, "to make yourself uneasy, the sea has become as smooth as a mirror since their departure."

"Ah, yes, I know that, my dear Mrs. Wolston, but when one has already undergone the perils of shipwreck, the impression always remains, and makes us see storms in a glass of water."

"I am certain," remarked Mr. Wolston, "the cause of their delay is a concession made to Willis."

"Very likely he would not consent to return, unless they went as far as possible."

"By the way, madam," said Mary, "now that you have got two great girls added to your establishment, I hope you are going to make them useful in some way — we can sew, knit, and spin."

"And know how to make preserves," added Sophia.

"Yes, and to eat them too," said her mother.

"If you can spin, my dears, we shall find plenty of work for you; we have here the Nankin cotton plant, and I intend to dress the whole colony with it."

"Delightful!" exclaimed Sophia, clapping her hands;

"Nankin dresses just as at the boarding-school, with a straw hat and a green veil."

"To be sure, it must be woven first," reflected Mrs. Becker; "but I dare say we shall be able to manage that."

"By the way, girls," said Mrs. Wolston, "have you forgotten your lessons in tapestry?"

"Not at all, mamma; and now that we think of it, we shall handsomely furnish a drawing-room for you."

"But where are the tables and chairs to come from?" inquired Mrs. Becker.

"Oh, the gentlemen will see to them."

"And the room, where is that to be?"

"There is the gallery, is there not?"

"And the wool for the carpet?"

"Have you not sheep?"

"That is true, children; you speak as if we had only to go and sit down in it."

"The piano, however, I fear will be wanting, unless we can pick up an Erard in the neighboring forest."

"True, mamma, all the overtures that we have had so much trouble in learning will have to go for nothing."

"But," said Mrs. Becker, "by way of compensation, there is the vegetable and fruit garden, the pantry, the kitchen, the dairy, and the poultry yard; these are all my charges, and you may have some of them if you like."

"Excellent, each shall have her own kingdom and subjects."

"It being understood," suggested Mrs. Wolston, "that you are not to eat everything up, should the fruit garden or pantry come under your charge."

"That is not fair, mamma; you are making us out to be a couple of cannibals."

"You see," continued Mrs. Wolston, "these young people have not the slightest objection to my parading their accomplishments, but the moment I touch their faults they feel aggrieved."

"I am persuaded," rejoined Mrs. Becker laughing, "that there are no calumniators in the world like mothers."

"Therefore, mamma, to punish you we shall come and kiss you."

And accordingly Mrs. Wolston was half stifled under the embraces of her two daughters.

"I am certainly not the offender," said Mrs. Becker, "but I should not object to receive a portion of the punishment; these great boys — pointing to Frank — are too heavy to hang on my neck now; you will replace them, my dears, will you not?"

"Most willingly, madam; but not to deprive them of their places in your affection."

"In case you should lose that, Master Frank," said Mrs. Wolston, "you must have recourse to mine."

"But now, my friends, what do you say to going down to the shore to meet the pinnace, and perhaps the *Nelson?*" said Mrs. Becker.

"Ah, yes," said Sophia; "and I will stay at home to wait upon father."

"No," said Mary; "I am the eldest — that is my right."

"Well, my children, do not quarrel about that," said Wolston; "I feel rather better; and I dare say a walk will do me good. Perhaps, when I get tired, Frank will lend me his arm."

"Better than that," hastily added Frank; "I shall saddle Blinky, and lead him gently, and you will be as comfortable as in an arm-chair."

"What is that you call Blinky?"

"Oh, one of our donkeys."

"Ah, very good; I was afraid you meant one of your ostriches, and I candidly admit that my experiences in equitation do not extend to riding a winged horse."

"In that case," said Mrs. Becker, "to keep Blinky's brother from being jealous, I shall charge him with a basket of provisions; and we shall lay a cloth under the mangoes, so that our ocean knights, as Jack will have it, may have something to refresh themselves withal as soon as they dismount."

The little caravan was soon on the march; the two dogs cleared the way, leaping, bounding, and scampering on before, sniffing the bushes with their intelligent noses; then, returning to their master, they read in his face what was next to be done. Mary walked by the side of Blinky, amusing her father with her prattle. Sophia, with her antelope, was gambolling around them, the one rivalling the other in the grace of their movements, not only without knowing it, but rather because they did not know it. The two mothers were keeping an eye on the donkey; whilst Frank, with his rifle charged, was ready to bring down a quail or encounter a hyena.

Some hours after the pinnace hove in sight, the voyagers landed, and received the warm congratulations of those on shore. When Willis had secured the boat, he took a final survey of the coast, penetrating with his eyes every creek and crevice.

" Is there no trace of the *Nelson?*" inquired Wolston.

" None !"

" Well, I had all along thought you would find it so; the wind for four days has been blowing that it would drive the *Nelson* to her destination. Captain Littlestone, being charged with important despatches, having already lost a fortnight here, has, no doubt, taken advantage of the gale, and made sail for the Cape, trusting to find us all alive here on his return voyage."

"Yes," said the Pilot, " I know very well that you have all good hearts, and that you are desirous of giving me all the consolation you can."

"Would you not have acted, under similar circumstances, precisely as we suppose Captain Littlestone to have done?"

"I admit that the thing is not only possible, but also that, if alive, it is just what he would have done. I trust, if it be so, that when he gets into port he will report me keel-hauled ?"

" Keel-hauled?"

" Yes, I mean dead. It is a thousand times better to pass for a dead man than a deserter."

" The wisest course he could pursue, it appears to me, would be to hold his tongue — probably you will not be missed."

"Ah! you think that her Majesty's blue jackets can disappear in that way, like musk-rats? But no such thing. When the captain in command at the station hails on board, every man and boy of the crew, from the powder-monkey to the first-lieutenant, are mustered in pipe-clay on the quarter-deck, and there, with the ship's commission in his hand, every one must report himself as he calls over the names.

"Then the captain will tell the simple truth."

"Well, you see, truth has nothing at all to do with the rules of the service, the questions printed in the orderly-book only will be asked, and he may not have an opportunity of stating the facts of the case ; besides, discipline on board a ship in commission could not be maintained if irregularities could be patched up by a few words from the captain. When it is found that I had been left on shore, the questions will be, ' Was the *Nelson* in want of repairs?' 'No.' 'Did she require water?' 'No.' 'Provisions?' 'No.' 'Then Willis has deserted?' 'Yes.' And his condemnation will follow as a matter of course."

"In that case, the Captain would be more to blame than you are."

"So he would, and it is for that reason I hope he will be able to show by the log that I was seized with cholera, tied up in a sack, and duly thrown overboard with a four-pound shot for ballast."

"I cannot conceive," said Becker, "that the discipline of any service can be so cruelly unreasonable as you would have us believe."

"No, perhaps you think that just before the anchor is heaved, and the ship about to start on a long voyage, the cabin boys are asked whether they have the colic — that lubbers, who wish to back out have only to say the word, and they are free — that the pilot may go a-hunting if he likes, and that the officers may stay on shore and amuse themselves in defiance of the rules of the service? In that case the navy would be rather jolly, but not much worth."

When Willis was once fairly started there was no stopping him.

"Dead," he continued; "that is to say, without a berth, pay, or even a name, nothing! My wife will have the right to marry again, my little Susan will have another father, and I shall only be able to breathe by stealth, and to consider that as more than I deserve. You must admit that all this is rather a poor look-out a-head."

"Really, Willis," said Mrs. Wolston, "you seem to take a pride in making things worse than they are, conjuring up phantoms that have no existence."

"It is true, madam, I may be going upon a wrong tack. Judging from all appearances, the sloop, instead of being on her way to the Cape, is tranquilly reposing at the bottom of the sea. But it is only death for death; hanged by a court-martial or drowned with the sloop, it comes, in the end, to the same thing."

"I dare say, Willis, had there really been an accident, and you had been on board, you would not have felt yourself entitled to escape?"

"Certainly not, madam; unless the crew could be saved, it would look anything but well for the pilot to escape alone."

Willis, however, to do him justice, seemed trying to smother his grief; and, in the meanwhile, the two girls had been spreading a pure white cloth on a neighboring rock, cutting fruit plates out of the thick mangoe leaves, cooling the Rockhouse malaga in the brook, and giving to the repast an air of elegance and refinement which had the effect of augmenting the appetite of the company. The viands were not better than they had been on many similar occasions, but they were now more artistically displayed, and consequently more inviting.

Who has not remarked, in passing through a street of dingy-looking houses, one of them distinguished from the others by its fresh and cheerful aspect, the windows garnished with a luxuriant screen of flowers, with curtains on either side of snowy whiteness and elaborate workmanship? Very likely the passer-by has asked himself, Why is this house not as neglected, tattered, and dirty as its wretched neighbors? The answer is simple; there dwells in this house a young girl, blithe, frolicsome, and joyous, singing with the lark, and, like a butterfly, floating from her book to her work-box—from her mother's cheek to her father's, leaving an impress of her youthfulness and purity on whatever she touches.

For a like reason the *al fresco* dinner of this day had a charm that no such feast had been observed to possess before.

5

"We are not presentable," said Fritz, referring to his seal-gut uniform.

"Ah," replied Mrs. Wolston, "it is your costume of war, brave knights; and, for my part, I admire you more in it than in the livery of Hyde Park or Bond Street."

"In that case," said Ernest, "we shall do as they do in China."

"And what is that?"

"Well, the most profound remark of respect a host can pay to his guests, is to go and dress after dinner."

"Just when they are about to leave?"

"Exactly so, madam."

"That is very decidedly a Chinese observance. Are they not somewhat behind in cookery?"

"By no means, madam; on the contrary, they have attained a very high degree of perfection in that branch of the arts. It is customary, at every ceremonious dinner, to serve up fifty-two distinct dishes. And when that course is cleared off, what do you think is produced next?"

"The dessert, I suppose."

"Eight kinds of soup, never either one more or one less. If the number were deficient, the guests would consider themselves grossly insulted, the number of dishes denoting the degree of respect entertained by the host for his guests."

"I beg, Mrs. Wolston," said Mrs. Becker laughing, "that you will not estimate our esteem for you by the dinner we offer you."

"Well," replied Mrs. Wolston in the same tone, "let me see; to be treated as we ought to be, there are fifty-seven dishes wanting, therefore we must go and dine at home. John, call my carriage."

At this sally they all laughed heartily, and even Willis chimed in with the general hilarity.

"Then, after the soups," continued Ernest, "comes the tea, and with that the dessert, as also sixty square pieces of silver paper to wipe the mouth. It is then that the host vanishes, to reappear in a brilliant robe of gold brocade and a vest of satin."

"These people ought all to perish of indigestion."

"No; they are moderate eaters, their dishes consist of small saucers, each containing only a few mouthfuls of meat, and, as for Europeans, the want of forks and spoons —— "

"What! have they no forks?"

"Not at table — nor knives either; but, on the other hand, they are exceedingly expert in the use of two slender sticks of ivory, which they hold in the first three fingers of the right hand, and with which they manage to convey solids, and even liquids, to their mouths."

"Ah! I see," said Jack; "the Europeans would be obliged, like Mrs. Wolston, to call their carriage, in spite of the fifty-two saucers of meat: it puts me in mind of the stork inviting the fox to dine with her out of a long-necked jar."

"We are apt to judge the Chinese by the pictures seen of them on their own porcelain, and copied upon our pottery," said Becker; "but this conveys only a ludicrous idea of them. They are the most industrious, but at the same time the vainest, most stupid, and most credulous people in the world; they worship the moon, fire, fortune, and a thousand other things; people go about amongst them selling wind, which they dispose of in vials of various sizes."

"That is a trade that will not require an extraordinary amount of capital."

"True; and besides, as they carry on their trade in the open air, they have no rent to pay."

"Their bonzes or priests," continued Becker, "to excite charity, perambulate the streets in chains, sometimes with some inflammable matter burning on their heads, whilst, instead of attempting to purify the souls of dying sinners, they put rice and gold in their mouths when the vital spark has fled. They have a very cruel mode of punishing renegade Lamas: these are pierced through the neck with a red-hot iron."

"What is a Lama, father?"

"It is a designation of the Tartar priests."

For some time Willis had been closely examining a particular point in the bay with increasing anxiety; at last he ran towards the shore and leapt into the sea. Becker and his four sons were on the point of starting off in pursuit of him.

"Stop," said Wolston, "I have been watching Willis's movements for the last ten minutes, and I guess his purpose — let him alone."

Willis swam to some object that was floating on the water, and returned in about a quarter of an hour, bringing with him a plank.

"Well," he inquired, on landing, "was I wrong?"

"Wrong about what?" inquired Wolston.

"The *Nelson* is gone."

"The proof, Willis."

"That plank."

"Well, what about the plank?"

"I recognise it."

"How, Willis?"

"How! Well," replied the obstinate pilot, "fish don't breed planks, and — and — I scarcely think this one could escape from a dockyard, and float here of its own accord."

"Then, Willis, according to you, there are no ships but the *Nelson*, no ships wrecked but the *Nelson*, and no planks but the *Nelson's*. Willis, you are a fool."

"Every one has his own ideas, Mr. Wolston."

Towards evening, when they were on their way back to Rockhouse, Sophia confidentially called Willis aside, and he cheerfully obeyed the summons.

"Pilot," said she, "I have made up my mind about one thing."

"And what is that, Miss Sophia?"

"Why, this — in future, when we are alone, as just now, you must call me Susan, as you used to call your own little girl when at home, not Miss Susan."

"Oh, I cannot do that, Miss Sophia."

"But I insist upon it."

"Well, Miss Sophia, I will try."

"What did you say?"

"Miss Sus——"

"What?"

"Susan, I mean."

"There now, that will do."

CHAPTER V.

AFTER some days more of anxious but fruitless expectation, it was finally concluded that either the *Nelson* had sailed for the Cape, or, as Willis would have it, she had gone to that unexplored and dread land where there were neither poles nor equator, and whence no mariner was ever known to return. It was necessary, therefore, to make arrangements for the surplus population of the colony — whether for a time or for ever, it was then impossible to say. At first sight, it might appear easy enough to provide accommodation for the eleven individuals that constituted the colony of New Switzerland. It is true that land might have been marked off, and each person made sovereign over a territory as large as some European kingdoms; but these sovereignties would have resembled the republic of St. Martin — there would have been no subjects. What, then, would they have governed? it may be asked. Themselves, might be answered; and it is said to be a far more difficult task to govern ourselves than to rule others.

Though space was ample enough as regards the colony in general, it was somewhat limited as regards detail. To live *pêle-mêle* in Rockhouse was entirely out of the question. Independently of accommodation, a thousand reasons of propriety opposed such an arrangement. Whether or not there might be another cave in the neighborhood, hollowed out by Nature, was not known; if there were, it had still to be discovered. Chance would not be chance, if it were undeviating and certain in its operations. To consign the Wolstons to **Falcon's Nest** or Prospect Hill, and leave them there alone, **even** though **under** the protection of Willis, could not be thought of; they knew nothing of the dangers that would surround them, and as **yet** they were ignorant of the topography of the island. It was, therefore, requisite that both families should continue **in** proximity, so as to aid **each** other **in moments** of peril, but without, **at the same** time, outraging propriety, or shackling individual freedom of action. Under ordinary circumstances, these difficulties might have been solved by taking apartments **on the opposite** side of the street, **or** renting a **house next door.** But, alas! the blessings of landlords and poor-rates **had not yet been bestowed on the island.**

One day **after dinner,** when **these** points were **under** consideration, Willis, who **was accustomed to** disappear after **each meal,** no one knew why or whereto, came and took his place amongst them under the gallery.

"As for myself," said the Pilot, "I do not wish to live anywhere. **Since I** am **in your house,** Mr. Becker, and cannot get away honestly for a quarter **of** an hour, I must of course remain; but as for becoming a mere dependant on your bounty, that I **will** not suffer."

"What you say **there is not very** complimentary to **me,"** said Mr. Wolston.

"Your position, Mr. Wolston, is a very different thing; besides, you are an invalid and require attention, whilst I am strong and healthy, for which I ought to be thankful."

"You are **not** in my house," replied Becker "**any more** than **I am in yours;** the place we are in is **a shelter provided** by **Providence** for us all, **and I venture to suppose** that such **a** host is rich enough to supply all our wants. I am only the humble instrument distributing the gifts **that** have been **so** lavishly bestowed on this island."

"What **you** say is very kind and very generous," **added** Willis, "but I mean to provide for myself — that is **my idea."**

"And not **a** bad one either," continued Becker; "but how? You are welcome here to do the work for four — if you like; and then, supposing you eat for two, I will be your debtor, **not you** mine."

" Work! and at what? walking about with a rifle on my shoulder; airing myself, as I am doing now under your gallery, in the midst of flowers, on the banks of a river : or opening my mouth for quails to jump down my throat ready roasted — would you call that work?"

" Look there, Willis — what do you see?"

" A bear-skin."

" Well, suppose, by way of a beginning, I were to introduce you to a fine live bear, with claws and tusks to match, ready to spring on you, having as much right to your skin as you have to his — now, were I to say to you, I want that animal's skin, to make a soft couch similar to the one you see yonder, would you call that work?"

" Certainly, Mr. Becker."

" Very good, then; it is in the midst of such labors that we pass our lives. Before we fell comfortably asleep on feather beds, those formidable bones which you see in our museum were flying in the air ; the cup which I now hold in my hand was a portion of the clay on which you sit; the canoe with which you ran away the other day was a live seal ; the hats that we wear, were running about the fields in the form of angola rabbits. So with everything you see about you ; for fifteen years, excepting the Sabbath, which is our day of rest and recreation as well as prayer, we have never relapsed from labor, and you are at liberty to adopt a similar course, if you feel so disposed."

" No want of variety," said Jack ; " if you do not like the saw-pit, you can have the tannery."

" Neither are very much in my line," replied Willis.

" What then do you say to pottery?"

" I have broken a good deal in my day."

" Yes, but there is a difference between breaking it and making it."

" What appears most needful," remarked Fritz, " is, three or four acres of fresh land, to double our agricultural produce."

" Is land dear in these parts?" inquired Mrs. Wolston, smiling.

" It is not to be had for nothing, madam ; there is the trouble of selecting it."

"And the labor of rendering it productive," added Ernest.

"But how do you manage for a lawyer to convey it?"

"I was advising Ernest to adopt that profession," said Mrs. Becker; "wills and contracts would be in harmony with his studious temperament."

"At present, the question before us," said Becker, "is the allotment of quarters; in the meantime, Mr. and Mrs. Wolston, with the young ladies, will continue to occupy our room."

"No, no," said Wolston "that would be downright expropriation."

"In that case the matter comes within the sphere of our lawyer, and I therefore request his advice."

To this Ernest replied, by slowly examining his pockets; after this operation was deliberately performed, he said, in a *nisi prius* tone, "That he had forgotten his spectacles, and consequently that it was impossible for him to look into the case in the way its importance demanded, otherwise he was quite of the same opinion as his learned brother — his father, he meant."

"And what if we refuse?" said Mrs. Wolston.

"If you refuse, Mrs. Wolston, there is only one other course to adopt."

"And what is that, Master Frank?"

"Why, simply this," and rising, he cried out lustily, "John, call Mrs. Wolston's carriage."

"Ah, to such an argument as that, there can be no reply; so I see you must be permitted to do what you like with us."

"Very good," continued Becker; "then there is one point decided: my wife and I will occupy the children's apartment."

"And the children," said Jack, "will occupy the open air. For my own part, I have no objection: that is a bedroom exactly to my taste."

"Spacious," remarked Ernest.

"Well-aired," suggested Fritz.

"Hangings of blue, inlaid with stars of gold," observed Frank.

" Any thing else ? " inquired Becker.

" No, father, I believe the extent of accommodation does not go beyond that."

" Therefore I have decided upon something less vast, but more comfortable for you ; you will go every night to our *villa* of Falcon's Nest."

" On foot ? "

" On horseback, if you like and under the direction of Willis, whom I name commander-in-chief of the cavalry."

" Of the cavalry ! " cried the sailor ; " what ! a pilot on horseback ? "

" Do not be uneasy, Willis," replied Jack, " we have no horses."

" Ah, well, that alters the case."

" But then we have zebras and ostriches."

" Ostriches ! worse and worse."

" Say not so, good Willis ; when once you have tried Lightfoot or Flyaway, you would never wish to travel otherwise : they run so fast that the wind is fairly distanced, and scarcely give us time to breathe — it is delightful."

" Thank you, but I would rather try and get the canoe to travel on land."

" Ah, Willis," said Fritz, " that would be an achievement that would do you infinite credit — if you only succeed."

" Will you allow me to make a request, Mrs. Becker ? "

" Listen to Willis," said Jack, " he has an idea."

" The request I have to urge is, that you will permit me to encamp on Shark's Island, and there establish a lighthouse for the guidance of the *Nelson*, in case she should return."

" What ! the commander-in-chief of cavalry on an island ? "

" No, not of the cavalry, but of the fleet ; it is only necessary for Mr. Becker to change my position into that of an admiral, which will not give him much extra trouble."

" I shall do so with pleasure, Willis."

" In that case, since I am an admiral, the first thing I shall do, is to pardon myself for the faults I committed whilst I was a pilot."

“ Capital ! ” said Ernest, “ that puts me in mind of Louis
XII., who, on ascending the throne, said that it was not
for the King of France to revenge the wrongs of the
Duke of Orleans.”

“ What, then, is to become of the boys ?   I intended to
make you their compass — on land, of course.”

“ The boys,” cried the latter, “ are willing to enlist as
seamen, and accompany the admiral on his cruise.”

“ You will spin yarns for us, Willis, will you not ? ”

“ Well, my lads, if you want a sleeping dose, I will
undertake to do that.”

“ But there are objections to this arrangement,” Mrs.
Becker hastily added.

“ What are they, mother ? ”

“ In the first place, a storm might arise some fine night
— one of those dreadful hurricanes that continue several
days, like the one that terrified us so much lately — and
then all communication would be cut off between us.”

“ You could always see one another.”

“ How so, Willis ? ”

“ From a distance — with the telescope.”

“ Then,” continued Mrs. Becker, “ you would be a prey
to famine, for though the telescope, good Master Willis,
might enable you to see our dinner — from a distance — I
doubt whether that would prevent you dying of starvation.”

“ We might easily guard against that, by taking over a
sufficient quantity of provisions with us every night, and
bringing them back next morning.”

“ But could you carry over my kisses, Willis, and dis-
tribute them amongst my children every morning and
evening, like rations of rice ? ”

“ If the arrangement will really make you uneasy, Mrs
Becker, I give it up,” said Willis, polishing with his arm
the surface of his oil-skin sou’-wester.

“ Not at all, Willis.   It is for me to give up my objections.   Besides, I observe Miss Sophia staring at me with
her great eyes ; she will never forgive me for tormenting
her sweetheart.”

“ Ah ! since I have been staring at you, I have only
now to eat you up like the wolf in Little Red Riding-

hood," and in a moment her slender arms were clasped round Mrs. Becker's neck.

" Good," said Becker, "there is another point settled — temporarily."

" In Europe," observed Wolston, "there is nothing so durable as the temporary."

" In Europe, yes, but not here. To-morrow morning we shall select a tree near Falcon's Nest, and in eight days you shall be permanently housed in an aerial tenement close to ours, so that we may chat to each other from our respective balconies."

" That will be a castle in the air a little more real than those I have built in Spain."

" Then you have been in Spain, papa ?"

" Every one has been less or more in the Spain I refer to, Sophy — it is the land of dreams."

" And of castanets," remarked Jack.

" Then my sweetheart will be alone on his island, like an exile ?"

" No, Miss Sophia, we are incapable of such ingratitude. After enjoying the hospitality of Willis in Shark's Island, he will surely deign to accept ours at Falcon's Nest; so, whether here or there, he shall always have four devoted followers to keep him company."

The Pilot shook Fritz by the hand, at the same time nearly dislocating his arm.

" I wonder why God, who is so good, has not made houses grow of themselves, like pumpkins and melons ?" said Ernest.

" Rather a lazy idea that," said his father; "our great Parent has clearly designed that we should do something for ourselves; he has given us the acorn whence we may obtain the oak."

" Nevertheless, there are uninhabited countries which are gorged with vegetation — the territory we are in, for example."

" True ; but still no plant has ever sprung up anywhere without a seed has been planted, either by the will of God or by the hands of man. With regard, however, to the distribution of vegetation in a natural state, that depends more upon the soil and climate than anything else;

wherever there is a fertile soil and moist air, there seeds will find their way."

" But how ?"

" The seeds of a great many plants are furnished with downy filaments, which act as wings; these are taken up by the wind and carried immense distances; others are inclosed in an elastic shell, from which, when ripe, they are ejected with considerable force."

" The propagation of plants that have wings or elastic shells may, in that way, be accounted for; but there are some seeds that fall, by their own weight, exactly at the foot of the vegetable kingdom that produces them."

" It is often these that make the longest voyages."

" By what conveyance, then ?"

" Well, my son, for a philosopher, I cannot say that your knowledge is very profound; seeds that have no wings borrow them."

" Not from the ant, I presume ?"

" No, not exactly; but from the quail, the woodcock, the swallow, and a thousand others, that are apparently more generous than the poor ant, to which Æsop has given a reputation for avarice that it will have some trouble to shake off. The birds swallow the seeds, many of which are covered with a hard, horny skin, that often resists digestion; these are carried by the inhabitants of the air across rivers, seas, and lakes, and are deposited by them in the neighborhood of their nests—it may be on the top of a mountain, or in the crevice of a rock."

" True, I never thought of that."

" There are a great many philosophers who know more about the motions of stars than these humbler operations of Nature."

" You are caught there," said Jack.

" There are philosophers, too, who can do nothing but ridicule the knowledge of others."

" Caught you there," retaliated Ernest.

" It was in this way that a bird of the Moluccas has restored the clove tree to the islands of this archipelago, in spite of the Dutch, who destroyed them everywhere, in order that they might enjoy the monopoly of the trade."

"Still, I must fall back upon my original idea; by sowing a brick, we ought to reap a wall."

"And if a wall, a house," suggested another of the young men.

"Or if a turret, a castle," proposed a third.

"Or a hall to produce a palace," remarked the fourth.

"There are four wishes worthy of the four heads that produced them! What do you think of those four great boys, Mrs. Wolston?"

"Well, madam, as they are wishing, at any rate they may as well wish that chinchillas and marmots wore their fur in the form of boas and muffs, that turkeys produced perigord pies, and that the fish were drawn out of the sea ready roasted or boiled."

"Or that the sheep walked about in the form of nicely grilled chops," suggested Becker.

"And you, young ladies, what would you wish?"

Mary, who was now beyond the age of dolls, and was fast approaching the period of young womanhood, felt that it was a duty incumbent upon her to be more reserved than her sister, and rarely took part in the conversation, unless she was directly addressed, ceased plying her needle, and replied, smiling,

"I wish I could make some potent elixir in the same way as gooseberry wine, that would restore sick people to health, then I would give a few drops to my father, and make him strong and well, as he used to be."

"Thank you for the intention, my dear child."

"And you, Miss Sophia? It is your turn."

"I wish that all the little children were collected together, and that every papa and mamma could pick out their own from amongst them."

Here Willis took out his pocket-handkerchief and appeared to be blowing his nose, it being an idea of his that a sailor ought not to be caught with a tear in his eye.

"Now then, Willis, we must have a wish from you."

"I wish three things: that there had not been a hurricane lately, that canoes could be converted into three masters, and that Miss Sophia may be Queen of England."

" Granted," cried Jack.

And laying hold of a wreath of violets that the young girl had been braiding, he solemnly placed it on her head.

" You will make her too vain," said Mrs. Wolston.

" Ah mamma, do not scold," and gracefully taking the crown from her own fair curls, she placed it on the silvery locks of her mother; " I abdicate in your favor, and, sweetheart, I thank you for placing our dynasty on the throne.   Mary, you are a princess."

. " Yes," she replied, and here is my sceptre," holding up her spindle.

" Well answered, my daughter, that is a woman's best sceptre, and her kingdom is her house."

" Our conversation," said Becker, " is like those small threads of water which, flowing humbly from the hollow of a rock, swell into brooks, then become rivers, and, finally, lose themselves in the ocean."

" It was Ernest that led us on."

" Well, it is time now to get back to your starting-point again.   God has said that we shall earn our bread by the sweat of our brow, and consequently that our enjoyments should be the result of our own industry; that is the reason that venison is given to us in the form of the swift stag, and palaces in the form of clay; man is endowed with reason, and may, by labor, convert all these blessings to his use."

" Your notion," said Mr. Wolston, "of drawing the fish out of the sea ready cooked, puts me in mind of an incident of college life which, with your permission, I will relate."

" Oh yes, papa, a story !"

" There was at Cambridge, when I was there, a young man, who, instead of study and sleep, spent his days and nights in pistol practice and playing on the French horn, much to the annoyance of an elderly maiden lady, who occupied the apartments that were immediately under his own."

" These are inconveniences that need not be dreaded here."

" Our police are too strict."

"And our young men too well-bred," added Mrs. Wolston.

"Not only that," continued Mr. Wolston, "this young student, who never thought of study, had a huge, shaggy Newfoundland dog, and the old lady possessed a chubby little pug, which she was intensely fond of; now, when these two brutes happened to meet on the stairs, the large one, by some accident or other, invariably sent the little one rolling head over heels to the bottom; and, much to the horror of the old lady, her favorite, that commenced its journey down stairs with four legs, had sometimes to make its way up again with three."

"I always understood that dogs were generous animals, and would not take advantage of an animal weaker than themselves; our dogs would not have acted so."

"Well, perhaps the dog was not quite so much to blame in these affairs as its master; besides, in making advances to its little friend, it might not have calculated its own force."

"Yes, and perhaps might have been sorry afterwards for the mischief it had done."

"Very likely; still the point was never clearly explained, and, whether or no, the elderly lady could not put up with this sort of thing any longer; she complained so often and so vigorously, that her troublesome neighbor was served in due form with a notice to quit. The young scapegrace was determined to be revenged in some way on the party who was the cause of his being so summarily ejected from his quarters. Now, right under his window there was a globe belonging to the old lady, well filled with good-sized gold fish. His eye by chance having fallen upon this, and spying at the same time his fishing-rod in a corner, the coincidence of vision was fatal to the gold-fish; they were very soon hooked up, rolled in flour, fried, and gently let down again one by one into the globe."

"I should like to have seen the old lady when she first became aware of this transformation!"

"Well, one of the fish had escaped, and was floating

about, evidently lamenting the fate of its finny companions."

" It was very cruel," observed Mary.

" Elderly ladies who have no family and live alone are very apt to bestow upon animals the love and affection that is inherent in us all."

" Which is very much to be deprecated."

"Why so, Master Frank?"

" Are there not always plenty of poor and helpless human beings upon whom to bestow their love? are there not orphans and homeless creatures whom they might adopt?"

" There are ; but it requires wealth for such benevolences, and the goddess Fortune is very capricious; whilst one must be very poor indeed that cannot spare a few crumbs of bread once a day. Besides, admitting that this mania is blamable when carried to excess, still it must be respected, for it behoves us to reverence age even in its foibles."

Frank, whose nature was so very susceptible, that a single grain of good seed soon ripened into a complete virtue, bent his head in token of acquiescence.

" Now the old lady loved these gold-fish as the apples of her eyes, and her astonishment and grief, in beholding the state they were in, was indescribable."

" And yet it was a loss that might have been easily repaired."

" Ah, you think so, Jack, do you? If you were to lose Knips, would the first monkey that came in your way replace him in your affections ? "

" That is a very different thing — I brought Knips up."

" No ; it is precisely the same thing. She had the fish when they were very small, had seen them grow, spoke to them, gave each of them a name, and believed them to be endowed with a supernatural intelligence."

" Therefore, I contend the student was a savage."

" Not he, my friend, he was one of the best-hearted fellows in the world : hasty, ardent, inconsiderate, he resisted commands and threats, but yielded readily to a tear or a prayer. As soon as he saw the sorrowful look of the old woman, he regretted what he had done, and undertook to restore the inhabitants of the globe to life."

"With what sort of magic wand did he propose to do that?"

"All the inhabitants of the house had collected round the old lady and her globe, endeavoring to console her, and at the same time trying to account for the phenomenon; some ascribed the transformation to lightning, others went so far as to suggest witchcraft. Our scapegrace now joined the throng, took the globe in his hands, gravely examined his victims, and declared, with the utmost coolness that they were not dead. 'Not dead, sir! are you sure?' 'Confident, madam; it is only a lethargy, a kind of coma or temporary transformation, that will be gradually shaken off; I have seen many cases of the same kind, and, if proper care be taken as to air, repose, and diet, particularly as regards the latter, your fish will be quite well again to-morrow.'"

"Did she believe that?"

"One readily believes what one wishes to be true; besides, in twenty-four hours, all doubt on the subject would be at an end; added to which, the young man was ostensibly a student of medicine, and had the credit in the house of having cured the washerwoman's canary of a sore throat."

"Well, how did he manage about the fish?"

"Very simply; he went and bought some exactly the same size that were not in a lethargy; he then, at the risk of breaking his neck or being taken for a burglar, scaled the balcony, and substituted them for the defunct. Next morning, when he called to inquire after his patients, he found the old lady quite joyful."

"Had she no doubts as to their identity?"

"Well, one was a little paler and another was a trifle thinner, but she was easily persuaded that this difference might arise from their convalescence. The young man immediately became a great favorite; and the old lady would rather have shared her own apartments with him,

than allow him to quit the house; he consequently remained."

"What, then, became of the pistols and the French
horn?" inquired Jack.

" From that time on there sprung up a close friendship
between the two; he was induced by her to convert his
weapons of war into pharmacopœas. Always, when she
made some nice compound of jelly and cream, he had a
share of it; he, on his side, scarcely ever passed her door
without softening his tread; and both himself and his dog
managed, eventually, to acquire the favor of the old lady's
pug."

" He appears to have been one of those medical gentlemen who profess to cure every conceivable disease by one
kind of medicine."

" And who generally contrive to remove both the
disease and the patient at the same time."

" You mistake the individual altogether; he is now one
of the most esteemed physicians in London, remarkable
alike for his skill and benevolence. It is even strongly
suspected by his friends that he is not a little indebted for
his present eminent position to his first patients — the
canary and the gold-fish."

It was now the usual hour for retiring to rest. After
the evening prayer, which Mary and Sophia said alternately
aloud, Willis and the four brothers prepared to start for
Shark's Island, to pass their first night in the store-room
and cattle-shed that had been erected there. Of course
they could not expect to be so comfortable in such quarters
as at Rockhouse or Falcon's Nest; but then novelty is to
young people what ease is to the aged. Black bread
appears delicious to those who habitually eat white; and
we ourselves have seen high-bred ladies delighted when
they found themselves compelled to dine in a wretched
hovel of the Tyrol — true, they were certain of a luxurious
supper at Inspruck. So grief breaks the monotony of joy,
just as a rock gives repose to level plain.

Whilst the pinnace was gradually leaving the shore,
loaded with mattresses and other movables adapted for a

temporary encampment, Jack signalled a parting adieu to Sophia, and, putting his fingers to his lips, seemed to enjoin silence.

"All right, Master Jack," cried she.

"What is all this signalling about?" inquired Mrs. Wolston.

"A secret," said the young girl, leaping with joy; "I have a secret!"

"And with a young man? that is very naughty, miss."

"Oh, mamma, you will know it to-morrow."

"What if I wanted to know it to-night?"

"Then, mamma, if you insisted — that is — absolutely —— "

"No, no, child, I shall wait till to-morrow; keep it till then — if you can."

"Sophia dear," said Mary to her sister, when their two heads, enveloped in snowy caps with an embroidered fringe, were reclining together on the same pillow, "you know I have always shared my *bon-bons* with you."

"Yes, sister."

"In that case, make me a partner in your secret."

"Will you promise not to speak of it?"

"Yes, I promise."

"To no one?"

"To no one."

"Not even to the paroquette Fritz gave you?"

"No, not even to my paroquette."

"Well, it is very likely I shall speak about it in my dreams — you listen and find it out."

"Slyboots!"

"Curiosity!"

Like those delicate flowers that shrink when they are touched, each then turned to her own side; but it would have cost both too much not to have fallen asleep as usual, with their arms round each other's necks; — consequently this tiff soon blew over, and, after a prolonged chat, their lips finally joined in the concluding "Good-night."

CHAPTER VI.

NEXT morning, Sophia came running in with a sealed
letter in her hand, which she opened and read as follows:—

"HEAD QUARTERS, SAFETY BAY, DAYBREAK.

"The Admiral commanding the Fleet stationed in Safety
Bay to her Most gracious Majesty Sophia, Queen of
Great Britain and Ireland.

"May it please your Majesty,

"The crews of your Majesty's yachts, the *Elizabeth*
and the *Morse*, are quite entire and in perfect health.
The enemy having kept at a respectful distance, we have
not had as yet an opportunity of proving our courage and
devotion. Mr. Midshipman Jack fell asleep on the carriage of a four-pounder, like Marshal Turenne before his
first battle; but, in all other respects, the conduct of the
officers has been most exemplary, and merits the utmost
commendation.

"It is the admiral's intention to push out a recon-
naissance towards the east, in the direction of Pearl Bay,
which he has not yet explored. If, however, your
Majesty should regard this expedition as likely to interfere with the good understanding that subsists between
that government and your own, it will be only necessary
to fire a gun, in which case we shall return to port.
Under other circumstances, the squadron will proceed
with the enterprise, and endeavor to obtain a collar for
your Majesty's doll."

"For my doll!" exclaimed Sophia angrily; "when did
Jack find out that I had a doll?"

" Is that, then, your secret ?" inquired her mother.

" Yes, mamma, Master Jack took a pigeon with him for the express purpose of playing me this trick."

" And what is worse, included yourself in the conspiracy.   Dreadful !"

" Is it not — to speak of a young person of thirteen's doll ?"

" Say nearer fourteen, my dear."

" Therefore, to punish your confederates, I shall fire a gun, and put a stop to their excursion," said Becker, turning to one of the six-pounders that flanked Rockhouse in the direction of the river.

" Clemency being one of the dearest rights of the royal prerogative," replied Sophia, " I shall pardon them, and I pray you not to throw any obstacle in the way of their expedition."

" Very good, your Majesty ; but there are state reasons which should be allowed to overrule the impulses of your heart ; those gentlemen have forgotten that we were to go and lay the first stone, or rather to cut, to-day, the first branch of your aerial residence at Falcon's Nest."

Admiral Willis and his officers having obeyed the preconcerted signal, the whole party started on their land enterprise.   One of the young men was harnessed to a sledge, containing saws, hatchets, a bamboo ladder that had formerly done duty as a staircase to the Nest, and everything else requisite for the contemplated project.

Jack had already started when Sophia called him back, and he hastily obeyed the summons.

" What are your Majesty's commands ?"

" Oh, nothing particular, only should you meet my doll in company with your go-cart, be pleased to pay my respects to them."   Saying this, she made a low curtsy, and turned her back upon him.

" Your Majesty's behests shall be obeyed," said Jack, and he ran off to rejoin the caravan.

The sad ravages of the tempest presented themselves as they proceeded ; tall chestnuts lay stretched on the ground, and seemed, by their appearance, to have struggled hard with the storm.

" After all," inquired Frank, " what is the wind?"

" Wind is nothing more than air rushing in masses from one point to another."

" And what causes this commotion in the elements?"

" The equilibrium of the atmosphere is disturbed by a variety of actions;—the diurnal motion of the sun, whose rays penetrate the air at various points; absorption and radiation, which varies according to the nature of the soil and the hour of the day; the inequality of the solar heat, according to seasons and latitude; the formation and condensation of vapor, that absorbs caloric in its formation, and disengages it when being resolved into liquid."

" I never thought," remarked Willis, " that there were so many mysteries in a sou'-easter. Does it blow? is it on the starboard or larboard? was all, in fact, that I cared about knowing."

" In a word, the various circumstances that change the actual density of the air, making it more rarefied at one point than another, produce currents, the force and direction of which depend upon the relative position of hot and cold atmospheric beds. Again, the winds acquire the temperature and characteristics of the regions they traverse."

" That," observed Frank, " is like human beings; you may generally judge, by the language and manners of a man, the places that he is accustomed to frequent."

" There are hot and cold winds, wet and dry; then there are the trade winds."

" Ah, yes," cried Willis, " these are the winds to talk of, especially when sailing with them — that is, from east to west; but when your course is different, they are rather awkward affairs to get ahead of. The way to catch them is to sail from Peru to the Philippines."

" Or from Mexico to China."

" Yes, either will do; then there is no necessity for tacking, you have only to rig your sails and smoke your pipe, or go to sleep; you may, in that way, run four thousand leagues in three months."

" Stiff sailing that, Willis."

" Yes, Master Ernest, but it does not come up to your

yarn about the stars, you recollect, ever so many millions of miles in a second!"

"The trade winds, I was going to observe," continued Becker, "that blow from the west coast of Africa, carry with them a stifling heat."

"That might be expected," remarked Frank, "since they pass over the hot sands of the desert."

"Well, can you tell me why the same wind is cooler on the east coast of America?"

"Because it has been refreshed on crossing the ocean that separates the two continents?"

"By taking a glass of grog on the way," suggested Willis.

"Yes; and so in Europe the north wind is cold because it carries, or rather consists of, air from the polar regions; and the same effect is produced by the south wind in the other hemisphere."

"It is for a like reason," suggested Ernest, "that the south wind in Europe, and particularly the south-west wind, is humid, and generally brings rain, because it is charged with vapor from the Atlantic Ocean."

"How is it, father, that the almanac makers can predict changes in the weather?"

"The almanac makers can only foresee one thing with absolute certainty, and that is, that there are always fools to believe what they say. A few meteorological phenomena may be predicted with tolerable accuracy; but these are few in number, and range within very narrow limits."

"Their predictions, nevertheless, sometimes turn out correct."

"Yes, when they predict by chance a hard frost on a particular day in January, it is just possible the prediction may be verified; out of a multitude of such prognostications a few may be successful, but the greater part of them fail. Their few successes, however, have the effect with weak minds of inspiring confidence, in defiance of the failures which they do not take the trouble to observe."

"At what rate does the wind travel?"

"The speed of the wind is very variable; when it is scarcely felt, the velocity does not exceed a foot a second;

but it is far otherwise in the cases of hurricanes and tornados, that sweep away trees and houses.

"And sink his Majesty's ships," observed Willis.

"In those cases the wind sometimes reaches the velocity of forty-five yards in a second, or about forty leagues in an hour."

"Therefore," remarked Jack, "the wind is a blessing that could very well be dispensed with."

"Your conclusions, Jack, do not always do credit to your understanding. The wind re-establishes the equilibrium of the temperature, and purifies the air by dispersing in the mass exhalations that would be pernicious if they remained in one spot; it clears away miasma, it dissipates the smoke of towns, it waters some countries by driving clouds to them, it condenses vapor on the frozen summits of mountains, and converts it into rivers that cover the land with fruitfulness."

"It likewise fills the sails of ships and creates pilots," observed Willis.

"And brings about shipwrecks," remarked Jack.

"It conveys the pollen of flowers, and, as I had occasion to state the other day, sows the seeds of Nature's fields and forests. It is likewise made available by man in some classes of manufactures—mills, for example."

"And it causes the simoon," persisted Jack, "that lifts the sand of the desert and overwhelms entire caravans; how can you justify such ravages?"

"I do not intend to plead the cause of either hurricanes or simoons; but I contend that, if the wind sometimes terrifies us by disasters, we have, on the other hand, to be grateful for the infinite good it does. In it, as in all other phenomena of the elements, the evils are rare and special, whilst the good is universal and constant."

Fritz, as usual, with the dogs and his rifle charged, acted as pioneer for the caravan, now and then bringing down a bird, sometimes adding a plant to their collection, and occasionally giving them some information as to the state of the surrounding country.

"Father," said he, "I chased this quail into our cornfield; the grain is lying on the ground as if it had been passed over by a roller, but I am happy to say that it is neither broken nor uprooted."

"Now, Jack, do you see how gallantly the wind behaves, prostrating the strong and sparing the weak? If you had been charged with the safety of the grain, no doubt you would have placed it on the tops of the highest trees."

"Very likely; and, until taught by experience, everybody else would have done precisely the same thing."

"True; therefore in this, as in all other things, we should admire the wisdom of Providence, and mistrust our own."

"Whoever would have thought of trusting the staff of human life to such slender support as stalks of straw?"

"If grain had been produced by forests, these, when destroyed by war, burned down by imprudence, uprooted by hurricanes, or washed away by inundations, we should have required ages to replace."

"Very true."

"The fruits of trees are, besides, more liable to rot than those of grain; the latter have their flowers in the form of spikes, often bearded with prickly fibres, which not only protect them from marauders, but likewise serve as little roofs to shelter them from the rain; and besides, as Fritz has just told us, owing to the pliancy of their stalks, strengthened at intervals by hard knots and the spear-shaped form of their leaves, these plants escape the fury of the winds."

"That," said Willis, "is like a wretched cock-boat, which often contrives to get out of a scrape when all the others are swamped."

"Therefore," continued Becker, "their weakness is of more service to them than the strength of the noblest trees, and they are spread and multiplied by the same tempests that devastate the forests. Added to this, the species to which this class of plants belong—the grasses—are remarkably varied in their characteristics, and better suited than any other for universal propagation."

"Which was remarked by Homer," observed Ernest, "who usually distinguishes a country by its peculiar fruit,

but speaks of the earth generally as *zeidoros,* or grain-
bearing."

"There, Willis," exclaimed Jack, "is another great
admiral for you."

"An admiral, Jack?"

"It was he who led the combined fleets of Agamemnon,
Diomedes, and others, to the city of Troy."

"Not in our time, I suppose?"

"How old are you, Willis?"

"Forty-seven."

"In that case it was before you entered the navy."

"I know that there is a Troy in the United States, but
I did not know it was a sea-port."

"There is another in France, Willis; but the Troy I
mean is, or rather was, in Asia Minor, capital of Lesser
Phrygia, sometimes called Ilion, its citadel bearing the
name of Pergamos."

"Never heard of it," said Willis.

"To return to grain," continued Becker, laughing.
"Nature has rendered it capable of growing in all climates,
from the line to the pole. There is a variety for the
humid soils of hot countries, as the rice of Asia; immense
quantities of which are produced in the basin of the Ganges. There is another variety for marshy and cold climates—as a kind of oat that grows wild on the banks of
the North American lakes, and of which the natives gather
abundant harvests."

"God has amply provided for us all," said Frank.

"Other varieties grow best in hot, dry soils, as the millet
in Africa, and maize or Indian corn in Brazil. In Europe,
wheat is cultivated universally, but prefers rich lands,
whilst rye takes more readily to a sandy soil; buckwheat
is most luxuriant where most exposed to rain; oats prefer
humid soils, and barley comes to perfection on rocky,
exposed lands, growing well on the cold, bleak plains of
the north. And, observe, that the grasses suffice for all
the wants of man."

"Yes," observed Ernest, "with the straw are fed his
sheep, his cows, his oxen, and his horses; with the seeds,

he prepares his food and his drinks. In the north, grain is converted into excellent beer and ale, and spirits are extracted from it as strong as brandy."

"The Chinese obtain from rice a liquor that they prefer to the finest wines of Spain."

"That is because they have not yet tasted our Rock-house malaga."

"Then of roasted oats, perfumed with vanilla, an excellent jelly may be made."

"Ah! we must get mamma to try that—it will delight the young ladies."

"And, no doubt, you will profit by the occasion to partake thereof yourself, Master Jack."

"Certainly; but I would not, for all that, seek to gratify my own appetite under pretence of paying a compliment to our friends."

"I know an animal," said Willis, "that, for general usefulness, beats grain all to pieces."

"Good! let us hear what it is, Willis."

"It is the seal of the Esquimaux; they live upon its flesh, and they drink its blood."

"I scarcely think," said Jack, "that I should often feel thirsty under such circumstances."

"The skin furnishes them with clothes, tents, and boats."

"Of which our canoe and life-preservers are a fair sample," said Fritz.

"The fat furnishes them with fire and candle, the muscles with thread and rope, the gut with windows and curtains, the bones with arrow heads and harness; in short, with everything they require."

"True, Willis, in so far as regards their degree of civilization, which is not very great, when we consider that they bury their sick whilst alive, because they are afraid of corpses; that they believe the sun, moon, and stars to be dead Esquimaux, who have been translated from earth to heaven."

Whilst chatting in this way, the party had imperceptibly arrived at Falcon's Nest, wherein they had not set foot for a fortnight previously.

Fritz went up first, and before the others had ascended,

came running down again as fast as his legs would carry him.

"Father," he cried, in an accent of alarm, "there is a fresh litter of leaves up stairs, which has been recently slept upon, and I miss a knife that I left the last time we were here!"

CHAPTER VII.

"HAVE any of you been at Falcon's Nest lately?" inquired Becker, when he had verified the truth of Fritz's intelligence.

"None of us," unanimously replied all the boys.

"You will understand that the question I put to you is, under the circumstances in which we are placed, one of the greatest moment. If, therefore, there is any unseemly joking, any trick, or secret project in contemplation, with which this affair is connected, do not conceal it any longer."

All the boys again reiterated their innocence of the matter in question.

Becker then called to mind the mysterious disappearances of Willis, and, although they were too short in duration to admit of his having been at Falcon's Nest, still he deemed it advisable to put the question to him individually.

Willis declared that the present was the first time he had been in the vicinity of the Nest, and his word was known to be sacred.

"There can be no mistake then," said Becker; "the traces are self-evident. This is altogether a circumstance calculated to give us serious uneasiness. Nevertheless, we must view the matter calmly, and consider what steps we should take to unravel the mystery."

"Let us instantly beat up the island," suggested Fritz.

7*

"It appears to me," remarked Willis, "that the *Nelson* has been wrecked after all, and that one of the men has escaped."

"That," replied Ernest, "is very unlikely. All the crew knew that the island was inhabited, and consequently, had any one of them been thrown on shore, he would have come at once to Rockhouse, and not stopped here."

"As regards the Captain or Lieutenant Dunsley," said Willis, "who were on shore, and could easily find their way, what you say is quite true; but the men were kept on board; and if we suppose that a sailor had been thrown on the opposite coast, he would not be able to determine his position in fifteen days."

"Much less could he expect to find a villa in a fig-tree."

"To say nothing of the light that has been kept burning recently on Shark's Island, nor of the buildings with which the land is strewn, nor the fields and plantations that are to be met with in all directions. For, although a swallow alone is sufficient to convey the seeds of a forest from one continent to another, still it requires the hand of man to arrange the trees in rows and furnish them with props."

"Perhaps we may have crossed each other on the way; and the stranger, after passing the night here, has steered, by some circuitous route, in the direction of Safety Bay."

"May it not have been a large monkey," suggested Jack, "who has resolved to play us a trick for having massacred its companions at Waldeck?"

"Monkeys," replied Ernest, "do not generally open doors, and, seeing no bed prepared for them, go down stairs and collect material for a mattress. You may just as well fancy that the monkey, in this case, came to pass the night at Falcon's Nest with a cigar in its mouth."

"Then he must have been dreadfully annoyed to find neither slippers nor a night-cap."

"There is, unquestionably, a wide field of supposition open for us," said Becker; "but that need not prevent us taking active measures to arrive at the truth. Our first duty is to care for the safety of the ladies; Mr. Wolston is still ailing and feeble, so that, if a stranger were sud-

denly to appear amongst them, they might be terribly
alarmed."

"There are six of us here," remarked Willis, "the
cream of our sea and land forces; we could divide ourselves into three squadrons, one of which might sail for
Rockhouse."

"Just so; let Fritz and Frank start for Rockhouse."

"And what shall we say to the ladies, father?" inquired
the latter; "it does not seem to me necessary to alarm our
mother, Mrs. Wolston, and the young ladies, until something more certain is ascertained."

"Your idea is good, my son, and I thank you for bringing it forward; it is one of those that arise from the heart
rather than the head."

"We have only to find a pretext for their sudden return," observed Ernest.

"Very well," said Jack, "they have only to say it is
too hot to work."

"Just as if it were not quite as hot for us as for them.
Your excuse, Jack, is not particularly artistic."

"Might they not as well say they had forgotten a tool
or a pocket handkerchief?"

"Or, better still, that they had forgotten to shut the
door when they left, and came back to repair the
omission."

"We shall say," replied Fritz, "that, finding there were
twelve strong arms here to do what my father accomplished
fifteen years ago by himself—for the assistance of us
boys could not then be reckoned—we were ashamed of
ourselves, and had returned to Rockhouse to make ourselves useful in repairing the damage to the gallery caused
by the tempest."

"Well, that excuse has, at least, the merit of being
reasonable; and let it be so. Fritz and Frank will return
to Rockhouse; Ernest and myself will continue the work
in hand, and receive the friend or enemy which God has
sent us, should he return to resume his quarters; Willis
and Jack will investigate the neighborhood."

"By land or water, Willis?" inquired Jack.

"By land, Master Jack, for this cruise. I shall abandon

the helm to you, for I know nothing of the shoals here-abouts."

"If," continued Becker, "though highly improbable, any thing important should have happened, or should happen at Rockhouse, you will fire a cannon, and we will be with you immediately. Willis and Jack will discharge a rifle if threatened with danger; and we shall do the same on our side, if we require assistance."

"It is a pity," remarked Jack, "that we had not two or three four-pounders amongst the provisions."

"I scarcely regard this matter as altogether a subject for joking," continued Becker, "and sincerely hope that all our precautions may prove useless. Take each of you a rifle and proceed with caution; above all, do not go far apart from each other; do not fire without taking good aim, and only in case of self-defence or absolute necessity; for this time it does not appear to be a question of bears and hyenas, but, as far as we are able to judge, one of our own species."

Two of the squadrons then hauled off in different directions, carefully examining the ground as they went, beating up the thickets, and endeavoring to obtain some further trace of the stranger, in order to confirm those at Falcon's Nest.

The squadron of observation, in the meanwhile set diligently to work. A tree having been selected at about fifteen paces from that already existing, it was necessary, as on the former occasion, to discharge an arrow carrying the end of a line, and in such a way that the cord might fall across some of the strongest branches; this done, the bamboo ladder was drawn up from the opposite side and held fast until Ernest had ascended and fastened it with nails to the top of the tree.

Ernest then commenced lopping off the branches to the right and left, so as to form a space in the centre for their contemplated dwelling; whilst Becker himself below was making an entrance into the trunk, taking care to avoid an accident that formerly happened, by assuring himself that a colony of bees had not already taken possession of the ground. The gigantic fig-trees at Falcon's Nest

being for the most part hollow, and supported in a great
measure by the bark — like the willows in Europe when
they reach a certain stage of their growth — it was easy
to erect a staircase in the interior ; still this was a work
of time, and Becker had resolved in the meantime to give
up the habitation already constructed to Wolston and his
family, at least until such time as an entrance was attached
to the new one that did not require any extraordinary
amount of gymnastics.

A portion of the day had been occupied in these operations, when Willis and Jack returned to the camp.

" We have seen no one," said the Pilot.

" But," said Jack, " we are on the track of Fritz's knife."

" Be good enough to explain yourself."

" Well, father, at the entrance to the cocoa-nut tree
wood we stumbled upon two sugar canes completely
divested of their juice."

" Which proves ——" said Ernest ; but his remark was
cut short by Jack, who continued —

" Not a bit of it ; a philosopher would have passed these
two worthless sugar canes just as a place-hunter passes an
overthrown minister, that is, as unworthy of notice."

" And what did you do ?"

" Well, I, the headless, the thoughtless, the stupid — for
these are the epithets I am usually favored with — I took
them up, scrutinized them carefully, and discovered ——"

" That they were sugar canes."

" In the first instance, yes."

" Very clever, that !"

" And then that they had not been torn up — *they had
been cut*."

" Is that all ?"

" Yes, most wise and learned brother, that is all ; and I
leave you to draw the inferences."

" I may add," observed the sailor, " that, as we were
steering for the plantation, myself on the starboard and
Jack on the larboard ——"

" On the what ?"

" Master Jack on the left and myself on the right."

" That I pitched right over these canes without ever
noticing them."

"Which is not much to be wondered at; Willis has been so long at sea that he has no confidence in the solidity of the land; during our cruise he kept a look-out after the wind, expecting, I suppose, that it would perform some of the wonderful things you spoke of this morning."

"After all," observed Becker, "this is another link in the chain of evidence, and I congratulate Jack on his sagacity in tracing it."

"But the affair is as much a mystery as ever."

"True; and the solution may probably be awaiting us at Rockhouse."

The united squadrons then started on their homeward voyage, Jack thrusting his nose into every bush, and carefully scanning all the stray objects that seemed to be out of their normal position.

"If these plants and bushes had tongues," said Jack, "they could probably give us the information we require."

"Do you think," inquired Ernest, "that plants and bushes are utterly without sensation?"

"Faith, I can't say," replied Jack; "perhaps they can speak if they liked — probably they have an idiom of their own. You, that know all languages, and a great many more besides, possibly can converse with them."

"I should like to know," said Becker, "why you two gentlemen are always snarling at each other; it is neither amusing nor amiable."

"Ernest is continually showing me up, father, and it is but fair that I should be allowed to retort now and then. But to return to plants, Ernest; you say they have nerves?"

"If they have," said Willis, "they do not seem to possess the bottle of salts that most nervous ladies usually have."

"No," replied Ernest, "they have no nerves, properly so called; but there are plants, and I may add many plants, which, by their qualities — I may almost say by their intelligence — seem to be placed much higher in the scale of creation than they really are. The sensitive plant, for example, shrinks when it is touched; tulips open their petals when the weather is fine, and shut them again at sunset or when it rains; wild barley, when placed on a table, often moves by itself, especially when it has been first warmed by the hand; the heliotrope always turns the face of its flowers to the sun."

"A still more singular instance of this kind was recently discovered in Carolina," remarked Becker; "it is called the *fly-trap*. Its round leaves secrete a sugary fluid, and are covered with a number of ridges which are extremely irritable: whenever a fly touches the surface the leaf immediately folds inwards, contracts, and continues this process till its victim is either pierced with its spines or stifled by the pressure."

"It is probably a Corsican plant," observed Jack, "whose ancestors have had a misunderstanding with the brotherhood of flies, and have left the *Vendetta* as a legacy to their descendants."

"There is nothing in Nature," continued Ernest, "so obstinate as a plant. Let us take one, for example, at its birth, that is, to-day, at the age when animals modify or acquire their instincts, and you will find that your own will must yield to that of the plant."

"If you mean to say that the plant will refuse to play on the flute or learn to dance, were I to wish it to do so, I am entirely of your opinion."

"No, but suppose you were to plant it upside down, with the plantule above and the radicle below; do you think it would grow that way?"

"Plantule and radicle are ambitious words, my dear brother; recollect that you are speaking to simple mortals."

"Well, I mean root uppermost."

"Right; I prefer that, don't you, Willis?"

"Yes, Master Jack."

"At first the radicle or root would begin by growing upwards, and the plantule or germ would descend."

"That is quite in accordance with my revolutionary idiosyncracies."

"You accused me just now of using ambitious words."

"Well, I understand a revolution to mean, placing those above who should be below."

"Nature then," continued Ernest, "very soon begins to assert her rights; the bud gradually twists itself round and ascends, whilst the root obeys a similar impulse and descends — is not this a proof of discernment?"

"I see nothing more in it than a proof of the wonderful mechanism God has allotted to the plant, and is analogous to the movements of a watch, the hands of which point out the hours, minutes, and seconds of time, and are yet not endowed with intelligence."

"Very good, Jack," said Becker.

"Suppose," continued Ernest, "that the ground in the neighborhood of your plant was of two very opposite qualities, that on the right, for example, damp, rich, and spongy; that on the left, dry, poor, and rocky; you would find that the roots, after growing for a time up or down, as the case might be, will very soon change their route, and take their course towards the rich and humid soil."

"And quite right too," said Willis; "they prefer to go where they will be best fed."

"If, then, these roots stretched out to points where they would withdraw the nourishment from other plants in the neighborhood — how could you prevent it?"

"By digging a ditch between them and the plants they threaten to impoverish."

"And do you suppose that would be sufficient?"

"Yes, unless the plant you refer to was an engineer."

"Therein lies the difficulty. Plants are engineers; they would send their roots along the bottom of the ditch, or they would creep under it — at all events, the roots would find their way to the coveted soil in spite of you; if you dug a mine, they would countermine it, and obtain supplies from the opposite territory, and revenge themselves there for the scurvy treatment to which they had been subjected. What could you do then?"

"In that case, I should admit myself defeated."

"If," continued Ernest, "we present a sponge saturated with water to the naked roots of a plant, they will slowly, but steadily, direct themselves towards it; and, turn the sponge whichever way you will, they will take the same direction."

"It has been concluded," remarked Becker, "from these incontestable facts, that plants are not devoid of sensibility; and, in fact, when we behold them lying down at sunset as if dead, and come to life again next morning, we are forced to recognise a degree of irritability in the vegetable organs which very closely resemble those of the animal economy."

"In future," said Jack, "I shall take care not to tread upon a weed, lest, being hurt, it should scream."

"On the other hand, they have not been found to possess any other sign of this supposed sensibility. All their other functions seem perfectly mechanical."

"Ah then, father," exclaimed Jack, "you are a believer in my system!"

"We make them grow and destroy them, without observing anything analogous to the sensation we feel in rearing, wounding, or killing an animal."

"But the fly-trap, father, what of that?"

"It is no exception. The fly-trap seizes any small body that touches it, as well as an insect, and with the same tenacity; hence, we may readily conclude that these actions, so apparently spontaneous, are in reality nothing more than remarkable developments of the laws of irritability peculiar to plants."

"It does not, then, spring from a family feud, as Jack supposed?" remarked Willis.

"Besides," continued Becker, "if plants really existed, possessing what is understood by the term sensation, they would be animals."

"For a like reason, animals without sensation would be plants."

"Evidently. Moreover, the transition from vegetable to animal life is almost imperceptible, so much so, that polypi, such as corals and sponges, were for a long time supposed to be marine plants."

"And what are they?" inquired Willis.

"Insects that live in communities that form a multitude of contiguous cells; some of these are begun at the bottom of the sea and accumulated perpendicularly, one layer being continually deposited over another till the surface is reached."

"Then the coral reefs, that render navigation so perilous in unknown seas, are the work of insects?"

" Exactly so, Willis."

" Might they not as well consist of multitudes of insects piled heaps upon heaps?"

" It is in a great measure as you say, Willis."

" Not I—I do not say it—quite the contrary."

" Well, Willis, you are at liberty to believe it or not, as you think proper."

" I hope so; we shall, therefore, put the polypi with Ernest's stars and Jack's admirals."

" So be it, Willis; but to resume the subject. There is a remarkable analogy in many respects between the lower orders of animals and plants, the bulb is to the latter what the egg is to the former. The germ does not pierce the bulb till it attains a certain organization, and it remains attached by fibres to the parent substance, from which, for a time, it receives nourishment."

" Not unlike the young of animals," remarked Willis.

" When the germ has shot out roots and a leaf or two, it then, but not till then, relinquishes the parent bulb. The plant then grows by an extension and multiplication of its parts, and this extension is accompanied by an increasing induration of the fibres. The same phenomena are observed as regards animals."

" Curious!" said Willis.

" Animals, however, are sometimes oviparous."

"Oviparous?" inquired Willis.

" Yes, that is, they lay eggs; others are viviparous, producing their young alive. A few are multiplied like plants by cuttings, as in the case of the polypi."

" Bother the polypi," said Willis, laughing, "since we have to thank them for destroying some of his Majesty's ships."

" Then again," continued Becker, "both plants and animals are subject to disease, decay, and death."

" But, father, if the analogies are remarkable, the differences are not less marked."

" Well, Ernest, I shall leave you to point them out."

" Without reckoning the faculty of feeling, that cannot

be denied to the one nor granted to the other, the most striking of these distinctions consists in the circumstance that animals can change place, whilst this faculty is absolutely refused to plants."

" If we except those," remarked Jack, " that insist upon travelling to the succulent parts of the earth, and are as indefatigable in digging tunnels as the renowned Brunel."

" Then plants are obliged to accept the nourishment that their fixed position furnishes to them; whilst animals, on the contrary, by means of their external organs, can range far and near in search of the aliments most congenial to their appetites."

" Which is often **very capricious**," remarked Willis.

" Then, considered with regard to magnitude, the two kingdoms present remarkable distinctions; the interval between a whale and a mite is greater than between the moss and the oak."

" Ho!" cried Jack, " there is Miss Sophia coming to meet us, Willis."

" Perhaps they have news at the grotto."

" Well," inquired the child, " have you seen them?"

" Good," thought Becker, " our chatterers have not been able to hold their tongues; I am surprised at that as regards Frank."

" We expected to have found them at Rockhouse."

" To have found whom?"

" The sailors from the wreck."

" What wreck?"

" The *Nelson.*"

" I sincerely hope that the *Nelson* has not been wrecked."

" In that case, whom do you refer to yourself, Miss Sophia?"

" To your go-cart and my doll, Master Jack."

CHAPTER VIII.

SOME days passed without anything having occurred to ruffle the tranquil existence of the island families. Every morning the *élite* of the sea and land forces continued to divide themselves into three squadrons of observation; one of which remained at Rockhouse on some pretext or other, whilst the other two were occupied in exploring the country, or in carrying on the works at Falcon's Nest.

The mysterious stranger, whether shipwrecked seaman, savage, or hobgoblin, who kept all the bearded inhabitants of Rockhouse on the alert, had reappeared in his old quarters, where another litter of leaves had been miraculously strewn exactly in the same place the former had occupied.

Beyond this, however, and sundry gashes here and there —of which Fritz's knife was clearly guilty, but which could not have been perpetrated without an accomplice — nothing had transpired to enable them to arrive at a satisfactory conclusion as to who or what this personage could be.

Though the hypothesis was highly improbable, still Willis persisted in his theory of the shipwreck; he only doubted whether the individual on shore was a marine or the cabin-boy, an officer or a foremast man, and, if the latter, whether it was Bill, Tom, Bob, or Ned.

Ernest rather inclined to think that the invisible stranger was an inhabitant of the moon, who, in consequence of a false step, had tumbled from his own to our planet.

The warlike Fritz was impatient and irritated. He would over and over again have preferred an immediate solution of the affair, even were it bathed in blood, rather than be kept any longer in suspense.

Frank, on the contrary, took a metaphysical view of the case; and, believing that Providence had not entirely dispensed with miracles in dealing with the things of this world, came to the conclusion that it was no earthly visitor they had to deal with; and he even went so far as to hint that prayer was a more efficacious means of solving the mystery than the methods his brothers were pursuing.

Jack, coinciding in some degree with Ernest, shifted his view from an ape to an anthropophagian, and blamed the latter for not coming earlier; when he and his brothers were younger, and consequently more tender, they would have made a better meal, and been more easily digested.

As to what opinion Becker himself entertained, with regard to the occurrence at Falcon's Nest that kept his sons in a feverish state of anxiety, and had awakened all the fears of the Pilot for the safety of his friends on board the *Nelson*, nothing could be clearly ascertained; in so far as this matter was concerned he kept his own counsel; and, to use an expression of Madame de Sevigné, "had thrown his tongue to the dogs."

The close of the day had, as usual, collected all the members of the family round the domestic hearth; and it may be stated here that Mrs. Wolston, Mary, and Mrs. Becker alternately undertook the preparations of the viands for the diurnal consumption of the community. By this means, uniformity, that palls the appetite, was entirely banished from their dishes. One day they would have the cooked, or rather half-cooked, British joints of Mrs. Wolston and her daughter, varied occasionally, to the great delight of Willis, with a tureen of hotch-potch or cocky-leekie. The next there would be a display of the cosmopolite and somewhat picturesque cookery of Mrs. Becker; there was her famous peccary pie, with ravansara sauce, followed by her delicious preserved mango and seaweed jelly. Nor did she hesitate to draw upon the raw material of the colony now and then for a new hash or soup, taking care, however, to keep in view the maxim that prudence is the mother of safety — an adage that was rather roughly handled by the renowned French linguist, Madame Dacier, who, on one occasion nearly poisoned her husband with a Lacedemonian stew, the receipt for which she had found in Xenophon.

Luckily Becker's wife did not know Greek, consequently he ran no risk of being entertained with a classic dinner; but he was often reminded by his thoughtful partner of Meg Dod's celebrated receipt: before you cook your hare, first — catch it.

Sophia desired earnestly to have a share in the culinary government; but having shown on her first trial, too decided a leaning towards puddings and pancakes, her second essay was put off till she became more thoroughly penetrated with the value of the eternal precept *utile dulci*, which signifies that, before dessert it is requisite to have something substantial.

As soon as they had finished their afternoon meal, Willis departed on one of his customary mysterious excursions; and Jack, who, like the birds that no sooner hop upon one branch than they leap upon another, had also disappeared. It was not long, however, before he made his appearance again; he came running in almost out of breath, and cried at the top of his voice,

"I have discovered him!"

"Whom?" exclaimed half a dozen voices.

"The inhabitant of the moon?" inquired Ernest.

"No."

"I know," said Sophia playfully, "your go-cart and my doll."

"No, I have discovered Willis' secret."

"If you have been watching him, it is very wrong."

"No, father; seeing some thin columns of smoke rising out of a thicket, I thought a bush was on fire; but on going nearer, I saw that it was only a tobacco-pipe."

"Was the pipe alone, brother?"

"No, not exactly, it was in Willis' mouth; and there he sat, so completely immersed in ideas and smoke, that he neither heard nor saw me."

" That he does not smoke here," remarked Becker, " I can easily understand ; but why conceal it ? "

" Ah," replied Mrs. Wolston, " you do not know Willis yet ; — beneath that rough exterior there are feelings that would grace a coronet : he is, no doubt, afraid of leading your sons into the habit."

" That is very thoughtful and considerate on his part."

" He was always smoking on board ship, and it must have been a great sacrifice for him to leave it off to the extent he has done lately."

" Then we shall not allow him to punish himself any longer ; and as for the danger of contagion from his smoking here, that evil may perhaps be avoided."

" Do not be afraid, father ; it will not be necessary to establish either a quarantine or a lazaretto on our account."

" Besides, any of the boys," said Mrs. Becker, " that acquire the habit, will, by so doing, voluntarily banish themselves from my levees."

" It is an extraordinary habit that, smoking," observed Mrs. Wolston.

" Yes," said Becker ; " and what makes the habit more singular is, that it holds out no allurements to seduce its votaries. Generally, the path to vice, or to a bad habit, is strewn with roses that hide their thorns, but such is not the case with smoking ; in order to acquire this habit, a variety of disagreeable difficulties have to be overcome, and a considerable amount of disgust and sickness must be borne before the stomach is tutored to withstand the nauseous fumes."

" In point of fact," observed Wolston, " if, instead of being made part and parcel of the appliances of a fashionable man, cigars and meershaums were classed in the pharmacopœia with emetics and cataplasms, there is not a human being but would bemoan his fate if compelled to undergo a dose."

" Just so," added Becker ; " the great and sole attraction of tobacco to young people consists in its being to them a forbidden thing ; the apple of Eve is of all time — it hangs from every tree, and takes myriads of shapes. If I had the honor of being principal of a college I should no

more think of forbidding the pupils to use tobacco than I
should think of commanding them not to use the birch for
purposes of self-chastisement."

"Perhaps you would be quite right."

"Instead of lecturing them on the pernicious effects of
tobacco, I should hang up a pipe of punishment in the
class-room, and oblige offending pupils to inhale a fixed
number of whiffs proportionate to the gravity of their
delinquency."

"An excellent idea," observed Wolston; "for it is often
only necessary to show some things in a different light in
order to give them a new aspect and value. This puts me
in mind of an illustration in point; these two girls, when
children, were the parties concerned, and I will relate the
circumstance to you."

"In that case," said Mary, "I shall go and feed the
fowls."

"And I," said Sophia, "must go and water the flowers."

"Oh, then," cried Jack laughing, "it is another doll
story, is it ? "

"No, Master Jack, it is not a doll story ; and, besides,
we girls were no bigger at the time than that."

On saying this Sophia placed her two hands about a
foot and a half from the floor and then the two girls
vanished.

"When Mary was about six years old," began Wolston,
"a slight rash threatened to develope itself, and the doctor
ordered a small blister to be applied to one of her arms.
Now, there was likely to be some difficulty about getting
her to submit quietly to this operation, so, after an instant's
reflection, I called both her and her sister, and told them
that the most diligent of the two should have a vesicatory
put on her arm at night. 'Oh,' cried both the girls quite
delighted, "it will be me, papa, I shall be so good.
Mamma, mamma — such a treat — papa has promised us
a vesicatory for to-night !"

"That was simplicity itself," said Mrs. Becker, laughing
till the tears came into her eyes.

"The day passed, the one endeavoring to excel the
other in the quantity of leaves they turned over; and,

from time to time, I heard the one asking the other in a low voice, 'Have you ever seen a vesicatory? What is it made of? Is it for eating? And each in turn regarded her arms, to judge in advance the effect of the marvellous ornament."

"I should like much to have seen them."

"Night came, and I declared gravely that the eldest was fairly entitled to the prize. The latter jumped about with joy, and Sophia began to cry. "Don't cry,' said Mary, 'if you are good, papa will, perhaps, give you one to-morrow, too.' Then the joyful patient, turning to me, said, 'On which arm, papa?" and I told her that the ceremony of placing it on must take place when she was in bed. To bed accordingly she went, the ornament was applied , she looked at it, was pleased with it, thanked me for it, and fell asleep as happy as a queen. But, alas! like that of many queens, the felicity did not last long; before morning, I heard her saying to her sister, in a doleful tone, "Soffy, will you have my vesicatory?' 'Oh, yes, just lend it to me for a tiny moment.' At this I hurried to the spot, and, as you may readily suppose, opposed the transfer."

" Poor Sophia!"

"Yes; she was quite heart-broken, and said, sobbing, 'It is always Mary that gets everything, nobody ever gives anything to me.'"

Next day, Willis laid hold of his sou'-wester, and was starting off on his customary pilgrimage, when Becker stopped him.

"Willis," said he, "have you any objections to state what the engagements are, that require you to leave us at pretty much the same hour every day?"

"I merely go for a walk, Mr. Becker."

"Ah!"

"You see I require to take a turn just after dinner for the sake of my health."

"A habit that you contracted on board ship; eh, Willis?"

"On board ship; yes Mr. Becker, that is to say——"

"Just so," observed Mrs. Wolston; "and by the way, Willis, I regret that you do not smoke now; they say there is plenty of tobacco on the island."

"Smoke!" cried Willis, raising his ears like a war-horse at the sound of the trumpet, "why so, Mrs. Wolston?"

"Because we are dreadfully tormented with those horrid mosquitoes, and you might help us to get rid of them. You smoked at sea, did you not?"

"Yes, madam; but then my constitution——"

"Bah!" said Wolston, "I thought you were as strong as a horse, Willis."

"Well, I have no cause to complain neither; but then they say tobacco would kill even a horse."

"Of course, Willis, your health is a most necessary consideration."

"Still for all that, if the mosquitoes really do annoy Mrs. Wolston, I should have no objection to take a whiff now and then."

"You must not put yourself about though, on our account, Willis."

"About; no, it would not put me about."

"Very good; then it only remains to be seen whether there is a pipe in the colony."

"Ah," said Willis, feeling his pockets, "yes, exactly — here is one."

"Curious how things do turn up, isn't it, Willis?" said Becker; "but the mosquitoes would not be frightened away by the smoke, if applied at long intervals, so you will have to repeat the dose at least two or three times every day, always supposing it does not affect your constitution."

"Sailors, you see," replied Willis, "are like chimneys, they always smoke when you want them, and sometimes a great deal more than you want them." And on turning round, he beheld Sophia holding a light, and a good-sized case of Maryland, which had been preserved from the wreck.

Ever after that time the mosquitoes had a most persevering enemy in Willis; and, notwithstanding his health, his daily walks entirely ceased.

For some time the Pilot and the four young men passed the night in a tent erected about midway between Rockhouse and the Jackal River. The apparent reason for this modification of their plans was the greater facility it afforded for their all meeting at daybreak, breakfasting together, and setting out for Falcon's Nest before the temperature reached ninety degrees in the shade, which junction could not be so easily effected with one party encamped at Rockhouse and the other bivouacked on Shark's Island, with an arm of the sea between them.

The real motive, however, was that all might be within hail of each other, and prepared for every emergency, in the event of the stranger appearing in a more palpable shape, and assuming a hostile attitude. We say the stranger, because, judging from the indications, there was only one — still that did not prove that there might not be several.

One night, as **Fritz was** lying with one eye open, he observed Mary's little black terrier suddenly prick up the fragments of its ears, and begin sniffing at the edge of the tent. This shaggy little **cur was** called Toby; it had accompanied the Wolstons on their voyage, and was Mary's exclusive property; but Fritz had found the way to the animal's heart as usual through its stomach, and **Mary** was in no way jealous of his attentions to her favorite, but rather the reverse.

Fritz, feeling convinced by the actions of the dog, which was of the true Scotch breed, that something extraordinary was passing outside the tent, seized his rifle, hastened out, and was just in time to distinguish a human figure on the opposite **bank of the Jackal River,** which, on seeing him, took to its heels and disappeared in the forest.

He was soon joined by the Pilot and his brothers; the dogs leaped about them, and the alarm became general throughout the encampment. Fritz re-established order, enjoined silence, and said,

"I am determined this **time to follow the affair up; who** will accompany me?"

"I will!" said all the four voices at once.

"Scouting parties ought not to be numerous," said Fritz; "I will, therefore, take Willis, in case this mystification has anything to do with the *Nelson.*"

"And me," said Jack, "to serve as a dessert, in case the individual should turn out to be an anthropophagian."

"Be it so; but no more. Frank and Ernest will remain to tranquilize our parents, in case we should not return before they are up."

"And if so, what shall we say?"

"Tell them the truth. We shall proceed direct to Falcon's Nest; and if the stranger — confiding in our habit of sleeping during the night — be there as usual, we shall do ourselves the honor of helping him to get up."

"Providing he does not nightly change his quarters like Oliver Cromwell — not so much to avoid enemies, as to calm his uneasy conscience."

"Well, we shall be no worse than before; we shall have tried to restore our wonted quietude, and, if we fail, we can say, like Francis I. at Pavia, '*All is lost except our honor.*'"

Some minutes after this conversation, three shadows might have been seen stealing through the glades in the direction of Falcon's Nest. Nothing was to be heard but the rustling of the leaves — the deafened beating of the sea upon the rocks — and, to use the words of Lamartine, "those unknown tongues that night and the wind whisper in the air." The trees were mirrored in the rays of the moon, and the ground, at intervals, seemed strewn with monstrous giants; their hearts beat, not with fear, but with that feverish impatience that anticipates decisive results.

When they arrived at the foot of the tree on which the aerial dwelling was situated, Fritz opened the door, and resolutely, but stealthily, ascended.

Willis and Jack followed him with military precision.

They reached the top of the staircase, and held the latch of the door that opened into the apartment.

A train of mice, in the strictest incognito, could not have performed these operations with a greater amount of secretiveness. On opening the door they stood and listened.

Not a sound. Jack fired off a pistol, and the fraudulent occupier of the room instantly started up on his feet. Fritz rushed forward, and clasped him tightly round the body.

"Ho, ho, comrade," said he, "this time you do not get off so easily!"

CHAPTER IX.

"THE chimpanzé or chimpanzee," says Buffon, the French naturalist, "is much more sagacious than the *ourang outang*, with which it has been inaccurately confounded; it likewise bears a more marked resemblance to the human being; the height is the same, and it has the same aspect, members, and strength; it always walks on two feet, with the head erect, has no tail, has calves to its legs, hair on its head, a beard on its chin, a face that Grimaldi would have envied, hands and nails like those of men, whose manners and habits it is susceptible of acquiring."

Buffon knew an individual of the species that sat demurely at table, taking his place with the other guests; like them he would spread out his napkin, and stick one corner of it into his button-hole just as they did, and he was exceedingly dexterous in the use of his knife, fork, and spoon. Spectators were not a little surprised to see him go to a bed made for him, tie up his head in a pocket-handkerchief, place it sideways on a pillow, tuck himself carefully in the bed-clothes, pretend to be sick, stretch out his pulse to be felt, and affect to undergo the process of being bled.

The naturalist adds that he is very easily taught, and may be made a useful domestic servant, at least as regards the humbler operations of the kitchen; he promptly obeys signs and the voice, whilst other species of apes only obey the stick; he will rinse glasses, serve at table, turn tl a spit, grind coffee, or carry water. Add to his virtues as a domestic, that he is not much addicted to chattering about the family affairs, has no followers, and is very accommodating in the matter of wages.

It was neither more nor less than a chimpanzee that Fritz had caught in the dark at Falcon's Nest.

"Now then, old fellow," said he, "you will help us to clear up this mysterious affair."

The caged stranger made no reply to this observation; Willis and Jack then questioned him, the one in English and the other in French.

Still no reply.

He did not submit, however, to be interrogated quietly; on the contrary, his struggles to get away were most vigorous, so much so that Fritz adopted the precaution of binding him.

"If it had been one of our sailors," said Willis, "he would have recognized my voice long ago."

"Who are you?" asked one.

"Where do you come from?" inquired another.

"Do not attempt to escape," said a third.

"We mean you no harm; on the contrary, we are friends, disposed to do you good if we can."

"If all his brothers and sisters are as talkative as himself," remarked Jack, "they must be a very amusing sort of people."

"He can walk at all events," said Fritz giving him a smart push.

The chimpanzee fell flat on the floor.

"It appears, sir, that you are determined to have your own way, we must therefore wait till daylight."

An hour passed in polyglot expostulations with the stranger on the score of his obstinacy, but all to no purpose; to use a popular expression, he was as dumb as the Doges. He deigned, however, to empty at a single draught a calabash of Malaga that Willis gave him, but there his condescension stopped.

The Pilot, who now encountered mosquitoes in all directions, made preparations for smoking; the light he struck,

however, instead of clearing up the mystery, only perplexed them more and more; there lay their new companion, stretched on the ground, staring at them with a
ludicrous grin.

If, on the one hand, it occurred to them this man was
an animal, on the other the animal was a man, and Buffon
did not happen to be there at the time to assign him
officially a place in the former kingdom.

The next difficulty that presented itself was, how they
were to get him along; when they broke in the onagra,
they ran a prong through his ear; in reducing the buffalo
to subjection, they did not feel the slightest compunction in
thrusting a pin through the cartilage of his nose; then, in
order to give elasticity to the legs of the ostrich, they
yoked him to two or three other animals, and, willing or
unwilling, he was compelled ultimately to yield obedience
to the lords of creation. But whether the creature before
them was a lower order of negro or a higher order of ape,
there was too great a resemblance between the captured
and the capturers to admit of any of these methods of
impulsion being adopted. It was, therefore, stretched on
a plank, like a nabob in his palanquin, that the chimpanzee
made his first appearance at Rockhouse.

When the cavalcade arrived there, all the family, with
the exception of Ernest and Frank, were still asleep.
The first thing they did was to clothe the creature they
had captured in a sailor's pantaloons and jacket, with
which he seemed rather pleased, and the result of this
operation was, that he began to assume a less ferocious
aspect, and behave more respectfully towards his captors.
All the family had sat down to breakfast, when Fritz and
Jack, taking him by the hands, led him gravely into the
gallery. A cord was attached to his legs, allowing him to
walk, but was so arranged that he could not run.

On his appearance the young girls fled at once; and,
more accustomed to drawing-rooms than the rude realities
of savage life, Mrs. Wolston's first impulse was to do the
same.

"Goodness gracious!" she cried with an air of alarm,
"what horror is that?"

"That, madam, is precisely what we have been anxious for the last two or three hours to find out," replied Fritz.

" Does the creature speak ? "

" Up till now, madam," replied Willis, " he has only opened his mouth to swallow my calabash of Malaga; beyond that, he has kept as close as a purser's locker."

When the first shock had passed, and the company had regained their self-possession, Jack related, with his customary originality, the incidents of the nocturnal expedition, of which Fritz was the originator, leader, and hero. The ladies then, for the first time, were made acquainted with the doubts, fears, perplexities, and battues, which, out of gallantry, they had hitherto been kept in ignorance of. Becker then, having carefully investigated the creature, pronounced it to be (as we already know) a full-grown specimen of a kind of ape, called by the Africans " the wild man of the woods," and by naturalists the *jocko* or chimpanzee.

" It is naturally very savage," added Becker ; "but this individual seems already to have received some degree of education."

As a proof of this, the chimpanzee seated himself amongst them very much at his ease ; he scanned the faces surrounding him with an air of curiosity, and seemed to search for a particular countenance that it annoyed him not to find. Some fruit and nuts that were given him put him in excellent humor.

"He has, without doubt, been on board some ship, wrecked on the coast," said Wolston, "for I recollect having read that his kindred are only found in Western Africa and the adjacent islands ; do you not recognize him, Willis, to belong to the *Nelson*, like the plank of the other day ? "

" No, sir."

" So much the better."

" We do not ship such cattle on board his Majesty's ships," added the Pilot.

The girls, ashamed of their fear, now came peeping in at the door, and, seeing that nobody had been devoured, took refuge by the side of their mother.

"Look here, father," said Ernest, feeling the creature's crania, after having facetiously begged pardon for the liberty, "its head is precisely like our own; that is very humiliating."

"Yes, my son, but his tongue and other organs are also exactly like ours, yet he cannot utter a word. His head is of the same form and proportion, but he does not for all that possess human intelligence. Is this not a very striking proof that mere matter, though perfectly organized, neither produces words nor thought; and that it requires a special manifestation of the Divine will to call these attributes into existence?"

"True; but, father, some writers say that apes have been observed to profit by fires lighted in the forest, and have gone and warmed themselves when the travellers left."

"That, my son, is instinct, nothing more; the operation of keeping up a fire, by throwing a few branches upon it, is exceedingly simple, but their instinct has never been known to rise to that amount of intelligence."

"You recollect, father, that heathcock we saw some years ago displaying his glossy plumage to the dazzled hens; is that not a well-marked proof of coquetry? and is not this coquetry an indication of something more than mere instinct?"

"You will permit me to believe, my son, at least till the contrary has been proved, that these actions to which you refer have nothing at all to do with coquetry. Those brilliant colors are designed for a purpose other than that which you suppose; they serve as signals to keep the community together, or, in other words, they are a common centre round which the hens may revolve."

"The transition from apes to heathcocks," remarked Jack, "appears to me somewhat abrupt."

"Not so abrupt as you think, Master Jack," said Wolston; "those who take the trouble to study Nature, observe an admirable gradation and easy progression from a simple to a complex organization. There is no race or species that is not connected by a perceptible link with that which precedes and that which follows."

9*

"What relation is there, for example," inquired Jack, "between an oyster and a horse?"

"No immediate relation certainly, but there are intermediate links by which the two are brought together: they may be regarded, however, as the opposite extremes of the brotherhood — the two poles in the chain of existence. A horse bears even less resemblance to a turnip than to an oyster; a relationship may, nevertheless, be traced, step by step, between them, dissimilar as they are. There is the polypus, that singular product of Nature, which, regarded in one light, performs all the functions of animal life, whilst, when regarded in another, it has the ordinary attributes of a plant; does this not clearly and distinctly mark the transition from the vegetable to the animal kingdom? Again, certain species of worms blend the animal with the insect tribe, those which are covered with a horny substance unite them with the crustaceæ. These approach fish on the one hand, and reptiles on the other, whilst reptiles in some species become moluscs."

"And what is a molusc?" inquired Willis.

"The term *molusc* is applied by naturalists to creatures which have no vertebræ, as for example, the cuttle fish and the oyster."

"I believe *you*, Mr. Wolston; but if I had asked Ernest or Jack, they would have told me that it was a commodore or an admiral."

"Reptiles, I was going to say, are connected at one end of the chain with moluscs by the slug, and at the other with fish by the eel. . From flying-fish to birds the transition is by no means abrupt. The ostrich, whose legs are like goat's, and runs rather than flies, connects birds with quadrupeds; these again return to fish through the cetacea."

"Yes, but the interval between such creatures and man is still great."

"True; to connect the two would be a process replete with insurmountable difficulties, and only possible to creative power. The projecting snout would have to be flattened, and the features of humanity imprinted upon it —that head bent upon the ground would have to be directed upwards — that narrow breast would have to be flattened out — those legs would have to be converted into flexible arms, and those horny hoofs into nimble fingers."

"To accomplish which," remarked Frank, "God had only to say, ' Let it be so.'"

"Assuredly ; and as there is nothing incongruous in Nature, as everything is admirably adapted for its purpose, as unity of design is perceptible in all things, as every effect proceeds from a cause, and becomes a cause in its turn of succeeding effects, so God has willed that there should be a chain of resemblance running through all his works, and the link that connects man with the animal kingdom — the highest type of the mammiferous race, and the nearest approach to humanity amongst the brutes — is the creature before you."

As if to illustrate this position, and prove his title to the place awarded him, the chimpanzee quietly laid hold of Mr. Wolston's straw hat and stuck it on his crispy head.

"He is, perhaps, afraid of catching cold," said Jack, thrusting a mat under his feet.

"Compare birds with quadrupeds," continued Mr. Wolston, "and you will find analogies at every step. Does the powerful and kingly eagle not resemble the noble and generous lion? — the cruel vulture, the ferocious tiger? — the kite, buzzard, and crow preying upon carrion, hyenas, jackals, and wolves?   Are not falcons, hawks, and other birds used in the chase, types of foxes and dogs? Is the owl, which prowls about only at night, not a type of the cat?   The cormorants and herons, that live upon fish, are they not the otters and beavers of the air?   Do not peacocks, turkeys, and the common barn-door fowl bear a striking affinity to oxen, cows, sheep, and other ruminating animals?"

During these remarks, Jack's monkey, Knips, had found its way into the gallery, and, observing the new-comer, went forward to accost him as if an old friend; the latter, however, uttered a menacing cry, and was about to seize Knips with evidently no amiable design, but was prevented by the cords that bound his legs. Knips leaped upon the back of one of the boys, and there, as if on the tower of an impregnable fortress, commenced making a series of grimaces at the chimpanzee, these being the only missiles within reach that he could launch at his relation. The enemy retorted, and kept up a smart fire of like ammunition.

"It appears," remarked Mrs Wolston, "that apes are something like men; the great and the little do not readily amalgamate."

"We must make them amalgamate," said Jack, taking one of Knips's paws, whilst Ernest held that of the chimpanzee; thus they compelled them to shake hands, but with what degree of cordiality we are unable to state.

"You ought to oblige them now to take an oath of fealty," said Mrs. Wolston

"Chimpanzee," said Jack, speaking for Knips, "I promise always to treat you in future with smiles, delicacies, and respect."

"Knips," replied the wild man of the woods, through the organs of Ernest, "I promise to have for you only the most generous intentions; to share with you the nuts I may have occasion to crack, that is, by giving you the shells and keeping the kernel; I promise, moreover, not to immolate you at the altar of my just rage, unless it is impossible for me to avoid an outburst of temper."

"Now the embrace of peace."

"Ah, madam," said Jack, "you must excuse that ceremony, their friendship is too new for such intimacy, and Knips don't much like being bitten."

"Need we other proofs," remarked Becker, when the scene between the monkeys was concluded, "that everything has been premeditated, weighed, and calculated? It was necessary for that most arid country, Arabia, that we should have a sober animal, susceptible of existing a long time without water, and capable of treading the hot sands of the desert. God has accordingly given us the camel."

"And the dromedary," remarked Ernest.

"So everywhere," continued Becker; "and add to these evidences of Divine wisdom the brilliant colors, the silken furs, the golden plumage, and the ever-varying forms, yet, in all this diversity, there is unison — a harmony. Like the various objects which a clever artist introduces into his sketch, they are placed without uniformity, but still with reference to their effect upon each other, and so to the unity of the general design."

"Therefore," remarked Ernest, "we have an animal whose skin is of stone, which it throws off annually to assume a new one — whose flesh is its tail and in its feet — whose hair is found inside in its breast — whose stomach is in its head, which, like the skin, is renewed every year, the first function of the new being to digest the old one."

Here the Pilot manifested some symptoms of incredulity.

"That is not all, Willis," continued Ernest, "the animal of which I speak carries its eggs in the interior of its body till they are hatched, and then transfers them to its tail. It has pebbles in its stomach, can throw off its limbs when they incommode it, and replace them with others more to its fancy. To finish the portrait, its eyes are placed at the tip of long flexible horns."

"Do you really mean me to believe that yarn?" inquired Willis.

"Yes, Willis, unless you intend to deny the existence of lobsters."

"Lobsters! Ah! you are talking of them, are you!"

"Have not," continued Ernest, "six thousand three hundred and sixty-two eyes been counted in one beetle? sixteen thousand in a fly? and as many as thirty-four thousand six hundred in a butterfly? Of course, facets understood."

"Supposing these facets myope or presbyte," observed Jack, "that gives seventeen thousand three hundred and twenty-five pairs of spectacles on one nose!"

"How wonderfully varied are the forms of Nature. If, from the mastodon and the fossil mammoth, to which Buffon attributes five or six times the bulk and size of the elephant, we descend to those animalculæ, of which Leuwenhoek estimates that a thousand millions of them would not occupy the place of an ordinary grain of sand."

Here Willis lost all patience and left the gallery, whistling as usual, under such circumstances, the "Mariner's March."

"Malesieu has detected animals by the microscope twenty-seven times smaller than a mite. A single drop of water under this instrument assumes the aspect of a lake, peopled by an infinite multitude of living creatures."

"Therefore," observed Wolston, "it is not the great works of Nature, or those of which the organization is most perfect, that alone presents to the mind of man the unfathomable mysteries of creation; atoms become to him problems, that utterly defy the utmost efforts of his intelligence."

"Which," suggested Becker, "does not prevent us believing ourselves a well of science, nor hinder us from piling Pelion on Ossa to scale the skies."

"What becomes, in the presence of these facts, of the metaphysics and cosmogonies that have succeeded each other for two thousand years? What of all the theories, from Ptolemy to Copernicus, from Copernicus to Galileo, Descartes and his zones, Leibnitz and his monads, Wolf and his fire forces, Maupertuis and his intelligent elements, Broussais, who, in his anatomical lectures, has oftener than once shown to his pupils, on the point of his scalpel, the source of thought; what, I say, becomes of all these?"

"There is less wisdom in such vain speculation than in these simple words: '*I believe in God the Father, the Creator of all things.*'"

"Worlds," says Isaiah, "are, before Him, like the dewdrops on a blade of grass."

"We are now, however, getting into the clouds," remarked Wolston; "let us return to the earth by the shortest route. What do you mean to do with the chimpanzee?"

"Why, we must cage him in some way," replied Becker; "to let him loose again would be to create fresh uneasiness for ourselves. To kill him would be almost a kind of homicide."

"Can I come in now?" inquired Willis, thrusting his head into the gallery.

"Yes, with perfect safety."

" You see, when Master Ernest begins to spin, he gets into the chapter of miracles, and forgets that we have ears."

" I cannot help seeing them sometimes though, Willis; when they are a little longer than usual, it is difficult to hide them altogether."

" Well," replied Willis, " I confess I am a bit of a fool, and as you are at a loss what to do with our friend here, I shall take him over with me to Shark's Island: there will be a pair of us there then."

" If you will undertake to be his guide and instructor, he is yours, Willis."

" What shall I call him ? "

"Jocko."

" It shall go hard with me if I do not make a gentleman of him in a month's time."

" I should like," said Frank, " if you could convert him into a tiger."

" A tiger ? "

" Yes, we want a footman in livery to fetch Mrs. Wolston's carriage next time she calls for it."

" I feel highly flattered by the compliment," said Mrs. Wolston, " but fear you will not be able to turn him out entire."

" Why so, madam ? "

" Where are the top boots to come from ? "

CHAPTER X.

WHEN a country is released from the presence of an
enemy that annoyed and harassed them, the people feel
as if a weight had been taken off their shoulders; so the
inhabitants of New Switzerland had breathed more freely
since the capture of the chimpanzee.

The works at Falcon's Nest were completed, and the
two families had taken possession of their aerial dwellings,
where they were perched like a pair of rookeries within
call of each other.

The confined air of towns has a tendency to plunge men
into lethargy and indolence, and to precipitate the deca-
dence of a constitution in which the seeds of disease have
been sown; whilst, on the other hand, the pure air of the
country braces the nerves, excites a healthy action in the
system, and invigorates a shattered frame; so it was with
Mr. Wolston — under the benign influences of the genial
climate and the refreshing sea breeze, he gradually, but
steadily, recovered health and strength.

A larger breadth of land had been cleared and fitted for
receiving grain, which it was susceptible of reproducing a
hundred-fold. Such is the sublime contract God has made
with man, that, in exchange for his labor and skill, a single
grain of wheat will produce seven or eight stalks, each
bearing an ear containing fifty grains; a single grain has
been known to yield twenty-eight ears, and Pliny states
that Nero received a grain bearing the enormous number

of three hundred and sixty ears. Strange that such a singular instance of fecundity should present itself during the domination of a man, or rather monster, who dared to wish that the Roman people had only one head, so that he might cut it off at a single blow!

Willis and the Wolstons were as yet ignorant of the extent and limits of the colony; there were two inclosed and cultivated sections, named respectively Waldeck and Prospect Hill, which they had not yet inspected. With a view to enable them to form a more accurate conception of the boundaries of the territory they inhabited, a grand excursion was decided upon that would enable them leisurely to investigate every nook and cranny of the settlement.

The storehouse was accordingly overhauled, and the ladies called in to prepare viands for the journey; they were likewise invited to furnish a supply of certain enchanted travelling bags, in which the gentlemen were often astonished to find, during their distant expeditions, a thousand and one useful things that they would never have dreamt of bringing with them of their own accord.

Becker, Wolston, Ernest, and Frank set about the construction of a vehicle on four wheels for the luggage and the ladies; they did not contemplate erecting a machine with elastic springs and gilded panels, like the Lord Mayor's state coach — their object was to produce a machine that would ease, without dislocating, the limbs of the travellers, and that would move at least more gently than a gardener's cart, loaded with hampers of greens for Covent Garden Market. It may readily be supposed that Ernest's Latin was not of much service in these operations, for even Wolston's mechanical skill was sorely tried in elaborating the design.

Fritz, Willis, and Jack had already started as pioneers of the expedition to examine the buildings, and to see that no more apes or other piratical marauders had established themselves on their premises; and, in compliance with a request made by Willis, who strongly objected to becoming a bushranger, they had gone by water. It was further arranged that, on their return, all should start together —

10

the entire community in one cavalcade, like an army on the march.

"The young ladies were as much pleased in anticipation with this journey as if the destination of the travellers had been Brighton or Ramsgate. To children of their age, change is always pleasing. Often, in consequence of a death, the collapse of a bank, the loss of a law-suit, or some dire disaster of that sort, parents have seen themselves compelled to abandon the home of their fathers, endeared to them by many gentle recollections, perhaps to embark for some far distant land; they stifle their sighs, and bid a mute farewell to each stone and each tree, familiar to them as household words; they depart with reluctance, and often turn to cast a lingering look behind at objects so dear to their memory. Not so the children; they issue from the door like a flock of caged pigeons just let loose; they sing and leap and laugh with glee; the old house has no charms for them, they are as glad to depart as their elders are wishful to stay; the trunk desires to multiply its roots on the soil, but the buds prefer to blow elsewhere — for the latter life resolves itself into the word FUTURE, and for the former into the word PAST.

Leaving Wolston, Becker, and his two sons hard at work on the carriage, let us turn to the pinnace which was now making its way along the shore under the guidance of the Pilot.

"I should like much," said Fritz, "to present Mr. and Mrs. Wolston with a couple of bear, leopard, or tiger skins."

"So should I," said Jack.

"I wish you could think of some other sort of gift," suggested Willis; "what do you say to a couple of seal or shark skins?"

"Won't do," replied both Fritz and Jack in one voice. "What objections have you to the others?"

"Well, you are in some sort consigned to my care; I should like you to return to your parents with your own skins entire."

"Then you think it is a terrific affair to kill a tiger or

two? You have been accustomed to the sea, and fancy landsmen are good for nothing but shooting crows and wild-cats; that is a mistake, however; we are familiar with larger game."

"Shiver my timbers! do you call bears and tigers game?"

"I am afraid, Willis, you are a bit of a milksop."

"Avast heaving there, Master Fritz! as it is, I am a half-hanged man already, so death has now no terrors for me; it is the first pang that is most felt."

"Yes; but in the case of tigers, they never give you time to feel a second pang; miss your aim, and it is all over with you."

"True; and therefore I wish you would give up the project. As for myself, I would face anything with a four pounder, but rifle practice on board ship is mostly confined to the marines; it is not that, however, I am troubled about; I am certain your worthy father would never forgive me if I countenance this project."

"You need not tell him anything about it."

"Where, then, are the skins to come from? Can you say you bought them at the furrier's? You must really hit upon some other fancy."

"But it is not a fancy, Willis, it is a necessity; it is not our own amusement we are consulting. Just imagine yourself what will happen during the excursion now being arranged. Our parents will, of course, offer their bear skins to Mr. and Mrs. Wolston; there will be refusals on the one side and entreaties on the other."

"And, as is usual in these sort of discussions," added Jack, "Mrs. Wolston will call her carriage."

"Yes," continued Fritz, "and my mother will most certainly deprive herself of a covering that is absolutely indispensable during the cold nights of this climate."

"There is reason in what you say," observed Willis, scratching his ear.

"You see, Willis, the thing ought and must be done."

"As you put it, yes; but it will take time to prepare the skins."

"They will not be ready in time for this expedition

certainly, and my mother must do without her skin this journey; but it is our duty to prevent anything of the sort happening in future."

"Were I to consent to this project," said Willis, "there is still something more required."

"What, Willis?"

"Why, the tigers and what's-a-names; it is necessary to find the brute before you can get its skin."

"Granted; there would be a difficulty in the case had we not here quite handy a magnificent covering of wild animals, all ready to kill or to be killed. Just steer a point to the east, Willis; there, that will do. Just beyond that bluff you see yonder, there is a low flat plain covered with brushwood and tufted with trees; on the left, this prairie is bounded by a chain of low hills, and on the right a broad river, which last we have named the St. John, because it bears some resemblance to a stream of that name in Florida; beyond this plain there is a swamp."

"And," added Jack, "behind this swamp there is a magnificent forest of cedars, peopled with the finest furs imaginable, but garnished, however, with formidable claws and rows of teeth."

"I was not aware," said Willis, "that we were within reach of such amiable neighbors."

"Oh, they cannot reach us; thanks to the conformation of that chain of hills you see yonder, there is only one pass that opens into our settlement, and that we have taken care to shut up and fortify."

"It appears then," said Willis, "that there will be no difficulty in finding the animals, but——"

"Come, Willis, no more buts; you hunt in your own way from morning till night, let us for once hunt in ours."

"I go a-hunting?"

"Yes, there you are, charging your piece just now."

"Oh, my pipe you mean; but look at the difference; mosquitoes bite human beings, they don't eat them!"

"And, you may add, their skins don't make bed-clothes. Besides, if my mother takes rheumatism or the ague, it will be you that is to blame."

"I would rather face all the tigers in Bengal and all the

lions in Africa than incur such a responsibility. I will, therefore, take a part in your cruise, and if any accident happens to either of you, I shall stay in the forest till nothing is left of me but my cap and my bones. In this way I will escape all reproach in this world, and I may as well, after all, rejoin my old commander, Captain Little-stone, by this road as by any other."

In the meantime, they had reached the coast of Waldeck, and having landed, they found the outhouses and sheds that had been erected there in satisfactory order; the apes had not forgotten a battue that had once been got up for their special behoof, as not an individual was to be seen in the neighborhood. A morass of the district that had been converted into a rice plantation, promised an abundant crop; and the cotton plants, that Frank had once mistaken for flakes of snow, reared their woolly blossoms, looking for all the world like the powdered heads of our ancestors. After a slight repast, the pinnace was once more in motion, and the party steering for Prospect Hill.

"Ah," sighed Willis, "I wish we had only Sir Marmaduke Travers' cage here."

"Cage!" cried Fritz, laughing, "what, to shut up the game first and shoot it afterwards?"

"No, quite the reverse: to shut up the hunters."

"Ah, you would serve us in the same way as Louis XI. served Cardinal Balue."

"I know nothing of either Louis XI. or Cardinal Balue; but the cage I speak of was an excellent invention, for all that."

"Which you would like to prove to us by caging ourselves, eh?"

"Sir Marmaduke Travers," continued Willis, "was an English gentleman, and he was travelling in Coromandel, no one knew why or for what purpose."

"For the fun of the thing, probably," suggested Jack; "the English are said to be great oddities."

"At that time there happened to be a Hindoo widow somewhere in those parts. This lady was very rich, very young, very beautiful, and very fond of tormenting her admirers. And, as fate would have it, the travelling

10*

Englishman was completely taken captive by this dark beauty; and taking advantage of the hold she had obtained upon his heart, she amused herself by making him do all sorts of out of the way things. Sometimes she would bid him let his moustache grow, then she would order him to cut it off; he had to worship Brahma, adopt the fashion of the Hindoos, and had even to undergo the indignity of having his head tied up in a dirty pocket-handkerchief."

" That is to say," remarked Jack, " that the lady, not having a pug or a monkey, made Sir Marmaduke a substitute for both."

" Very likely, but still Sir Marmaduke was no fool ; he was on the contrary, a gentleman and a philosopher."

" I doubt that," said Jack.

" You are wrong, then. You have been brought up in an out of the way part of the world, and are not familiar with the usages of civilized society. When once a man has allowed the tender passion to take root in his breast, it cannot afterwards be extinguished at will; it grows and grows like an oil spot, so that what might easily have been mastered at first, makes us in time its devoted slave."

" I cannot admit," said Fritz, " that any sensible man would allow himself to be treated in the way you state."

" The wisest and bravest have often, for all that, been obliged to bend their heads to such circumstances ; in fact, those only escape whose hearts have been steeled by time or adversity. Well, nothing would please the lady in one of her caprices short of Sir Marmaduke's going alone to the jungle and killing a tiger or two for her. This caused him some little uneasiness."

" I should think so," remarked Jack, " unless he had been accustomed to face the animals."

" However, the widow's hand was to be the reward of the achievement, and the thing must consequently be done. Being, however, as I have said, a bit of a philosopher, he considered with himself that if, by chance, he should perish in the attempt, he would lose the widow all the same, and that he could not think of with any thing like equanimity. To extricate himself from this dilemma

he sent a despatch to an enterprising friend of his, then
stationed with his regiment at Calcutta, requesting his
advice."

" And this friend, no doubt, sent him a couple of tigers
all ready trussed ? "

" No, better than that ; he sent him a strong iron cage
fifteen feet square, very solid. This was shipped on board
a cutter commanded by Captain Littlestone, and I was
entrusted with the task of erecting it on shore, whilst an
express was sent off to Sir Marmaduke."

" Ah ! " said Jack, " I begin to understand now."

" Well, he rigged himself in tiger-hunting costume, went
and bade the lady good-bye, who coolly wished him good
sport, mounted a horse, and rode off to conquer a lady
who, as a proof of her affection, had so cavalierly consigned
him to the tender mercies of the wild beasts."

" Why, it was dooming him to certain destruction," said
Fritz.

" In the meantime the cage had been conveyed to a
valley surrounded with mountains, the caves of which
were known to shelter entire colonies of tigers. Here
also came Sir Marmaduke. The cage was firmly embedded
in the soil, the exterior was thickly studded over with
sharp spikes screwed into the bars ; inside were placed a
table and a sofa, with crimson velvet cushions."

" A lady's boudoir in the wilderness," said Jack.

" In one corner there was a case containing a dozen
bottles of pale ale, and as many of champagne ; in another
was a second case containing curry pies and a variety of
preserved meats ; in a third case were five and twenty
loaded rifles, together with a complete magazine in minia-
ture of powder and shot. On the table were sundry cases
of havannahs, a box of *allumettes*, the last number of the
Edinburgh Review, and a copy of the *Times*."

" What is the *Times* ? " inquired Jack.

" It is a furlong of paper, folded up and covered with
news, advertisements, and letters from the oldest inhabitant
of everywhere. Leaving, then, Sir Marmaduke seated in
the centre of his cage, we towards night returned to the
cutter, first scattering two or three quarters of fresh beef
in the vicinity of the cage."

"That should have assembled all the tigers in Coromandel," said Fritz.

"Anyhow, it brought enough. Towards midnight Sir Marmaduke could count thirty noble brutes capering in the moonlight and feasting upon the beef that had been provided for them."

"What did the Englishman do then?"

"He took aim at the most magnificent specimen of the herd and fired. No sooner had he done this than the whole pack came scampering towards the cage, thinking, doubtless, they had nothing to do but scrunch the bones of the solitary hunter. This was the signal for a regular slaughter. Sir Marmaduke discharged his rifles point blank in the noses of the animals that environed him on all sides; those who were not wounded by the balls were severely injured by the spikes of the cage in their furious efforts to seize their enemy. The howling, yelling, and fury was quite a new sensation for Sir Marmaduke; he rather enjoyed the thing whilst the excitement lasted. However, all things must have an end; when the sun appeared on the horizon the wounded retired, leaving the dead masters of the situation."

"I suppose, in the meantime," remarked Fritz, "that the amiable Hindoo was considering whether or not, under the circumstances, she should wear mourning for her defunct cavalier."

"Be that as it may, the defunct made his appearance, safe and sound, that same day, whilst the cutter stood out to sea with every vestige of the cage except the dead tigers. Shortly after, the widow was astonished to see an army of coolies marching in procession towards her door, all, like the slaves of Aladdin, heavily laden; and she was not awakened from her surprise till the master of the ceremonies had placed the following letter in her hands:

"'MADAM,— With this you will receive seventeen full-grown tigers, which I have had the honour of shooting for you.

"MARMADUKE TRAVERS."

"That was a choice bijou for a lady," said Jack.

"Yes," added Fritz; "and if the ladies of Coromandel have stands in their drawing-rooms, to display the tributes to their charms, Sir Marmaduke's present afforded abundant material for adorning those of the widow."

"Well, the consequence was, that Sir Marmaduke's name rung from one end of India to the other. The feat of killing, single-handed, seventeen tigers, converted him into a hero of the first magnitude. No festival was complete without him, he was courted by the fashionables and worshipped by the mob; some enthusiasts even proposed to erect a tomb for him, that being the way they honor their great men in eastern nations."

"Every country," remarked Fritz, "has its own peculiarities in this respect. The memory of the illustrious men of Greece and Rome was perpetuated in the intrinsic merit of the works of art erected in their names. In England quantity takes the place of quality; there is said to be in London a statue of a hero disguised as Achilles, six yards in height, and perched upon a pedestal twelve yards high."

"Making in all," remarked Jack, "exactly eighteen yards of fame."

"The handsome Hindoo," continued Willis, "was proud of the feat her charms had inspired. She gloried in showing off the redoubtable tiger-slayer at her *réunions*, and ended in being completely fascinated herself with her former slave. The match that she had formerly sneezed at she now earnestly desired, and, as Sir Marmaduke did not declare himself so speedily as she desired, she determined to give him a little encouragement by sending one of the most inviting and most odoriferous of notes."

"Sir Marmaduke must then have considered himself one of the happiest of men," said Fritz.

"Well," continued Willis, "neither man nor woman can, in affairs of this kind, depend upon themselves for two consecutive hours. The aspirations of a whole lifetime may be dispelled in five minutes, and the wishes of to-day may become the detestations of to-morrow. The new sensations awakened in Sir Marmaduke by the affair of the cage—his recollection of the ferocious brutes as they clung

with expiring energy to the bars of the cage, their streaked
skins streaming with blood, the fearful howling and terrific
death yells, the formidable claws that were often within an
inch of his face—had, somehow or other, chased the passion he had felt **for the** widow completely **out** of his
breast."

"Oh, the scamp of **a Travers !**" said Jack, energetically.

" He began to ask himself coolly what a lady, who had
made such extraordinary demands upon him before marriage, might not require him to do after ; and the result of
his cogitations is expressed in the following reply that **he
sent to the now** smiling **widow :—**

"' Sir Marmaduke Travers is highly flattered **by** the
charming note of the adorable daughter of Brahma; he
shall gladly continue to bask in the sunshine of her smiles,
out his ambition desires and will accept nothing more.'"

" Flowery and laconic," said Fritz.

" Well," inquired Willis, " was I not right in **wishing to**
aave the cage of Sir Marmaduke here ?"

" Yes, but we cannot get it. We have no ingenious
friend at Calcutta to send us such a machine, and furnish
it with crimson-cushioned sofas and pale ale, **so** we shall
have to rest satisfied with our own ingenuity, tact, and
agility."

Fritz **and Jack** were justified in relying upon their own
resources. **They had** been **often** sorely tried, and never
had been found wanting **in cases of** emergency. Since
the arrival of the Wolstons their courage had become
almost temerity; previous to that event, they **had been**
content to meet danger bravely when it was inevitable, **and
never** went deliberately in search of it. Now, however,
if we apply the glass of which Sterne speaks to their
breasts and spy what is passing therein, we shall find that
an imperious desire to become heroes had taken possession
of their inward souls—a determination to make themselves conspicuous at all hazards was burning within them;
that, in fact, they were courting the admiration of the new
audience that Providence had sent to the colony, the praise
of which found more favor in their hearts than the pater-
nal admonitions.

This was far from being commendable; but, although
emulation and vanity have some features in common, still
they must not be confounded: the former consists in generous efforts to equal or surpass some one in something
praiseworthy; the second is a kind of self-love, that seeks
to purchase respect or flattery at no matter what cost;—
the one is a vice, the other a virtue.

Fritz and Jack were not actuated by vanity; they were
urged on by their impulses, without weighing the circumstances that gave them rise; and indeed they were not
even conscious of being more desirous of renown now than
they had been hitherto.

The temperament of Ernest and Frank was of another
kind. Their natures were much less excitable, and it did
not appear that the recent arrivals had altered their outward demeanor in the slightest degree; they continued
calm, staid, and reflective, as they had ever been.

All four were a singular mixture of the child and the
man—knowing many things that young people are ignorant of, they were yet almost totally unacquainted with the
ordinary attributes of social life—unsophisticated and
naive to an extreme degree, they would have appeared in
a fashionable drawing-room downright fools. On the other
hand, they possessed great clearness of perception, presence of mind in danger, promptitude in action, and the
utmost coolness in the face of apparently insurmountable
obstacles—qualities that would have utterly confounded
the young men who shine in the saloons of Europe, whose
chief merit often consists in their being familiar with the
unmeaning conventionalisms of fashionable life.

At Prospect Hill they found the outhouses and plantations in much the same position as at Waldeck. Here the
crimson flowers of the caper plant, the white flowers of the
tea plant, and the rich blossoms of the clove tree, perfumed
the air and promised a fragrant harvest. This was a
charming caravansary, all ready with its smiles to welcome
the illustrious colonists as soon as they presented themselves.

These points being settled to the satisfaction of the three
pioneers, a sheep was taken on board the pinnace at the
request of Willis—who seemed to have taken a violent

fancy for mutton chops — and they set sail towards the east.

In the first instance they made for a projecting headland that seemed to bar their progress in that direction, and, much to the astonishment of the Pilot, they entered a cavern that formed the entrance to a natural tunnel. This, besides being an interesting feature in the coast scenery, was one of the treasures of the colony, for it contained vast quantities of edible birds' nests, so much prized by the Chinese. The voyagers did not, however, tarry here; these were not the objects they were now in search of. Nautilus Bay and the Bay of Pearls were likewise traversed unheeded, nor could the attractive banks of the St. John, fringed with verdant foliage, divert them from the project they had in contemplation.

Wise men, when they indulge in folly, are often more foolish than real fools; so it was with Willis: now that he had joined in the scheme, he evinced more ardor in its execution than the young men themselves. He said that it would not be enough to capture skins for Mr. and Mrs. Wolston, they must also capture one a-piece for Mary and Sophia likewise, and talked as if the adventure of Sir Marmaduke and his seventeen tigers had been a bagatelle.

Some hours before dark they landed at a spot well known to both Fritz and Jack; it was a place where Becker and his sons had some time before been engaged in deadly conflict with a herd of lions, and where one of their dogs had fallen a victim to the enraged monarchs of the forest.

"My plan," said Willis, "is to kill the sheep and place the quarters on the shore, just as bait is thrown into the water to bring the fish within the net."

"A reminiscence of Sir Marmaduke," said Jack.

"Then," continued Willis, "we shall light a fire to take the place of the sun, who is about to retire for the night. This done, I propose that we should return to the pinnace, keep the mutton within rifle range, and riddle the skins that come to feast upon it."

After some opposition on the part of Fritz and Jack, who preferred to encounter their antagonists on more equal terms, the proposal of Willis was ultimately agreed to.

CHAPTER XI.

As is usual in tropical climates, a blazing hot day was succeeded by an intensely dark night. The fire that the hunters had made on shore cast a lurid glare on the prominent objects round about. The flames, as they fitfully lit up the landscape into that dim distinctness termed by artists the *chiar oscuro*, made the bushes and trunks of trees appear like monsters issuing stealthily from the forest that lined the background. There seemed to be some attraction, however, elsewhere for the real monsters, not a single wild beast having as yet appeared on the scene.

The two young men were eagerly straining their eyes from the stern of the pinnace, whilst the dogs kept diligently wagging their tails in expectation of a signal for the onset. The position of Willis could be ascertained now and then by an eye of fire, which opened and shut as he inhaled or exhaled the fumes of his Maryland. The ripple beat gently on the sea-line of the boat, which oscillated with the regularity and softness of a cradle.

"It is always so," said Jack, impatiently; "if we don't want wild beasts, there are shoals of them to be seen; but if we do want them, then they are all off to their dens."

"Perhaps, there are none now," suggested Willis.

"Say rather," observed Fritz, "that there ought to be thousands; for on the one hand they multiply rapidly, and on the other there is no one to destroy them.　The Spaniards once left a few cattle on St. Domingo, and they increased at such a rate, that the island very soon would not have been able to support them, had they not been kept down by constant slaughter."

"Besides," remarked Jack, "the bovine race reproduce themselves more slowly than other animals; a single sow, according to a calculation made by Vauban, if allowed to live eleven years, would produce six millions of pigs."

"What a cargo of legs of pork and sides of bacon!" exclaimed Willis, laughing.

"Then fish; there are more than a hundred and sixty thousand eggs in a single carp.　A sturgeon contains a million four hundred and sixty-seven thousand eight hundred and fifty, whilst in some codfish the number exceeds nine millions."

"Oh, you need not favor us with the 'Mariner's March,' Willis; what my brother says is perfectly correct."

"What, then, do these shoals of creatures live upon?"

"The big ones upon the little ones; fish devour each other."

"A beautiful harmony of Nature," remarked Fritz drily.

"Then plants," continued Jack, "are still more prolific than animals.　Some trees can produce as many of their kind as they have branches, or even leaves.　An elm tree, twelve years old, yields sometimes five hundred thousand pods; and, by the way, Willis, to encourage you in carrying on the war against the mosquitoes, a single stalk of tobacco produces four thousand seeds."

"The leaves, however, are of more use to me than the seeds," replied Willis.

"This admirable proportion between the productiveness of the two kingdoms demonstrates the far-seeing wisdom of Providence.　If the power of multiplication in vegetables had been less considerable, the fields, gardens, and prairies would have been deserts, with only a plant here and there to hide the nakedness of the land.　Had God permitted animals to multiply in excess of plants, the entire vegetation would soon have been devoured, and then the animals themselves would of necessity have ceased to exist."

"How is it, then," inquired Willis, "with this continual multiplication always going on, the inhabitants of land and sea do not get over-crowded?"

"Why, as regards man, for example, if thirteen or fourteen human beings are born within a given period, death removes ten or eleven others; but though this leaves a regular increase, still the population of the globe always continues about the same."

"It may be so, Master Jack, but when I was a little boy at school, I generally came in for a whipping, if I made out two and two to be anything else than four."

"And served you right too, Willis; but if the human family did not continually increase, if the number of deaths exceeded continually that of the births, at the end of a few centuries the world would be unpeopled."

"Very good; but if, on the other hand, there is a continual increase, how can the population continue the same?"

"Because the increase supposes a normal state; that is to say, the births are only estimated as compared with deaths from disease or old age. But then there are shipwrecks, inundations, plagues, and war, which sometimes exterminate entire communities at one fell swoop. Then whole nations die out and give place to the redundant populations of others; phenomena now observed in the cases of the aborigines of Australia and America."

"Very true."

"No signs of furs yet," cried Fritz, who was every now and then levelling his rifle at the phantoms on shore.

"We need not dread," continued Jack, "ever being hustled or jostled on the earth; life will fail us before space. There are now eight hundred millions of human beings in existence, and, according to the most moderate computation, room enough for twice that number. As it is, the most fertile sections of the earth are not the most populous; there are four hundred millions in Asia, sixty millions in Africa, forty in America, two hundred and thirty in Europe, and only seventy millions in the islands and continent of Oceanica!"

"To which," remarked Fritz, "you may add the eleven inhabitants of New Switzerland."

"Assuming, then, this calculation to be nearly accurate, though authorities vary materially in their computations of the earth's inhabitants, and regarding it in connexion with the average duration of human life, a thousand millions of mortals must perish in thirty-three years; to descend to detail, thirty millions every year, three thousand four hundred every hour, sixty every minute, or ONE EVERY SECOND."

"Aye," remarked Willis, "we are here to-day and gone to-morrow."

"Suppose, then, that the population of the earth were twice as great, cultivation would be extended, territories that are now lying waste would be teeming with life and covered with fertile fields, but the same beautiful equilibrium would be maintained."

"And the inhabitants of the planets," said Fritz, "what are they about?"

"What planets do you mean?" inquired Willis.

"Well, all in general; the moon, for example, in particular."

"The moon," replied Jack, "has, in the first place, no atmosphere. This we know, because the rays of the stars passing behind her are not, in the slightest degree, refracted; and this proves that neither men, nor animals, nor vegetables of any kind, are to be found in that planet, for they could not exist without air."

"That should settle the question," remarked Willis.

"Yes," remarked Fritz; "but some theorists, nevertheless, insist that there may be living creatures in the moon, for all that — of course, differently constituted from the inhabitants of our earth, and susceptible of existing without air. There is, however, no evidence of any kind to support such a theory; it is a mere fancy, the dream of an imaginative brain. Upon the same grounds, it may be argued, that the interior of the earth is inhabited, and that elves and gnomes are possible beings. Besides, the telescope has been brought to so high a degree of perfection, that objects the size of a house can now be detected in the moon."

"It seems, I am afraid," remarked Jack, who, like his brother, was getting annoyed by the phantasmagoria on shore, "that we were about as well supplied with wild beasts here as they are with men in the planets."

"In speaking of the moon, however," continued Fritz, "I do not imply all the planets; for, certain as **we** are that the moon has no atmosphere, **so we** are equally certain that some of the planets possess that attribute. Still there are **other circumstances** that render **the** notion of their being inhabited by beings like ourselves exceedingly improbable. Mercury, for example, is so embarrassed by the solar rays, that lead must always be in a state of fusion, and **water,** if not reduced to a state of vapor, will be hot enough **to** boil the fish that are in it. Uranus, at the other extremity of the system, receives four hundred times less heat and light than we do, consequently neither water nor any thing else can exist **there** in a liquid state; what is fluid on our earth must be frozen up into a solid mass. Good, I declare **my** brother has fallen asleep!"

"It is very — interesting — however," said Willis, making ineffectual efforts to smother a yawn.

"The same difficulty with comets; **there must** have been some very urgent necessity for human beings in order to have peopled them. When they pass the perihelion——"

"The what?" inquired Willis.

"The point where they approach nearest the sun—— **when** they pass the perihelion, I was going to say, the heat they endure must be terrific; when on the other hand, at their extreme distance from that body, the cold must be intense. The comet of 1680 did not approach within five thousand *myriamètres* of the sun."

"Friends coming within that distance of each other should at least shake hands," said Willis.

"Still, even at that distance, the heat, according to Newton, must be like red-hot iron, and if constituted like **our** earth, when heated **to that** degree, must take fifty thousand years to cool."

"Fifty thousand years!" said Willis, yawning from ear to ear.

"The central position between these extremes, which would either congeal our earth into a mass of ice or burn it up into a heap of cinders, is therefore the most

11*

congenial to such beings as ourselves. Whence I conclude ——"

Here the crimson flashes of Willis's pipe, which had
been gradually diminishing in brilliance suddenly ceased;
contralto notes issued from the profundities of his breast,
and it became evident to the orator that all his audience
were sound asleep.

"Whence I conclude," said Fritz, addressing himself,
"that my orations must be somewhat soporiferous."

Being thus left alone to keep a look-out on shore, his
thoughts gradually receded within his own breast, where
all was rose-colored and smiling, for at his age rust has
not had time to corrupt, nor moths to eat away. And it
was not long before he himself, like his two companions,
was fast locked in the arms of sleep.

How long this state of things lasted the chronicle saith
not; but the three sleepers were eventually awakened by
a simultaneous howl of the dogs. They were instantly on
their feet, with their rifles levelled.

It was too late; day had broken, and there was light
enough to convince them that nothing was to be seen.
The sheep's quarters had, however, entirely disappeared,
and they had the satisfaction of knowing that they had
politely given the denizens of the forest a feast gratis.

"Ah, they shall pay us for it yet," said Jack.

"This is a case of the hunters being caught instead of
the game," remarked Fritz.

"The poor sheep! If Ernest had been here, he would
have erected a monument to its memory."

"I doubt that; epitaphs are generally made rather to
please the living than to compliment the defunct. But,
Willis, we must deprive you of your office of huntsman
in chief—I shall go into the forest and revenge this
insult."

"I have no objection to abdicate the office of huntsman,
but must retain that of admiral, in which capacity I
announce to you that there will be a storm presently, and
that we shall just have time to make Rockhouse before it
overtakes us."

"That is rather a reason for our remaining where we
are."

" We have come for skins, and skins we must have."

" Besides, we are two to one, and in all constitutional governments the majority rules."

" Have you both made up your minds?" inquired Willis.

" Yes, we are quite decided."

" In that case," said Willis, " let us hoist the anchor and be off home."

" Home! but we are determined to have the skins first."

" No, you are not," said Willis; " I know you better than you know yourselves. You are both brave fellows, but I know you would not, for all the skins in the world, have your good mother suppose that you were buffeted about by the waves in a storm."

" True; up with the anchor, Willis," said Fritz.

" Be it so," said Jack, shaking his fist menacingly at the silent forest, " but we shall lose nothing by waiting."

The sailor had not erred in his calculations, for they had scarcely unfurled the sail before they heard the distant rumbling of the storm. As soon as the first flash of lightning shot across the sky, Jack put his forefinger of one hand on the wrist of the other, and began counting one — two — three.

" Do you feel feverish?" inquired Willis.

" No, not personally," replied Jack; " I am feeling the pulse of the storm — twenty-four — twenty-five — twenty-six — it is a mile off."

" Aye! how do you make that out? "

" Very easily; you recollect Ernest telling us that light travelled so rapidly, that the time it occupied in passing from one point to another of the earth's surface was scarcely perceptible to our senses? "

" Yes, but I thought he was spinning a yarn at the time."

" You were wrong, Willis; he likewise told us that sound travels at the rate of four hundred yards in a second."

" Well, but —— "

" Have patience, Willis! When the lightning flashes, the electric spark is discharged, is it not?"

“Well, I was never high enough aloft to see.”

“But others have been; Newton and Franklin have seen it. Now, if the sound reaches our ears a second after the flash, it has travelled four hundred yards. If we hear it twelve or thirteen seconds after, it has travelled twelve or thirteen times four hundred yards, or about half a mile, and so on.”

“But what has that to do with your pulse?”

“In the first place, I am in perfect health, am I not?”

“I hope so, Master Jack.”

“Then when our systems are in good order, the pulse, keeping fractions out of view, beats once in every second; and consequently, though we do not always carry a watch, we always have our arteries about us, and may therefore always reckon time.”

“Now I understand.”

“Ah! then we are to escape this time without the ‘Mariner’s March.’”

“It appears, Master Jack, that you have turned philosopher as well as your brothers. Can you tell me what causes lightning?”

“Yes, I can, Willis. You must know, in the first place, that all the layers of the atmosphere are, more or less, charged with electricity.”

“Ask him how,” said Fritz drily.

“Ah, you hope to puzzle me,” replied Jack, “but thanks to Mr. Wolston, I am too well up in physics to be easily driven off my perch, and therefore may safely take my turn in philosophising.”

“Well, we are listening.”

“The air, by means of the vapor it contains, absorbs electricity from terrestrial bodies, and so becomes a sort of reservoir of this invisible fluid. All chemical combinations evolve electricity, the air collects it and stores it up in the clouds. There, worshipful brother, your question is answered.”

“Good, go on.”

“Well, Willis, you must know, in the second place, the clouds are very good fellows, and share with each other the good things they possess. When one cloud meets another, the one over-supplied with this fluid and the other in its normal state, there is an immediate interchange of courtesies, the negative electricity of the one is exchanged for the positive of the other."

"There does not appear, however, to be much generosity in this transaction, since the surcharged cloud does not cede its superfluous abundance without a consideration."

"It is very rarely that philanthropy amongst us goes much further," remarked Fritz.

"No, everybody is not like Willis," rejoined Jack, "who acts like a prince, and gives legs of mutton gratis to hyenas and tigers. The discharges of electricity from one cloud to another are the flashes of lightning, and it is to be observed that the thunder is nothing more than the noise made by the fluid rushing through the air."

"What, then, is the thunderbolt?"

"There is no such thing as what is popularly understood by the term thunderbolt. The lightning itself, however, often does mischief. This happens when the discharge, instead of being between two clouds in the air, takes place between a cloud and the ground—a cloud surcharged with electricity understood. Then all intervening objects are struck by the fluid."

"There, however, you are wrong," said Fritz. "All objects are not struck; on the contrary, the fluid avoids some things and searches out others, even moving in a zig-zag direction to manifest these caprices; it often discharges itself on or into hard substances, and passes by those which are soft or feeble."

"I might say this arose from a sentiment of generosity," added Jack, "but I have other reasons to assign."

"So much the better," said Fritz, "as I should scarcely be satisfied with the first."

"Well," continued Jack, "lightning has its likings and dislikings."

"Like men and women," suggested Willis.

"It has a partiality for metal."

"An affection that is not returned, however," observed Fritz.

" If the fluid enters a room, for example, it runs along the bell wires, inspects the works of the clock, and sometimes has the audacity to pounce upon the money in your purse, even though a policeman should happen to be in the kitchen at the time."

" Perhaps," remarked Willis, " it is Socialist or Red Republican in its notions." .

" It does not, however, patronise war," replied Jack; " I once heard of it having melted a sword and left the scabbard intact."

" That, to say the least of it, is improbable," remarked Fritz.   " The hilt, or even the point, might have been fused; but even supposing the electric fluid to have been capable of such flagrant preference, the scabbard could not have held molten metal without being itself consumed."

" Aye," remarked Willis, " there are plenty of nonsensical stories of that kind in circulation, because nobody takes the trouble to test their truth.   Still, according to your own account, a man or woman runs no danger from the lightning."

" I beg your pardon there, Willis; the electric fluid does not go out of its way to attack a human being, but if one should happen to be in its way, it does not take time to request that individual to stand aside, it simply passes through him, and leaves him or her, as the case may be, a coagulated mass of inanimate tissues."

" What a variety of ways there are of getting out of the world!" said Willis lugubriously.

" Again," continued Jack, " anything that happens to be in the vicinity of the clouds when this interchange of courtesies is going on, is apt to draw the storm upon itself, hence the continual war that is carried on between the lightning and the steeples."

" Something like an individual coming within range of a cloud of mosquitoes," suggested Willis.

" A learned German — one of us," said the scapegrace, laughing, " calculated, in 1783, that in the space of thirty-three years there had been, to his own knowledge, three hundred and eighty-six spires struck, and a hundred and twenty bell-ringers killed by lightning, without reckoning a much larger number wounded."

"And yet," remarked Willis, "I never heard of an insurance against accidents by lightning."

"There are plenty of them, however, in Roman Catholic countries," said Fritz. "Every village has one, and the charge is almost nominal."

"How, then, do these companies make it pay?"

"They find it answer somehow, and they never collapse."

"Then everybody ought to insure."

"Yes, but there are some obstinate people who do not see the good of it."

"If my life had not already been forfeited, I should insure it. But how is it done?"

"Well, you have only to go into a church, fall down on your knees before the priest, he will make you invulnerable by a sign of the cross; then, come storms that pulverize the body or crush the mind, you are perfectly safe."

"Ah! that is the way you insure your lives, is it, trusting to the priests rather than to Providence? For my own part, I should prefer a policy of insurance — that is to say, if my life were of any value."

"Next to steeples," continued Jack, "come tall trees, such as poplars and pines. Should you ever be caught by a storm in the open country, Willis, never take shelter under a tree; face the storm bravely, and submit to be deluged by the rain. Dread even bushes, if they are isolated. An entire forest is less dangerous than a single reed when it stands alone."

"But you forget, brother, that when a man stands alone he is quite as prominent an object as the trunk of a tree four or five feet high, particularly in an open plain."

"Quite so. It is therefore advisable, when severe storms are close upon us, to lie down flat on the ground."

"Suppose," remarked Fritz, smiling, "a brigade of soldiers on the march suddenly to collapse in this way, as if before a discharge of grape,"

"And why not? If it is done in the case of grape-shot, why may it not be done when the artillery is a thousand times more effective?"

" Well, I suspect it would rather astonish the commanding officer, that is all."

" Then, Willis, continued Jack, " you must not run during a storm, because the air you put in motion by so doing may draw the electricity into the current."

" Do the conductors not prevent the lightning from doing harm ?"

" Yes, but you cannot carry one of them on your hat. These rods are only useful in protecting buildings, and then to nothing more than double the area of their length; it is for this last reason that roofs of public buildings have them projecting in all directions."

" They are a sort of trap set for the lightning, are they not ?"

" Yes, and into which it is pretty sure to fall. Franklin, of whom I spoke just now, was the first to suggest that bars of steel would draw lightning out of a cloud surcharged with electricity."

" What becomes of it when it is caught ?"

" Keeping in view its partiality for bell-pulls, a wire is attached to the rod down which the unconscious fluid glides."

" Like a powder-monkey from the main-top."

" Exactly; till it enters a well, and there it is left at the bottom in company with Truth."

A practical storm had begun to mix itself up with the theory as developed by Jack, but not before they had very nearly reached their destination, where they were waited for with the greatest anxiety.

No sooner had they landed than Sophia ran to meet Willis, who was advancing with Jack.

" Ah, sweetheart," she said, " Susan has been so uneasy about you."

" You are a good girl, Miss Soph — Susan."

" Oh, if you only knew how frightened we have been !"

" What, do you admit fear to be one of your accomplishments, Miss Sophia ?" inquired Jack.

" Certainly, when others are concerned, Master Jack. But, by the way, do you recollect the chimpanzee ?"

" Yes, what about the rascal ?"

"Oh, I must not tell you, mamma would call me a chatterbox; you will know by-and-by."

In the meanwhile Mary, on her side, was congratulating Toby, who kept scampering between herself and Fritz, at one moment receiving the caresses of the one and at the next of the other, with every demonstration of joy. This had become an established mode of communication between the young people when Fritz arrived from a lengthened ramble; the intelligent brute, in point of fact, had assumed the office of dragoman.

"Ah, ah, Becker, glad to see you again," said Willis. "Your sons are fountains of knowledge, whilst I am——"

"A very worthy fellow, Willis, and I know it," replied Becker, shaking him heartily by the hand.

12

CHAPTER XII.

To the storm succeeded one of those diluvian showers that have already been described. Rain being merely a result of evaporation, it was evident that sea and land in those climates must perspire at an enormous rate to effect such cataclysms. In consequence of this deluge, the proposed excursion was indefinitely postponed. The provisions, the marvellous kits, the waggon, were all ready; but Nature, as often happens under such circumstances, had assumed a menacing attitude, and for the present forbade the execution of the project.

A sort of vague sadness, that generally accompanies a gloomy atmosphere, weighed upon the spirits of the colonists. Recollections of the *Nelson* and her sudden disappearance thrust themselves more vividly than ever upon their memory; and Willis was observed to throw his sou'-wester unconsciously on the ground — a proof that remembrances of the past occupied his thoughts.

One of the ladies was occupied in the needful domestic operations of the household, whilst the other sat with a stocking on her left arm, busily occupied in repairing the ravages of tear and wear upon that useful though humble garment. The two young ladies spun, as used to do the great ladies of the court of King Alfred, and as Hercules himself is said to have done when he changed his club and lion's skin for a spindle and distaff with the Queen of Lybia; Jack was apparently sketching, Fritz had a collection of hunting apparatus before him, and the other two young men, each with a book, were deeply immersed in study.

This state of things was by no means cheerful, and Wolston determined to break up the monotony by introducing a subject of conversation likely to interest them all, the old as well as the young.

"By the way, gentlemen," said he, "it occurs to me that you have not yet thought of selecting a profession; your future career seems at present somewhat obscure."

"What would you have?" inquired Jack; "there is no use for lawyers and judges in our colony, except to try plundering monkeys or protect jackal orphans."

"True; but suppose you were to find yourselves, by some chance, again in the great world, there it is necessary to possess a qualification of some kind; a blacksmith or a carpenter, expert in his handicraft, has a better chance of acquiring wealth and position than a man without a profession, however great his talents may be; an idler is a mere clog in the social machine, and is often thrust aside to browse in a corner with monks and donkeys."

"But to acquire a profession, is not instruction and practice necessary?"

"Certainly; it is impossible to become a proficient in any art or science by mere study alone; but before sowing a field, what is done?"

"It is ploughed and manured."

"And should there be only a few seeds?"

"We can sow what we have, and reserve the harvest till next season. By economising each crop in this way, we shall soon have seeds enough to cover any extent of land."

"May I request you, Master Ernest, to draw a conclusion from that as regards sowing the seeds of a future career?"

"I would infer, from your suggestion, that we might adapt ourselves for such and such a profession by preparing our minds to receive instruction in it, and we might also avail ourselves in the meantime of such sources of information regarding it as are at present open to us. The physician in prospective, for example, might make himself familiar with the medical properties of such plants as are within his reach; he might likewise examine the bones of an ape, and thus, by analogy, become acquainted with the framework of the human body. The would-be lawyer might, in the same way, avail himself of the library to obtain an insight into those social mysteries that bind men in communities and necessitate human laws for the preservation of peace and order. Thus, by directing our thoughts into one line of study, we may form a basis upon which the superstructure may be easily erected, and the necessary academical degrees or sanction of the university obtained."

"And, when you see this, why not adopt so commendable a course?"

"Because we may probably be destined to remain here, where, according to Jack, the learned professions, at least, are not likely to be much in demand."

"The study of a particular science or art has charms in itself, which amply compensate the student for his labor. But, even admitting you do not return to the Old World, you forget that it is your intention to colonise this territory."

"It seems, however, that God has willed it otherwise."

"What God does not will in one way, he may bring about in another. What reason have you for supposing that the *Nelson* may not return with colonists?"

"It will be from the other world then," said Willis.

"Yes, from the other world," replied Jack, "but not in the sense you imply."

"Besides, should the *Nelson* not reappear, that is no reason why another accident may not drive another ship upon the coast that will be more fortunate; what has happened to-day may surely happen again to-morrow. And in the event of colonists arriving, will there not be sick to cure, boundaries to determine, differences of opinion to decide, and opposing claims to adjudge."

"Certainly, Mr. Wolston."

"Well, admitting these necessities, what profession will each of you select? Let us begin with you, Master Fritz."

"The career," replied Fritz, "that would be most congenial to my taste is that of a conqueror."

" A conqueror!"

"Yes; Alexander, Scipio, Timour the Tartar, and Gengis Khan are the sort of men I should like to resemble. They have made a tolerable figure in the world, and I should have no objection to follow in their footsteps."

"But you forget that their footsteps are marked with tears, disasters, terror, and bloodshed."

"These are indispensable."

"Why?"

"Once, when a great commander was asked the same question, he replied, that you cannot make omelets without breaking eggs."

"Yes," remarked Becker, "but if you had read the anecdote entire, you would have seen that he was asked in return, ' What use there was for so many omelets.' "

"Added to which," continued Wolston, "that is not a normal career; there is no diploma required for it; it is an accident arising out of adventitious circumstances, sometimes fostered by ambition, but no course of study can produce a conqueror."

"What, then, is the use of military schools?"

"They are, to the best of my knowledge, instituted for rearing defenders for one's country, and not with a view to the subjugation of another's."

"My poor Fritz," said Mrs. Becker laughing, "I hope when you conquer half the world, you will find an occupation for your mother more in consonance with your dignity than mending your stockings."

"Then, again," continued Wolston, "war cannot be waged by a single individual."

"There must be an enemy somewhere," suggested Willis.

"The difficulty does not, however, lie there," observed Jack; "for, if we have no enemies, it is easy enough to make them."

"There must, at all events, be armies, magazines, and a treasury — or eggs, as the great commander in question hinted."

"True," replied Fritz; "but there is the same difficulty

12*

as regards all professions; there can be no barristers without briefs, no physicians without patients."

" You will admit, however, that clients and patients are not so rare as hundreds of thousands of armed men and millions of money."

" Brother," said Jack, "your cavalry are routed and your infantry outflanked."

" If you are determined to be a conqueror, let it be by the pen rather than by the sword — or, what do you say to oratory? It is not easier, perhaps, but, at all events, eloquence is not denied to ordinary mortals. You will not then, to be sure, rank with the Hannibals, the Tamerlanes, or the Cæsars; but you may attain a place with Demosthenes, who was more dreaded by Philip of Macedon than an army of soldiers."

" Or Cicero," remarked Becker, "who preserved his country from the rapacity of Cataline."

" Or Peter the Hermit," remarked Frank, "who by his eloquence roused Europe against the Saracens."

" Or Bossuet," added Wolston, " and then you may venture to assert in the face of kings that *God alone is Great*, should they, like Louis XIV., assume the sun as an emblem, and adopt such a silly scroll as ' *Nec pluribus impar.*' "

" Bossuet, Peter the Hermit, Cicero, and Demosthenes, are not so bad, after all, as a last resource," remarked Mrs. Wolston, "and I would recommend you to enrol yourself in that list of conquerors, Master Fritz."

" The more especially," observed Jack, "as you have no impediment in your voice, and would not have to undergo a course of pebbles like Demosthenes."

" So far as that goes, Jack," replied Fritz, "you would possess a like advantage for the profession as myself; but I will take time to reflect." Then, turning towards his mother, he said, "Conqueror or Jack Pudding, mother, you shall always find me a dutiful son."

His mother was more gratified by this expression of attachment than she would have been had he laid at her feet the four thousand golden spurs found, in 1302, on the field of Courtray.

"And now, Ernest, what profession do you intend to adopt? what is your dream of the future?"

"I, Mr. Wolston! Well, having no taste for artillery, brilliant charges, blood-stained ruins, and the other *agrémens* of war, I cannot be a hero. Do you know when I feel most happy?"

"No, let us hear."

"It is towards evening, when I am reposing tranquilly on the banks of the Jackal."

"Ah, I thought so," cried Jack; "no position so congenial to the true philosopher as the horizontal."

"When the sun," continued Ernest, gravely, "is retiring behind the forest of cedars that bounds the horizon; when the palms, the mangoes, and gum trees, mass their verdure in distinct and isolated groups; when nature is making herself heard in a thousand melodious voices; when the hum of the insect is ringing in my ears, and the breeze is gently murmuring through the foliage; when thousands of birds are fluttering from grove to grove, sometimes breaking with their wings the smooth surface of the river; when the fish, leaping out of their own element, reflect for an instant from their silvery scales the departing rays of the sun; when the sea, stretching away like a vast plain of boundless space, loses itself in the distance, then my eyes and thoughts are sometimes turned upwards towards the azure of the firmament, and sometimes towards the objects around me, and I feel as if my mind were in search of something which has hitherto eluded its grasp, but which it is sure of eventually finding. Under these circumstances, I assure you, I would not exchange the moss on which I sat for the greatest throne in Christendom."

"But surely you do not call such a poetical exordium a profession?" remarked Becker.

"It must be admitted," said Wolston, "that the sun and trees have their uses, especially when the one protects us from the other; the sun, for example, dries up the moisture that falls from the trees, and the trees shelter us from the burning rays of the sun. Still, I am at a loss myself to connect these things with a profession in a social point of view."

"What would you have thought," inquired Ernest, "if you had seen Newton and Kepler gazing at the sky, before the one had determined the movements of the celestial bodies, and the other the laws of gravitation? What would you have thought of Parmentier passing hours and days in manipulating a rough-looking bulb, that possessed no kind of value in the eyes of the vulgar, but which afterwards, as the potato, became the chief food of two-thirds of the population of Europe? What would you think of Jenner, with his finger on his brow, searching for a means of preserving humanity from the scourge of the small-pox?"

"But these men had an object in view."

"Jenner, yes; but not the other two. They thought, studied, contemplated, and reflected, satisfied that one day their thoughts, calculations, and reflections would aid in disclosing some mystery of Nature; but it would have perplexed them sorely to have named beforehand the nature and scope of their discoveries."

"According to you, then," said Jack, "there could not be a more dignified profession than that of the scarecrow. The greatest dunderhead in Christendom might simply, by going a star-gazing, pass himself off as an adept in the occult sciences, and claim the right of being a benefactor of mankind in embryo."

"At all events," replied Ernest, "you will admit that, so long as I am ready to bear my share of the common burdens, and take my part in providing for the common wants, and in warding of the common dangers, it is immaterial whether I occupy my leisure hours in reflection or in rifle practice."

"Well," said Jack, "when you have made some discovery that will enrol your name with Descartes, Huygens, Cassini, and such gentlemen, you will do us the honor of letting us know."

"With the greatest pleasure."

"It is a pity that Herschell has invented the telescope: he might have left you a chance for the glory of that invention."

" If I have not discovered a new star, brother, I discovered long ago that you would never be one."

" Well, I hope not ; their temperature is too unequal for me — they are either freezing or boiling: at least, so said Fritz the other day, whilst we were——ah, what were we doing, Willis ? "

" We were supposed to be hunting."

" Ah, so we were."

" Now, Master Jack, it is your turn to enlighten us as to your future career."

" It is quite clear, Mr. Wolston, that, since my brothers are to be so illustrious, I cannot be an ordinary mortal; the honor of the family is concerned, and must be consulted. I am, therefore, resolved to become either a great composer, like Haydn, Mozart, and Beethoven; a renowned painter, like Titian, Carrache, or Veronese ; or a great poet, like Homer, Virgil, Shakspeare, Dante, Milton, Goethe, and Racine."

" That is to say," remarked Mrs. Wolston, " that you are resolved to be a great something or other."

" Decidedly, madam ; on reflection, however, as I value my eyesight, I must except Homer and Milton."

" But have you not determined to which of the muses you will throw the handkerchief? "

" I thought of music at first. It must be a grand thing, said I to myself, that can charm, delight, and draw tears from the eyes of the multitude — that can inspire faith, courage, patriotism, devotion and energy, and that, too, by means of little black dots with tails, interspersed with quavers, crotchets, sharps and flats."

" Have you composed a sonata yet? "

" No, madam ; I was going to do so, but it occurred to me that I should require an orchestra to play it."

" And not having that, you abandoned the idea?"

" Exactly, madam. I then turned to poetry. That is an art fit for the gods ; it puts you on a level with kings, and makes you in history even more illustrious than them. You ascend the capitol, and there you are crowned with laurel, like the hero of a hundred fights."

"What is the subject of your principal work in this line?"

"Well, madam, I once finished a verse, and was going on with a second, but, somehow or other, I could not get the words to rhyme."

"Then it occurred to you that you had neither a printer nor readers, and you broke your lyre?"

"I was about to reproach you, Master Jack," said Wolston, "for undertaking too many things at once; but I see the ranks are beginning to thin."

"Beautiful as poetry may be," continued Jack, "one gets tired of reading and re-reading one's own effusions."

"It is even often intensely insipid the very first time," remarked Mrs. Wolston.

"There still remains painting," continued Jack. "Painting is vastly superior to either music or poetry. In the first place, it requires no interpreter between itself and the public; — what, for example, remains of a melody after a concert? nothing but the recollection. Poesy may excite admiration in the retirement of one's chamber; your nostrils are, as it were, reposing on the bouquet, though often you have still a difficulty in smelling anything. But if once you give life to canvas, it is eternal."

"Eternal is scarcely the proper word," remarked Wolston: "the celebrated fresco of Leonardo da Vinci, in the refectory of the Dominicans at Milan, is nothing but a confused mass of colors and figures."

"I answer that by saying that the painting in question is only a fresco. Besides, I use the word eternal in a modified or relative sense. A painting is preserved from generation to generation, whilst its successive races of admirers are mingled with the dust. Then suppose a painter in his studio; he cannot look around him without awakening some memory of the past. He can associate with those he loves when they are absent, nay, even when they are dead, and they always remain young and beautiful as when he first delineated them."

"Take care," cried Ernest, pushing back his seat, "if you go on at that rate you will take fire."

"No fear of that, brother, unless you have a star or a comet in your pocket, in which case you are not far enough away yet."

These occasional bickerings between Ernest and Jack were always given and taken in good part, and had only the effect of raising a good-humored laugh.

"Let the painter," he continued, "fall in with a spot that pleases him, he can take it with him and have it always before his eyes. The hand of God or of man may alter the original, the forest may lose its trees, the old castle may be destroyed by fire or time, the green meadow may be converted into a dismal swamp, but to him the landscape always retains its pristine freshness, the same butterfly still flutters about the same bush, the same bee still sucks at the same flower."

"Really," said Mrs. Wolston, "it is a pity, after all, that you did not achieve your second verse."

"And yet," continued Jack, "that is only a copy. How much more sublime when we regard the painter as a creator! If there is in the past or present a heroic deed —if there is in the infinity of his life one moment more blessed than another, like Pygmalion he breathes into it the breath of life, and it becomes imperishable. Who would think a century or two hence of the victories of Fritz, unless the skill of the painter be called in to immortalize them!"

"I agree with you in thinking that the arts you name are the source of beautiful and legitimate emotions. But generally it is better to view them as a recreation or pastime, rather than a profession. They have doubtless made a few men live in posterity, but, on the other hand, they have embittered and shortened the lives of thousands."

"You will never guess what led me to adopt this art in preference to the two others. It was the discovery, that we made some years ago, of a gum tree, the name of which I do not recollect."

"The myrica cerifera," said Ernest.

"From the gum of this tree the varnish may be made. Now, like my brother, who, when he sees the sun overhead, considers he ought to profit by the circumstance and become a discoverer, so I said to myself: You have varnish, all you want, therefore, to produce a magnificent painting is canvas, colors, and talent ; consequently, you must not allow such an opportunity to pass — it would be unpardonable. Accordingly, I set to work with an energy never before equalled ; and," added he, showing the design he had just finished, " here are two eyes and a nose, that I do not think want expression."

" Capital !" said Mrs. Wolston ; " your painting will be in admirable keeping with the hangings my daughters have promised to work for your mamma."

" Nobody can deny," continued Jack, laughing, " that the colony is advancing in civilization; it already possesses a conqueror, a member of the Royal Society minus the diploma, and an Apelles in embryo."

" It is now your turn, Frank."

" I," replied Frank, in his mild but penetrating voice, " if I may be allowed to liken the flowers of the garden to the occupations of human life, I should prefer the part of the violet."

" It hides itself," said Mrs. Wolston, " but its presence is not the less felt."

" When I have allowed myself to indulge in dreams of the future, I have pictured myself dwelling in a modest cottage, partially shrouded in ivy, not very far from the village church. My coat is a little threadbare."

" Why threadbare ?" inquired Sophia.

" Because there are a number of very poor people all round me, and I cannot make up my mind to lay out money on myself when it is wanted by them."

" Such a coat would be sacred in our eyes," said Mrs. Wolston.

" In the morning I take a walk in my little garden ; I inspect the flowers one after the other; chide my dog, who is not much of a florist; then, perhaps, I retire to my study, where I am always ready to receive those who may require my aid, my advice, or my personal services."

Here Mrs. Wolston shook Frank very warmly by the hand.

" Sometimes I go amongst the laborers in the fields,

talk to them of the rain, of the fine weather, and of HIM
who gives both. I enter the home of the artizan, cheer
him in his labors, and interest myself in the affairs of his
family; I call the children by their names, caress them,
and make them my friends. I talk to them of our
Redeemer, and thus, in familiarly conversing with the
young, I find means of instructing the old. They, perhaps,
tell me of a sick neighbor; I direct my steps there, and
endeavor to mitigate the pangs of disease by words of
consolation and hope; I strive to pour balm on the
wounded spirit, and, if the mind has been led away by the
temptations of the world, I urge repentance as a means of
grace. If death should step in, then I kneel with those
around, and join them in soliciting a place amongst the
blessed for the departed soul."

"We shall all gladly aid you in such labors of love,"
said Mrs. Wolston.

"When death has deprived a family of its chief support, then I appeal to those whom God has blessed with
the things of this world for the means of assisting the
widow and the fatherless. To one I say, "You regret
having no children, or bemoan those you have lost; here
are some that God has sent you.' I say to another, ' You
have only one child, whilst you have the means of sup-
porting ten; you can at least charge yourself with two.'
Thus I excite the charity of some and the pity of others,
till the bereaved family is provided for. I obtain work
for those that are desirous of earning an honest living, I
bring back to the fold the sheep that are straying, and
rescue those that are tottering on the brink of infidelity."

Here the girls came forward and volunteered to assist
Frank in such works of mercy.

"I accept your proffered aid, my dear girls, but, as yet,
I am only picturing a future career for myself. After a
day devoted to such labors as these, I return to my home,
perhaps to be welcomed by a little circle of my own, for
I hope to be received as a minister of the Protestant
Church, and, as such, may look forward to a partner in my
joys and troubles. Should Providence, however, shape my
13

destiny otherwise, I shall have the poor and afflicted —
always a numerous family — to bestow my affections upon.
But, whilst much of my time is thus passed amongst the
sorrowing and the sick, still there are hours of gaiety
amongst the gloom — there are weddings, christenings, and
merrymakings — there are happy faces to greet me as well
as sad ones — and I am no ascetic. I take part in all the
innocent amusements that are not inconsistent with my
years or the gravity of my profession — but you seem
sad, Mrs. Wolston."

"Yes, Frank; you have recalled my absent son, Richard,
so vividly to my memory, that I cannot help shedding a
tear."

"Is your son in orders then, madam?"

"He is precisely what you have pictured yourself to be,
a minister of the gospel, and a most exemplary young
man."

"If," remarked Becker, "we have hitherto refrained
from inquiring after your son, madam, it was because we
had no wish to recal to your mind the distance that separated you from him, and we should be glad to know his
history."

"There is little to relate ; he is very young yet, and as
soon as he had obtained his ordination, he was offered a
mission to Oregon, which he accepted ; but the ship
having been detained at the Cape of Good Hope, he regarded the accident as a divine message, to convert the
heathen of Kafraria, where he now is."

"It is no sinecure to live amongst these copper-colored
rascals," said Willis ; "they are constantly stealing the
cattle of the Dutch settlers in their neighborhood. About
twelve years ago, our ship was stationed at the Cape, and
I was sent with a party of blue jackets into the interior,
as far as Fort Wiltshire, on the Krieskamma, the most
remote point of the British possessions in South Africa.
There we dispersed a cloud of them that had been for
weeks living upon other people's property. They are tall,
wiry fellows, as hardy as a pine tree, and as daring as buc-
caneers. The chief of the *kraals*, or huts, wear leopard

or panther skins, and profess to have the power of causing rain to fall, besides an endless number of other miraculous attributes. Amongst them, a wife of the ordinary class costs eight head of cattle, but the price of a young lady of the higher ranks runs as high as twenty cows. When a Kafir is suspected of a crime, his tongue is touched seven times with hot iron, and if it is not burnt he is declared innocent."

"I am afraid," said Jack, "if they were all subjected to that test, they would be found to be a very bad lot. But now, since we have all decided upon a profession, let us hear what the young ladies intend doing with themselves; let them consult their imagination for a beautiful future gilded with sunshine, and embroidered with gold."

"There is only one occupation for women," said Mrs. Becker, "and that is too well defined to admit of speculation, and too important to admit of fanciful embellishments."

"Well, then, mother, let us hear what it is."

"It is to nurse you, and rear you, when you are unable to help yourselves; to guide your first steps, and teach you to lisp your first syllables. For this purpose, God has given her qualities that attract sympathy and engender love. She is so constituted as to impart a charm to your lives, to share in your labors, to soothe you when you are ruffled, to smooth your pillow when you are in pain, and to cherish you in old age; bestowing upon you, to your last hour, cares that no other love could yield. These, gentlemen, are the duties and occupations of women; and you must admit, that if it is not our province to command armies, or to add new planets to the galaxy of the firmament; that if we have not produced an Iliad or an Ænead, a Jerusalem Delivered, or a Paradise Lost, an Oratorio of the Creation, a Transfiguration, or a Laocoon, we have not the less our modest utility."

"I should think so, mother," replied Jack; "it would take no end of philosophers to do the work of one of you."

"It surprises me," said Willis, "that not one of you

has selected the finest profession in the world — that of a sailor."

"The finest profession of the sea, you mean, Willis. There is no doubt of its being the finest that can be exercised on the ocean, since it is the only one. If it is the best, Willis, it is also the worst."

"It has also produced great men," continued Willis; "there are Columbus, Vasco de Gama, and Captain Cook, to whom you are indebted for a new world."

"No thanks to them for that," said Jack; "if they had not discovered a new world we should have been in an old one."

"That does not follow," remarked Ernest; "the new world would have existed even if it had not been discovered, and you might have found your way there all the same."

"Not very likely," replied Jack, "unless one of the stars you intend to discover had shown us the way; otherwise it would only have existed in conjecture; and as nobody under such circumstances would have dreamt of settling in it, they would not have been shipwrecked during the voyage."

"Very true," remarked Fritz; "if we had not been here we should, very probably, have been somewhere else, and perhaps in a much worse plight. Let me ask if there is any one here who regrets his present position?"

Willis was about to reply to this question, but Sophia observing that there was something wrong with the handkerchief that he wore round his neck, hastened towards him to put it to rights, and he was silent.

The hour had now arrived when the families separated for the night. Mary was preparing as usual to recite the evening prayer, but before doing so she whispered a few words in her mother's ear.

"Yes, my child;" and, turning to Frank, she added, "Since you are determined to adopt the ministry as a profession, it is but right that we should for the future entrust ourselves to your prayers."

The two families were now located in their respective

eyries; and Jack, whilst escorting the Wolstons to the foot of their tree, said to Sophia,

"I thought the chimpanzee had been playing some prank."

"So he has. Has nobody told you of it?"

"No, not a soul."

"Then I will be as discreet as my neighbors; good night, Master Jack."

13*

CHAPTER XIII.

NEXT day the sky was shrouded in dense masses of cloud, some grey as lead, some livid as copper, and some black as ink. Towards evening the two families, as usual, resolved themselves into a talking party, and Wolston, requesting them to listen, began as follows :—

"There were two rich merchants in Bristol, between whom a very close intimacy had for a long time existed. One of them, whom I shall call Henry Foster, had a daughter; and the other, Nicholas Philipson, had a son, and the two fathers had destined these children for one another. The boy was a little older than the girl, and their tastes, habits, and dispositions seemed to fit them admirably for each other, and so to ratify the decision of the parents. Little Herbert and Cecilia were almost constantly together. They had a purse in common, into which they put all the pieces of bright gold they received as presents on birthdays and other festive occasions. In summer, when the two families retired to a retreat that one of them had in the country, the children were permitted to visit the cottagers, and to assist the distressed, if they chose, out of their own funds — a permission which they availed themselves of so liberally that they were called by the country people the two little angels."

"What a pity there are no poor people here!" said Sophia, dolefully.

"Why?" inquired her mother.

"Because we might assist them, mamma."

"It is much better, however, as it is, my child; our assistance might mitigate the evils of poverty, but might not be sufficient to remove them."

This reasoning did not seem conclusive to Sophia, who shook her head and commenced plying her wheel with redoubled energy.

When Herbert Philipson was twelve years of age he was sent off to school, and Cecilia was confided to the care of a governess, who, under the direction of Mrs. Foster, was to undertake her education. But neither music nor drawing, needlework, grammars nor exercises, could make little Cecilia forget her absent companion. Absence, that cools older friendships, had a contrary effect on her heart; the months, weeks, days, and hours that were to elapse before Herbert returned for the holidays, were counted and recounted. When that period — so anxiously desired — at length arrived, there was no end of rejoicing: she told Herbert of all the little boys and little girls she had clothed and fed, of the old people she had relieved, of the tears she had shed over tales of woe and misery, how she had carried every week a little basket covered with a white napkin to widow Robson, how often she had gone into the damp and dismal cottage of the dying miner, and how happy she always made his wife and their nine pitiful looking children."

"That is a way of conquering human hearts," remarked Mrs. Becker, "often more effective than those referred to the other day."

"Once, when Herbert was at home for the holidays, he accompanied Cecilia on her charitable visits, and was greatly surprised to find that blessings were showered upon his own head wherever they went; people, whom he had never seen before, insisted upon his being their benefactor. This he could not make out. At last, by an accident, he discovered the secret — Cecilia had been distributing her gifts in his name! He remonstrated warmly against this, declaring that he had no wish to be praised and blessed for doing things that he had no hand in.

Finding that his protestations were of no avail, he determined, on the eve of his returning to school, to have his revenge."

"He did not buy Cecilia a doll, did he?" inquired Jack.

"No; he collected all the eatables, clothing, blankets, and money he could obtain; went amongst the poorest of the cottages, and distributed the whole in Cecilia's name."

"Ah," remarked Mrs. Becker, "it is a pity we could not all remain at the age of these children, with the same purity, the same innocence, and the same freshness of sensation; the world would then be a veritable Paradise."

"For some years this state of things continued, the affection between the young people strengthened as they grew older, the occasional holiday time was always the happiest of their lives. Herbert, in due course, was transferred from school to college, where he obtained a degree, and rapidly verged into manhood. Cecilia from the girl at length bloomed into the young lady. A day was finally fixed when they were to be bound together by the holy ties of the church; everything was prepared for their union, when the commercial world was startled by the announcement that Philipson was a ruined man. A ship in which he had embarked a valuable freight had been wrecked, and an agent to whom he had entrusted a large sum of money had suddenly disappeared."

"How deplorable!" cried Fritz.

"Not so very unfortunate, after all," remarked Mary.

"What makes you think so?"

"Because nothing had occurred to interrupt the marriage; only one of the families was ruined, and there was still enough left for both."

"But," said Fritz, "even admitting that the friendship between the two families continued uninterrupted, and that the father of Cecilia was willing to share his property with the father of Herbert, still the young man, in the parlance of society, was a beggar; and it is always hard for a man to owe his position to a woman, and to become, as it were, the *protégé* of her whom he ought rather to protect."

"If that is the view you take, Master Fritz, then I agree

with you that the misfortune was deplorable," said Mary, bending at the same time to hide her blushes, under pretence of mending a broken thread.

"And what if Cecilia's father had been ruined instead of Herbert's?" inquired Jack.

"I should say," replied Sophia, "that we have as much right to be proud and dignified as you have."

"The best way in such a case," observed Willis, laughing, "would be for both parties to get ruined together."

"Herbert," continued Wolston, "was a youth of resolution and energy. He entertained the same opinion as Fritz; and instead of wasting his time in idle despondency, got together some articles of merchandise, and sailed for the Indian Archipelago, promising his friends that he would return to his native land in two years."

"Two years is a long time," remarked Mary; "but sometimes it passes away very quickly."

"Ah!" observed Sophia, "Cecilia, in the meantime, would redouble her charities and her prayers."

"The two years passed away, then a third, and then a fourth, but not a single word had either been heard of or from the absentee. Cecilia was rich, and her hand was sought by many wealthy suitors, but hitherto she had rejected them all."

"The dear, good Cecilia," cried Sophia.

"Up till this period the family had permitted her to have her own way. But as it is necessary for authority to prevent excesses of all kinds, they thought it time now to interfere; they could not allow her to sacrifice her whole life for a shadow. Her parents, therefore, insisted upon her making a choice of one or other of the suitors for her hand. She requested grace for one year more, which was granted."

"Come back, truant, quick; come back, Master Herbert!" cried Sophia.

"There now, Willis," cried Jack, "you see the effect of your new world; people go away there, and never come back again."

"Oh, but you must bring him back in time, father; you must indeed," urged Sophia.

"If it were only a romance I were relating to you, Sophia, I could very easily bring him back; but the narrative I am giving you is a matter of fact, which I cannot alter at will. There would be no difficulty in bringing a richly-laden East Indiaman, commanded by Captain Philipson, into the Severn, and making Herbert and Cecilia conclude the story in each other's arms, but it would not be true."

"Then if I had been Cecilia, I should have become a nun," said Mary, timidly.

"Exaggeration, my daughter, is an enemy to truth. It is easy to say, 'I would become a nun,' and in Roman Catholic countries it is quite as easy to become one; but, though it may be sublime to retire in this way from the world, it is frightful when a woman has afterwards to regret the inconsiderate step she has taken, and which is often the case with these poor creatures."

"As you said of myself," remarked Willis, "it is a crime to go down with a sinking ship so long as there is a straw to cling to."

"I presume," continued Wolston, "that during this year poor Cecilia prayed fervently for the return of her old playfellow; but her prayers were all in vain, the year expired, and still no news of the young man; at last she despaired of ever seeing him again, and, after a severe struggle with herself, she decided upon complying with the desire of her parents and her friends. A few months after the expiring of the year of grace, she was the affianced bride of a highly respectable, well-to-do, middle-aged gentleman. John Lindsey, her intended husband, could not boast of his good looks; he was little, rather stout, was deeply pitted in the face with the small-pox, and had a very red nose, but he was considered by the ladies of Bristol as a very good match for all that."

"Oh, Cecilia, how ridiculous!" exclaimed Sophia.

"Better, at all events, than turning nun," said Jack.

"The family this season had gone to pass the summer at the sea-coast; and one day that Cecilia and her intended were taking their accustomed walk along the shore ——"

"Holloa!" cried Jack, "the truant is going to appear, after all."

"John Lindsey, observing a ring of some value upon Cecilia's finger, politely asked her if she had any objections to tell him its history. She replied that she had none, and told him it was a gift of young Philipson's. 'I am well acquainted with your story, said Lindsey, 'and do not blame the constancy with which you have treasured the memory of that young man; on the contrary, I respect you for it — in fact, it was the knowledge of your self-sacrifice to this affection and all its attendant circumstances, that led me to solicit the honor of your hand; for, said I to myself, one who has evinced so much devotion for a mere sentiment, is never likely to prove unfaithful to sacred vows pledged at the altar.' 'Come what may, you may at least rely upon that, sir,' she answered. 'Then,' continued Lindsey, 'as an eternal barrier is about to be placed between yourself and your past affections, perhaps you will pardon my desire to separate you, as much as possible, from everything that is likely to recal them to your mind.' Saying that, he gently drew the ring from her finger, and threw it into the sea."

It was strongly suspected that Mary shed a tear at this point of the recital.

"It is all over with you now, Herbert," cried Fritz.

"You had better make a bonfire of your ships, like Fernando Cortez in Mexico; or, if you are on your way home, better pray for a hurricane to swallow you up, than have all your bright hopes dashed to atoms, when you arrive in port."

"I am only a little girl," said Sophia; "but I know what I should have said, if the gentleman had done the same thing to me."

"And what would you have said, child?" inquired her mother.

"I should have said, that I was not the Doge of Venice, and had no intention of marrying the British Channel."

"Can you describe the ceremony to which you refer?"

"Yes; but it would interrupt papa's story, and Jack would laugh at me."

"Never mind my story," replied her father, "there is plenty of time to finish that."

"And as for me," said Jack, "though I do not wear a cocked hat and knee breeches, and though, in other respects, my tailor has rather neglected my outward man, still I know what is due to a lady and a queen."

"There, he begins already!" said Sophia.

"Never mind him, child; go on with your account of the marriage."

"Well," began Sophia, "for a long time, there had been disputes between the states of Bologna, Ancona, and Venice, as to which possessed the sovereignty of the Adriatic."

"If it had been a dispute about the Sovereignty of the ocean in general," remarked Willis, "there would have been another competitor."

"Venice," continued Sophia, "carried the day, and about 1275 or 76 she resolved to celebrate her victory by an annual ceremony. For this purpose, a magnificent galley was built, encrusted with gold, silver, and precious stones. This floating *bijou* was called the *Bucentaure*, was guarded in the arsenal, whence it was removed on the eve of the Ascension. Next day the Doge, the patriarch, and the Council of Ten embarked, and the galley was towed out to the open sea, but not far from the shore. There, in the presence of the foreign ambassadors, whilst the clergy chanted the marriage service, the Doge advanced majestically to the front of the galley, and there formally wedded the sea."

"He might have done worse," observed Willis.

"The ceremony," continued Sophia, "consisted in the Doge throwing a ring into the sea, saying, ' We wed thee, O sea! to mark the real and perpetual dominion we possess over thee.'"

"And it may be added," observed Becker, "that the history of Venice shows how religiously the spouses of the Adriatic kept their vows."

"Now," said Sophia, "that I have told my tale, let us hear what became of Cecilia."

"Well, the marriage took place the morning after Herbert's ring had been thrown to the fishes. Whilst the bride, bridegroom, and their friends were congratulating each other over the wedding breakfast, as is usual in England on such occasions, Cecilia's father was called out of the room."

"Too late," remarked Fritz.

"Herbert Philipson had arrived that same morning; but, as Fritz observes, he was just an hour too late. He had acquired a fortune, but his long-cherished hopes of happiness were completely blasted."

"Why did he stay away five years without writing?" inquired Mrs. Wolston.

"He had written several times, but at that time no regular post had been established, and his letters had never reached their destination."

"When did he find out that Cecilia was married?"

"Well, some people think it more humane to kill a man by inches rather than by a single blow of the axe. Not so with Herbert's friends; the first news that greeted him on landing were, that his ever-remembered Cecilia was probably at that moment before the altar pledging her vows to another."

"I should rather have had a chimney-pot tumble on my head," remarked Willis.

"Herbert was a man in every sense of the word — the mode of his departure proves that. On hearing this painful intelligence, he simply covered his face with his hands, and, after a moment's thought, resolved to see his lost bride at least once more."

"Poor Herbert!" sighed Mary.

"Foster was thunderstruck when the stranger declared himself to be the son of his old friend; and, after cordially bidding him welcome, sorrowfully asked him what he meant to do. 'I should wish to see Mrs. Lindsey in presence of her husband,' he replied, 'providing you have no objections to introduce me to the company.'"

"Bravo!" ejaculated Willis.

"Foster could not refuse this favor to an unfortunate, who had just been disinherited of his dearest hopes. He, therefore, took Herbert by the hand and led him into the room. Nobody recognized him. 'Ladies and gentlemen,'

14

said he, 'permit me to introduce Mr. Herbert Philipson, who has just arrived from Sumatra.' You may readily conceive the dismay this unexpected announcement called up into the countenances of the guests. There was only one person in the room who was calm, tranquil, and unmoved — that person was Cecilia herself. She rose courteously, bade him welcome, hoped he was well, coolly asked him why he had not written to his friends, and politely asked him to take a seat beside herself and husband, just, for all the world, as if he had been some country cousin or poor relation to whom she wished to show a little attention."

"I would rather have been at the bottom of the sea than in her place, for all that," said Mary.

"Why? She had nothing to reproach herself with. Had she not waited long enough for him?"

"Young heads," remarked Becker, "are not always stored with sense. A foolish pledge, given in a moment of thoughtlessness is often obstinately adhered to in spite of reason and argument. The young idea delights in miraculous instances of fidelity. What more charming to a young and ardent mind than the loves of Dante and Beatrix, of Eleonora and Tasso, of Petrarch and Laura, of Abelard and Heloise, or of Dean Swift and Stella? Young people do not reflect that most of these stories are apocryphal, and that the men who figure in them sought to add to their renown the prestige of originality; they put on a passion as ordinary mortals put on a new dress, they yielded to imagination and not to the law of the heart, and almost all of them paid by a life of wretchedness the penalty of their dreams."

"That is, I presume," remarked Mrs. Wolston, "you do not object to any reasonable amount of constancy, but you object to its being carried to an unwarrantable excess."

"Exactly so, madam," replied Becker; "constancy, like every thing else when reasonable limits are exceeded, becomes a vice."

"The merriments of the marriage breakfast," continued Wolston "slightly interrupted by the arrival of the new guest, were resumed. Fresh dishes were brought in, and, amongst others, a fine turbot was placed on the table. The gentleman who was engaged in carving the turbot struck the fish-knife against a hard substance."

"I know what!" exclaimed two or three voices.

"I rather think not," said Wolston, drily.

"Oh, yes, the ring! the ring!"

"No, it was merely the bone that runs from the head to the tail of the fish."

"Oh, father," cried Sophia, "how can you tease us so?"

"If they had found the ring," replied Wolston, laughing, "I should have no motive for concealing it. Fruit was afterwards placed before Herbert, and, when nobody was looking, he pulled a clasped dagger out of his pocket."

Here Sophia pressed her hands closely on her ears, in order to avoid hearing what followed.

"It was a very beautiful poignard," continued Wolston, "and rather a bijou than a weapon; and, as the servants had neglected to hand him a fruit-knife, he made use of it in paring an apple."

"Is it all over?" inquired Sophia, removing a hand from one ear.

"Alas! yes!" said Jack, lugubriously, "he has been and done it."

"O the monster!"

"Travelling carriages having arrived at the door for the bridal party, Herbert quietly departed."

"What!" exclaimed Sophia, "did they not arrest and drag him to prison?"

"Oh," replied Jack, "the crime was not so atrocious as it appears."

"Not atrocious!"

"No; you must bear in mind that young Philipson had passed the preceding five years of his life amongst demi-savages, whose manners and customs he had, to a certain extent, necessarily contracted. In some countries, what we call crimes are only regarded as peccadillos. In France, for example, till very lately, there existed what was called the law of *combette*, by right of which pardon might be obtained for any misdeed on payment of a certain sum of money. There was a fixed price for every imaginable crime. A man might consequently be a Blue Beard if he liked, it was only necessary to consult the tariff in the first instance, and see to what extent his means would enable him to indulge his fancy for horrors."

"On quitting the house," continued Wolston, "Herbert Philipson bent his way to the shore, and shortly after was observed to plunge into the sea."

"So much the better," exclaimed Sophia; "it saved his friends a more dreadful spectacle."

"The weather being fine and the water warm, Herbert enjoyed his bath immensely; he then returned to his hotel, went early to bed, and slept soundly till next morning."

"The wretch!" cried Sophia, "to sleep soundly after assassinating his old playfellow, who had suffered so much on his account."

"It is pretty certain," continued Wolston, "that, if Philipson had been left entirely to himself, he would always have shown the same degree of moderation he had hitherto displayed."

"Oh, yes, moderation!" said Sophia.

"But his friends began to prate to him about the shameful way he had been jilted by Cecilia, and, by constantly reiterating the same thing, they at last succeeded in persuading him that he was an ill-used man. His self-esteem being roused by this silly chatter, he began to affect a ridiculous desolation, and to perpetrate all manner of outrageous extravagances."

"Bad friends," remarked Willis, "are like sinking ships; they drag you down to their own level."

"The first absurd thing he did was to purchase a yacht, and when a storm arose that forced the hardy fishermen to take shelter in port, he went out to sea, and it is quite a miracle that he escaped drowning. Then, if there were a doubtful scheme afloat, he was sure to take shares in it. Nothing delighted him more than to go up in a balloon; he would have gladly swung himself on the car outside if the proprietor had allowed him."

"I have often seen balloons in the air," remarked Willis, "but I could never make out their dead reckoning."

"A balloon," replied Ernest, "is nothing more than an

artificial cloud, and its power of ascension depends upon the volume of air it displaces.

"Very good, Master Ernest, so far as the balloon itself is concerned; but then there is the weight of the car, passengers, provisions, and apparatus to account for."

"Hydrogen gas, used in the inflation of balloons, is forty times lighter than air. If a balloon is made large enough, the weight of the car and all that it contains, added to that of the gas, will fall considerably short of the weight of the air displaced by the machine."

"I suppose it rises in the air just as an empty bottle well corked rises in the water?"

"Very nearly. Air is lighter than water; consequently, any vessel filled with the one will rise to the surface of the other. So in the case of balloons. The gas, in the first place, must be inclosed in an envelope through which it cannot escape. Silk prepared with India-rubber is the material usually employed. As the balloon rises, the gas in the interior distends, because the air becomes lighter the less it is condensed by its superincumbent masses; hence it is requisite to leave a margin for this increase in the volume of the gas, otherwise the balloon would burst in the air."

"If a balloon were allowed to ascend without hindrance where would it stop?"

"It would continue ascending till it reached a layer of air as light as the gas; beyond that point it could not go."

"And if the voyagers do not wish to go quite so far?"

"Then there is a valve by which the gas may be allowed to escape, till the weight of the machine and its volume of air are equal, when it ceases to ascend. If a little more is permitted to escape, the balloon descends."

"And should it land on the roof of a house or the top of a tree, the voyagers have their necks broken."

"That can only happen to bunglers; there is not the least necessity for landing where danger is to be apprehended. When the aeronaut is near the ground, and sees that the spot is unfavorable for debarkation, he drops a little ballast, the balloon mounts, and he comes down again somewhere else."

"The fellow that made the first voyage must have been very daring."

"The first ascent was made by Montgolfier in 1782, and he was followed by Rosiers and d'Arlandes."

"With your permission, father," said Ernest, "I will claim priority in aerial travelling for Icarus, Dœdalus, and Phæton."

"Certainly; you are justified in doing so. Gay-Lussac, a philosophic Frenchman, rose, in 1804, to the height of seven thousand yards."

"He must have felt a little giddy," remarked Jack.

"Most of the functions of the body were affected, more or less, by the extreme rarity of the air at that height. Its dryness caused wet parchment to crisp. He observed that the action of the magnetic needle diminished as he ascended, sounds gradually ceased to reach his ear, and the wind itself ceased to be felt."

"That, of course," remarked Ernest, "was when he was travelling in the same direction and at the same speed."

"Well," said Jack, "we can find materials here for a balloon; the ladies have silk dresses, there is plenty of India-rubber — we used to make boots and shoes of it; hydrogen gas can be obtained from a variety of substances. What, then, is to prevent us paying a visit to some of Ernest's friends in the skies?"

"Unfortunately for your project, Jack, no one has discovered the art of guiding a balloon; consequently, instead of finding yourself at *Cassiope*, you might land at *Sirius*, where your reception would be somewhat cool."

"But what became of Herbert?" inquired one of the ladies.

"Singularly enough, he escaped all the dangers he so recklessly braved, and all the bad speculations he embarked in turned out good. Somehow or other, the moment he took part in a desperate scheme it became profitable."

"Ah!" exclaimed Sophia, "his victim, like a guardian angel, continued to watch over him."

"When the cholera appeared in England, he was sure to be found where the cases were most numerous. He followed up the pest with so much pertinacity and publicity, that it was no unusual thing to find it announced in the newspapers that Philipson and the cholera had arrived in such and such a town."

"The bane and the antidote," remarked Jack.

"If Cecilia had been one of those women who delight in horse-racing, fox-hunting, opera-boxes, and public executions, she would have been highly amused to see her old friend's name constantly turning up under such extraordinary circumstances."

"Is she not dead, then?" inquired Sophia, with astonishment.

"It appears that her wounds were not mortal," quietly replied her mother.

"Besides," observed Jack, "there are human frames so constituted that they can bear an immense amount of cutting and slashing. So in the case of animals; there, for instance, is the fresh-water polypus — if you cut this creature lengthwise straight through the middle, a right side will grow on the one half and a left side on the other, so that there will be two polypi instead of one. The same thing occurs if you cut one through the middle crosswise, a head grows on the one half and a tail on the other, so that you have two entire polypi either way."

"And you may add," observed Ernest, "since so interesting a subject is on the *tapis*, that if two of these polypi happen to quarrel over their prey, the largest generally swallows the smallest, in order to get it out of the way; and the latter, with the exception of being a little cramped for space, is not in the slightest degree injured by the operation."

"And does that state of matters continue any length of time?"

"The polypus that is inside the other may probably get tired of confinement, in which case it makes its exit by the same route it entered; but, if too lazy to do that, it makes a hole in the body of its antagonist and gets out that way. But, what is most curious of all, these processes do not appear to put either of the creatures to the slightest inconvenience."

"I am quite at a loss to make you all out," said Sophia.

"Well, my child," replied her mother, "you should not close up your ears in the middle of a story."

"Cecilia, or rather Mrs. Lindsey, however," continued Wolston, "was a pious, painstaking, simple-minded woman, who devoted her whole attention to her domestic duties. Notwithstanding her fortune, she did not neglect the humblest affairs of the household, and thought only of making her husband pleased with his home. When she was told of the vagaries of Philipson, she prayed in private that he might be led from his evil ways, and could not help thanking Providence that she was not the wife of such a dreadful scapegrace."

"I should think so," remarked Mrs. Becker.

"At last, Herbert Philipson astonished even his own companions by a crowning act of folly. There was then a young woman in Bristol, of good parentage, but an unmitigated virago; her family were thoroughly ashamed of her temper and her exploits. They allowed her to have her own way, simply for fear that, through contradiction, she might plunge herself into even worse courses than those she now habitually followed. In short, she was the talk and jest of the whole town."

"What a charming creature!" remarked Mrs. Becker.

"No servant of her own sex could put up with her for two days together; she styled everybody that came near her fools and asses, and did not hesitate to strike them if they ventured to contradict her. She got on, however, tolerably well with ostlers, stable-boys, cabmen, and such like, because they could treat her in her own style, and were not ruffled by her abuse."

"How amiable!" exclaimed Mrs. Wolston.

"Herbert heard of this young person, and, through a fast friend of his own, obtained an introduction to her, and on the very first interview he offered her his hand. He was known still to be a wealthy man, so neither the lady herself nor anybody connected with her made the slightest objection to the match, thinking probably that, if there were six of the one, there were at least half a dozen of the other."

"They ought to have gone to Bedlam, instead of to church," said Willis; "that is my idea."

"Nevertheless, they went to church; and, after the marriage, Cecilia sought and obtained an introduction to the lady, and, whether by entreaties or by her good example, I cannot say; be this as it may, the unpromising personage in question became one of the best wives and the best mothers that ever graced a domestic circle — in this respect even excelling the pattern Cecilia herself; and, what is still more to the purpose, she succeeded in completely reforming her husband. When I left England there was not a more prosperous merchant, nor a more estimable man in the whole city of Bristol, than Herbert Philipson."

"From which we may conclude," remarked Mrs. Becker, "it is always advisable to have angels for friends."

"We may also conclude," remarked Mrs. Wolston, "that when a stroke of adversity, or any other misfortune, overturns the edifice of happiness we had erected for the future, we may build a new structure with fresh material, which may prove more durable than the first."

"Talking of having angels for friends," said Becker, "puts me in mind of the association of Saint Louis Gonzaga, at Rome. On the anniversary of this saint, the young and merry phalanx forming the association march in procession to one of the public gardens. In the centre of this garden a magnificent altar has been previously erected, on which is placed a chafing-dish filled with burning coals. The procession forms itself into an immense ring round the altar, broken here and there by a band of music. These bands play hymns in honor of the saints, and other *morceaux* of a sacred character. Each member of the association holds a letter inclosed in an embossed and highly ornamented envelope, bound round with gay-colored ribbons and threads of gold. These letters are messages from the young correspondents to their friends in heaven, and are addressed to 'Il Santo Giovane Luigi Gonzaga, in Paradiso.' At a given signal, the letters, in the midst of profound silence, are placed on the chafing-dish. This done, the music resounds on all sides, and the assembly burst out into loud acclamations, during which the letters are supposed to be carried up into heaven by the angels."

"A curious and interesting ceremony," remarked Mrs. Wolston, "and one that may possibly do good, inasmuch as it may induce the young people composing the association to persevere in generous resolutions."

The two families again separated for the night. And whilst the young men were escorting the Wolstons to their tree, Sophia went towards Jack. "Will you tell me," inquired she, "what happened whilst I had my ears closed up, Jack?"

"Yes, with all my heart, if you will tell me first what the chimpanzee had been about during our absence."

"Well, he got up into our tree when we were out of the way. After soaping his chin, he had taken one of papa's razors, and just as he was beginning to shave himself, some one entered and caught him."

"Oh, is that all? What I have to tell you is a great deal more appalling than that."

"Well, then, be quick."

"But I am afraid you will be shocked."

"Is it very dreadful?"

"More so than you would imagine. If you dream about it during the night, you will not be angry with me for telling you?"

"No, I will be courageous, and am prepared to hear the worst."

"What was your father saying when you shut up your ears?"

"Herbert had just pulled out a dagger."

"And when you took your hands away?"

"All was then over; Herbert had done some dreadful thing with the dagger, and I want to know what it was."

"He pared an apple with it," replied Jack, bursting into a roar of laughter, and, running off, he left Sophia to her reflections.

A few seconds after he returned. This time he had almost a solemn air, the laughter had vanished from his visage, like breath from polished steel.

"Miss Sophia," inquired he gravely, "are you rich?"

"I don't know, Master Jack; are you?"

"Well, I have not the slightest idea either."

CHAPTER XIV.

AT daybreak next morning, all the eyes in the colony
were busily engaged in scrutinizing the sky. This time
the operation seemed satisfactory, for immediately afterwards, all the hands were, with equal diligence, occupied
in packing up and making other preparations for the
meditated excursion to the remote dependencies of New
Switzerland.

The dense veil that the day before had shrouded them
in gloom was now broken up into shreds. The azure
depths beyond had assumed the appearance of a blue
tunic bespattered with white, and the clouds suggested the
idea of a celestial shepherd, driving myriads of sheep to
the pasture. Children alone can dry up their tears with
the rapidity of Nature in the tropics; perhaps we may
have already made the remark, and must, therefore, beg
pardon for repeating the simile a second time.

In a short time, the two families were assembled on the
lawn, in front of the domestic trees of Falcon's Nest,
ready to start on their journey. The cow and the buffalo
were yoked to the carriage, which was snugly covered
over with a tarpauling, thrown across circular girds, like
the old-fashioned waggons of country carriers. Frank
mounted the box in front; Mrs. Becker, Wolston, and
Sophia got inside; whilst Ernest and Jack, mounted on
ostriches that had been trained and broken in as riding
horses, took up a position on each side, where the doors

of the vehicle ought to have been. These dispositions made, after a few lashes from the whip, this party started off at a brisk rate in the direction of Waldeck.

It had been previously arranged that one half of the expedition should go by land, and the other half by water, and that on their return this order should be reversed, so that both the interior and the coast might be inspected at one and the same time. The only exception was made in favor of Willis, who was permitted both to go and return by sea.

The second party, consisting of Mrs. Wolston, Becker, Mary, and Fritz, started on foot in the direction of the coast. They had not gone far before Becker observed a large broadside plastered on a tree.

"What is that?" he inquired.

Nobody could give a satisfactory reply.

"Perhaps," suggested Mrs. Wolston, "paper grows ready made on the trees of this wonderful country."

"They all approached, and, much to their astonishment, read as follows:—

"TAKE NOTICE.

"The renowned Professor Ernest Becker is about to enlighten the benighted inhabitants of this country, by giving a course of lectures on optics. The agonizing doubts that have hitherto enveloped astronomical science, particularly as regards the interiors of the moon and the stars, have arisen from the absurd practice of looking at them during the night. These doubts are about to be removed for ever by the aforesaid professor, as he intends to exhibit the luminaries in question in open day. He will also place Charles's Wain* at the disposal of any one who is desirous of taking a drive in the Milky Way. The learned professor will likewise stand for an indefinite period on his head; and whilst in this position will clearly demonstrate the rotundity of the earth, and the tendency

---

* The constellation known in astronomy as the *Great Bear* is in some parts of England termed the *Plough*, and in others *Charles's Wain* or *Waggon*. It may be added, that the same constellation is popularly known in France as the *Chariot of David*

of heavy bodies to the centre of gravity. In order that
the prices of admission may be in accordance with the
intrinsic value of the lectures, nothing will be charged for
the boxes, the entrance to the pit will be gratis, and the
gallery will be thrown open for the free entry of the
people. The audience will be expected to assume a horizontal position. Persons given to snoring are invited to
stay at home."

"I rather think I should know that style," remarked
Willis.

"It is a pity Ernest is not with us," observed Fritz;
"but the placard will keep for a day or two."

"They say laughing is good for digestion," remarked
Mrs. Wolston; "and if so, it must be confessed that Master
Jack is a useful member of the colony in a sanitary point
of view."

The party had scarcely advanced a hundred paces farther, when Fritz called out,

"Holloa! there is another broadside in sight."

"This one was headed by a smart conflict between two
ferocious looking hussars, and was couched in the following
terms : —

" PROCLAMATION.

" All the inhabitants of this colony capable of bearing
arms, who are panting after glory, are invited to the Fig
Tree, at Falcon's Nest, there to enrol themselves in the
registry of Fritz Becker, who is about to undertake the
conquest of the world. Nobody is compelled to volunteer,
but those who hold back will be reckoned contumacious,
and will be taken into custody, and kept on raw coffee till
such time as they evince a serious desire to enlist. There
will be no objection to recruits returning home at the end
of the war, if they come out of it alive. Neither will there
be any objections to the survivors bringing back a marshal's baton, if they can get one. The Commander-in-
chief will charge himself with the fruits of the victory.
Surgical operations will be performed at his cost, and cork
legs will be served out with the rations. In the event of

15

a profitable campaign, a monument will be erected to the memory of the defunct, by way of a reward for their heroism on the field of battle."

"Well, Fritz," said Becker, with a merry twinkle in his eye, "you were sorry that Ernest was not present to hear the last placard read; fortunately, you are on the spot yourself this time."

Fritz tried to look amused, but the attempt was a decided failure.

When the party had gone a little farther, another announcement met their gaze; all were curious to know whose turn was come now; as they approached, the following interesting question, in large letters, stared them in the face :—

"HAVE YOU HAD YOUR PORTRAIT TAKEN YET?

"It has been reserved for the present age, and for this prolific territory, so exuberant in cabbages, turnips, and other potables, to produce the greatest of living artists — a real genius — who is destined to outshine all the Michel Angelos and Rubenses of former ages. Not that these men were entirely devoid of talent, but because they could do nothing without their palette and their paint brushes. Now that illustrious *maestro*, Mr. Jack Becker, has both genius and ingenuity, for he has succeeded in dispensing with the aforementioned troublesome auxiliaries of his art. His plan which has the advantage of not being patented, consists in placing his subject before a mirror, where he is permitted to stay till the portrait takes root in the glass. By this novel method the original and the copy will be subject alike to the ravages of time, so that no one, on seeing a portrait, will be liable to mistake the grandmother for the grand-daughter. Likenesses guaranteed. Payments, under all circumstances, to be made in advance."

"Ah, well," said Becker, laughing, "it appears that the scapegrace has not spared himself."

"I hope there is not a fourth proclamation," said Mrs. Wolston.

"There are no more trees on our route, at all events," replied Becker.

"Glad to hear that; Jack must respect the avocation chosen by Frank, since he sees nothing in it to ridicule."

As they drew near the Jackal River, in which the pinnace was moored, Mary and Fritz were a little in advance of the party.

"Are you really determined to turn the world upside down, Master Fritz?"

"At present, Miss Wolston, I am myself the sum and substance of my army, in addition to which I have not yet quite made up my mind."

"It is an odd fancy to entertain to say the least of it."

"Does it displease you?"

"In order that it could do that, I must first have the right to judge your projects."

"And if I gave you that right?"

"I should find the responsibility too great to accept it. Besides, a determination cannot be properly judged, without putting one's self in the position of the person that makes it. You imagine happiness consists in witnessing the shock of armies, whilst I fancy enjoyment to consist in the calm tranquility of one's home. You see our views of felicity are widely different."

"Not so very widely different as you seem to think, Miss Wolston. As yet my victories are *nil;* I have not yet come to an issue with my allies; to put my troops on the peace establishment I have only to disembody myself, and I disembody myself accordingly."

"Oh!" exclaimed Mary, "you are very easily turned from your purpose."

"Easily! no, Miss Wolston, not easily; you cannot admit that an objection urged by yourself is a matter of no moment, or one that can be slighted with impunity."

"Ah! here we are at the end of our journey."

"Already! the road has never appeared so short to me before."

"What!" exclaimed Mrs. Wolston, coming up to her daughter, "you appear very merry."

"Well, not without reason, mamma; I have just restored peace to the world."

The pinnace was soon launched, and, under the guidance of Willis, was making way in the direction of Waldeck. The sea had not yet recovered from the effects of the recent storm; it was still, to use an expression of Willis, "a trifle ugly." Occasionally the waves would catch the frail craft amidships, and make it lurch in an uncomfortable fashion, especially as regarded the ladies, which obliged Willis to keep closer in shore than was quite to his taste. The briny element still bore traces of its recent rage, just as anger lingers on the human face, even after it has quitted the heart.

Whilst the pinnace was in the midst of a series of irregular gyrations, a shrill scream suddenly rent the air, and at the same instant Fritz and Willis leaped overboard.

Mary had fallen into the sea.

Becker strained every nerve to stay the boat. Mrs. Wolston fell on her knees with outstretched hands, but, though in the attitude of prayer, not a word escaped her pallid lips.

The two men floated for a moment over the spot where the poor girl had sunk; suddenly Fritz disappeared, his keen eye had been of service here, for it enabled him to descry the object sought. In a few seconds he rose to the surface with Mary's inanimate body in his left arm. Willis hastened to assist him in bearing the precious burden to the boat, and Becker's powerful arms drew it on deck.

The joy that all naturally would have felt when this was accomplished had no time to enter their breasts, for they saw that the body evinced no signs of life, and a fear that the vital spark had already fled caused every frame to shudder. They felt that not a moment was to be lost; the resources of the boat were hastily put in requisition; mattresses, sheets, blankets, and dry clothes were strewn upon the deck. Mrs. Wolston had altogether lost her presence of mind, and could do nothing but press the dripping form of her daughter to her bosom.

" Friction must be tried instantly," cried Becker; "here, take this flannel and rub her body smartly with it — particularly her breast and back."

Mrs. Wolston instinctively followed these directions.

"It is of importance to warm her feet," continued Becker; "but, unfortunately, we have no means on board to make a fire."

Mrs. Wolston, in her trepidation, began breathing upon them.

"I have heard," said the Pilot, "that persons rescued from drowning are held up by the feet to allow the water to run out."

"Nonsense, Willis; a sure means of killing them outright. It is not from water that any danger is to be apprehended, but from want of air, or, rather, the power of respiration. What we have to do is to try and revive this power by such means as are within our reach."

The Pilot, meantime, endeavored to introduce a few drops of brandy between the lips of the patient. Fritz stood trembling like an aspen leaf and deadly pale; he regarded these operations as if his own life were at stake, and not the patient's.

"There remains only one other course to adopt, Mrs. Wolston," said Becker, "you must endeavor to bring your daughter to life by means of your own breath."

"Only tell me what to do, Mr. Becker, and, if every drop of blood in my body is wanted, all is at your disposal."

"You must apply your mouth to that of your daughter, and, whilst her nostrils are compressed, breathe at intervals into her breast, and so imitate the act of natural respiration."

Stronger lungs than those of a woman might have been urgent under such circumstances, but maternal love supplied what was wanting in physical strength.

The Pilot had turned the prow of the pinnace towards home; he felt that, in the present case at least, the comforts of the land were preferable to the charms of the sea.

"This time it is not my breath, but her own," said Mrs. Wolston.

"Her pulse beats," said Becker; "she lives."

"Thank God!" exclaimed Fritz and Willis in one voice.

A quarter of an hour had scarcely yet elapsed since the

15*

patient's first immersion in the sea; but this brief interval had been an age of agony to them all. As yet, her head lay quiescent on her mother's bosom, that first pillow, common alike to rich and poor, at the threshold of life.

The signs of returning animation gradually became more and more evident; at length, the patient gently raised her head, and glanced vacantly from one object to another; then, her eyes were turned upon herself, and finally rested upon Fritz and Willis, who still bore obvious traces of their recent struggle with the waves. Here she seemed to become conscious, for her body trembled, as if some terrible thought had crossed her mind. After this paroxysm had passed, she feebly inclined her head, as if to say—"I understand—you have saved my life—I thank you." Then, like those jets of flame that are no sooner alight than they are extinguished, she again became insensible.

As soon as they reached the shore, Fritz hastened to Rockhouse, and made up a sort of palanquin of such materials as were at hand, into which Mary was placed, and thus was conveyed, with all possible care and speed, on the shoulders of the men to Falcon's Nest. A few hours afterwards she returned to consciousness and found herself in a warm bed, surrounded with all the comforts that maternal anxiety and Becker's intelligent mind could suggest.

Fritz was unceasing in his exertions; no amount of fatigue seemed to wear him out. As soon as he saw that everything had been done for the invalid that their united skill could accomplish, he bridled an untrained ostrich, and rode or rather flew off in search of the land portion of the expedition.

"Mary is saved," he cried, as he came up with them.

"From what?" inquired Wolston, anxiously.

"From the sea, that was about to swallow her up."

"And by whom?"

"By Willis, myself, and us all."

The same evening, the two families were again assembled at Falcon's Nest, and thus, for a second time, the long talked-of expedition was brought to an abrupt conclusion.

"Ah," said Willis, "we must cast anchor for a bit;

yesterday it was the sky, to-day it was the sea, to-morrow it will be the land, perhaps — the wind is clearly against us."

How often does it not happen, in our pilgrimage through life, that we have the wind against us? We make a resolute determination, we set out on our journey, but the object we seek recedes as we advance; it is no use going any farther — the wind is against us. We re-commence ten, twenty, a hundred times, but the result is invariably the same. How is this? No one can tell. What are the obstacles? It is difficult to say. Perhaps, we meet with a friend who detains us; perhaps, a recollection that our memory has called, induces us to swerve from the path — the blind man that sung under our window may have something to do with it — perhaps, it was merely a fly, less than nothing.

It is not our minor undertakings, but rather our most important enterprises, that are frustrated by such trifles as these; for it must be allowed that we strive less tenaciously against an obstacle that debars us from a pleasure, than against one that separates us from a duty — in the one case we have to stem the torrent, in the other we sail with the current.

When we observe some deplorable instance of a wrecked career — when we see a man starting in life with the most brilliant prospects collapsing into a dead-weight on his fellows, we are apt to suppose that some insurmountable barrier must have crossed his path — some Himalaya, or formidable wall, like that which does not now separate China from Tartary; but no such thing. Trace the cause to its source, and what think you is invariably found? A grain of sand; the unfortunate wretch has had the wind against him — nothing more.

Rescued from the sea, Mary Wolston was now a prey to a raging fever. Ill or well, at her age there is no medium, either exuberant health or complete prostration; the juices then are turbulent and the blood is ardent.

Somehow or other, a good action attaches the doer to the recipient; so, in the case of Fritz, apart from the brotherly affection which he had vaguely vowed to entertain for the two young girls that had so unexpectedly appeared amongst them, he now regarded the life of Mary as identical with his own, and felt that her death would inevitably shorten his own existence; "for," said he to himself, "should she die, I was too late in drawing her out of the water." In his tribulation and irreflection, he drew no line between the present and the past, but simply concluded, that if he saved her too late, he did not save her at all. Hope, nevertheless, did not altogether abandon him. He would sometimes fancy her restored to her wonted health, abounding in life and vigour. Then the pleasing thought would cross his mind that, but for himself, that charming being, in all probability, would have been a tenant of the tomb. Would that those who do evil only knew the delight that sometimes wells up in the breasts of those who do good!

The first day of Mary's illness, Fritz bore up manfully. On the second, he joined his father and brothers in their field labors; but, whilst driving some nails into a fence, he had so effectually fixed himself to a stake that it was only with some difficulty that he could be detached. The third day, at sunrise, he called Mary's dog, shouldered his rifle, and was about to quit the house.

"Where are you going?" inquired Jack.

"I don't know — anywhere."

"Anywhere! Well, I am rather partial to that sort of place; I will go with you."

"But I must do something that will divert my thoughts. There may be danger."

"Well I can help you to look up a difficulty."

Every day the two brothers departed at sunrise, and returned together again in the evening. Mrs. Becker felt acutely their sufferings. She watched anxiously for the return of the two wanderers, and generally went a little way to meet them when they appeared in the distance.

"She does not run to meet us," said Fritz, one day; "that is a bad sign."

"Not a bit of it," replied Jack. "If she had any bad news to give us, she would not come at all."

CHAPTER XV.

SOME men, when they regard the sinister side of events, are apt to call in question the axiom, Nothing is accomplished without the will of God. Why, they ask, do the wicked triumph? Why are the just oppressed? Why this evil? What is the use of that disaster? Was it necessary that Mary Wolston should be thrown into the sea, and that she should afterwards die in consequence of the accident?

To these questions we reply, that God does not interrupt the ordinary course of His works. Man is a free agent in so far as regards his own actions; were it otherwise, we should not be responsible for our own crimes. We might as well plunge into vice as adhere to virtue; for we could not be called upon to expiate the one, nor could we hope to be rewarded for the other. It is not to be expected that God is to perform miracles at every instant for our individual benefit. It is unreasonable in us to suppose that, in obedience to our wishes or desires, He will alter His immutable laws.

A foot slips on the brink of a precipice, and we are dashed to atoms. Our boat is upset in a squall, and we are drowned. Like Stanislaus Leszinsky, King of Poland, we fall asleep in the corner of a chimney, our clothes take fire, and we are burned to death. We go a hunting; we mistake a grey overcoat for the fur of a deer, and we kill our friend or his gamekeeper, as once happened to the son of Louis XV., who in consequence almost died of grief, and renounced forever a sport of which he was passionately fond. Did Providence will, **exact**, or pre-ordain all these calamities? Certainly not; **but our** Creator has seen fit to tolerate and permit them, **since** he did not interpose to prevent them.

The government of God is a conception **so** wonderful, so sublime, that none but Himself **can** fathom its depths. Human intelligence is too finite to penetrate or comprehend a system so complex, and yet so uniform. The mind of man can only form a just idea of a cause when the effect has been made manifest to his understanding. There might have been a reason for the death of Mary Wolston — who knows? But if it were **so**, that reason was beyond the pale of mortal ken.

Let us not, however, anticipate. Mary **Wolston** is not yet dead. On the contrary, when the ninth day of her illness had passed, Fritz and Jack were returning **from an** expedition, the nature of which was only known to themselves, but which, to judge from the packs that **they bore** on their backs, had been tolerably productive. The **two** young men observed their mother advancing, **as usual, to** meet them, but this time *she ran.* They had no need to be told in words that Mary Wolston was now **out of** danger; the serenity of their mother's countenance was more eloquent than the most elaborate discourse that ever stirred human souls.

Mrs. Becker herself felt that words were superfluous, so she quietly took her son's arm, and they walked gently homewards, whilst Jack strode on before. On turning a corner of the road, the latter stumbled upon Wolston and Ernest, who, in the exuberance of their joy, had also come out to meet the hunters. They were, however, a little behind; but that was nothing new. These two members of the colony had become quite remarkable for procrastination and absence of mind. When Wolston the mechanician, and Ernest the philosopher, travelled in company, it was rare that some pebble or plant, or question in physics, did not induce them to deviate from their route or tarry on their way. One day they both started for Rockhouse to fetch provisions for the family dinner, but instead of bringing back the needful supplies of beef and mutton, they returned in great glee with the solution of an intricate problem in geometry. All fared very indifferently on that occasion, and, in consequence, Wolston and Ernest were, from that time on, deprived of the office of purveyors.

In the present instance, instead of running like Mrs. Becker, they had philosophically seated themselves on the trunk of a tree. At their feet was a diagram that Wolston had traced with the end of his stick; this was neither a tangent nor a triangle, as might have been expected, but a figure denoting how to carve one's way to a position, amidst the rugged defiles of life.

" In all things," observed Wolston, " in morals as well as physics, the shortest road from one point to another, is the straight line."

"Unless," objected Ernest, " the straight line were encumbered with obstacles, that would require more time to surmount than to go round. Two leagues of clear road would be better than one only a single league in length, if intersected by ditches and strewn with wild beasts."

"Bah!" cried Jack, who had just come up out of breath, "you might leap the one and shoot the others."

"Your argument," replied Wolston, "is that of the savage, who can imagine no obstacles that are not solid and tangible. The obstacles that retard our progress in life neither display yawning chasms nor rows of teeth; they dwell within our own minds — they are versatility, disgust, ennui, thirst after the unknown, and love of change. These lead us to take bye-paths and long turnings, and fritter away the strength that should be used in promoting a single aim. Hence arise a multiplicity of hermaphrodite avocations and desultory studies, that terminate in nothing but vexation of spirit. Let us suppose, for example, that Peter has made up his mind to be a lawyer."

"I do not see any particular reason why Peter should not be a lawyer," said Jack.

" Nor I either; but unfortunately when Peter has pored

a certain time over Coke upon Littleton, and other abstruse legal authorities, he accidentally witnesses a review; he throws down his books, and resolves to become a soldier."

" After the manner and style of our Fritz," suggested Jack.

" He changes the Pandects for Polybius, and Gray's Inn for a military school. All goes well for awhile; the idea of uniform helps him over the rudiments of fortification and the platoon exercise. He passes two examinations creditably, but breaks down at the third, in consequence of which he throws away his sword in disgust. He does not like now to rejoin his old companions in the Inn, who have been working steadily during the years he has lost. He therefore, perhaps, adopts a middle course, and gets himself enrolled in the society of solicitors, which does not exact a very elaborate diploma."

" Well, after all, the difference between a barrister and a solicitor is not so great."

" True; but the exercises to which he has been accustomed previously unfit him for the drudgeries of his new employment, and he soon abandons that, just as he abandoned the other two."

" Your friend Peter is somewhat difficult to please," said Jack.

" He then goes into business, a term which may mean a great deal or nothing at all; it admits of one's going about idle with the appearance of being fully occupied. Then a few unsuccessful speculations bring him back, at the end of his days, to the point whence he started — that is, zero."

" Ah, yes, I see now," cried Jack, whilst he traced a diagram on the ground. " Poor Peter has always stopped in the middle of each profession and gone back to the starting point of another, thus passing his life in making zigzags, and only moving from one zero to another."

" Exactly," added Wolston: " whilst those who persevered in following up the profession they chose at first finally succeeded in attaining a position, and that simply by adhering to a straight line."

Here Fritz and his mother arrived, arm in arm.

" Ha! there you are," cried Ernest. " We were on our way to meet you."

"You surely do not call sitting down there being on your way to meet us, do you?"

"Well, yes, mother," suggested Jack, "on the principle that two bodies coming into contact meet each other."

Like those flowers that droop during a storm, but recover their brilliancy with the first rays of the sun, so a few days more sufficed to restore Mary Wolston to better health than she had ever enjoyed in her life before. Some months now elapsed without giving rise to any event of note. All the men, women, and children in the colony had been busily employed from early morn to late at e'en. No sooner had one field been sown than there was another to plant; then came the grain harvest and its hard but healthy toil; next, much to the delight of Willis, herrings appeared on the coast, followed by their attendant demons, the sea-dogs; salmon-fishing, hunting ortolans, the foundries and manufactories, likewise exacted a portion of their time. Frequently parties were occupied for weeks together in the remote districts; so that, with the exception of one day each week — the Sabbath — the two families had of late been rarely assembled together in one spot.

The hope of ever again beholding the *Nelson* had gradually ceased to be entertained by anybody. Like an echo that resounds from rock to rock until it is lost in the distance, this hope had died away in their breasts. Willis nevertheless continued to keep the beacon on Shark's Island alight; but he regarded it more as a sepulchral lamp in commemoration of the dead, than as a signal for the living.

One morning, the break of day was announced by a cannon-shot. All instantly started on their feet and gazed inquiringly in each other's faces. One thing forced itself upon all their thoughts — daybreak generally arrives without noise; it is not accustomed to announce itself with gunpowder; like real merit, it requires no flourish of trumpets to announce its advent.

"Good," said Becker; "Fritz and Jack are not visible, therefore we may easily guess who fired that shot."

"Particularly," added Wolston, "as this is the first of

16

January. Last night I observed an unusual amount of going backwards and forwards, so, I suppose, nobody need be much at a loss to solve the mystery."

"Aye," sighed Willis, "New Year's Day brings pleasing recollections to many, but sad ones to those who are far away from their own homes."

Shortly after, the absentees arrived, each mounted on his favorite ostrich.

"Mrs. Wolston," said Fritz, spreading out a fine leopard's skin, "be good enough to accept this, with the compliments of the season."

"Mr. Wolston," said Jack, at the same time, "here is the outer covering of a panther, who, stifling with heat, commissioned me to present you with his overcoat."

"I am very proud of your gift, Master Fritz," said Mrs. Wolston; "it is really very handsome."

"It may, perhaps, be useful at all events, madam," said Fritz; "for, in the absence of universal pills and such things, it is a capital preventative of coughs and colds."

"You have been over the way again, then?" inquired Willis.

"Yes; but, as you see, we adopted a more efficacious mode of operations than the one you suggested."

"Ah," replied Willis, drily, "you did not light a fire this time to frighten the brutes away, and go to sleep when it went out!"

Sophia then presented Willis with a handsome tobaccco pouch, on which the words, "From Susan," were embroidered.

"Bless your dear little heart!" said the sailor, whilst a tear sparkled in the corner of his eye, "you make me almost think I am in Old England again."

"What is the matter?" inquired Mrs. Wolston, as Mary came running in.

"Oh, such a miracle, mamma! my parrot commenced talking this morning."

"And what did it say, child?"

Here Mary blushed and hesitated; Mrs. Wolston glanced at Fritz, and thought it might be as well not to inquire any further.

“ Perhaps somebody has changed it,” suggested Jack.

“ Not very likely that a strange parrot could pronounce my own name.”

“ Well, perhaps your own has been learning to spell for a long time, and has just succeeded in getting into words of two or more syllables. These creatures abound in self-esteem; and yours, perhaps, would not speak till it could speak well.”

“ Odd, that it should pitch upon New Year’s morning to say all sorts of pretty things. They do not carry an almanack in their pockets, do they?”

“ Well,” remarked Willis, “parrots do say and do odd things. I heard of one that once frightened away a burglar, by screaming out, ‘The Campbells are coming;’ so, Miss Wolston, perhaps yours does keep a log.”

“ By counting its knuckles,” suggested Jack.

“ Counting one’s knuckles is an ingenious, but rather a clumsy substitute for the calendar,” remarked Wolston.

“ And who invented the calendar?” inquired Willis.

“ I am not aware that the calendar was ever invented,” replied Wolston. “ Fruit commences by being a seed, the admiral springs from the cabin-boy, words and language succeed naturally the babble of the infant; so, I presume, the calendar has grown up spontaneously to its present degree of perfection.”

“ Yes, Mr. Wolston, but some one must have laid the first plank.”

“ The motions of the sun, moon, and stars would, in all probability, suggest to the early inhabitants of our globe a natural means of measuring time. God, in creating the heavenly bodies, seems to have reflected that man would require some index to regulate his labors and the acts of his civil life. The primary and most elementary subdivisions of time are day and night, and it demanded no great stretch of human ingenuity to divide the day into two sections, called forenoon and afternoon, or into twelve sections, called hours. Such subdivisions of time would probably suggest themselves simultaneously to all the nations of the earth. Necessity, who is the mother of all invention, doubtless called the germs of our calendar into existence.”

"Yes, so far as the days and hours are concerned. There are other divisions — weeks, for example."

"The division of time into weeks is a matter that belongs entirely to revelation; the Jews keep the last day of every seven as a day of rest, in accordance with the law of Moses, and the Christians dedicate the first day of every seven to our Lord and Saviour Jesus Christ."

"Then there are months."

"The month is another natural division. The return of the moon in conjunction with the sun, was observed to occur at regular intervals of twenty-nine days, twelve hours, and some minutes. This interval is called the *lunar month*, which for a long time was regarded as the **radical** unit in the admeasurement of time."

"But the year is now the unit, is it not?"

"Yes, in course of time the moon, in this respect, **gave** place to the sun. It was observed that the earth, **in** performing her revolution round the sun, always arrived at the same point of her orbit at the end of three hundred and sixty-five days, five hours, fifty-eight minutes, and forty-five seconds."

"Does the earth invariably pass the same point **at that** interval?"

"Yes, invariably; and the interval in question is termed the solar year."

"After all," remarked Jack, "the perseverance of the earth is very much to be admired. It goes on eternally, always performing the same journey, never deviates from its path, and is never a minute too late."

"If the earth had performed her annual voyage in **a** certain number of entire days, the solar year would have been an exact unit of time; but the odd fraction defied all our systems of calculation. Originally, we reckoned the year to consist of three hundred and sixty-five days."

"And left the fraction to shift for itself!"

"Yes, but the consequence was, that the civil year was always nearly a quarter of a day behind; so that at the end of a hundred and twenty-one years the civil year had become an entire month behind. The first month of winter found itself in autumn, the first month of spring in the middle of winter, and so on."

"Rather a lubberly sort of log, that," remarked Willis.

"This confusion became, with time, more and more embarrassing. Another evil was, likewise, eventually to be apprehended, for it was seen that, on the expiring of fourteen hundred and sixty revolutions of the earth round the sun, fourteen hundred and sixty-one civil years would be counted."

"But where would have been the evil?"

"All relations between the dates and the seasons would have been obliterated, astronomical calculations would have become inaccurate, and the calendar virtually useless."

"Well, Willis, you that are so fertile in ideas, what would you have done in such a case?" inquired Jack.

"I! Way I scarcely know — perhaps run out a fresh cable and commenced a new log."

"Your remedy," continued Wolston, "might, perhaps, have obviated the difficulty; but Julius Cæsar thought of another that answered the purpose equally well. It was simply to add to every fourth civil year an additional day, making it to consist of three hundred and sixty-six instead of three hundred and sixty-five, This supplementary day was given to the month of February."

"Why February?"

"Because February, at that time, was reckoned the last month of the year. It was only in the reign of Charles IX. of France, or in the second half of the sixteenth century, that the civil year was made to begin on the 1st of January. As the end of February was five days before the 1st or kalends of March, the extra day was known by the phrase *bis sexto (ante) calendus martii*. Hence the fourth year is termed in the calendar *bissextile*, but is more usually called by us in England *leap year*."

"The remedy is certainly simple; but are your figures perfectly square? If you add a day every four years, do you not overleap the earth's fraction?"

"Yes, from ten to eleven minutes."

"And what becomes of these minutes? Are they allowed to run up another score?"

"No, not exactly. In 1582, the civil year had got ten

clear days the start of the solar year, and Pope Gregory XIII. resolved to cancel them, which he effected by calling the day after the 4th of October the 15th." ·

"That manner of altering the rig and squaring the yards," said Willis laughing, "would make the people that lived then ten days older. If it had been ten years, the matter would have been serious. Had the Pope said to me privately, 'Willis, you are now only forty-seven, but to-morrow, my boy, you will fill your sails and steer right into fifty-seven,' I should have turned 'bout ship and cleared off. Few men care about being put upon a short allowance of life, any more than we sailors on short rations of rum."

"But you forget, Willis, that, though ten years were added to your age, you would not have died a day sooner for all that."

"Still, it is my idea that the Pope was not much smarter at taking a latitude than Mr. Julius Cæsar — but what are you laughing at?"

"Nothing; only Julius Cæsar is not generally honored with the prefix *Mr.* It is something like the French, who insist upon talking of *Sir Newton* and *Mr. William Shakespeare;* the latter, however, by way of amends, they sometimes style the *immortal Williams.*"

"Not so bad, though, as a Frenchman I once met, who firmly believed the Yankees lived on a soup made of bunkum and soft-sawder. But who was Julius Cæsar."

"Julius Cæsar," replied Jack, sententiously, "was first of all an author, having published at Rome an Easy Introduction to the Latin Language; he afterwards turned general, conquered France and England, and gave *Mr.* Pompey a sound thrashing at the battle of Pharsalia." ·

"He must have been a clever fellow to do all that; still, my idea continues the same. When he began to caulk the calendar, he ought to have finished the business in a workmanlike manner."

"That, however," continued Wolston, "he left to Pope Gregory, who decreed that three leap years should be suppressed in four centuries. Thus, the years 1700 and 1800, which should have been leap years, did not reckon the extra day; so the years 2000 and 2400 will likewise be deprived of their supplementary four-and-twenty hours."

"There is one difficulty about this mode of stowing away extra days; these leap years may be forgotten."

"Not if you keep in mind that leap years alone admit of being divided by four."

"Did the Pope manage to get entirely rid of the fraction?"

"Not entirely; but the error does not exceed one day in four thousand years, and is so small that it is not likely to derange ordinary calculations; and so, Willis, you now know the origin of the calendar, and likewise how time came to be divided into weeks, months, and years."

"You have only spoken of the Christian calendar," remarked Ernest. "There have been several other systems in use. Those curious people that call themselves the children of the sun and moon, possess a mode of reckoning that carries them back to a period anterior to the creation of the world. Then, the Greeks computed by Olympiads, or periods of four years. The Romans reckoned by lustri of five years, the first of which corresponds with the 117th year of the foundation of Rome."

"And when does our calendar begin?"

"It dates only from the birth of Christ, but may be carried back to the creation, which event, to the best of our knowledge, occurred four thousand and four years before the birth of our Savior. This period, added to the date of the present, or any future year, gives us, as nearly as we can ascertain, the interval that has elapsed since our first parents found themselves in the garden of Eden."

"Our calendar," remarked Jack; "appears simple enough; it is to be regretted that there have been, and are, so many other modes of reckoning extant. What with the Greek Olympiads, the Roman lustres, the Mahometan hegira, and Chinese moonshine, there is nothing but perplexity and confusion."

"It is possible, however," said Becker, "to accommodate all these systems with each other. Leaving the Chinese out of the question, we have only to bear in mind, that the Christian era begins on the first year of the 194th

Olympiad, 753 years after the building of Rome, and 622 years before the Mahometan hegira.   These three figures will serve us as flambeaux to all the dates of both ancient and modern history."

The discourse was here interrupted by Toby, who entered the room, and was gleefully frisking and bounding round Mary.

"Really," observed Mrs. Becker, "Toby does seem to know that this is New Year's Day, he looks so lively and so smart."

The animal, in point of fact, wore a new collar, and seemed conscious that he was more than usually attractive that particular morning.   At a sign from Mary, the intelligent brute went and wagged his tail to Fritz.   Hereupon the young man, observing the collar more closely, noticed the following words embroidered upon it : *I belong now entirely to Master Fritz, who rescued my mistress from the sea.*

"Ah, Miss Wolston," said Fritz, "you forget I only did my duty ; you must not allow your gratitude to overestimate the service I rendered you."

"Well, I declare," cried Mrs. Wolston, laughing "here is another animal that speaks."

"The age of Æsop revived," suggested Mrs. Becker.

"What do you say, Master Jack ? " inquired Mrs. Wolston.   "Do you suppose that Toby has learned embroidery in the same way that the parrot learned grammar ? "

"Oh, more astonishing things than that have happened ! Mr. Wolston there will tell you that he has seen a wooden figure playing at chess ; why, therefore, should the most sagacious of all the brutes not learn knitting ? "

"I fear, in speaking so highly of the dog," replied Mrs. Wolston, "you are doing injustice to other animals Marvellous instances of sagacity, gratitude, and affection, have been shown by other brutes beside the dog.   A horse of Caligula's was elevated to the dignified office of consul."

"Yes, and talking of the affection of animals," observed Ernest, "puts me in mind of an anecdote related by Au-

lus Gellius. It seems that a little boy, the son of a fisherman, who had to go from Baiæ to his school at Puzzoli,
used to stop at the same hour each day on the brink of the
Lucrine lake. Here he often threw a bit of his breakfast to a Dolphin that he called Simon, and if the creature
was not waiting for him when he arrived, he had only to
pronounce this name, and it instantly appeared."

"Nothing very wonderful in that," said Jack; "the common gudgeon, which is the stupidest fish to be found in
fresh water, would do that much."

"Yes; but listen a moment. The dolphin, after having
received his pittance, presented his back to the boy, after
having tacked in all his spines and prickles as well as he
could, and carried him right across the lake, thus saving
the little fellow a long roundabout walk; and not only
that, but after school hours it was waiting to carry him
back again. This continued almost daily for a year or
two; but at last the boy died, and the dolphin, after waiting day after day for his reappearance, pined away, and
was found dead at the usual place of rendezvous. The
affectionate creature was taken out of the lake, and buried
beside its friend.*

"And, on the other hand," added Jack, "if animals
sometimes attach themselves to us, we attach ourselves to
them. We are told that Crassus wore mourning for a
dead ferret, the death of which grieved him as much as if
it had been his own daughter.† Augustus crucified one of
his slaves, who had roasted and eaten a quail, that had
fought and conquered in the circus.‡ Antonia, daughter-
in-law of Tiberius, fastened ear-rings to some lampreys
that she was passionately fond of."§

"That, at all events, was attachment in one sense of the
word," said Mrs. Wolston.

"Without reference to the dog in particular," continued
Jack, "proofs of sagacity in animals are very numerous.
The nautilus, when he wants to take an airing, capsizes
his shell, and converts it into a gondola; then he hoists a

* Aulus Gellius, VII., 8.　　† Macrobius, *Saturn*, XI., 4.
‡ Plutarch.　　§ Pliny, IX., 53.

thin membrane that serves for a sail; two of his arms are
resolved into oars, and his tail performs the functions of a
rudder. There are insects ingenious enough to make
dwellings for themselves in the body of a leaf as thin as
paper. At the approach of a storm some spiders take in
a reef or two of their webs, so as to be 'less at the mercy
of the wind. Beavers will erect walls, and construct
houses more skilfully than our ablest architects. Chim-
panzees have been known spontaneously to sit themselves
down, and perform the operation of shaving."

"Stop, Jack," cried Mrs. Wolston; "I must yield to
such a deluge of argument, and admit that Toby may have
acquired the art of embroidery with or without a master,
only I should like to see some other specimen of his
skill."

"Probably you will by-and-by," replied Jack, laughing,
"if you keep your eyes open."

Here Sophia came into the room leading her gazelle.

"Ah, just in time," said Mrs. Wolston; "here is another
animal that probably has something to say."

"Wrong, mamma," replied Sophia; "my gazelle is as
mute as a mermaid. Very provoking, is it not, when all
the other animals in the house talk?"

"You had better apply to Master Jack; he may, probably, be able to hit upon a plan to make your gazelle
communicative."

"Will you, Master Jack?"

"Certainly, Miss Sophia. The plan I would suggest is
very simple. Feed him for a week or two with nouns,
adjectives, and verbs."

Here Sophia, addressing her gazelle, said, "Master Jack
Becker is a goose."

Meantime Fritz was leaning on the back of Mary's
chair.

"Miss Wolston," said he, "did you not tell me that you
had brought Toby up, and that you were very fond of
him?"

"Yes, Fritz."

"Then it would be unfair in me to withdraw his
allegiance from you now, and, consequently, I must refuse
your present."

“But where would have been the merit of the gift if I did not hold him in some esteem? Besides, I thought you were fond of Toby.”

“So I am, Miss Wolston.”

“Then you will not be indebted to me for anything — I owe you much.”

“No such thing; you owe me nothing.”

“My life, then, is nothing?”

“Oh, I did not mean that; I must beg your pardon.”

“Which I will only grant on condition you accept my gift.”

“Well, if you insist upon it, I will.”

“I can see him as before; the only difference will be that you are his master, in all other respects he will belong to us both.”

“May I know what your knight-errant is saying to you, Mary?” inquired Mrs. Becker.

“Oh, I have been so angry with him; he was going to refuse my present.”

“That was very naughty of him, certainly.”

“He has, however, consented, like a dutiful squire, to obey my behests.”

“Yes, mother, Toby is henceforth to be divided between us.”

“Divided?”

“Yes; that is, he is to be nominally mine, but virtually to belong to us both. Is it not so, Miss Wolston?”

“Yes, Master Fritz.”

On his side, Jack had approached Miss Sophia.

“So you won’t give me your gazelle?” he whispered.

“No, certainly not, Mr. Jack,’ replied Sophia; “if you had saved my life, as Fritz saved my sister’s, I should then have had the right to make you a present. But you know it is not my fault.”

“Nor mine either,” said Jack.

“Perhaps not; but if I had fallen into the sea, you would have allowed the sharks to swallow me, would you not?”

“I only wish we had been attacked by a hyena or a bear on our way to Waldeck.”

"God be thanked, that we were not!"

"Well, but look here, Miss Sophia; let me paint the scene. You have fainted, as a matter of course, and fallen prostrate on the ground, insensible."

"That is likely enough, if we had encountered one of the animals you mention."

"Then I throw myself between you and the savage brute."

"Supposing you were not half a mile off at the time."

"No fear of that — he rises on his hind legs, and glares."

"Is it a hyena or a bear?"

"Oh, whichever you like — he opens his jaws, and growls."

"Like the wolf at Little Red Riding Hood."

"I plunge my arm down his throat and choke him."

"Clever, very; but are you not wounded?"

"I beg your pardon, however; all my thoughts are centred in you — I think of nothing else."

"I am insensible, am I not?"

"Yes, more than ever — we all run towards you, and exert ourselves to bring you back to your senses."

"Then I come to life again."

"No, stop a bit."

"But it is tiresome to be so long insensible."

"My mother has luckily a bottle of salts, which she holds to your nose — I run off to the nearest brook, and return with water in the crown of my cap, with which I bathe your temples."

"Oh, in that case, I should open one eye at least. Which eye is opened first after fainting?"

"I really don't know."

"In that case, to avoid mistakes, I should open both."

"It is only then, when I find you are recovering, that I discover the brute has severely bitten my arm."

"Then comes my turn to nurse you."

"You express your thanks in your sweetest tones, and I forget my wounds."

"Sweet tones do no harm, if they are accompanied with salves and ointment."

"In short, I am obliged to carry my arm in a sling for three months after."

"Is that not rather long?"

"No; because your arm, in some sort, supplies, meantime, the place of mine."

"Your picture has, at least, the merit of being poetic. Is it finished?"

"Not till next New Year's Day, when you present me with an embroidered scarf, as the ladies of yore used to do to the knights that defended them from dragons and that sort of thing."

"What a pity all this should be only a dream!"

"Well, I am not particularly extravagant, at all events; others dream of fortune, honor, and glory."

"Whilst you confine your aspirations to a bear, a bite, and a scarf."

"You see nothing was wanted but the opportunity."

"And foresight."

"Foresight?"

"Yes; if you had previously made arrangements with a bear, the whole scene might have been realized."

"You are joking, whilst I am taking the matter *au sérieux*."

"That order is usually reversed; generally you are the quiz and I am the quizzee."

"You will admit, at all events, that I would not have permitted the bear to eat you."

Here Sophia burst into a peal of laughter, and vanished with her gazelle.

17

CHAPTER XVI.

WINTER was now drawing near, with its storms and
deluges. Becker therefore felt that it was necessary to
make some alterations in their domestic arrangements;
and he saw that, for this season at all events, the two
families must be separated — this was to create a desert
within a desert; but propriety and convenience demanded
the sacrifice.

It was decided that Wolston and his family should be
quartered at Rockhouse, whilst Becker and his family
should pass the rainy season at Falcon's Nest, where,
though these aerial dwellings were but indifferently
adapted for winter habitations, they had passed the first
year of their sojourn in the colony. The rains came and
submerged the country between the two families, thus,
for a time, cutting off all communication between them.
The barriers that separated the Guelphs from the Ghibe-
lines, the Montagues from the Capulets, the Burgundians
from the Armagnacs, and the House of York from that of
Lancaster, could not have been more impenetrable than
that which now existed between the Wolstons and Beckers.

Whenever a lull occurred in the storm, or a ray of
sunshine shot through the murky clouds, all eyes were
mechanically turned to the window, but only to turn them
away again with a sigh; so completely had the waters
invaded the land, that nothing short of the dove from

Noah's Ark could have performed the journey between Rockhouse and Falcon's Nest.

Dulness and dreariness reigned triumphant at both localities. The calm tranquility that Becker's family formerly enjoyed under similar circumstances had fled. They felt that happiness was no longer to be enjoyed within the limits of their own circle. Study and conversation had lost their charms; and if they laughed now, the smile never extended beyond the tips of their lips. The young people often wished they possessed Fortunatus's cap, or Aladdin's wonderful lamp, to transport them from the one dwelling to the other; but as they could obtain no such occult mode of conveyance, there was no remedy for their miseries but patience. To the Wolstons this interval of compulsory separation was particularly irksome, as this was the first time in their lives that they had been entirely isolated for any length of time.

At Falcon's Nest, Ernest was the most popular member of the domestic circle. His astronomical predilections made him the Sir Oracle of the storm, and he was constantly being asked for information relative to the progress and probable duration of the rains. Every morning he was called upon for a report as to the state of the weather; but, with all his skill, he could afford them very little consolation.

But all things come to an end, as well as regards our troubles as our joys. One morning, Ernest reported that less rain had fallen during the preceding than any former night of the season; the next morning a still more favorable report was presented; and on the third morning the floods had subsided, but had left a substratum of mud that obliterated all traces of the roads. Notwithstanding this, and a smart shower that continued to fall, Fritz and Jack determined to force a passage to Rockhouse.

Towards evening, the two young men returned, soaking with wet and covered with mud, but with light hearts, for they had found their companions in the enjoyment of perfect health and in the best spirits. They brought back with them a missive, couched in the following terms:—

"Mr. and Mrs. Wolston, greeting, desire the favor of

Mr. and Mrs. Becker's company to dinner, together with their entire family, this day se'nnight, weather permitting."

Ernest was hereupon consulted, and stated that, in so far as the rain was concerned, they should in eight days be able to undertake the journey to Rockhouse. This assurance was not, however, entirely relied upon, for between this and then many an anxious eye was turned skywards, as if in search of some more conclusive evidence. Those who possess a garden—and he who has not, were it only a box of mignionette at the window—will often have observed, in consequence of absence or forgetfulness, that their flowers have begun to droop; they hasten to sprinkle them with water, then watch anxiously for signs of their revival. So both families continued unceasingly during these eight days to note the ever-varying modifications of the clouds.

At length the much wished-for day arrived; the morning broke with a blaze of sunshine, and though hidden with a dense mist, the ground was sufficiently hardened to bear their weight. Wolston awaited his guests at a bridge of planks that had been thrown across the Jackal River, where he and Willis had erected a sort of triumphal arch of mangoe leaves and palm branches. Here Becker and his family were welcomed, as if the one party had just arrived from Tobolsk, and the other from Chandernagor, after an absence of ten years.

Another warm reception awaited them at Rockhouse, where an abundant repast was already spread in the gallery. Mrs. Becker had often intended to work herself a pair of gloves, but the increasing demand for stockings had hitherto prevented her. She was pleased, therefore, on sitting down to dinner, to discover a couple of pairs under her plate, with her own initials embroidered upon them.

"Ah," said she, "I was almost afraid I had lost my daughters, but I have found them again."

After dinner the girls showed her a quantity of cotton they had spun, which proved that, though they might have been dull, they had, at least, been industrious.

"Mary span the most of it," said Sophia; "but you know, Mrs. Becker, she is the biggest."

"Oh, then," said Jack. "the power of spinning depends
upon the bulk of the spinner?"

"Oh, Master Jack, I thought you had been ill, that you
h. not commenced quizzing us before."

"Never mind him, Soffy," said her father; "to quote
Hudibras,

"There's nothing on earth hath so perfect a phiz,
  As not to give birth to a passable quiz."

Here Willis led in the chimpanzee, who made a grimace
to the assembled company.

"Now, ladies and gentlemen," said Willis, "Jocko is
about to show you the progress he has made in splicing
and bracing."

"Good!" said Becker, "you have been able to make
something of him, then?"

"You will see presently. Jocko, bring me a plate."

Hereupon the chimpanzee seized a bottle of Rockhouse
malaga, and filled a glass.

"He has erred on the safe side there," said Jack, drily.

"Well," added Willis, laughing, "we must let that pass.
Jocko," said he, assuming a sententious tone, "I asked you
for a plate."

The chimpanzee looked at him, hesitated a moment,
then seized the glass, and drank the contents off at a single
draught. A box on the ears then sent him gibbering into
a corner.

"Your servant," remarked Mrs. Wolston, "has been
taking lessons from Dean Swift as well as yourself, Willis."

"I will serve him out for that, the swab; he does not
play any of those tricks when we are alone. I must admit,
however, that I am generally in the habit of helping myself."

Here attention was called to the parrot, who was
screaming out lustily, "I love Mary, I love Sophia."

"Holloa," exclaimed Fritz, "Polly loves everybody
now, does she?"

"Well, you see," replied Sophia, "I grew tired of hearing him scream always that he loved my sister, so by means of a little coaxing, and a good deal of sugar, I got him to love me too."

The poultry were next mustered for the inspection of their old masters. These did not consist of the ordinary domestic fowls alone; amongst them **were a** beautiful flamingo, some cranes, bustards, and **a variety** of tame tropical birds. With the fowls came the pigeons, which were perching about them in all directions.

"We are now something **like** the court **of** France in the fourteenth century," said Wolston.

"How **so?**" inquired Becker.

"In the reign of Charles V., they were obliged to place **a** trellis at the windows of the Palace of St. Paul to prevent the poultry **from** invading the dining room."

"Rural anyhow," observed Jack.

"Of course, most other features of the palace were **in** unison with this primitive state of matters. The courtiers sat on stools. There was only one chair in the palace, that was the arm-chair of the king, which was covered with red leather, and ornamented with silk fringes."

"So that we may console ourselves with the reflection, that we are as comfortable here as kings were at that epoch in Europe," remarked Ernest.

"Yes; historians report, that when Alphonso **V.** of Portugal went to Paris to solicit **the** aid of Louis XI. against the King of Arragon, who had taken Castile from him, the French monarch **received him** with great honor, and endeavored to make his stay as agreeable as possible."

"Reviews, I suppose, feasts, tournaments, spectacles, and so forth."

"A residence was assigned him in the Rue de Prouvaires, at the house of one Laurent Herbelot, a grocer."

"What! amongst dried peas and preserved plums?"

"Precisely; but the house of Herbelot might then have been one of the most commodious buildings in all Paris. Alphonso was afterwards conducted to the palace, where he pleaded his cause before the king. Next day he was entertained at the archiepiscopal residence, where he witnessed the induction of a doctor in theology. The day after that a procession to the university was organized, which passed under the grocer's windows."

"These were singular marvels to entertain a king withal," said Jack.

"Such were the amusements peculiar to the epoch. It must be observed that the Louis in question was somewhat close-fisted, and rarely drew his purse-strings unless he was certain of a good interest for his money. But courts in those days were very simple and frugal. The sumptuary laws of Philip le Bel (1285) had fixed supper at three dishes and a lard soup. The king's own dinner was likewise limited to three dishes."

"These three dishes might, however, have yielded a better repast than the fifty-two saucers of the Chinese," remarked Jack.

"No one could obtain permission to give his wife four dresses a year, unless he had an income of six thousand francs."

"What business had the laws to interfere with these things, I should like to know?" inquired Mrs. Wolston.

"Those who possessed two thousand francs income were only allowed to wear one dress a year, the cloth for which was not permitted to exceed tenpence a yard; but ladies of rank could go as high as fifteenpence."

"Philip le Bel must have been an old woman," insisted Mrs. Wolston.

"No private citizen was permitted to use a carriage, and such persons were likewise interdicted the use of flambeaux."

"They were permitted to break their necks at all events, that is something."

"In England, the same primitive simplicity prevailed; Queen Elizabeth is said to have breakfasted on a gallon of ale, her dining-room floor was strewn every day with fresh straw or rushes, and she had only one pair of silk stockings in her entire wardrobe."

"At the same time," observed Ernest, "these usages stand in singular contradiction to those that prevailed at an earlier age. The supper of Lucullus rarely cost him less than thirty thousand francs, and he could entertain five and twenty thousand guests. Six citizens of Rome possessed a great part of Africa. Domitius had an estate in France of eighty thousand acres."

" Poor fellow !"

" When Nero went to Baiæ he was accompanied by a thousand chariots and two thousand mules caparisoned with silver. Poppæa followed him with five hundred she asses to furnish milk for her bath. Cicero purchased a dining-room table that cost him a million sesterces, or about two hundred thousand francs. I can understand the progress of civilization, and I can also understand civilization remaining stationary for a given period; but I cannot understand why a citizen of ancient Rome should be able to lodge twenty-five thousand men, whilst a king of France could scarcely keep the ducks from waddling about his apartments, and a queen of England could fare no better than a ploughman."

" If," replied Frank, " there were no other criterion of civilization than luxury and riches, you would have good grounds for surprise; but such is not the case. Between ancient and modern times, Christianity arose, and that has tended in some degree to keep down the ostentation of the rich, and to augment, at the same time, the comforts of the poor. In place of the heroes, Hercules and Achilles, we have had the apostles Peter and Paul; so Luther and Calvin have been substituted for Semiramis and Nero. Pride has given place to charity, and corruption to virtue."

" Would that it were so, Frank," continued Ernest. " Christianity has, doubtless, effected many beneficial changes, and produced many able men; but in this last respect antiquity has not been behind. It has also its sages: Thales, Socrates, and Pythagoras, for example."

" True," replied Frank, " antiquity has produced some virtuous men, but their virtue was ideal, and their creed a dream."

" And the Stoics ?"

" The Stoics despised suffering, and Christians resign themselves to its chastisements; this constitutes one of the lines of demarcation between ancient and modern theology."

" But there were many signal instances of virtue manifested in ancient times."

" Yes; but for the most part, it was either exaggerated or false; unyielding pride, obstinate courage, implacable resentment of injuries. Errors promenaded in robes under the porticos. Ambition was honored in Alexander, suicide in Cato, and assassination in Brutus."

" But what say you to Plato ? "

" The immolation of ill-formed children, and of those born without the permission of the laws, prosecution of strangers and slavery; such were the bases of his boasted republic, and the gospel of his philosophy."

" Why, then, are these men held up as models for our imitation ? "

" Because they are distant and dead; likewise, because they were, in many respects, great and wise, considering the paganism and darkness with which they were surrounded. Life was then only sacred to the few; the many were treated as beasts of burden. The Emperor Claudian even felt bound to issue an edict prohibiting slaves from being slain *when they were old and feeble.*"

" Which leaves a margin for us to suppose that they might be slain when they were young and strong," observed Jack.

" By the constitution of Constantine certain cases were defined, where a master might suspend his slave by the feet, have him torn by wild beasts, or tortured by slow fire."

" Does slavery and its horrors not still exist, for example, in Russia and the United States of America ? "

" Slavery does exist, to the great disgrace of modern civilization, in the countries you mention; but, so far as I am aware, its horrors are not recognized by the laws."

" There, Mr. Frank," said Wolston, " I am very sorry to be under the necessity of contradicting you. I have visited the slave states of North America, and have witnessed atrocities perhaps less brutal, but not less heart-rending, than those you mention."

" But do the laws recognize them ? "

" Yes, tacitly; the testimony of the slaves themselves is not received as evidence."

"Why do a people that call their country a refuge for the down-trodden nations of Europe suffer such abominations?"

"Well, according to themselves, it is entirely a question of the *almighty dollar*. If there were no slaves, the swamps and morasses of the south could not be cultivated. It has been found that the negro will dance, and sing, and starve, but he will not work in the fields when free. Besides, they assert, that the slaves are generally well cared for, and that it is only a few detestable masters that beat them cruelly."

"Then, at all events, dollars are preferred to humanity by the United States men, in spite of their vaunted emblems — liberty and equality."

"Quite so. In all matters of internal policy, the dollar reigns supreme."

"Admitting," continued Frank, "that the evils of slavery may exist in a section of the American Union, and amongst the barbarous hordes of Russia, these evils are trifling in comparison with others that stain the annals of antiquity. We are told that a hundred and twenty persons applied to Otho to be rewarded for killing Galba. That so many men should contend for the honor of premeditated murder, is sufficiently characteristic of the epoch. There was then no corruption, no brutal passion, that had not its temple and its high priest. In the midst of all this wickedness and vice there appeared a man, poor and humble, who accomplished what no man ever did before, and what no man will ever do again — he founded a moral and eternal civilization. Judaism and the religion of Zoroaster were overthrown. The gods of Tyre and Carthage were destroyed. The beliefs of Miltiades and of Pericles, of Scipio and Seneca, were disavowed. The thousands that flocked annually to worship the Eleusinian Ceres ceased their pilgrimage. Odin and his disciples have all perished. The very language of Osiris, which was afterwards spoken by the Ptolemies, is no longer known to his descendants. The paganisms which still exist in the East are rapidly yielding to the march of western intelligence. Christianity alone, amidst all these tottering and fallen fabrics, retains its original vitality, for, like its author, it is imperishable."

"It is a curious thing what we call conversation," observed Mrs. Wolston. "No sooner is one subject broached than another is introduced; and we go on from one thing to another until the original idea is lost sight of. Leaving the palace of Charles V., to go with the King of Portugal to a grocer's shop in some street or other of Paris, we cross the Alps, the Himalaya, and the Atlantic. Lucullus, Nero, Achilles, Peter, Paul, Tyre and Sidon, Semiramis and Elizabeth — queens, saints, and philosophers, are all passed in review, and why? Because the pigeons put my husband in mind of the Palace of St. Paul!"

"No wonder," observed Jack; "these pigeons are carriers, and naturally suggest wandering."

Once more seated round the table, Fritz, observing that the misunderstanding between Willis and the chimpanzee still continued, thrust a plate into the hand of the latter, and pointed with his finger to Willis. This time Jocko obeyed, for the language was intelligible, and he went and placed the plate before his master.

"Ho, ho!" cried Willis, "so you have come to your senses at last, have you? Well, that saves you an extra lesson to-morrow, you lubber you."

"He takes rather long to obey your orders, though, Willis; it is rather awkward to wait an hour for anything you ask for. What system do you pursue in educating him — the Pestalozzian or the parochial?"

"I follow the system in fashion aboard ship," replied Willis.

"And what does that consist of?"

"A rope's end."

"Oh, then, you are an advocate for the birch, are you?" said Wolston; "it is, doubtless, a very good thing when moderately and judiciously administered. That puts me in mind of the missionary and the king of the Kuruman negroes."

"A tribe of Southern Africa, is it not?"

"Yes, the missionary and the king were great friends,

The king not only permitted him to baptize his subjects, but offered to whip them all into Christianity in a week. This summary mode of proselytism did not, however, coincide with the Englishman's ideas, and he refused the offer, although the king insisted that it was the only kind of argument that could ever reach their understandings."

The day at length drew to a close, and, though no one asked the time, yet all felt that the moment of departure was approaching; whether they were willing to go was doubtful, but that they were loth to depart was certain.

"It is time to return now," said Becker, rising.

"Already!"

"There are some clouds in the distance that bode no good."

"Nothing more than a little rain at worst," said Jack.

"And your mother?" inquired Becker.

"Oh! we can make a palanquin for her."

"Your plan, Jack, is not particularly bright; it puts me in mind of some genius or other that took shelter in the water to keep out of the wet."

"Very odd," said Jack, "we are always wishing for rain, and when it comes, we do all we can to keep out of its way."

"That is, because we are neither green pease nor gooseberries," said Ernest, drily.

"True, brother; and as the rain is your affair, perhaps you will be good enough to delay it for an hour or so."

"I am sorry on my own account, as well as yours, that I have not yet discovered the art of controlling the skies."

Here Fritz whispered a few words in his mother's ear, that called up one of those ineffable smiles that the maternal heart alone can produce.

"Well," said Mrs. Becker, "if you think so, deliver the message yourself."

"Mrs. Wolston," said Fritz, "I am charged to invite you and your family to Falcon's Nest this day week."

"The invitation is accepted, unless my daughters have any objections to urge."

"How can you fancy such a thing, mamma?" said both girls.

" The fact is, that my daughters have got such a dread of cold water, that they dread to wet the soles of their shoes, unless one or other of you gentlemen is within hail."

" Mamma does so love to tease us," said Mary; " we are afraid of nothing but putting you to inconvenience."

" Well, in that case, we shall be at Falcon's Nest on the appointed day, unless the roads are positively submerged."

" In that case," said Jack, " a line of canoes will be placed upon the highway, between the two localities."

As the prospect of a prize incites the young scholar to increased exertion — as the prospect of worldly honors urges the ambitious man on in his career — as the oasis cheers the weary traveller on his journey through the desert, and makes him forget hunger and thirst — as the dreams of comfort and home warm the blood of a way-farer amongst snow and ice — as hope smooths the rugged-ness of poverty and softens the calamities of adversity, so the prospect of meeting again mitigates the regrets of parting.

18

CHAPTER XVII.

THE old saw, *Where there's a will there's a way,* means
—if it means anything—that a great deal may be effected
by energy. A man without energy is a helpless character,
and invariably lags behind his fellow mortals in the stream
of life; like a cork in an eddy, he is rebuffed here and
jostled there, and goes on travelling in a circle to the end
of the chapter. Not so the man of action; no jostling
thwarts him, no rebuffs retard him; he breaks through all
sorts of obstacles, and floats along with the current.

Such a man was Becker. Though surrounded with
dangers, and harassed by the elements, almost alone he
had converted a wilderness into fertile fields; he pursued
the track that his judgment suggested, and followed it up
with invincible resolution; he manfully resisted the sever-
est trials, and cheerfully bore the heaviest burdens; his
reliance on Truth or Virtue and on God were unfaltering;
but had he provided for every emergency? Is mortal power
capable of overcoming every difficulty? We shall see.

A day or two after the entertainment at Rockhouse,
Becker whispered to the Pilot—

"Willis, take a rifle, and come along with me; I have
something to say to you."

They walked a quarter of an hour or so without uttering a word, when Willis broke the silence.

"You seem sad, Mr. Becker."

"Yes, Willis, I am almost distracted."

"Still, you seem well enough; you are as hale and hearty as if you had just been keel-hauled and got a new rig."

"It is not my body that is suffering, Willis; it is my mind."

"Whatever is the matter?"

"Willis, *my wife is dying.*"

And so it was. For a long period Becker's wife had been a prey to racking pains, which, so to speak, she hid from herself, the better to conceal them from others, just as if suffering had been a crime. After having resisted for fourteen years the afflictions of exile, long and perilous expeditions, nights passed under tents, humid winters and fierce burning summers, her health had, at length, succumbed, not all at once, like fabrics sapped by gunpowder, but little by little, like those that are demolished piecemeal with the pickaxe of the workman. Day by day she grew more and more feeble, without those who were constantly by her side observing the insidious workings of disease. Like Mucius Scævola, who held his hands in a burning brazier without uttering a word, she so effectually hid her griefs within the recesses of her own bosom, that no one even suspected her illness.

"But, Mr. Becker," said Willis, "I saw your wife this morning, and she seemed as well as usual."

"Yes, *seemed*, Willis, that is true enough; not to give us pain, she has concealed her illness from us all. It is only within the last twelve hours that I accidentally discovered that she has been long laboring under some fearful malady."

"Do you know the nature of the disease?"

"No, that I have no means of ascertaining; it may be a distinct form of disease, or it may be a complication of disorders, which I know not."

"It would not signify about the name if we only knew a remedy."

"True; but I dread some malady of a cancerous type, which could not be eradicated without surgical skill."

"I wish I had been born a doctor instead of a pilot," sighed Willis.

"I cannot see her perish before my eyes."

"Certainly not, Mr. Becker; it would never do to allow a ship to sink if she can be saved."

"Well, what is to be done?"

"There lies the difficulty; had it been a question of anything that floats on the water, I might have suggested a remedy; but, in this case, I am fairly run aground."

"I know too well what must be done, Willis. In cases of ordinary maladies, with care and due precaution, proper nourishment and time, Nature will generally effect a cure."

"Nature has no diploma, but she accomplishes more cures than those that have."

"Unfortunately this is not a malady that can be cured by such means; and, unless its progress be checked in time, it may ultimately assume a form that will render a cure impossible."

"Is death, then, inevitable?"

"A patient may retain a languishing life under such circumstances for some time; but if the disease be cancer, a cure is hopeless without instruments and scientific skill."

"I thought I was the only wretched being in the colony," said Willis, sighing, "but I find I am not alone."

"There are no hopes of the *Nelson*, are there?" inquired Becker.

"None now; for some time Mr. Wolston and yourself almost persuaded me that she had escaped; but had she reached the Cape, we should have heard of her ere now."

"The probabilities of another vessel touching here are small, are they not?"

"We are not in the direct track to anywhere; therefore, unless a ship has been driven out of her course by a gale, there is not a chance."

"Unfortunate that I am!" exclaimed Becker, covering his face with his hands. "Brutus, Manlius Torquatus, and Peter the Great, condemned their sons to death, but they were guilty; still the sacrifice must be made."

Here Willis stared aghast, and began to fear Becker's intellect had been affected by his troubles.

"I do not exactly understand you, Mr. Becker."

"Two of my sons have gone on before us; they were to

embark in the canoe for Shark's Island, and wait for us there. I must have courage, and you also, Willis."

This exordium did not tend to alter the Pilot's impression. They walked on for some time in silence towards the coast.

"Do you know the latitude and longitude of this coast, Willis?"

"Good!" thought the Pilot, "he has changed the subject."

"Yes; we are in the South Sea, and no great distance from the line."

"What continent is nearest us?"

"We cannot be very far off the south coast of New Holland, or, as it is named in some charts, Australia. You know that the *Nelson* hailed from Botany Bay, or Sydney, as the convict colony which the English Government has just founded there is called."

"How far do you suppose we are from Sydney?"

"Well, I should say, with a fair wind and a smart craft, Sydney is not above two months' sail, if so much."

"Is the coast inhabited?"

"Yes."

"What character do the inhabitants bear?"

"According to the Dutch sailors, who have been on the coast, they are the most plundering and lubberly set of rascals to be met with anywhere."

"They are not acquainted with the use of fire-arms, are they?"

"No, not of fire-arms; but they have a machine of their own that they call a waddy, or something of that sort, which they throw like a harpoon; but the thing takes a twist in the air, and strikes behind them."

"Is the coast accessible?"

"No; it is fringed with reefs, and, in some places, the surf runs for miles out to sea."

"The navigation along shore, then, is extremely perilous?"

"Whatever can he be driving at?" thought Willis.

"Yes; such a lee shore in a gale would terrify the Flying Dutchman himself."

Here Becker shook his head dolefully, and they walked on a little further in silence.

" What islands do you suppose are nearest us, Willis?"

" I should say we are in or near the group marked in the chart Papuasia ; beyond them is the territory of New Guinea, and a point to nor'ard are a whole nest of islands discovered by the celebrated buccaneer, Dampière."

" And their inhabitants? "

" Oh, some of them are pretty fair ; but, taking them in the lump, they are a bad lot."

" The islands to the west are those discovered by Cook, Vancouver, and Bougainville, are they not? "

" They are marked Polynesia in the charts."

" Do you know of any European settlements on these islands ? "

" Well, there is a fort of the Hudson's Bay Company on Vancouver's Island, but that is a long way north ; and, I believe, a factory has recently been anchored in New Zealand, but that is a long way south."

" And what are the principal islands between? "

" There is New Caledonia, the New Hebrides, the Friendly Islands, the Societies' Islands, the Marquesas, Tahite, and the Pelew Islands ; but each navigator gives them a new name, so that it is hard to say which is which ; all you can do is to say that there is an island in latitude so and so and longitude so and so, but the name is almost out of the question." .

" And the natives? "

" Some of them are remarkably tame, and trade freely with strangers ; but others have strongly marked cannibal propensities, and dote upon a white-skin feast when they can get one,"

Here Becker shuddered, and uttered an exclamation of horror.

" That would be a terrible fate, Willis."

" Whatever can he mean? " thought the Pilot.

" Willis, to reach Europe from here, what course do you think would be best? "

" Now I think I shall fix him at last," said the Pilot, levelling his rifle at an imaginary bird.

"You will only waste gunpowder," said Becker; "I see nothing."

"You asked me just now what course I should steer for Europe, did you not?"

"Yes."

"Well, the **most** direct **course** would be **to make the** Straits of Macassar, and then **steer for Java.**"

"And when **there?**"

"You would then be fifteen or sixteen hundred leagues from the Cape."

"So much?"

"Yes, that is about the distance in a straight line **across** the Indian Ocean. When at the Cape, another fifteen days' sail will bring you to the line; five or six weeks after that St. Helena will heave in sight; then you fall in with the Island of Ascension; leaving which a week or two will bring **you to the Straits of** Gibraltar, where you get the first glimpse of Europe. But if you are bound for England, **your** daughter may commence working a pair of slippers for **you;** they will be ready by the time you get there."

They **had** now arrived at the point of the Jackal River **where** the pinnace **was** moored.

"What do you think of this boat?" inquired Becker.

"The pinnace is well enough for fair weather; but it is **not the** sort of craft I should like to command in a storm **at sea.**"

"So that to venture **to sea in it** would be to incur imminent danger?"

"There is **no** denying **that, Mr.** Becker; if she shipped a moderately heavy sea, down she must go to the bottom, like a four and twenty pound shot; and if she should spring a leak, you cannot land to put her to rights; the waves are by no means solid."

"Just as I thought!" exclaimed Becker; "I was right in judging that it would be a sacrifice. It is almost certain death; but they must go."

"Where?" inquired Willis.

"To Europe if need be, if God in his mercy spares the pinnace."

" What for ? "

" I have the means of purchasing surgical skill, and I must use all the sacrifices at my command to obtain it."

" Avast heaving, Mr. Becker," cried Willis ; " now I understand ; the thing is as clear as the tackle of the best bower, and when a resolution is once formed, nothing like paying it out at the word of command.   When shall we start ? "

" I am not talking of either you or myself, Willis."

" Of whom then, may I ask ? "

" Fritz and Jack.   Fritz knows something of navigation ; and if they succeed, they will have saved their mother ; if they perish, they will have died to save her."

" Fritz, as you say, does know something of navigation, particularly as regards coasting ; but here you have a pilot, accustomed to salt water, quite handy, why not engage him also ? "

" Willis, you have yourself said that the undertaking is perilous in the extreme, and your life is not bound up like theirs in that of their mother."

" True ; but do you not see that I am sick of dry land, and that I am getting rusty for the want of a little sea air ? "

" I felt ashamed to ask you to share in so desperate an enterprise, otherwise I would have proposed it to you, Willis."

" But you might have seen that I was growing thin, absolutely pining away, and drying up on land.   There are ducks that can live without water, but I am not one of them."

" Am I, then, to understand that you offer to risk your life in this forlorn hope ? "

" Certainly, Mr. Becker ; a man condemned to be hanged, running the risk of being drowned is no great sacrifice."

" Willis, I accept your offer, to share in the dangers of this enterprise, most gratefully.   I thank you in the name of my sons and of their mother, and trust that God may enable me to recompense you for your devotion to them and to myself."

" You forget," added Willis, wiping a tear from the

corner of his eye, that he ascribed to a grain of dust, " you forget that I was on the point of venturing out to sea in the canoe, had you yourself and Mr. Wolston not prevented me. There is work to be done, I admit; and it is not impossible to cross even the Indian Ocean in the pinnace. But we may find a doctor, perhaps, at some of the settlements — for instance, at Manilla, in the Philippines."

"That is not to be hoped for, Willis; there is, probably, only one skilful medical man in each colony, and he will be prevented leaving by Government engagements."

"True; then we had better hoist sail for Europe direct, and trust to falling in with a ship now and then."

"Alas!" sighed Becker, "in a path so wide as the ocean, it would be unwise to trust to such chances; you will have to rely, I fear, entirely upon the resources of the pinnace alone."

"Well, I dare say, though we may have to put up with half rations, we shall not starve on the voyage, at all events."

They had unmoored the pinnace, and were on their way to Shark's Island.

"You are about to announce to your sons their departure?" said Willis, inquiringly.

"Yes; but my heart almost fails me."

"The iron must be struck while it is hot. Will you commission me to whisper a few words in their ear?"

"Thanks, Willis; but what right have I to expect courage from them, if I exhibit weakness myself? No, my friend, I may shed tears in your presence, but not before them."

"A man ought never to allow his feelings to get the better of his courage," said Willis, in whose eyes, however, the dust was evidently playing sad havoc.

"These boys have almost never been absent from me. I have watched them grow up from infancy to adolescence, and from adolescence to manhood; they have always been dutiful and obedient, and with gratitude I have blessed them every night of their lives. But stern are the decrees of Fate; I must command them to depart from me — perhaps for ever!"

" There are evils that lead to good," said Willis, " even though these evils be the Straits of Magellan or the storms of the Indian Ocean."

Here the pinnace reached the offing of Shark's Island, where Fritz and Jack, leaning on the battery, watched the progress of the boat.

" Do you observe how downcast my father looks ?" said Fritz.

" Willis does not look much gayer," remarked Jack.

" Do you believe in omens, Jack ? "

" Now and then."

" Well, mark me, there is a screw loose somewhere, or I am no oracle."

CHAPTER XVIII.

ON their return from Shark's Island, Fritz and Jack
were deeply affected, not by the dread of the perils they
were destined to encounter — these never gave them a
moment's uneasiness — but by the knowledge that a merciless vulture was preying upon the vitals of their beloved
mother.

Willis on the contrary, appeared as lively as if he had
just received notice of promotion ; but whether the idea
of again dwelling on the open sea had really elevated his
spirits, or whether this gaiety was only assumed to encourage Becker and his sons, was best known to himself.

It was arranged amongst them that no one, under any
circumstances, should be made acquainted with the design
they had in contemplation. By this means all opposition
would be vanquished, and the regrets of separation would,
in some degree, be avoided. Besides, if the project were
divulged, might not Frank and Ernest insist upon their
right to share its dangers? This eventuality alone was
sufficient to impress upon them all the urgency of secrecy.
The really strong man knows his weakness, and therefore
dislikes to run the risk of exposing it, so Becker dreaded
the tears and entreaties that this desperate undertaking
would inevitably exercise, were it generally known beforehand to the rest of the family ; whereas, if once the pinnace were fairly at sea, it could not be recalled, and time
would do the rest.

Since, then, all the preparations had to be made in such a way as not to excite suspicion that any thing extraordinary was on foot, the progress was necessarily slow. Willis, under pretext of amusing himself, refitted the pinnace, and strengthened it so far as he could without impairing its sailing efficiency. He called to mind that, when Captain Cook reached Batavia, after his first voyage round the world, he observed with astonishment that a large portion of the sides of his famous ship the *Endeavor* was, under the water line, no thicker than the sole of a shoe.

As soon as the weather had settled, and the tropical heats set in, the Wolstons resumed their abode at Falcon's Nest ; whilst, under some plausible pretext or other, Willis, Fritz, and Jack took up their quarters at Rockhouse. This arrangement gave the destined navigators the means of carrying on their operations unobserved, especially as regards salting provisions and baking for the voyage.

Along with the stores, a portion of the valuables, that still remained in the magazines of Rockhouse, were placed on board the pinnace ; for, though gold and precious stones were not of much value in New Switzerland, Becker had not forgotten that such was not the case in other portions of the world ; he reflected that his sons must be furnished with the means of returning to the colony with comfort. There was also a man of science and education to be bought, and that, he knew, could not be done without as the French proverb has it, having some hay in one's boots.

Storms are usually heralded by some premonitory symptoms : the atmosphere becomes oppressive, the clouds increase in density, the sky gradually becomes obscure and large drops of rain begin to fall, then follows the deluge, and the elements commence their strife. It is much the same with impending misfortunes : gloom gathers on the countenance, our movements become constrained, our thoughts wander, and a tear lingers in the corner of the eye. Fritz and Jack endeavored in vain to appear unconcerned, but, in spite of their efforts, it was painfully evident that their minds were burdened by some heavy weight. They were more tender and more affectionate, particularly towards their mother. Towards evening, when they quitted the family circle for Rockhouse, their adieus were so earnest, so warm, and so often repeated, that it almost appeared as if they were laying in a stock of them for their voyage, to store up and preserve with the bacon and biscuits. Even the animals came in for an extra share of caresses, and, if they were capable of reflection, it must have puzzled them sorely to account for all the endearments that were lavished upon them by the two brothers.

Becker himself was no less affected than his sons; sometimes, when the latter were busily occupied with some preparation for the voyage, he would fix his eyes sadly upon them, just as if every trait of these cherished features had not already been deeply graven on his soul.

During the preceding rainy season, the two young men felt the days long and tedious, and wished in their inmost hearts that they would pass away more swiftly; now, the hours seemed to fly with unaccountable rapidity, and they would gladly have lengthened them if **they had had the power.** But no one can arrest

> Le temps, cette image mobile
> De l'immobile éternité.

And time is right in holding on the **even** tenor of its **way**; for if it once yielded to the desires of mortals, there would be no end of confusion and perplexity. It takes unto itself wings and flies away, say the fortunate; it lags at a snail's pace, say the unfortunate. The idler knows not how to pass it away. The **man** of action does not observe its progress. Those who are looking forward to some favorite amusement exclaim, "Would that it were to-morrow!" but how many there are that might well ejaculate, **from** the bottom of their souls, "Would that to-morrow may never arrive!" How, then, could such wishes be met in a way to satisfy all?

A day at length arrived when everything was ready for departure, and when nothing was wanted to weigh anchor but courage on the part of the voyagers. The pinnace was laden to the gunwale, the compass was in its place, the casks were filled with fresh water from the Jackal River, and Willis reported that both wind and sea were propitious for a start.

The morning of that day was lovely in the extreme. Willis, Fritz, and Jack were early at Falcon's Nest; the two families breakfasted together under the trees in the open air. After breakfast an adjournment to the umbrageous shade of the bananas was proposed and agreed to.

"Mother," said Fritz, taking Mrs. Becker's arm, " I want you all to myself."

" I object to that, if you please," cried Jack, taking her other arm.

" Why, you boys seem extravagantly fond of your mother to-day," said Mrs. Becker, gaily.

" Well, you see, mother, we have the right to have an idea now and then — Willis has one every week."

" So long as your ideas are about myself, I have no reason to object to them," said Mrs. Becker, smiling.

" We have always been dutiful sons, have we not, mother?" inquired Fritz.

" Yes, always."

" You are well pleased with us then ?"

" Yes, surely."

" We have never caused you any uneasiness, have we?" inquired Jack.

" That is to say, inadvertently," added Fritz; "designedly is out of the question."

" No, not even inadvertently," replied their mother.

" Were you very sorry when Frank and Ernest were going to leave us ?"

" Yes, my children, the tears still burn my cheek."

" Nevertheless, you knew that it was for the common welfare, and you felt resigned to the separation."

" But why do you ask such a question now ?"

" Well, à propos de rien, mother," replied Jack, "simply because we love you, and, like misers, we treasure your love."

Towards the afternoon both families were again assembled under the trees at Falcon's Nest. This time it was dinner that brought them together; the repast consisted of cold meats of various kinds, but the chief dish was a wonderful salad, the rich, fresh odor of which perfumed the air. Wolston, Frank, and Ernest kept up a lively conversation, yet, though all seemed happy and pleased, there were bursting hearts at the table that day."

"I am going to take a turn in the pinnace to-morrow," said Willis, quietly; "who will go with me?"

"I will!" cried all the four brothers.

"I shall require you, Frank and Ernest, to take a look at the rice plantation to-morrow," said Becker, "so I wish you to put off the excursion till another time."

"We are at your orders, father," replied the two young men.

"Where are you going, Willis?" inquired Mrs. Wolston.

"Well, I am anxious to discover whether we inhabit an island or a continent, and may, consequently, extend the survey beyond the points already known; so you must not be disappointed should we not return the same night."

"But what is the good of such an expedition?" inquired Mrs. Becker.

"The country may be inhabited, or there may be inhabited islands in the vicinity," replied Willis.

"If there be natives anywhere near," said Mrs. Becker, "they have left us at peace hitherto, and, in my opinion, since the dog sleeps, it will be prudent for us to let it lie."

"It is not a question of creating any inconvenience," suggested Becker, "but only to ascertain more accurately our geographical position: such a knowledge can do us no possible harm, but, some day, it may be of immense service to us."

"What if you should fall in with a ship?" inquired Mrs. Wolston.

"In that case we shall give your compliments to the commander," replied Jack.

"You may do that if you like, but try and bring it back with you if you can."

"Do you wish to leave us?"

"I do not mean that," hastily added Mrs. Wolston,

"but I am beginning to get anxious about my son, poor fellow. If the *Nelson* has not arrived at the Cape, then he will suppose we are all drowned, and I should like to fall in with some means of assuring him of our safety."

"Oh yes," cried the two girls, "do try and fall in with a ship; our poor brother will be so wretched."

"You might say our brother as well," added the two young men.

Here the two mothers interchanged a glance of intelligence, which might mean very little, but which likewise might signify a great deal.

A moment of intense anxiety had now arrived for Becker and his two sons; they could scarcely refrain from shedding tears, but they felt that the slightest imprudence of that nature would divulge everything.

"Come now, my lads, look alive," cried Willis, in a voice which he meant to be gruff; "if you intend to take a few hours' repose before we start in the morning, it is time to be off."

Fritz and Jack, had it been to save their lives, could not now have helped throwing more than usual energy into their parting embraces that particular afternoon; but they passed through the ordeal with tolerable firmness, and then with heavy hearts turned towards the door.

"I think I will walk with you as far as Rockhouse," said Becker.

All four then departed; and when the party were about fifty yards from Falcon's Nest, Fritz and Jack turned round and waved a final adieu to those loved beings whom probably, they might never see again.

"It is well," said Becker. "I am satisfied with your conduct throughout this trying interval."

It was now an hour when there is something indescribably sombre about the country; day was declining, the outlines of the larger objects in the landscape were becoming less distinct, and the trees were assuming any sort of fantastical shape that the mind chose to assign to them. Here and there a bird rustled in the foliage, but otherwise the silence was only broken by footsteps of the four men.

In ordinary life children quit the parental home by easy and almost imperceptible gradations. First, there is the school, then college; next, perhaps, the requirements of the profession they have adopted. Thus they readily abandon the domestic hearth; friends, intercourse, and society divide their affection, and the separation from home rarely, if ever, costs them a pang. Not so with Becker's two sons; their world was New Switzerland; therefore, like the rays of the sun absorbed by the mirror of Archimedes, all their affections were concentrated on one point.

On the former occasion when the family-ties were on the eve of being rent asunder, the case was very different. It is true, Frank and Ernest were about to leave for an indefinite period of time; but then, every comfort that the most fastidious voyager could desire was awaiting them on board the *Nelson;* for a well-appointed ship is like a well-appointed inn on shore, all your wants are ministered to with the utmost celerity. Besides, Captain Littlestone had taken the young men under his special protection, and had promised to see them properly introduced and cared for in Europe. How dissimilar was the position of Fritz and his brother; they were about to tumble into the old world should they be so fortunate as to reach it, much as if they had dropped from the skies, without a guide and without a friend. They were about to entrust themselves to the ocean, separated from its treacherous floods by a few wretched planks; to be exposed for months, almost unsheltered, to wind, rain, and the mercy of pitiless storms.

"If God in His mercy preserves you, my sons," said Becker, breaking at last the silence, "you will find yourselves launched in an ocean still more turbulent than that you have escaped — an ocean where falsehood and cunning assume the names of policy and tact; where results always justify the means, whatever these may be; where everything is sacrificed to personal interest and ambition; where fortune is honored as a virtue that dispenses with all others, and where profligacies of the most odious kinds are decorated with gay and seductive colors. It is difficult for me to foresee the various circumstances amidst which

19*

you may be placed; but there are certain rules of conduct that provide for nearly every emergency. I have no need to urge loyalty or courage — these qualities are inseparable from your hearts. Strive only for what is just and honest. Submit to be cheated rather than be cheats yourselves; ill-gotten gains never made any one rich. Put your trust in Providence. Seek aid from on high, when you find yourselves surrounded with difficulties. Never forget that there is no corner on the earth's surface, however obscure, that the eyes of the Lord are not there to behold your actions. Act promptly and with energy. Bear in mind that every moment lost will be to your mother an age of suffering, and that her life is suspended on the fragile thread of your return."

The party had now reached the banks of the Jackal River, where the pinnace was moored. Fritz and Jack were shedding tears unrestrainedly, and had dropped on their knees at their father's feet.

"I call," said Becker, in a trembling voice, "the benediction of Heaven upon your heads, my sons."

"Oh, but they must not go!" cried Mrs. Becker, rushing out from behind some tall brushwood that hid her from their view; "they shall not go!"

Fritz and Jack were instantly inclosed within their mother's arms.

"Ah!" cried she, pushing aside the hair from their brows, the better to observe their features, "you thought to deceive your mother, did you?"

"Pardon!" exclaimed both the young men.

Here Becker thought it necessary to interfere; and, summoning all the courage he could muster to the task, said —

"Why should they not go? Is this the first expedition they have undertaken?"

"No, it is not the first expedition they have undertaken, but it is the first time their eyes and their looks betokened an eternal adieu. It is the first time that I felt they were forsaking me for ever, and it is the first time you ever addressed them with the words 'you just now uttered."

Becker saw that it was useless to attempt to carry deceit any further; he therefore withdrew his eyes from the piercing glance of his wife. Willis, caught in the act, as it were, was completely thrown off his guard, and had not a word to say for himself. Fritz and Jack had again fallen on their knees, this time at the feet of their mother.

"Ah! I begin to understand," she screamed, as she glanced around on the scared group that surrounded her, like a wounded lioness whose cubs were being carried off; "now the bandage begins to drop from my eyes. A thousand inexplicable things dart into my mind. You are sending the boys on an impracticable voyage to secure the safety of their mother; but you did not think that in order to prolong my existence for a few years, you would kill me instantly with grief! What right have you to impose a remedy upon me that is a thousand times worse than the malady? Have I ever complained? May my sufferings not be agreeable to me? May I not like them? Is pain and suffering not our lot from the cradle to the tomb? But I am not ill, I was never better in my life than I am at this moment."

Here she was seized with a paroxysm of nervous tremors that convulsed her frame most fearfully, and completely belied her words. Becker rushed forward and held her firmly in his arms.

"God give me strength!" he murmured. "Go, my children, where your duty calls you; go, my friend, do not prolong this terrible scene an instant longer."

Not another word was spoken, the pinnace was unmoored; Fritz, Jack, and Willis embarked. When at some little distance from the shore, there was just light enough for Fritz to notice that his father was directing the feeble steps of his mother in the direction of Falcon's Nest. In a few moments more all the objects on shore were one confused mass of unfathomable shadow. The pinnace dropped anchor at Shark's Island, where some few final preparations for the voyage had to be made. Fritz here took a pen and wrote:

"We part. We are gone. When you read this letter, the sea, for some distance, will extend between us. We shall live and move elsewhere, but our hearts are still with you. We wish that Ernest and Frank would erect a flag-staff on the spot where we last parted with our parents. It may be to us what the celestial standard bearing the scroll, *in hoc signo vinces* was to the Emperor Constantine. The place is already sacred, and may be hallowed by your prayers for us. Our confidence in the divine mercy is boundless. Do not despair of seeing us again. We have no misgivings, not one of us but anticipates confidently the period when we shall return and bring with us health, happiness, and prosperity to you all.

"Let me add a word," said Jack.

"The sea is calm, our hearts are firm, our enterprise is under the protection of Heaven — there never was an undertaking commenced under more favorable auspices. Farewell then, once more, farewell. All our aspirations are for you.

" Fritz.
" Jack.

"P.S. — Willis was going to write a line or two when, lo and behold! a big tear rolled upon the paper. 'Ha!' said he, 'that is enough, I will not write a word, they will understand that, I think,' and he threw down the pen."

"How is the letter to be sent on shore?" inquired Fritz.

"There is a cage of pigeons on board the pinnace," replied Jack, "but I do not want them to know that, for, if they should expect to hear from us, and some accident happen to the pigeons, they might be dreadfully dis-appointed."

"We can return on shore," observed Willis, "and place it on the spot, where we embarked; they are sure to be there to-morrow."

This suggestion was incontinently adopted. The letter was attached to a small cross, and fixed in the ground. The voyagers had all re-embarked in the pinnace. which was destined to bear even more than Cæsar and his fortunes. Willis had already loosened the warp, when a thought crossed the mind of Fritz.

" I must revisit Falcon's Nest once more," said he.

" What ! " cried Willis, " you are not going to get up such another scene as we witnessed an hour or two ago? "

" No, Willis, I mean to go by stealth like the Indian trapper, so as to be seen by no mortal eye. I wish to take one more look at the old familiar trees, and endeavor to ascertain whether my mother has reached home in safety."

" But the dogs? " objected Willis.

" The dogs know me too well to give the slightest alarm at my approach. I shall not be long gone ; but really I must go, the desire is too powerful within me to be resisted."

" I will go with you," said Jack.

Here Willis shook his head and reflected an instant.

" You are not angry with us, Willis, are you ? "

" Not at all," he replied, " and I think the best thing I can do, under the circumstances, is to go too."

" Very well, make fast that warp again, and come along."

The party then disappeared amongst the brushwood.

" Some time ago," remarked Fritz, " we followed this track about the same hour ; there was danger to be apprehended, but the enterprise was bloodless, though successful."

" You mean the chimpanzee affair," said Willis.

" Yes ; this time we have only an emotion to conquer, but I am afraid it is too strong for us."

" These are the trees," said Jack, as they debouched upon the road, " that I stuck my proclamations upon. We had very little to think of in those days."

As the party drew near Falcon's Nest, the dogs approached and welcomed them with the usual canine demonstrations of joy.

" I have half a mind to carry off Toby," said Fritz ; " but I fear Mary would miss him."

Externally all appeared tranquil at Falcon's Nest ; this satisfied the young men that their mother had succeeded in reaching home, at least, in safety ; a light streaming through the window of Becker's dwelling, however, showed that the family had not yet retired for the night.

"If they only knew we were so near them!" remarked Jack.

The entire party then sat down upon a rustic bench, shrouded with flowering orchis and Spanish jasmine.

"How often, on returning from the fields or the chase, we have seen our mother at work on this very seat," observed Fritz.

"Aye," added Jack; "once I observed she had fallen asleep whilst knitting stockings. I advanced on tip-toe, removed gently her knitting apparatus, stockings, and all, and placed on her lap some ortolans that I had caught and strangled; but I first plucked one of them, and scattered the feathers all about, and then retreated into a thicket to watch the *dénouement* of my scheme. She awoke, put down her hand to take up a stocking, and laid hold of a bird. She stared, rubbed her eyes, stared again, looked about, and could find nothing but the ortolan feathers. I then ran forward and embraced her, looking as if I had just come from unearthing turnips. 'Well, I declare,' she said with a bewildered air, 'I could have sworn that I was knitting just now, and here I find myself plucking ortolans; and what is more, I have not the slightest idea where, in all the world, the birds have come from!' Of course, I looked as innocent as possible; so that the more she stared and reflected, the less she could make the matter out. At last, she went on plucking the birds, and when this was done she stuck them on the spit. When the ortolans were roasted and ready to be served up, I went into the kitchen, carried them off, and put my mother's knitting apparatus on the spit. Imagine her surprise when she beheld her worsted and stockings at the fire, knowing, at the same time, that four hungry stomachs were waiting for their dinners! At last, fearing that she was going to ascribe the metamorphosis to some hallucination of her own, I went up to her, threw my arms round her neck, told her the whole story, and we both of us enjoyed a hearty laugh over it."

"Aye, Jack, those were laughing times," said Fritz, sadly.

"Not only that, but our mother was always so even-tempered; she was never ruffled in the slightest degree by my nonsense; though she often had the right to be very angry, yet she never once took offence. On another occasion, Mary and Sophia Wolston were working here at those mysterious embroideries which they always hid when we came near."

"Toby's collar, I suppose," remarked Fritz.

"My tobacco pouch," suggested Willis.

"I approached," continued Jack, "with the muffled softness of a cat, and was just on the point of discovering their secret, when my monkey, Knips, who was cracking nuts at their feet, made a spring, and drew a bobbin of silk after it; this caused them to look round, and great was my astonishment to find myself caught at the very moment I expected to surprise them. They commenced scolding me at an immense rate, but then it was so delightful to be scolded!"

"Aye," murmured Fritz, "that is all over now."

Like a file of sheep, one recollection dragged another after it, so that the whole of the past recurred to their memories. Some faint streaks of light now warned them that day was about to break; the cocks began to crow one after the other, and to fill the air with their shrill voices.

"Now," said Willis, "it is high time to be off."

Jack hastily gathered two bouquets of flowers, which he suspended to the lintel of each dwelling.

"These," said he, "will show them that we have paid them another visit."

They then bent down all three on their knees, uttered a short prayer, and afterwards disappeared amidst the shadows of the chestnut trees.

"Listen!" said Willis, seeing that his companions were about to make a halt, "if you stop again, or speak of returning any more, I will cease to regard you as men."

Half an hour afterwards, on the morning of the 8th March, 1812, the pinnace bore out to sea, and when day broke, the crew could not descry a single trace of New Switzerland on any point of the horizon.

CHAPTER XIX.

AT the date of the events narrated in the preceeding chapter, comparatively little was known of Oceania, that is, of the islands and continents that are scattered about the Pacific Ocean. Most of them had been discovered, named, and marked correctly enough in the charts, but beyond this all was supposition, hypothesis, and mystery. The mighty empire of England in the east was then only in its infancy, Sutteeism and Thuggism were still rampant on the banks of the Ganges, but the power of the descendants of the Great Mogul was on the wane. California was only known as the hunting-ground of a savage race of wild Indians. The now rich and flourishing colonies of Australia were represented by the convict settlement of Sydney. The Dutch had asserted that the territory of New Holland was utterly uninhabitable, and this was still the belief of the civilized world; nor was it without considerable opposition on the part of *soi-disant* philanthropists that the English government succeeded in establishing a prison depot on what at the time was considered the sole spot in that vast territory susceptible of cultivation. At the present time, these formerly-despised

regions send *one hundred tons of pure gold* to England.
The political state of Europe itself had at this time assumed a singular aspect. Napoleon had made himself
master of nearly all the continental states; Spain, Portugal, Belgium, Holland, and a part **of Germany were at**
his feet; **and, by the** Peace of Tilsit, he **had secured the**
coöperation of Alexander, Emperor **of** Russia, **in his**
schemes to ruin the trade **and** commerce of Great Britain.
England, by her opportune seizure of the Danish fleet,
broke up the first great northern confederacy that was
formed against her. This act, though much impugned by
the politicians of the day, **is** now known not only to have
been perfectly justifiable, but also highly creditable to the
political foresight of Canning and Castlereagh, by whom it
was suggested, to say nothing of the daring and boldness
that Nelson displayed in executing the manœuvre. When
news of this event reached the Russian Emperor it threw
him into a paroxysm of rage. and he declared war against
England in violent language. He had the insolence to
make peace with France the *sina qua non* of his friendship. At the distance of nearly half a century, the actual
language employed has a peculiar flavor. The emperor,
after detailing his grievances, declares that henceforth
there shall be no connection between the two countries,
and calls on his Britannic Majesty to dismiss his ministers,
and conclude a peace forthwith. The British Government replied to this by ordering Nelson to set sail forthwith for the mouth of the Neva. A bitter and scorching
manifesto was at the time forwarded to the emperor. It
accused **him** flatly **of** duplicity, and boldly defied him and
all his legions. The whole document is well worthy of
perusal in these lackadaisical times. It is dated West-
minister, December 18, 1807. It sets forth anew the
principles of maritime war, which England had then rig-
idly in force. Napoleon had declared the whole of the
British Islands in a state of blockade. The British Government replied by blockading *de facto* the whole of Europe. This was done by those celebrated orders in council, which, more than anything else, precipitated the down-
fall of Napoleon. They threw the trade of the world into

'he hands of England. Of course, Russia was deeply affected, so was Spain and all the other maritime states; and they were all, one way or another, in open hostility with this country. But England laughed all their threats to scorn; and in the whole history of the country, there was not a more brilliant period in her eventful history. She stood alone against the world in arms. Even the blusterings of the United States were unheeded, and in no degree disturbed her stern equanimity. She saw the road to victory, and resolved to pursue it. But England then had great statesmen, and, of them all, Lord Castlereagh was the greatest, although he served a Prince Regent who cared no more for England or the English people, than the Irish member, who, when reproached for selling his country, thanked God that he had a country to sell.

At length the ill-will of the Americans resolved itself into open warfare, and the United States was numbered with the overt enemies of England. This resulted in British troops marching up to Washington and burning the Capitol, or Congress House, about the ears of the members who had stirred up the strife. Meanwhile, all the islands of France in the east and west had been taken possession of; the British flag waved on the Spanish island of Cuba, and in the no less valuable possessions of Holland, in Java. Everywhere on the ocean England held undisputed sway. This state of things gave rise to one great evil — the sea swarmed with cruisers and privateers, English, French, and American; so that no vessel, unless sailing under convoy, heavily armed, or a very swift sailer, but ran risk of capture.

The *Mary* — for so Fritz now called the pinnace — had been ten days at sea, the wind had died away, and for some time scarcely a zephyr had ruffled the surface of the water, the sails were lazily flapping against the mast, and but for the currents, the voyagers would have been almost stationary. It may readily be supposed that, under such circumstances, their progress was somewhat slow, and, as Jack observed, to judge from their actual rate of sailing, they ought to have started when very young, in order to arrive at the termination of the voyage before they became bald-headed old men.

They prayed for a breeze, a gale, or even a storm ; their
fresh water was beginning to get sour, and they reflected
that, if the calm continued any length of time, their provisions would eventually run short, and the ordinary
resource of eating one another would stare them in the
face. Jack, being the youngest, would probably disappear
first, next Fritz, then Willis would be left to eat himself,
in order to avoid dying of hunger, just as the unfortunate
Count Ugolino devoured his own children to save them
from orphanage.

As yet, however, there were no symptoms of such a
dire disaster ; they were in excellent health and tolerable
spirits ; they had provisions enough to last them for six
months at least, and consequently had not as yet, at all
events, the slightest occasion to manifest a tendency to
anthropophagism.

"I can understand the sea," remarked Jack, "as I
understand the land and the sky ; God created them, that
is enough ; but I cannot understand how a mighty river
like the Nile or the Ganges can continue eternally dis-
charging immense deluges of water into the sea without
becoming exhausted. From what fathomless reservoirs
do the Amazon and the Mississippi receive their endless
torrents ? "

"The reservoirs of the greatest rivers," replied Fritz,
" are nothing more than drops of water that fall from the
crevice of some rock on or near the summit of a hill ; these
are collected together in a pool or hollow, from which they
issue in the form of a slender rivulet. At first, the
smallest pebble is sufficient to arrest the course of this
thread of water ; but it turns upon itself, gathers strength,
finally surmounts the obstacle, dashes over it, unites itself
with other rivulets, reaches the plain, scoops out a bed,
and goes on, as you say, for ever emptying its waters into
the sea."

" Yes ; but it is the source of these sources that I want
to know the origin of. You speak of hills, whilst we know
that water naturally, by reason of its weight and fluidity,
seeks to secrete itself in the lowest beds of the earth."

" It is scarcely necessary for me to observe that water

may come down a hill, although it never goes up. Rain, snow, dew, and generally all the vapors that fall from the atmosphere, furnish the enormous masses of water that are constantly flowing into the sea. The vapor alone that is absorbed in the air from the sea is more than sufficient to feed all the rivers on the face of the earth. Mountains, by their formation, arrest these vapors, collect them in a hole here and in a cavern there, and permit them to filter by a million of threads from rock to rock, fertilizing the land and nourishing the rivers that intersect it. If, therefore, you were to suppress the Alps that rise between France and Italy, you would, at the same time, extinguish the Rhone and the Po."

"It would be a pity to do that," said Jack; "there was a time though when there were no Pyrenees."

"That must have been, then, at a period prior to the formation of granite, which is esteemed the oldest of rocks."

"No such thing," insisted Jack; "it was so late as 1713, when, by the peace of Utrecht, the crown of Spain was secured to the Duke of Anjou, grandson of Louis XIV."

"Howsomever," remarked Willis, "all the mariners in the French fleet could not convince me that the Pyrenean mountains are only a hundred years old."

"My brother is only speaking metaphorically," said Fritz; "when the crown of Spain was assigned to the Duke of Anjou, his grandfather said— *Qu il n'y avait plus de Pyrénées.* He meant by that simply, that France and Spain being governed by the same prince, the moral barrier between them existed no longer. The formidable mountains still stood for all that, and he who removes them would certainly be possessed of extraordinary power."

"I am always putting my foot in it," said Willis, "when the yarn is about the land; let us talk of the sea for a bit. Who built the first ship?"

"Well," replied Fritz, "I should say that the first ship was the ark."

"Whence we may infer," added Jack, "that Noah was the first admiral."

"We learn from the Scriptures," continued Fritz, "that the first navigators were the children of Noah, and it appears from profane history that the earliest attempts at navigation were manifested near where the ark rested; consequently, we may fairly presume that the art of ship-building arose from the traditions of the deluge and the ark."

"In that case, the art in question dates very far back."

"Yes, since it dates from 2348 years before the birth of Christ; but the human race degenerated, the traditions were forgotten, and navigation was confined to planks, rafts, bark canoes, or the trunk of a tree hollowed out by fire."

"That is the sort of craft used by the inhabitants of Polynesia at the present day," remarked Willis.

"It appears, however, by the Book of Job, that pirates existed in those days, and that they went to sea in ships and captured merchantmen, which proves, to a certain extent, that there were merchantmen to conquer. We know also that David and Solomon equipped large fleets, and even fought battles on sea."

"Whether an ancient or modern, a Jew or a Gentile," said Willis, "he must have been a brave fellow who launched the first ship, and risked himself and his goods at sea in it."

"True," continued Fritz; "but when once the equilibrium of a floating body was known, there would be no longer any risk; as soon as it came to be understood that any solid body would float if it were lighter than its bulk of water, the matter was simple enough."

"Very good," interrupted Jack; "but the words 'when' and 'as soon as' imply a great deal; *when*, or *as soon as*, we know anything, the mystery of course disappears. But before! there is the difficulty. Particles of water do not cohere—how is it, then, that a ship of war, that often weighs two millions of pounds, does not sink through them, and go to the bottom? Individuals, like myself for example, who are not members of a learned society, may be pardoned for not knowing how water bears the weight of a seventy-four."

"The seventy-four would, most undoubtedly, sink if it

20*

were heavier than the weight of water it displaced; but this is not the case; wood is generally lighter than water."

"The wood, yes; but the cannon, the cargo, and the crew?"

"You forget the cabooses, the cockpits, and the cabins, that do not weigh anything. Allowing for everything, the weight of a ship, cargo and all, is much lighter than its bulk of water, and consequently it cannot sink."

"But how is it, then, that the immense bulk of a seventy-four moves so easily in the water? One would think that its prodigious weight would make it stick fast, and continue immoveable."

"When the seventy-four in question has displaced its weight of water, its own weight is substituted for the water, and is in consequence virtually annihilated; it does not, in point of fact, weigh anything at all, and therefore is easily impelled by the wind."

"When there is any, understood," added Jack.

"And a yard or so of canvas." suggested Willis.

"True," continued Fritz, "a sail or two would be very desirable; these instruments of propulsion do not appear, however, to have been used by the ancients. We first hear of a sail being employed at the time when Isis went in search of her husband Osiris, who was killed by his brother Typhon, and whose quarters were scattered in the Nile. This lady, it seems, took off the veil that covered her head, and fastened it to an upright shaft stuck in the middle of the boat, and, much to her astonishment, it impelled her onwards at a marvellous speed."

"A clever young woman that," said Willis; "but I doubt whether veils would answer the purpose on board a seventy-four, particularly as regards the mainsail and mizentops."

"The Phœnicians were the most enterprising of the early navigators. They appeared to have sailed round Africa without a compass, for they embarked on the Red Sea and reäppeared at the mouth of the Nile, and the compass was not invented till the fourteenth century."

"And who was the inventor of the compass?" inquired Willis.

"According to some authorities, it was invented by a Neapolitan named Jean Goya; according to others, the inventor was a certain Hugues de Bercy."

"Then," said Jack, "you do not admit the claims of the Chinese and Hindoos, who assert priority in the discovery?"

"I neither deny nor admit their claims, because I do not know the grounds upon which they are founded; like the invention of gunpowder and printing, the discovery of the compass has many rival claimants."

"I am of opinion," said Jack, "that Guttenberg is entitled to the honor of discovering printing, and that Berthold Schwartz invented gunpowder."

"Perhaps you are right; but there is scarcely any invention of importance that has not two or three names fastened to it as inventors; they stick to it like barnacles, and there is no way to shake any of them off. So, in the case of illustrious men, nations dispute the honor of giving them birth; there are six or seven towns in Asia Minor that claim to be the birth-place of Homer. National vanities justly desire to possess the largest amount of genius; hence, no sooner does anything useful make its appearance in the world, than half a dozen nations or individuals start up to claim it as their offspring. The wisest course, under such circumstances, is to side with the best accredited opinion, which I have done in the case of the compass."

"It was no joke," said Willis, "to circumnavigate Africa without a compass."

"You are quite right, Willis, if you judge the navigation of those days by the modern standard; but it is to be borne in mind that the ancients never lost sight of the coast. They steered from cape to promontory, and from promontory to cape, dropping their anchor every night and remaining well in-shore till morning. If by accident they were driven out into the open sea, and the stars happened to be hidden by fog or clouds, they were lost beyond recovery, even though within a day's sail of a harbor; because, whilst supposing they were making for the coast, they might, in all probability, be steering in precisely the opposite direction."

"It is certainly marvellous," said Jack, "that a piece of iron stuck upon a board should be a safe and sure guide to the mariner through the trackless ocean, even when the stars are enveloped in obscurity and darkness!"

"It is a symbol of faith," remarked Willis, "that supplies the doubts and incertitudes of reason."

As for the ships, or rather galleys, of the ancients," continued Fritz, "with the exception of the ambitious fleets of the Greeks and Romans that fought at Salamis and Actium, one of the modern ships of war could sweep them all out of the sea with its rudder."

Yes," said Jack, "at the period of which you speak, the ancients possessed a great advantage over us. The winds in those days were personages, and were very well known; they were called Æolus, Boreas, and so forth. They were to be found in caves or islands, and, if treated with civility, were remarkably condescending. Queen Dido, through one of these potentates, obtained contrary winds, to prevent Æneas from leaving her."

"By the way," said Willis, "there is, or at least was, in one of the Scottish rivers, a ship without either oars or sails."

"Yes, very likely; but it did not move."

"It did though, and, what is more, against both wind and tide."

"I wish we had your wonderful ship here just now, it is just the thing to suit us under present circumstances," said Jack.

"So it would, Master Jack, for it sails against currents, up rivers, and the crew care no more about the wind than I do about the color of the clouds when I am lighting my pipe."

"You don't happen to mean that the *Flying Dutchman* has appeared on the Scotch coast, do you, Willis?"

"Not a bit of it, I mean just exactly what I say. It is a real ship, with a real stern and a real figure-head, but manned by blacksmiths instead of mariners."

"Well, but how does it move? Does somebody go behind and push it, or is it dragged in front by sea-horses and water-kelpies?"

"No, it moves by steam."

"But how?"

"Aye, there lies the mystery. The affair has often been discussed by us sailors on board ship; some have suggested one way and some another."

"Neither of which throws much light on the subject," observed Jack; "at least, in so far as we are concerned."

"All I can tell you," said Willis, "is, that the steam is obtained by boiling water in a large cauldron, and that the power so obtained is very powerful."

"That it certainly is, if it could be controlled, for steam occupies seventeen or eighteen hundred times the space of the water in its liquid state; but then, if the vessel that contains the boiling water has no outlet, the steam will burst it."

"It appears that it **can be** prevented doing that, though," replied Willis, "even **though** additional heat be applied to the vapor itself."

"By heating the steam, the vapor may acquire a volume forty thousand times greater than that of the water; all that is well known; but as soon as it comes in contact with the air, nothing is left of it but a cloud, which collapses again into a few drops of water."

"That may be all very true, Master Fritz, if the steam were allowed to escape into the air; but it is only permitted to do that after it has done duty on board ship. It appears that steam is very elastic, and may be compressed like India-rubber, but has a tendency to resist the pressure and set itself free. Imagine, for example, a headstrong young man, for a long time kept in restraint by parental control, suddenly let loose, and allowed scope to follow the bent of his own inclinations."

"Very good, Willis; for argument's sake, let us take your headstrong young man, or rather the steam, for granted, and let us admit that it is as elastic as ever you please — but what then?"

"Then you must imagine a piston in a cylinder, forced upwards when the steam is heated, and falling downwards when the steam is cooled. Next fancy this upward and downward motion regulated by a number of wheels and cranks that turn two wheels on each side of the ship, keeping up a constant jangling and clanking, the wheels or paddles splashing in the water, and then you may form a slight idea of the thing."

"Oh!" cried Jack, "we invented a machine of that kind for our canoe, with a turnspit. Do you recollect it, Fritz?"

"Yes, I recollect it well enough; and I also recollect that the canoe went much better without than with it."

"You spoke just now," continued Willis, "of rival nations, who pounce like birds of prey upon every new invention; and so it is with the steamship. An American, named Fulton, made a trial in the Hudson with one in 1807 — that is about five years ago — and I believe the Yankees, in consequence, are laying claim to the invention."

"Now that you bring the thing to my recollection," said Fritz, "the idea of applying steam in the arts is by no means new, although, I must candidly admit, I never heard of it being used in propelling ships before. The Spaniards assert that a captain of one of their vessels, named Don Blas de Garay, discovered, as early as the sixteenth century, the art of making steam a motive power."

"I don't believe that," said Jack.

"Why?"

"Because a real Spaniard has never less than thirty-six words in his name. If you had said that the steam engine was discovered by Don Pedrillo y Alvares y Toledo y Concha y Alonzo y Martinez y Xacarillo, or something of that sort, then I could believe the man to have been a genuine Spaniard, but not otherwise."

"Spaniard or no Spaniard, the Spanish claim the discovery of steam through Don Blas; the Italians likewise claim the discovery for a mechanician, named Bianca;

the Germans assign its discovery to Solomon de Causs the French urge Denis Papin; and the English claim the invention for Roger Bacon."

"You have forgotten the Swiss," said Jack.

"The Swiss," replied Fritz, with an air of dignity, "put forward no candidate: steam and vapor and smoke are not much in their line. They discovered something infinitely better — the world is indebted to them for the invention of liberty. I mean rational, intelligent, and true liberty — not the savagery and mob tyranny of red republicanism. The three discoverers of this noble invention were Melchthal, Furst, and William Tell."

"You can have no idea," continued Willis, "of the stir that steam was creating in Europe the last time I was there. Of course there were plenty of incredulous people who said that it was no good; that it would never be of any use; and that if it were, it would not pay for the fuel consumed. On the other hand, the enthusiasts held that, eventually, it would be used for everything; that in the air we should have steam balloons; on the sea, steam ships, steam guns, and perhaps steam men to work them; that on land there would be steam coaches driven by steam horses. Journeys, say they, will be performed in no time, that is, as soon as you start for a place you arrive at it, just like an arrow, that no sooner leaves the bow than you see it stuck in the bull's eye."

"In that case," observed Jack, "it will be necessary to do away with respiration, as well as horses."

"A Londoner will be able to say to his wife, My dear, I am going to Birmingham to-day, but I will be back to dinner; and if a Parisian lights his cigar at Paris, it will burn till he arrives at Bordeaux."

"Holloa, Willis, you have fairly converted Fritz and me into marines at last."

"I am only speaking of what will be, not of what is — that makes all the difference you know. It is expected that there will be steam coaches on every turnpike-road; so that, instead of hiring a post-chaise, you will have to order a locomotive, and instead of postboys, you will have to engage an engineer and stoker."

"Then, instead of saying, Put the horses to," remarked Jack, "we shall have to say, Get the steam up."

"Exactly; and when you go on a pleasure excursion, you will be whisked from one point to another without having time to see whether you pass through a desert or a flower-garden."

"What, then, is to become of adventures by the way, road-side inns, and banditti?"

"All to be suppressed."

"So it appears," said Jack; "men are to be carried about from place to place like flocks of sheep; perhaps they will invent steam dogs as well to run after stragglers, and bring them into the fold by the calf of the leg. Your new mode of going a-pleasuring may be a very excellent thing in its way, Willis; but it would not suit my taste."

"Probably not; nor mine either, for the matter of that, Master Jack."

"At all events," said Fritz, "you would run no danger of being upset on the road."

"No; but, by way of compensation, you may be blown up."

"True, I forgot that."

"This conversation has carried us along another knot," said Jack, opening the log, which he had been appointed to keep; "and now, by your leave, I will read over some of my entries to refresh your memories as to our proceedings.

"March 9th. — Wind fair and fresh — steered to north-west — a flock of seals under our lee bow — feel rather squeamish.

"10th. — No wind — fall in with a largish island and four little ones, give them the name of Willis's Archipelago.

"11th. — A dead calm — sea smooth as a mirror — all of us dull and sleepy.

"12th. — Heat 90 deg. — shot a boobie, roasted and ate him, rather fishy — passed the night amongst some reefs.

"13th. — Same as the 12th, but no boobie.

"14th. — Same as the 13th.

"Dreadfully tiresome, is it not," said Jack; "no wonder they call this ocean the Pacific."

"Alas!" sighed Willis, thinking of the *Nelson*, "it does not always justify the name."

"15th.—Hailed a low island, surrounded with breakers, named it Sophia's Island."

"But all these islands have been named half a dozen times already," said Willis.

"Oh, never mind that, another name or two will not break their backs."

"16th.—Current bearing us rapidly to westward—caught a sea cow, and had it converted into pemican."

"17th.—Shot another boobie, which we put in the pot to remind us that we were no worse off than the subjects of Henry IV. No wind—sea blazing like a furnace."

"You will have to turn over a new leaf in your log by-and-by," said Willis, "or I am very much mistaken."

"Well, I hope you are not mistaken, Willis, for I am tired of this sort of thing."

A red haze now began to shroud the sun, the heat of the air became almost stifling, but the muffled roar of distant thunder and bright flashes of light warned the voyagers to prepare for a change. Willis reefed the canvas close to the mast, and suggested that everything likely to spoil should be put under hatches. This was scarcely done before the storm had reached them, and they were soon in the midst of a tropical deluge. At first, a light breeze sprung up, blowing towards the south-east, which continued till midnight, when it chopped round. Towards morning, it blew a heavy gale from east to east-south-east, with a heavy sea running. In the meantime, the pinnace labored heavily, and several seas broke over her. Willis now saw that their only chance of safety lay in altering their course. All the canvas was already braced up except the jib, which was necessary to give the craft headway, and with this sail alone they were soon after speeding at a rapid rate in the direction of the Polynesian Islands. The gale continued almost without intermission for three weeks, during which period Willis considered they must have been driven some hundreds, of miles to the north-west.

The gale at length ceased, the sea resumed its tranquility, and the wind became favorable. The pinnace had, however, been a good deal battered by the storm, and their fresh water was getting low, and it was decided they should still keep a westerly course till they reached an island where they could refit before resuming their voyage.

"The gale has not done us much good," said Jack, sadly; "if it had blown the other way, we might have been in the Indian Ocean by this time."

"Cheer up," said Willis, taking the glass from his eye, "I see land about three miles to leeward, and the landing appears easy."

"But the savages?" inquired Jack.

"The islands of this latitude are not all inhabited," replied Fritz; "besides, under our present circumstances, we have no alternative but to take our chance with them."

"Well, I do not know that," objected Jack; "it would be better for us to do without fresh water than to run the risk of being eaten."

"What a beautiful coast!" cried Willis, who still kept the telescope at his eye. "Near the shore the land is flat, and appears cultivated; but behind, it rises gradually, and is closed in with a range of hills, covered with trees. There is a beautiful bay in front of us, which appears to invite us ashore. But the place is inhabited; the shore is strewn with huts, and I can see clumps of the bread-fruit tree growing near them."

"What sort of vegetable is the bread-fruit?" inquired Fritz.

"It is a very excellent thing, and supplies the natives with bread without the intervention of grain, flour-mills, or bakers. It can be eaten either raw, or baked, or boiled; either way, it is palatable. The tree itself is like our apple trees; but the fruit is as large as a pine-apple — when it is ripe, it is yellow and soft. The natives, however, generally gather it before it is ripe; it is then cooked in an oven; the skin is burnt or peeled off — the inside is tender and white, like the crumb of bread or the flour of the potato."

"Let me have the telescope an instant," said Fritz; "I should like to see what the natives are like. Ah, I see a troop of them collecting on shore; some of them seem to be covered with a kind of wrought-steel armor."

"Perhaps the descendants of the Crusaders," remarked Jack, "returning from the Holy Land by way of the Pacific Ocean!"

"Others wear striped pantaloons," continued Fritz.

"That is to say," observed Willis, "the whole lot of them are as naked as posts. What you suppose to be cuirasses and pantaloons, are their tabooed breasts and legs."

"Are you sure of that, Willis?"

"Not a doubt about it."

"Such garments are both durable and economical," remarked Jack; "but I scarcely think they are suitable for stormy weather. But do you think it is safe to land amongst such a set of barebacked rascals, Willis?"

"I should not like to take the responsibility of guaranteeing our safety; but I do not see what other course we can adopt."

They had now approached within musket-shot of the shore. They could see that a venerable-looking old man stood a few paces in front of the group of natives. He held a green branch in one hand, and pressed with the other a long flowing white beard to his breast.

"According to universal grammar," said Jack, "these signs should mean peace and amity."

"Yes," replied the Pilot; "the more so that the rearguard are pouring water on their heads, which is the greatest mark of courtesy the natives of Polynesia can show to strangers."

"Gentlemen," cried Jack, taking off his cap and making a low bow, "we are your most obedient servants."

"We must be on our guard," said Willis; "these savages are very deceitful, and sometimes let fly their arrows under a show of friendship. I will go on shore alone, whilst you keep at a little distance off, ready to fire to cover my retreat, if need be."

The young men objected to Willis incurring danger that

they did not share; but on this point Willis was inexorable, so they were obliged to suffer him to depart alone. By good chance, they had shipped a small cask of glass beads on board the pinnace. The Pilot took a few of these with him, and, placing a cask and a couple of calabashes in the canoe, he rowed ashore.

The natives were evidently in great commotion; there was an immense amount of running backwards and forwards. Something important was, obviously enough, going forward; but, whether the excitement was caused by curiosity or admiration, it was hard to say. They might be preparing a friendly reception for the stranger, or they might be preparing to eat him — which of the two was an interesting question that Willis did not care about probing too deeply at that particular moment.

Fritz and Jack anxiously watched the operations of the natives from the bay. They could not with safety abandon the pinnace; but to leave Willis to the mercy of the sinister-looking people on shore was not to be thought of either. The *Mary* was, therefore, run in as close as possible, and Jack leaped on the sands a few minutes after the Pilot.

Willis marched boldly on towards the natives, and when he arrived beside the old man, the crowd opened up and formed an avenue through which a chief advanced, followed by a number of men, seemingly priests, who carried a grotesque-looking figure that Jack presumed to be an idol. The figure was made up of wicker-work — was of colossal height — the features, which represented nothing on earth beneath nor heaven above, were inconceivably hideous — the eyes were discs of mother-of-pearl, with a nut in the centre — the teeth were apparently those of a shark, and the body was covered with a mantle of red feathers.

At the command of the chief, some of the natives advanced and placed a quantity of bananas, bread-fruits, and other vegetables at the Pilot's feet; the priests then came forward and knelt down before him, and seemed to worship after the fashion of the ancients when they paid their devotions to the Eleusinian goddess, or the statue of Apollo. Meanwhile, Jack, on his side, was likewise surrounded by the natives, who was treated with much less ceremony than Willis. Instead of falling down on their knees, each of them, one after the other, rubbed their noses against his, and then danced round him with every demonstration of savage joy.

Jack had now an opportunity of observing the personages about him more in detail. They were mostly tall and well-formed; their features bore some resemblance to those of a negro, their nose being flat and their lips thick; on the other hand, they had the high cheek-bones of the North American Indian and the forehead of the Malay. Nearly all of them were entirely naked, but wore a necklace and bracelets of shells. They were armed with a sort of spear and an axe of hard wood edged with stone. Their skins were tattooed all over with lines and circles, and painted; these decorations, in some instances, exhibiting careful execution and no inconsiderable degree of artistic skill. These observations made, Jack pushed his way to the spot where Willis was receiving the homage of the priests.

"What! you here?" said the Pilot.

"Yes, Willis, I have come to see what detained you. By the way, is there anything the matter with my nose?"

"Nothing that I can see; but the natives of New Zealand rub their noses against each other, and probably the same usage is fashion here."

"Why, then, do they make you an exception?"

"I have not the remotest idea."

The priests at length rose, and the chief advanced. This dignitary addressed a long discourse to Willis in a sing-song tone, which lasted nearly half an hour. After this, he stood aside, and looked at Willis, as if he expected a reply.

"Illustrious chief, king, prince, or nabob," said Willis, "I am highly flattered by all the fine things you have just said to me. It is true, I have not understood a single word, but the fruits you have placed before me speak a language that I can understand. Howsomever, most mighty potentate, we are not in want of provisions; but if

21*

you can show us a spring of good water, you will confer upon us an everlasting favor."

"You might just as well ask him to show you what o'clock it is by the dial of his cathedral," said Jack.

"They would only point to the sun if I did."

"But suppose the sun invisible."

"Then they would be in the same position as we are when we forget to wind up our watches. Gentlemen savages," he said, turning to the natives and handing them the glass beads, "accept these trifles as a token of our esteem."

The natives required no pressing, but accepted the proffered gifts with great good-will. The dancing and singing then recommenced with redoubled fury, and poor Jack's nose was almost obliterated by the constant rubbing it underwent.

Suddenly the hubbub ceased, and a profound silence reigned throughout the assembly. The oldest of the priests brought a mantle of red feathers, similar to the one that covered the idol. This was thrown over the Pilot's shoulders; a tuft of feathers, something resembling a funeral plume, was placed upon his head, and a large semi-circular fan was thrust into his hand. Thus equipped, a procession was formed, one half before and the other half behind him. The *cortége* began to move slowly in the direction of the interior, but the operation was disconcerted by Willis, who remained stock-still.

"Thank you," he said, "I would rather not go far away from the shore."

As soon as the natives saw clearly that Willis was not disposed to move, the chief issued a mandate, and four stout fellows immediately removed the idol from its position, and Willis was placed upon the vacant pedestal.

The kind of adoration with which all these proceedings were accompanied greatly perplexed the voyagers. What could it all mean? Was this a common mode of welcoming strangers? It occurred to Jack that the Romans were accustomed to decorate with flowers the victims they designed as sacrifices to the altars of their gods before immolating them. This reminiscence made his flesh creep with horror, and filled him with the utmost dismay.

"Willis!" he cried to the Pilot, whom they were now leading off in triumph, "let us try the effects of our rifles on this rabble; you jump over the heads of your worshippers, and we will charge through them to shore. I will shoot the first man that pursues us, and signal Fritz to discharge the four-pounder amongst them."

"Impossible," replied Willis; "we should both be stuck all over with arrows and lances before we could reach the pinnace. Did I not tell you not to come ashore?"

"True, Willis, but did you suppose I had no heart? How could I look on quietly whilst you were surrounded by a mob of ferocious-looking men?"

"Well, well, Master Jack, say no more about it; I do not suppose they mean to do me any harm; but there would be danger in rousing the passions of such a multitude of people. They seem, luckily, to direct their attentions exclusively to me, so you had better go back and look after the canoe."

"No; I shall follow you wherever you go, Willis, even into the soup-kettles of the wretches."

"In that case," said Willis, "the wine is poured out, and, such as it is, we must drink it."

CHAPTER XX.

WAS he on his way to the Capitol or to the Gemoniæ?
The solution of this question became, for the moment, of
greater importance to Willis than the "to be or not to be"
of Hamlet to the State of Denmark. This incertitude
was all the more painful, that it was accompanied by
myriads of insects, created by the recent rains; these
swarmed in the air to such an extent, that it was utterly
impossible to inhale the one without swallowing the other.
The sailor, notwithstanding his elevated and somewhat
perilous position, true to his instincts and tormented by
the flies, took out his pipe, filled it, and struck a light.
As soon as the first column of smoke issued from his
mouth, the cavalcade halted spontaneously, the natives fell
on their faces, their noses touching the ground, and in an
attitude of the profoundest fear and apprehension. Jupiter thundering never created such a sensation as Willis
smoking. The savages seemed glued to the earth with
terror. If the Pilot had thought it advisable to escape,
he might have walked over the prostrate bodies of his
captors, not one of whom would have been bold enough
to follow what appeared to be a human volcano, vomiting
fire and smoke, — the fire of course being understood.

Willis, however, now saw that he possessed in his pipe a ready means of awing them. Besides, it was clear that, through some fortunate coincidence, the natives had mistaken him for a divinity. There was, consequently, no immediate danger to be apprehended; he therefore became himself again, and began to enjoy the novelty of his new dignity.

It was certainly a curious contrast. Willis, seated on a sort of throne, crowned with a waving plume of feathers, shrouded in a fiery mantle, and surrounded by a crowd of prostrate figures, was quietly puffing ribbons of smoke from the tips of his lips. There he sat, for all the world like a crane in a duck-pond.

From time to time the more daring of the worshippers slightly raised their heads to see whether Jupiter was still thundering; but when their eye caught a whiff of smoke, they speedily resumed their former posture. Some of them even thrust their heads into holes, or behind stones, as if more effectually to shelter themselves from the fury of the fiery furnace. At last the eruption ceased, Willis knocked the ashes out of his pipe, replaced it in his pocket, and the convoy resumed its route.

After half an hour's march, the procession halted near a clump of plantains, in front of a structure more ambitious than any of those in the neighborhood. A female, laden with rude ornaments, was standing at the door. This lady, who rivalled the celebrated Daniel Lambert in dimensions, would have created quite a *furore* at Bartholomew Fair; according to Jack, she was so amazingly fat, that it would have taken full five minutes to walk round her. She took the Pilot respectfully by the hand, and led him into the interior of the building, which was crowded with images of various forms, and was evidently a temple. Willis, at a sign from his conductress, seated himself in a chair, raised on a dais, and surmounted by a terrific figure similar to the one already described, but draped in white feathers instead of red.

The fat lady, or rather the high priestess — for she was the reigning potentate in this magazine of idols — took a sucking pig that was held by one of the priests. After muttering a prayer or homily of some sort, she strangled the poor animal, and returned it to the priest. By and by, the pig was brought in again cooked, and presented with great ceremony to Willis. There were likewise sundry dishes of fruit, nuts, and several small cups containing some kind of liquid. One of the priests cut up the pig, **and lifted pieces of it to Willis's mouth;** these, however, he refused to eat. The fat priestess, **observing** this, chewed one or **two** mouthfuls, which she afterwards handed to the Pilot. This was putting the sailor's gallantry to rather a rude test. He was equal to the **emergency,** and did not refuse the offering. But he must have felt at **the time, that** being a divinity was not entirely without its attendant inconveniences.

Nor was this the only infliction of the kind **he was** doomed to withstand. One of the priests took up a piece of kava-root, put it into his mouth, chewed it, and then dropped a bit into each of the cups already noticed. One of these, containing this nectar, was presented to Willis by the fat Hebe who presided at the feast, and he had the fortitude to taste it. Another of the cups was handed to **Jack.**

" No, I thank you," said he, shaking his head; "I breakfasted rather late this morning."

Meantime, another personage had entered upon the scene. After having performed an obeisance to Willis like the rest, this individual backed himself to where Jack was standing, by this means adroitly avoiding both the kava and the nose-rubbings. He was distinguished from the other natives by an ornament round his waist, which fell to his knees. His skin seemed a trifle less dark, his features less marked ; but his body was tattooed and stained after the common fashion.

The new comer turned out to be a Portuguese deserter, who had abandoned his ship twenty years before, and had married the daughter of a chief of the island on which he **now** was. **At** the present moment, he filled the part of prime minister to the king, an office he could not have held in his own ungrateful country, since he could neither read nor write. These accomplishments, it appeared, were

not, however, absolutely indispensable in Polynesia. It
has been found that when a savage is transferred to Europe,
he readily acquires the habits of civilized life. By a similar adaptation of things to circumstances, this European
had identified himself with the savages. He had adopted
their manners, their customs, and their costume. When
he thought of his own country, it was only to wonder why
he ever submitted to the constraint of a coat, or put himself to the trouble of handling a fork and spoon.

He had not, however, entirely forgotten his mother
tongue, and, moreover, still retained in his memory a few
English words. He was likewise very communicative, and
told Jack that they were in the Island of Hawai; that the
name of the king was Toubowrai Tamaidi, who, he added,
intended visiting the pinnace with the queen next day,
to pay his respects in person to the great Rono.

" His Majesty," said the Portuguese, " would have been
amongst the first to throw himself at his feet, but unfortunately the royal residence is a good way off; and though
both the king and the queen are on the way, running as
fast as they can, it may take them some time yet to reach
the shore."

" But who is the great Rono?" inquired Jack.

" Well," replied the prime minister, " you ought to know
best, since you arrived with him."

Jack felt that he was touching on delicate ground, and
saw that it was necessary to diplomatise a little.

" True," said he; " but I am not acquainted with the
position that illustrious person holds in relation to Hawai."

The Portuguese then made a very long, rambling, and
not very lucid statement, from which Jack gleaned the
following details. About a hundred years before, during
the reign of one of the first kings, there lived a great war-
rior, whose name was Rono. This chief was very popular,
but he was very jealous. In a moment of anger he killed
his wife, of whom he was passionately fond. The regret
and grief that resulted from this act drove him out of his
senses: he wandered disconsolately about the island, fought
and quarrelled with every one that came near him. At
last, in a fit of despair, he embarked in a large canoe, and,

after promising to return at the expiration of twelve hundred moons, with a white face and on a floating island, he put out to sea, and was never heard of more.

This tradition, it appears, had been piously handed down from family to family. The natives of Hawai—who are not more extravagant in the matter of idols than some nations who boast a larger amount of civilization, but who do not destroy them so often—enrolled Rono amongst the list of their divinities. An image of him was set up, sacrifices were instituted in his honor. Every year the day of his departure was kept sacred, and devoted to religious ceremonies. The twelfth hundred moon had just set, when a large boat appeared in the bay, and a man came ashore. The high priest of the temple, Raou, and his daughter, On La, priestess of Rono, solemnly declared that the man in question was Rono himself, who had returned at the precise time named, and in the manner he promised.

It was, therefore, clear from this statement that Willis was to be henceforward Rono the Great.

Jack was rather pleased than otherwise to learn that he was the companion of a real live divinity. It assured him, in the first place, that the danger of his being converted into a stew or a fricassee was not imminent. He did not forget, however, that the consequences might be perilous if, by any chance, the illusion ceased; for he knew that the greater the height from which a man falls, the less the mercy shown to him when he is down. As soon, therefore, as the ceremonies had a little relaxed, and Willis was left some freedom of action, Jack went forward, and knelt before him in his turn.

"O sublime Rono," said he, "I know now why your nose has escaped all the rubbings that mine has had to undergo."

"Do you?" said Willis; "glad to hear it, for I am as much in the dark as ever."

Jack then related to him the fabulous legend he had just heard.

After a while, Willis shook off his *entourage* as gently as possible, and succeeded in getting out of the temple. Accompanied by Jack, he proceeded towards the shore, receiving, as he went, the adoration of the people. The route was strewn with fruit, cocoa-nuts, and pigs, and the natives were highly delighted when any of their offerings were accepted by the deified Rono.

The islanders appeared mild, docile, and intelligent, notwithstanding the singular delusion that possessed them. Living from day to day, they were, doubtless, ignorant of those continual cares and calculations for the future that in the old world pursue us even into the hours of sleep. Were they happier in consequence? Yes, if the child is happier than the man, and if we admit that we often loose in tranquillity and happiness what we gain in knowledge and perfection: yes, if happiness is not exclusively attached to certain peoples and certain climates; yes, if it is true that, with contentment, happiness is everywhere to be found.

The houses of the Hawaians are singular structures, and scarcely can be called dwellings. They consist of three rows of posts, two on each side and one in the middle, the whole covered with a slanting roof, but without any kind of wall whatever.

They do not bury their dead, but swing them up in a sort of hammock, abundantly supplied with provisions. It is supposed that this is done with a view to enable the souls of the departed to take their flight more readily to heaven. The practice, consequently, seems to indicate that the natives possess a confused idea of a future state. When a child dies, flowers are placed in the hammock along with the provisions—a touch of the nature common to us all. They express deep grief by inflicting wounds upon their faces with a shark's tooth; and, when they feel themselves in danger of dying, they cut off a joint of the little finger to appease the anger of the Divinity. There was scarcely one of the adult islanders who was not mutilated in this way.

Though the worshippers of the great Rono appeared gentle and peaceable enough, there were to be seen here and there a human jaw-bone, seemingly fresh, with the teeth entire, suspended over the entrances to the huts. These ghastly objects sent a shudder quivering through

Jack's frame, and made Willis aware that it would not be advisable rashly to throw off his sacred character.

As it was now late, and as they knew that Fritz would be uneasy about them, they put off laying in their stock of water till next day. Jack told the prime minister that the great Rono would be prepared to receive their majesties whenever they chose to visit him. This done, Willis and his companion seated themselves in the canoe, and rowed out to the pinnace.

"God be thanked, you have returned in safety!" cried Fritz; "I never was so uneasy in the whole course of my life."

"Well, brother, we have not been without our anxieties as well, and had we not happened to have had a divinity amongst us, we might not have come off scathless."

Jack then related their adventures, which gradually brought a smile to the pale lips of Fritz.

"But the water?" inquired Fritz, after he had heard the story.

"Oh, water; they offered us something to drink on shore that will prevent us being thirsty for a month to come, but we shall see to that to-morrow."

Towards dark, some fireworks were discharged on board the pinnace, by way of demonstrating that Willis's pipe was not the only fiery terror the great Rono had at his command.

Early next morning a flotilla of canoes were observed rounding one of the points that formed the bay. The one in advance was larger than the others, and was evidently the trunk of a large tree hollowed out. Jack's new friend, the Portuguese, hailed the pinnace, and announced the King and Queen of Hawai, who thereupon scrambled into the pinnace. His majesty King Toubowrai had probably felt it incumbent upon himself to do honor to the illustrious Rono, for he wore an old uniform coat, very likely the produce of a wreck, through the sleeves of which the angular knobs of his copper-colored elbows projected. He did not seem very much at his ease in this garment, which contrasted oddly with the tight-fitting tattooed skin that served him for pantaloons.

"His wife, Queen Tonico, princess-like was half stifled in a thick blanket or mat of cocoa-nut fibre. Her ears were heavily laden with teeth and ornaments of various kinds, made out of bone, mother of pearl, and tortoise-shell. Her nails were two or three inches long; and, to judge by the number of finger-joints that were wanting, she was either troubled with delicate nerves, or was slightly hypochondriac.

The royal pair were accompanied by a band of music: fortunately, this remained in the regal barge. It consisted of a flute with four holes, a nondescript instrument, seemingly made of stones; a drum made out of the hollow trunk of a tree, covered at each end with skin, of what kind it is needless to inquire. The sounds emitted by this orchestra were of an ear-rending nature, and of a kind graphically termed by the Germans Katzenmusik.

"Illustrious Rono," cried Jack, "for goodness sake, tell these gentlemen you are not a lover of sweet sounds."

"Belay there!" roared Willis.

This command, however, had no effect; the artists continued thumping and blowing away as before. Willis, thinking to make himself better heard, placed his hands on his mouth, and roared the same order through them. This action seemed to be received as a mark of approbation, for the noise became absolutely terrific.

"No use," said Willis: "I can make nothing of them. You try what you can do."

"Very good," said Jack, lighting what is technically termed an *artichoke*, but better known as a zig-zag cracker; "if they do not understand English, perhaps they may comprehend pyrotechnics."

The artichoke was thrown into the royal barge. At first there was only a slight whiz, finally it gave an angry bound and leaped into the midst of the musicians. Startled, they tried to get out of its way; but they were no sooner at what they thought to be a safe distance, than the thing was amongst them again. Their majesties, who were just then engaged in kissing the Rono's feet, started up in alarm; but when they saw the danger did not menace themselves, they burst into a hearty laugh at the antics of their suite.

This episode over, and the orchestra silenced, the Sovereign of Hawai proceeded to inspect the pinnace. He expressed his delight every now and then by uttering the syllables "*ta-ta.*" Fritz handed one of those shaving glasses to the Queen that lengthen the objects they reflect. This astonished her Majesty vastly, and caused her to *ta-ta* at a great rate. She looked behind the mirror, turned **it** upside down, and at last, when she felt assured that it was the royal person it caricatured, she commenced measuring her cheeks to account for the extraordinary disproportion.

They next all sat down to a repast that was spread on deck. Their Majesties observing Rono use a fork, did so likewise; but though they stuck a piece of meat on the end of it, and held it in one hand, they continued carrying the viands to their mouths with the other. At the conclusion of the feast, Willis took a pinch of snuff out of a canister. Their Majesties insisted upon doing so likewise. Willis handed them the canister, and they filled their noses with the treacherous powder. Then followed a duet of sneezing, accompanied with facial contortions. The royal personages thinking, probably, that they were poisoned, leaped into the sea like a couple of frogs, and swam to the royal barge.

" Holloa, sire," cried Jack, " where are you off to?"

This was answered by the barge paddling away rapidly towards land. Hitherto, the whole affair had been a farce; but now the natives, who had collected in great numbers along the shore, seeing their king and queen leap into the water with a terrified air, supposed that an attempt had been made to cut short their royal lives, and, under this impression, discharged a cloud of arrows at the pinnace, and matters began to assume a serious aspect.

" What!" exclaimed Jack, " shooting at the great Rono!"

" That," said Fritz, " only proves they are men like ourselves. He who is covered with incense one day, is very often immolated the next."

" And that simply because Rono treated Mr. and Mrs.

What's-their-names to a pinch of snuff. Serve them right to discharge the contents of the four-pounder amongst them."

"No, no," cried Willis; "the worthy people are, perhaps, fond of their king and queen."

"Worthy people or not," said Fritz, drawing out an arrow that had sunk into the capstan, "it is very likely that if this dart had hit one of us, there would only have been two instead of three in the crew of the pinnace."

"Well," said Willis, "Master Jack thought the voyage rather dull; now something has turned up to relieve the monotony of his log."

"We are still without fresh water though, Willis; I wish you could say that had turned up as well."

"It will be prudent to go in search of that somewhere else now," said Willis, unfurling the sails. "Fortunately the wind is fresh, and we can make considerable headway before night."

As they steered gently out of the bay a second cloud of arrows was sent after them, but this time they fell short.

"The belief in Rono is about to be seriously compromised," remarked Fritz; "I should advise the priestess to retire into private life."

"Impossible."

"Why?"

"Because she is too fat to live in an ordinary house, she could only breathe in a temple. But, O human vicissitudes!" added Jack, rolling himself up in a sail after the manner of the Roman senators; "behold Rono the Great banished from his country, and compelled to go and pillow his head on a foreign sail, like Marius at Minturnus — like Coriolanus amongst the Volcians — like Hannibal at the house of Antiochus — like Alcibiades at the castle of Grunium in Phrygia, given to him out of charity by the benevolent Pharnabazus, and in which he was burnt alive by his countrymen — like Cimon, voted into exile by ballot and universal suffrage — like Aristides, whom the people got tired of hearing called the Just, and many others."

"Who are all these personages?" inquired Willis.

"They were worthies of another age," replied Fritz;

"very excellent men in their way, and you are in no way dishonored by being numbered amongst them."

"Yesterday," continued Jack, "an entire people were upon their knees before you; they offered up sacrifices, and poured out incense on their altars for you; fruit and pigs were scattered in heaps, like flowers, upon your path; the crowd were prostrated by the fumes of your pipe. To-day — alas, the change! — a cloud of arrows, and not a single glass of cold water!"

"That gives you an opportunity of quenching your thirst with the nectar offered to you yesterday," said Fritz; "as for myself, I have no such resource."

"Yes, that was a posset to quench one's thirst withal; I only wish I had a cupful to give you. I do not regret having had an opportunity of becoming acquainted with the people though. They have enabled me to rectify some erroneous notions I formerly entertained. If, for example, I were to ask you what air consists of? you would, no doubt, reply that is a compound body made of oxygen and hydrogen or azote, in the proportion of twenty-one of the one to seventy-nine of the other."

"Yes, most undoubtedly."

"Well, such is not the case; there are other elements in the air besides these."

"If you mean that the air accidentally, or even permanently, holds in solution a certain quantity of water, or a portion of carbonic acid gas, and possibly some particles of dust arising from terrestrial bodies, then I grant your premises."

"No; what I mean is, that the air of Hawai is composed of three distinct elements."

"Possibly; but if so, the air in question is not known to chemists."

"These three elements are oxygen, hydrogen, and insects."

"Ah, insects! I might have fancied you were driving at some hypothesis of that sort."

"I intend to communicate this discovery to the first learned society we fall in with."

"In the Pacific Ocean?"

" Yes ; there or elsewhere."

" I always understood," observed Willis, " that air was a sort of cloud, one and indivisible."

" A cloud if you like, Willis ; but do you know the weight of it you carry on your shoulders ? "

" Well, it cannot be very great, otherwise I should feel it."

" What do you say to a ton or so, old fellow ? "

" If you wish me to believe that, you will have to explain how, where, when, why, and wherefore."

" Very good, Willis ; you have bathed sometimes ?"

" Yes, certainly."

" In the sea ? "

" Yes."

" Do you know what water weighs ? "

" No, but I know that it is heavy."

" Well, a square yard of air weighs two pounds and a half, but a square yard of water weighs two thousand pounds. Now, can you calculate the weight of the water that is on your back and pressing on your sides when you swim ? "

" No, I cannot."

" You are not sufficiently up in arithmetic to do that, Willis ? "

" No."

" Nor am I either, Willis ; but let me ask you how it is that the waves do not carry you along with them ? "

" Because one wave neutralises the effect of another."

" Very good ; but how is it that these ponderous waves, coming down upon you, do not crush you to atoms by their mere weight ? "

" Well, I suppose that liquids do not operate in the same way as solids : perhaps there is something in our bodies that counterbalances the effect of the water."

" Very likely ; and if such be the case as regards water, may it not be so also as regards air ?"

" But I do not feel air ; whereas, if I go into water, I not only feel it, but taste it sometimes, and I cannot force my way through it without considerable exertion."

"That is because you are organized to live in air and not in water. You ask the smallest sprat or sticklebake if it does not, in the same way feel the air obstruct its progress."

"But would the stickleback answer me, Master Fritz?"

"Why not, if it is polite and well bred?"

"By the way, Willis," inquired Jack, "do you ever recollect having lived without breathing?"

"Can't say I do."

"Very well, then; had you felt the weight of the air at any given moment, it must have produced an impression you never felt before; but you have not, because circumstances have never varied. A sensation supposes a contrast, whilst, ever since you existed, you have always been subject to atmospheric pressure."

"Ah, now I begin to get at the gist of your argument. You mean, for example, that I would never have appreciated the delicate flavor of Maryland or Havanna, had I not been accustomed to smoke the cabbage-leaf manufactured in Whitechapel."

"Precisely so; and take for another example the farm of Antisana, which is situated about midway up the Cordilleras, mountains of South America. When travellers, arriving there from the summits which are covered with perpetual snow, meet others arriving from the plain where the heat is intense, those that descend are invariably bathed in perspiration, whilst those that have come up are shivering with cold and covered with furs. The reason of this is, that we cannot feel warm till we have been cold, and *vice versâ.*"

"Our bodies," resumed Fritz, "however much the thermometer descends, never mark less than thirty-five degrees above zero. In winter the skin shrinks, and becomes a bad conductor of heat from without; but, at the same time, does not allow so much gas and vapor to escape from within. In summer, on the contrary, the skin dilates and allows perspiration to form, a process that consumes a considerable amount of latent heat. Starting from this principle, it has been calculated that a man, breathing twenty times in a minute, generates as much heat in

twenty-four hours as would boil a bucket of water taken
at zero."

"If means could be found," remarked Jack, "to furnish
him with a boiler, by fixing a piston here and a pipe there
man might be converted into one of the machines we were
talking about the other day."

"Were I disposed to philosophize," added Fritz, "I
might prove to you that for a long time men have been
little else than mere machines."

Before night they had run about thirty miles further to
the north-east, without seeing any thing beyond a formidable bluff, guarded by a fringe of breakers, that would
soon have swallowed up the *Mary* had she ventured to
reach the land. It was necessary however to obtain fresh
water at any price before they resumed their voyage.

It was to be feared that all the islanders of the Pacific
were not in expectation of a great Rono, consequently
Willis suggested that it would be as well to search for an
uninhabited spot. The only question was, how long they
might have to search before they succeeded; for they
knew that there were plenty of small islands in these
latitudes unencumbered by savages, and furnished with
pools and springs of water.

Night at length closed in upon them, and with it came
a dense mist, that enveloped the *Mary* as if in a triple
veil of muslin.

"Willis," inquired Jack, "what difference is there
between a mist and a cloud?"

"None that I know of," replied the Pilot, "except that
a cloud which we are in is mist, and mist that we are not
in is a cloud. And now, my lads," he added, "you may
turn in, for I intend to take the first watch."

Before turning in, however, all three joined in a short
prayer. The young men had not yet forgotten the pious
precepts of their father. Prayer is beautiful everywhere,
but nowhere is it so beautiful as on the open sea, with
infinity above and an abyss beneath. Then, when all is
silent save the roar of the waves and the howling of the
winds, it is sublime to hear the humble voice of the sailor
murmuring, "Star of the night, pray for us!"

That night the star of the night did pray for the three voyagers, for the rays of the moon burst through the darkness and the mist, and fell upon a long line of reefs under the lee of the pinnace. Had they held on their course a few minutes longer, our story would have been ended.

CHAPTER XXI.

THE glimpse of moonshine only lasted a second, but it
was sufficient to light up the valley of the shadow of death.
All around was again enveloped in obscurity. The moon,
like a modest benefactor who hides himself from those to
whose wants he has ministered, concealed itself behind
its screen of blackness.

The pinnace was thrown into stays, and they resolved
to lie-to till daybreak. There might be rocks to windward
as well as to leeward; at all events, they felt that their
safest course lay in maintaining, as far as possible, their
actual position; and, after having returned thanks for
their almost miraculous escape, they made the usual arrangements for passing the night.

Next morning they found themselves in the midst of a
labyrinth of rocks, from which, with the help of Providence, they succeeded in extricating themselves. The
rocks, or rather reefs, amongst which they were entangled,
are very common in these seas. As they are scarcely
visible at high water, they are extremely dangerous, and
often baffle the skill of the most expert navigator.

Whilst Willis steered the pinnace amongst the islands
and rocks of the Hawaian Archipelago, Fritz kept a look-
out for savages, fresh water, and eligible landing-places.
And Jack, after having posted up his log, set about in-
diting a letter for home.

"The voyage," said he, "has lately been so prolific in
adventure, that I scarcely know where to begin."

"Begin by saluting them all round," suggested Fritz.

"But, brother of mine, that is usually done at the end of the letter," objected Jack.

"What then? you can repeat the salutations at the end, and you might also, for that matter, put them in the middle as well."

"I have written lots of letters on board ship for my comrades," remarked Willis, "and I invariably commenced by saying — *I take a pen in my hand to let you know I am well, hoping you are the same.*"

"What else could you take in your hand for such a purpose, O Rono?" inquired Jack.

"Sometimes, after this preamble, I added, '*but I am afraid.*'"

"I thought you old salts were never afraid of anything, short of the Flying Dutchman."

"Yes; but the letters I put that in were for young lubbers, who, instead of sending home half their pay, were writing for extra supplies, and were naturally in great fear that their requests would be refused."

"I scarcely think I shall adopt that style, Willis, even though it were recognized by the navy regulations."

"Do you think the pigeon will find its way with the letter from here to New Switzerland?" inquired Willis.

"I have no doubt about that," replied Fritz, "it naturally returns to its nest and its affections. If you had wings, would you not fly straight off in the direction of the Bass Rock or Ailsa Craig, to hunt up your old armchair?"

"Don't speak of it; I feel my heart go pit-pat when I think of home, sweet home."

"So do the birds. When they soften the grain before they throw it into the maw of their fledgelings — when they fly off and return laden with midges to their nests — when they tear the down from their breasts to protect their eggs and their young, do you think their hearts do not beat as well as yours?"

"But all that is said to be instinct."

. "Heart or instinct, where is the difference? The Abbé Spallanzani saw two swallows that were carried to

Milan return to Pavia in fifteen minutes, and the distance
between the two cities is seven leagues."

"That I can easily believe."

"When you see a little, insignificant bird flying backwards and forwards, perching on one branch and hopping
off to another, whistling, carolling, perching here and
there, you think that it has no cares, that it does not reflect, and that it does not love!"

"Well, I have heard in my time a great many wonderful stories of robin-redbreasts and jenny-wrens, but I always understood that they were intended only to amuse
little boys and girls."

"You consider, doubtless, that a field-sparrow is not a
creature of much importance; but do you know that he
consumes half a bushel of corn annually?"

"If that is his only merit, the farmers, I dare say,
would be glad to get rid of him."

"But it is not his only merit. What do you think of
his killing three thousand insects a week."

"That is more to the purpose. But, to return to the
pigeon, supposing it is possible for it to find its way, how
long do you suppose it will take to get there?"

"It is estimated that birds of passage fly over two hundred miles a day, if they keep on the wing for six hours."

"Two hundred miles in six hours is fast sailing, anyhow."

"Swallows have been seen in Senegal on the 9th of
October, that is, eight or nine days after they leave Europe; and that journey they repeat every year."

"They must surely make some preparations for such a
lengthy excursion."

"When the period of departure approaches, they collect
together in troops on the chimneys or roofs of houses, and
on the tops of trees. During this operation, they keep up
an incessant cry, which brings families of them from all
quarters. The young ones try the strength of their wings
under the eyes of the parents. Finally, they make some
strategic dispositions, and elect a chief."

"You talk of the swallows as if they were an army preparing for battle, with flags flying, trumpets sounding, and ready to march at the word of command."

"The resemblance between flocks of birds and serried masses of men in martial array is striking. Wild ducks, swans, and cranes fly in a kind of regimental order; their battalions assume the form of a triangle or wedge, so as to cut through the air with greater facility, and diminish the resistance it presents to their flight.

" But how do you know it is for that ? "

" What else could it be for ? The leader gives notice, by a peculiar cry, of the route it is about to take. This cry is repeated by the flock, as if to say that they will follow, and keep the direction indicated. When they meet with a bird of prey whose attacks they may have to repulse, the ranks fall in so as to present a solid phalanx to the enemy."

" If they had a commissariat in the rear and a few sappers in front, the resemblance would be complete."

" If a storm arises," continued Fritz, without noticing Willis's commentary, "they lower their flight and approach the ground."

" Forgotten their umbrellas, perhaps."

" When they make a halt, outposts are established to keep a look out while the troop sleeps."

" And, in cases of alarm, the outposts fire and fall in as a matter of course."

" Great Rono," said Jack, " you are become a downright quiz. I have finished my letter whilst you have been discussing the poultry," he added, handing the pen to his brother, "and it only waits your postscriptum." Fritz having added a few lines, the epistle was sealed, and was then attached to one of the pigeons, which, after hovering a short time round the pinnace, took a flight upwards and disappeared in the clouds.

They were now in sight of a large island, which bore no traces of habitation. There was a heavy surf beating on the shore, but the case was urgent, so Willis and Jack embarked in the canoe, and, after a hard fight with the waves, landed on the beach.

Each of them were armed with a double-barrelled rifle,

and furnished with a boatswain's whistle. The whistle
was to signal the discovery of water, and a rifle shot was
to bring them together in case of danger. These arrangements being made, Jack proceeded in the direction of a
thicket, which stood at the distance of some hundred yards
from the shore. He had no sooner reached the cover in
the vicinity of the trees than he was pounced upon by two
ferocious-looking savages. They gave him no time to level
his rifle or to draw a knife. One of his captors held his
hands firmly behind his back, whilst the other dragged him
towards the wood. At this moment the Pilot's whistle
rang sharply through the air. This put an end to any
hopes that Jack might have entertained of being rescued
through that means. Had he sounded the whistle, it would
only have led Willis to suppose that he had heard the signal, and was on his way to join him.

Poor Jack judged, from the aspect of the men who held
him, that they were cannibals, and consequently that his
fate was sealed, for if his surmises were correct, there was
little chance of the wretches relinquishing their prey.
Jack had often amused himself at the expense of the
anthropophagi, but here he was actually within their grasp.
Though death terminates the sorrows and the sufferings of
man, and though the result is the same in whatever shape
it comes, yet there are circumstances which cause its
approach to be regarded with terror and dismay. In one's
bed, exhausted by old age or disease, the lips only open to
give utterance to a sigh of pain; life, then, is a burden
that is laid down without reluctance; we glide imperceptibly and almost voluntarily into eternity.

At twenty years of age, however, when we are full of
health and ardor, the case is very different. Then we are
at the threshold of hope and happiness; our illusions have
not had time to fade, the future is a brilliant meteor
sparkling in sunshine. At that age our seas are always
calm, and the rocks and shoals are all concealed. Our
barks glide jauntily along, the sailors sing merrily, the
perils are shrouded in romance, and the flag flutters gaily
in the breeze. Then life is not abandoned without a tear
of regret.

To die in the midst of one's friends is not to quit them entirely. They come to see us through the marble or stone in which we are shrouded. It is another thing to have no other sepulchre than the æsophagus of a cannibal. How the recollections of the past darted into Jack's mind! He felt that he loved those whom he was on the point of leaving a thousand times more than he did before. What would he not have given for the power to bid them one last adieu? The idea of quitting life thus was horrible.

It was in vain that he tried to shake off his assailants; his adolescent strength was as nothing in the arms of steel that bound him. He saw that he was powerless in their hands, and at length ceased making any further attempts to escape.

The savages, finding that he had relaxed his struggles, commenced to rifle and strip him. They tore off his upper garments, and discovered a small locket, containing a medallion of his mother, which the unfortunate youth wore round his neck. This prize, which the savages no doubt regarded as a talisman of some sort, they both desired to possess. They quarrelled about it, and commenced fighting over it. Jack's hands were left at liberty. In an instant he had seized his rifle. He ran a few paces back, turned, took deliberate aim at the most powerful of his adversaries, who, with a shriek, fell to the ground. The other savage, scared by the report of the shot and its effects upon his companion, took to flight, but he carried off the locket with him.

Jack had now regained his courage. He felt, like Telemachus in the midst of his battles, that God was with him, and he flew, perhaps imprudently, after the fugitive. Seeing, however, that he had no chance with him as regards speed, he discharged his second rifle. The shot did not take effect, but the report brought the savage to his knees. The frightened wretch pressed his hands together in an attitude of supplication. Jack stopped at a little distance, and, by an imperious gesture, gave him to understand that he wanted the locket. The sign was comprehended, for the savage laid the talisman on the ground.

"Now," said Jack, "in the name of my mother I give you your life."

By another sign, he signified to the man that he was at liberty, which he no sooner understood than he vanished like an arrow.

Great was the consternation of Fritz when he heard the reports; he feared that the whole island was in commotion, and that both his brother and the Pilot were surrounded by a legion of copper-colored devils. From the conformation of the coast he could see nothing, and, like Sisiphus on his rock, he was tied by imperious necessity to his post.

The Pilot, on hearing the first shot, ran to the spot, and both he and Jack arrived at the same instant, where the savage lay bleeding on the ground.

"You are safe and sound, I hope?" said Willis, anxiously.

"With the exception of some slight contusions, and the loss of my clothes, thank God, I am all right, Willis."

"We are born to bad luck, it seems."

"Say rather we are the spoilt children of Providence. I have just passed through the eye of a needle."

"Is this the only savage you have seen?"

"No, there were two of them; and, to judge from their actions, I verily believe the rascals intended to eat me. As for this one, he is more frightened than hurt."

And so it was, he had escaped with some slugs in his shoulders; but he seemed, by the contortions of his face, to think that he was dying.

"Fortunately," said Jack, "my rifle was not loaded with ball. I should be sorry to have the death of a human being on my conscience."

"Well," said Willis, "I am not naturally cruel, but, beset as you have been, I should have shot both the fellows without the slightest compunction."

"Still," said Jack, giving the wounded savage a mouthful of brandy, "we ought to have mercy on the vanquished —they are men like ourselves, at all events."

"Yes, they have flesh and bone, arms, legs, hands, and

teeth like us; but I doubt whether they are possessed of souls and hearts."

"The chances are that they possess both, Willis; only neither the one nor the other has been trained to regard the things of this world in a proper light. Their notions as to diet, for example, arise from ignorance as to what substances are fit and proper for human food."

"As you like," said Willis; "but let us be off; there may be more of them lurking about."

"What! again without water?."

"No, this time I have taken care to fill the casks; the canoe is laden with fresh water."

"Fritz must be very uneasy about us; but this man may die if we leave him so."

"Very likely," said the Pilot; "but that is no business of ours."

"Good bye," said Jack, lifting up the wounded savage, and propping him against a tree; "I may never have the pleasure of seeing you again, and am sorry to leave you in such a plight; but it will be a lesson for you, and a hint to be a little more hospitable for the future in your reception of strangers."

The savage raised his eyes for an instant, as if to thank Jack for his good offices, and then relapsed into his former attitude of dejection.

Twenty minutes later the canoe was aboard the pinnace.

"Fritz," said Jack, throwing his arms round his brother's neck, "I am delighted to see you again; half an hour ago I had not the shadow of a chance of ever beholding you more."

CHAPTER XXII.

THE UTILITY OF ADVERSITY — AN ENCOUNTER — THE HOBOKEN
— BILL ALIAS BOB.

A LIGHT but favorable breeze carried them away from
land, and they were once again on the open sea.   Willis,
after a prolonged investigation of the sun's position, taken
in relation to some observations he had made the day
before, concluded that the best course to pursue, under
existing circumstances, was to steer for the Marian Islands.*
In addition to the distance they had originally to traverse,
all the way lost during the storm was now before them.
As regards provisions, they had little to fear; they could
rely upon falling in with a boobie or sea-cow occasionally,
and fresh fish were to be had at any time.   Their supply
of water, however, gave them some uneasiness, for the
quantity was limited, and they might be retarded by calms
and contrary winds.   The chances of meeting a European
ship were too slender to enter for anything into their
calculations.

"It appears to me," said Jack, one beautiful evening,
when they were some hundreds of miles from any habit-
able spot, "that, having escaped so many dangers, the
watchful eye of Providence must be guarding us from
evil."

"Very possibly," replied Fritz; "one of the early
chroniclers of the Christian Church says that Lazarus,
whom our Saviour resuscitated at the gates of Jerusalem,
became afterwards one of the most popular preachers of
Christianity, and in consequence the Jews regarded him
with implacable hatred."

"But what, in all the world, has that to do with the
Pacific Ocean?" inquired Jack.

* Sometimes called the *Ladrones* or *Archipelago of Saint Lazarus.*

"Very little with the Pacific in particular, but a great deal with the ocean in general. Lazarus, his sisters, and some of his friends, were thrown into prison, tried, and condemned."

" And stoned or crucified," added Jack.

" No ; the high priest of the temple had a great variety of punishments on hand besides these. He resolved to expose them to the mercy of the waves, without provisions, and without a mast, sail, or rudder."

"Thank goodness, we are not so badly off as that."

" *He*, for whom Lazarus suffered, and who is the same that nourishes the birds of the air and feeds the beasts of the field, watched over the forlorn craft ; under his guidance, the little colony of martyrs were wafted in safety to the fertile coasts of Provence. They landed, according to the tradition, at Marseilles, of whom Lazarus was the first bishop, and has always been the patron saint. Who knows? — the same good. fortune may perhaps await us."

" We are not martyrs."

"True ; but Providence does not always measure its favors by the merits of those upon whom they are bestowed — misfortune, alone, is often a sufficient claim ; so it is well for us to be patient under a little suffering, for sweet often is the reward."

" A little hardship, now and then," added Jack, "is, no doubt, salutary. The Italians say : ' *Le avversità sono per l'animo cio ch' è un temporale per l'aria.*' Suffering teaches us to prize health and happiness ; were there no such things as pain and grief, we should be apt to regard these blessings as valueless, and to estimate them as our legitimate rights. For my own part, I was never so happy in my whole life as when I embraced you the other day, after escaping out of the clutches of the savages."

" There are many charms in life that are almost without alloy : the perfume of flowers — music — the singing of birds — the riches of art — the intercourse of society — the delights of the family circle — the treasures of imagination and memory. Some of the most beneficent gifts of Nature we only know the existence of when we are deprived of them; occasional darkness alone enables us to appreciate the unspeakable blessing of light. Man has a multitude of enjoyments at his command; but so many sweets would be utterly insipid without a few bitters."

"The rheumatism, for example," said Willis, rubbing his shoulders.

"Many enjoyments," continued Fritz, "spring from the heart alone; the affections, benevolence, love of order, a sense of the beautiful, of truth, of honesty, and of justice."

"On the other hand," said Willis, "there are dishonesty, injustice, disappointment, and blighted hopes; but you are too young to know much about these. When you have seen as much of the world on sea and on land as I have, perhaps you will be disposed to look at life from another point of view. In old stagers like myself, the tender emotions are all used up; it is only when we are amongst you youngsters that we forget the present in the past; when we see you struggling with difficulties, it recalls our own trials to our mind, rouses in us sentiments of commiseration, and softens the asperities of our years."

"According to you, then," said Fritz, levelling his rifle at a petrel, "the misfortunes of the one constitute the happiness of the other?"

"Unquestionably," said Jack; "for instance, if you miss that bird, so much the worse for you, and so much the better for the petrel."

"It is very rarely, brother, that you do not interrupt a serious conversation with some nonsense."

"Keep your temper, Fritz; I am about to propose a serious question myself. How is it that the petrel you are aiming at does not come and perch itself quietly on the barrel of your rifle?"

"Jack, Jack, you are incorrigible."

"Did you ever see a hare or a pheasant come and stare you in the face when you were going to shoot it?"

"Stunsails and tops!" cried Willis, "if I do not see something stranger than that staring us in the face."

"The sea-serpent, perhaps," said Jack.

"I thought it was a sea-bird at first," said Willis,

"but they do not increase in size the longer you look at them."

"They naturally appear to increase as they approach," observed Fritz.

"Yes, but the increase must have a limit, and I never saw a bird with such singular upper-works before. Just take a cast of the glass yourself, Master Fritz."

"Halls of Æolus!" cried Fritz, "these wings are sails."

"So I thought!" exclaimed Willis, throwing his sou'-wester into the air, and uttering a loud hurrah.

"If it is the *Nelson*," said Jack, "it would be a singular encounter."

"The *Nelson!*" sighed Willis, "in the latitude of Hawai; no, that is impossible."

"She is bearing down upon us," said Fritz.

"Just let me see a moment whether I can make out her figure-head," said Willis. "Aye, aye!"

"Can you make it out?"

"No; but, from the sheer of the hull, I think the ship is British built."

"Thank God!" exclaimed both the young men.

"Yes, you may say 'Thank God;' but, if it turns out to be a man-of-war, I must report myself on board, and I doubt whether my story will go down with the captain."

"But if it is the *Nelson?*" insisted Jack.

"Aye, aye; the *Nelson*," replied Willis, "is not going to turn up here to oblige us, you may take my word for that."

"I have better eyes than you, Willis; just let me see if I can make her out. No, impossible; nothing but the hull and sails."

"It is just possible," persisted Jack, "that the *Nelson* may have been detained at the Cape, and afterwards blown out of her course like ourselves."

"All I can say is," replied Willis, "that if Captain Littlestone be on board that ship, it will make me the happiest man that ever mixed a ration of grog. But these things only turn up in novels, so it is no use talking."

"She has hoisted a flag at the mizzen," cried Fritz.

"Can you make it out?"

"Well, let me see — yes, it must be so."

"What, the Union Jack?" cried Willis.

"No, a red ground striped with blue."

"The United States, as I am a sinner!" cried Willis. "Well, it might have been worse. We can go to America; there are surgeons there as well as in Europe — at all events, we can get a ship there for England. But let me see, we must hoist a bit of bunting; unfortunately, we have only British colors aboard, and I am afraid they are not in particularly high favor with our Yankee cousins just now."

"Never mind a flag," said Fritz.

"Oh, that will never do, they have hoisted a flag and are waiting a reply. But let me see," added Willis, rummaging amongst some stores, "here is one of our Shark's Island signals — that, I think, will puzzle the Yankee considerably."

The Pilot's signal was answered by a gun, the report of which rang through the air. The strange ship's sails were thrown back and she stood still. A boat then put off with a young man in uniform and six rowers on board.

"Pinnace ahoy!" cried the officer through a speaking trumpet, "who are you?"

"Shipwrecked mariners," cried Fritz, in reply.

"What is the name of your craft?"

"The *Mary*."

"What country?"

"Switzerland."

"I was not aware that Switzerland was a naval power," observed Willis.

"She has no seaport," said Jack, "but she has a fleet — of row boats."

"Where do you hail from?" inquired the officer.

"New Switzerland."

"That gentleman is very curious," observed Jack.

Here a silence of some minutes ensued; the officer seemed at fault in his geography.

"Where away?" at last resounded from the trumpet.

"Bound for Europe," replied Fritz.

This reply elicited an expression of doubt, accompanied

with such a tremendous exjurgation as made both Fritz and Jack almost shrink into the hold.

A few minutes after the Yankee in command stepped on board, and explanations were entered into that perfectly satisfied the republican officer. He continued, however, to eye Willis curiously.

The *Hoboken*, for that was the name of the strange ship, was an American cruiser, carrying twelve ship guns and a long paixhan. She was attached to the Chinese station, but had recently obtained information that war had been declared between England and the States. She was now making her way to the west by a circuitous route to avoid the British squadron, and, at the same time, with a view to pick up an English merchantman or two.

Fritz and Jack being citizens of a sister republic, and subjects of a neutral power, were received on board with a hearty welcome, and with the hospitality due to their interesting position. Willis also received some attention, and was treated with all the courtesy that could be shown to the native of an enemy's country.

The pinnace was taken in tow till the young men made up their minds as to the course they would adopt. A free passage to the States was kindly offered to them, and even pressed upon their acceptance; but the captain left the matter entirely to their own option.

Fritz and Jack were delighted with the warmth of their reception; and, after being so long cooped up in the narrow quarters of the pinnace, looked upon the Yankee cruiser, with its men and officers in uniform, as a sort of floating palace. The *Nelson* having been only a despatch-boat, it had given them but an indifferent idea of a man-of-war. On board the Yankee everything was kept in apple-pie order. Discipline was maintained with martinet strictness. The fittings shone like a mirror. The brass cappings glistened in the sun. Complicated rolls of cable were profusely scattered about, but without confusion. The deck always seemed as fresh as if it had been planked the day before. The sails overhead seemed to obey the word of command of their own accord. The boatswain's whistle seemed to act upon the men like electricity. The seamen's cabins, six feet long by six feet broad, in which a hammock, locker, and washing apparatus were conveniently stowed, were something very different from the accommodation on board the pinnace. These things were regarded by Fritz and Jack with great interest; and nowhere is the genius of man so brilliantly displayed as on board a well-appointed ship of war.

The young men, however, when they sat down to dinner in the captain's cabin, and beheld a long table flanked with cushioned seats, commanded at each end by arm-chairs, the side-board plentifully garnished with plate and crystal of various kinds, fastened with copper nails to prevent damage from the ship's pitching, they did not reflect that they were in the crater of a volcano, and that two paces from where they sat there was powder enough to blow the ship and all its crew up into the air.

They were likewise highly amused by the perpetual "guessing," "calculating," "reckoning," and inexhaustible curiosity of the crew; but their admiration of the ship, her guns, her stores, and her tackle, were boundless; they felt that their pinnace was a mere toy in comparison. The urbanity of the officers also was a source of much gratification to them; Jack even declared that all the civilization of Europe had been shipped on board the *Hoboken*, and in so far as that was concerned, they had no occasion to go on much further.

The object of this expedition, however, was a surgeon. There was one on board. Would he go to New Switzerland? Jack determined to try, and accordingly he walked straight off to the personage in question.

"Doctor," said he, "would you do myself and my brother a great favor?"

"Certainly; and, if it is in my power, you may consider it done."

"Well, will you embark with us for New Switzerland?"

"For what purpose, my friend?"

"My mother is laboring under a malady, which there is every reason to fear is cancer."

"And suppose a fever was to break out in this ship,

whilst I am absent, what do you imagine is to become of the officers and crew?"

"There are no symptoms of disease on board; but my mother is dying."

"You forget, young man, that disease may make its appearance at any moment. There are many sons on board whose lives are as dear to their mothers as your mother's is to you, and for every one of these lives I am officially accountable."

Jack hung down his head and was silent.

"No, my good friend, it is impossible for me to grant such a request; but, from what I know of your history, and the means at your command, you may be able to obtain the services of a competent medical man. I would, therefore, recommend you to abandon your boat, and proceed with us to our destination."

After a lengthy consultation, the two brothers and Willis determined to adopt this course. The cargo of the pinnace was accordingly transferred to the hold of the *Hoboken*. A short summary of their history was written, corked up in a bottle, and fastened to the mast of the *Mary*, which was then cut adrift. A tear gathered on the cheeks of the young men as they saw their old friend in adversity dropping slowly behind, and they did not withdraw their eyes from it till every vestige of its hull was lost in the shadows of the waters.

As Fritz and Jack were thus engaged in gazing listlessly on the ocean, and reflecting upon their altered prospects, and perhaps trying to penetrate the veil of the future, Willis came towards them rubbing his breast, as if he had been seized with a violent internal spasm.

"Hilloa," cried Jack, "the Pilot is sea-sick! Shall I run for some brandy, Willis?"

"No, stop a bit; we were in hopes of falling in with Captain Littlestone, were we not?"

"Yes; but what then?"

"We were disappointed, were we not?"

"Yes. That has not made you ill, has it?"

"No; somebody else has turned up; there is one of the *Nelson's* crew on board this ship."

"One of the *Nelson's* crew?"

"Aye, and if you only knew how my heart beat when I saw him."

"I can easily conceive your feelings," said Jack, "for my own heart has almost leaped into my mouth."

"And I am thunderstruck," added Fritz.

"I went towards my old friend," continued Willis, "with tears in my eyes, threw my arms round him, and gave him a hearty but affectionate hug."

"And what did he say?"

"Nothing, at first; but, as soon as I left his arms at liberty, he gave me such a punch in the ribs as almost doubled me in two; it was enough to knock the in'ards out of a rhinoceros — ugh!"

"A blow in earnest?" exclaimed Fritz in astonishment.

"Yes; there was no mistake about it; it was a real, good, earnest John Bull knock-down thump; it put me in mind of Portsmouth on a pay day — ugh!"

"Extremely touching," said Jack, smiling.

"Then, when I called him by his name Bill Stubbs, and asked what had become of the sloop, he said that he knew nothing at all about the sloop, and swore that he had never set his eyes on my figure-head before, the varmint — ugh!"

"Odd," remarked Jack.

"Are you sure of your man?" inquired Fritz.

"But you say his name is Bill, whilst he declares his name is Bob."

"Aye, he has evidently been up to some mischief, and changed his ticket."

"Then what conclusion do you draw from the affair."

"I am completely bewildered, and scarcely know what to think; perhaps the crew has mutinied, and turned Captain Littlestone adrift on a desert island. That is sometimes done. Perhaps——"

"It is no use perhapsing those sort of melancholy things," said Fritz; "we may as well suppose, for the present, that Captain Littlestone is safe, and that your friend has been put on shore for some misdemeanour."

"May be, may be, Master Fritz; and I hope and trust

it is so. But to have an old comrade amongst us, who could give us all the information we want, and yet not to be able to get a single thing out of him ——"

"Except a punch in the ribs," suggested Jack.

"Exactly; and a punch that will not let me forget the lubber in a hurry," added Willis, clenching his fist; "but I intend, in the meantime, to keep my weather eye open."

A few weeks after this episode the *Hoboken* was slowly wending her way along the bights of the Bahamas. Fritz, Jack, and Willis were walking and chatting on the quarter-deck. The sky was of a deep azure. The sea was covered with herbs and flowers as far as the eye could reach — sometimes in compact masses of several miles in extent, and at other times in long straight ribbons, as regular as if they had been spread by some West Indian Le Notre. The ship seemed merely displaying her graces in the sunshine, so gentle was she moving in the water. The air was laden with perfumes, and a soft dreamy languor stole over the friends, which they were trying in vain to shake off. In one direction rose the misty heights of St. Domingo, and in another the cloud-capped summits of Cuba. Sometimes the highest peaks of the latter pierced the veil that enveloped them, and seemed like islands floating in the sky, or heads of a race of giants.

"The air here is almost as balmy and fragant as that of New Switzerland," remarked Fritz.

"Aye, aye," said the Pilot; "but it is not all gold that glitters: in these sweet smells a nasty fever is concealed, with which I have no wish to renew my acquaintance."

"By the way, talking about acquaintances, Willis, have you obtained any further intelligence from your friend Bill, *alias* Bob?" inquired Jack.

"No, not a syllable; the viper is as cunning as a fox, and keeps his mouth as close as a mouse-trap."

"He seems as obstinate as a mule, and as obdurate as a Chinaman into the bargain."

"All that, and more than that; but," added Willis, "I have found out from the mate that he was pressed on board this ship at New Orleans."

"Pressed on board?" said Fritz, inquiringly.

"Yes; that is a mode of recruiting for the navy peculiar to England and the United States. Would you like to hear something about how the system is carried out?"

"Yes, Willis, very much."

"The transactions, however, that I shall have to relate are in no way creditable, either to myself or anybody else connected with them; and I am afraid, when you hear the particulars, you will be ready to turn round and say, your friend the Pilot is no good after all."

"Have you, then, been desperately wicked, Willis?"

"Well, that depends entirely upon the view you take of what I am to tell you. Listen."

24*

CHAPTER XXIII.

"When I was a youngster, about a year or two older than you are now, Master Fritz, I shipped on board the brig *Norfolk* as boatswain's mate. The ship at the time was short of hands, so there was no immediate probability of her weighing anchor; but on the same day I scratched my name on the books a despatch arrived, in consequence of which we left the harbor, and proceeded out to sea under sealed orders. One day, when off the Irish coast, I was called aft by the first lieutenant.

"'You know something of Cork, my man, I believe?' said he.

"'Yes, your honor, I have been ashore there once or twice,' said I.

"'Very good,' said he; 'get ready to go ashore there again as quick as you like.'

"Leave to go on shore is always agreeable to a sailor. He prefers the sea, but likes to stretch himself on land now and then, just to enjoy a change of air, and look about him a bit; so it was with all possible expedition that I made the requisite preparations.

"When I re-appeared, I found a party of twenty men mustered on deck in pipe-clay order. A full ration of small arms was served out to them, and, under the command of the lieutenant, we embarked in the long-boat and rowed ashore. We landed at a point of the coast some miles distant from Cork, and it was dark before we reached the military barracks of that town, which, for the present, appeared to be our destination.

"I had not the slightest idea of what we were to do on shore. From our being so heavily armed, I knew it was no mere escort or parade duty that was in question, and began to think there was work of some kind on hand. This gave me no kind of uneasiness. I only wondered whatever it could be, for there was clearly a mystery of some kind or other. Were we going to besiege Paddy, in his own peaceable city of Cork? Had some of the peep-o'-day boys been burning down farmer Magrath's ricks again? or was there a private still to be routed out and demolished? I could not tell.

"Half an hour after our arrival, I was called into a private room by the lieutenant, who was seated at a table with a package of clothes beside him. The first lieutenant of the *Norfolk*, I must remark, was a bit of an original. He had won his way up to the rank he then held from before the mast. His build was rather squat, and his face was garnished with a pair of fiery red whiskers, so he was no beauty, added to which he was reckoned one of the most rigid martinets in the service; yet, for all that, his crew liked him, for they knew his heart was in the right place.

"'See, my man,' said he, 'take this package, and rig yourself out in the toggery it contains.'

"I obeyed this order, and soon after stood before him, in a pair of jack-boots, with a slouching sort of tarpauling hat on my head, so that I might either have passed for a mariner out of luck or a dustman.

"'Well,' said the lieutenant, laughing, 'now you have quite the air of the hulks about you.'

"This remark not being very complimentary, I did not feel called upon to make any reply.

"'You know,' he continued, 'that the brig is short about a dozen hands, and I want you to pick up a few likely lads here. I understand there are a number of able-bodied seamen skulking about the public-houses, where they will likely remain as long as their money lasts. I should like to secure as many of them as possible, and then capture a few stout landsmen to make up the number; but, in the first place, I want you to go and find out the best place to make a razzia.'

"I stared when I found myself all at once promoted to

the post of pioneer for a party of kidnappers, and muttered something or other about honor.

"'Honor, sir!' roared the lieutenant, 'what has honor to do with it, sir? It is duty, sir. It is the laws of the service, sir, and you must obey them, sir.'

"'But it is hard, your honor,' said I, 'that the laws of the service should force men to do what they think is wrong.'

"'And what right, sir, have you to think it is wrong, or to judge the acts of your superiors? If the laws of the service order you fifty lashes at the yard-arm to-morrow, you will find that you will get them. Do you want to be handed over to the drummer, and to cultivate an acquaintance with the cat?'

"'No, your honor,' said I, laughing.

"The lieutenant's face by this time was as red as his whiskers, and, though he was in a towering rage, he quickly calmed down again, like boiling milk when it is taken off the fire.

"'Then,' said he, quietly, 'am I to understand you refuse?'

"'No, your honor,' said I. 'If it is my duty, I must obey; but you will pardon the liberty, when I say that it is hard to be forced to drag away a lot of poor fellows against their wills.'

"'Look ye,' replied the lieutenant, 'I tolerate your freedom of speech for two reasons—the first, because we are here alone, and no harm is done; the second, because I entertain the same opinion myself; but, mind you, we are both bound by the regulations of the service, and it is mutiny for either of us to disobey.'

"According to the moral law, the mission with which I was charged could scarcely be considered honorable; but, according to the laws of the land, or rather of the sea, it was perfectly unexceptionable. Amongst the seamen, a foray amongst the landlubbers was regarded more in the light of a spree than anything else. If, indeed, it were possible to pick up the lazy and idle amongst the population, this mode of enlistment might be useful; but often the industrious head of a family was seized, whilst the idle

escaped. It was rare, however, that a ship's crew were employed in this sort of duty; men were more usually obtained through the crimps on shore, who often fearfully abused the authority with which they were invested for the purpose. As for myself, the lieutenant's arguments removed all my scruples, if I ever had any.

"I then suggested a plan of operations, which was approved. The men were to be kept ready for action, and the lieutenant himself was to await my report at the ' Green Dragon,' one of the hotels in the town.

"At that time there was in the outskirts of Cork a sort of tavern and lodging-house, called the 'Molly Bawn.' This establishment was frequented by the lowest class of seamen and 'tramps.' Thither I wended my way. It was late when I arrived in front of the place; and whilst hesitating whether I should venture into such a precious menagerie, I happened to look round, and, by the light of a dim lamp that burned at the corner of the street, I caught a glimpse of the lieutenant leaning against the wall, quietly smoking an Irish dudeen."

"Like Rono the Great in the island of Hawai," suggested Jack.

"Something. This, however, cut short my deliberations. I walked in. There was a crowd of men and women drinking and smoking about the bar. These, however, were not the people I sought. The regular tenants of the house were not amongst that lot, and it was essential for me to find out in what part of the premises they were stowed. I commenced proceedings by ordering a noggin of whisky, and making love to the damsel that brought it in. After having formally made her an offer of marriage, I asked after the landlord. She told me he was engaged with some customers, but offered to take a message to him.

"'Then,' said I, 'just tell him that a friend of One-eyed Dick's would like to have a parley with him.'"

"And who was One-eyed Dick?" inquired Fritz.

"One of the crew of a piratical craft captured by one of our cruisers a few months before, and who at that time was safely lodged in Portsmouth jail.

"The girl soon returned. She told me to walk with

her, and led me through some narrow passages into what appeared to be another house. She knocked at a door that was strongly barred and fastened inside. A slight glance at these precautions made me aware that there was no chance of making a capture here without creating a great disturbance. So, after reflecting an instant, I decided upon adopting some other course.

"When the door was opened I could see nothing distinctly; there was a turf-fire throwing a red glare out of the chimney, a dim oil-lamp hung from the roof, but everything was hidden in a dense cloud of tobacco smoke, through which the light was not sufficiently powerful to penetrate."

"The atmosphere must have been stifling," observed Fritz,

"Yes, it puts me in mind of your remark about the air, which, you said, consists of — let me see ——"

"Oxygen and hydrogen."

"Just so; but the air a sailor breathes when he is at home consists almost entirely of tobacco smoke. At last, I could make out twenty or thirty rough-looking fellows seated on each side of a long deal table covered with bottles, glasses, and pipes. Dan Hooligan, the landlord, sat at the top — a fit president for such an assembly. He was partly a smuggler, partly a publican, and wholly a sinner. I should say that the liquor consumed at that table did not much good to the revenue. How Dan contrived to escape the laws, was a mystery perhaps best known to the police."

"'So you are a pal of One-eyed Dick's, are you?' said he.

"'Rather,' said I, adopting the slang of the place.

"'Well,' said he, 'Dick has been a good customer of mine, and all his pals are welcome at the 'Molly.' I have not seen him lately, however — how goes it with him now?'

"'Right as a trivet,' said I, 'and making lots of rhino.'

"'Glad to hear it; and what latitude does he hail in now?'

"'That,' said I, 'is private and confidential.'

"'Oh,' said he, 'there are no outsiders here, we are all sworn friends of Dick's, every mother's son of us.'

"'Then,' said I, 'Dick is off the Cove in the schooner *Nancy*, of Brest.'"

"Holloa, Willis," cried Jack, "there was a fib!"

"Well, I told you to look out for something of that sort when I began."

"'What!' cried the landlord, 'Dick in a schooner off the Irish coast?'

"'Yes,' said I; 'and aboard that schooner there is as tight a cargo of brandy and tobacco as ever you set eyes upon.'

"Here the landlord pricked up his ears, and the rest of the company began to listen attentively. The fellow that sat next me coolly told me that both he and Dick had been lagged for horse-stealing, and had subsequently broken out of prison and escaped. He further told me that most of the gentlemen present had been all, one way or another, mixed up with Dick's doings; from which I concluded they were a rare parcel of scamps, and resolved, within myself, to try and bag the whole squad. They were all stout fellows enough, most of them seamen. I thought they might be able to 'do the State some service,' and determined to convert them into honest men, if I could.'

"'Dick cannot come ashore,' said I; 'some one of his old pals here has peached, and there is a warrant out against him.'

"This information threw the assembly into a state of violent commotion. They rose up, and swore terrible vengeance against the head of the unfortunate culprit when they caught him. The oaths rather alarmed me at first, for they were of a most ferocious stamp.

"'Yes,' continued I, 'Dick is aboard the schooner, but, as there are two or three warrants out against him, he does not care about coming ashore; so said he to me, 'We want a lugger and a few hands to run the cargo ashore'; and if you look in at the 'Molly,' and see my old pal, Dan, perhaps you will find some lads there willing to give us a turn. The captain said, if the thing was done clean off, he would stand something handsome."

"'Just the thing for us!' shouted half a dozen voices.

"'But the lugger?' said I.

"'Oh, Phil Doolan, at the Cove, has a craft that has landed as many cargoes as there are planks in her hull. Besides, he has stowage for a fleet of East Indiamen.'

"'Well, gentlemen,' said I, 'the chaplain, One-eyed Dick, and myself, will be at Phil Doolan's to-morrow at midnight ; do you agree to meet us there?'

"This question was answered by a universal 'Yes;' and by way of clenching the affair, I ordered a couple of gallons of the stiffest potheen in the house. This was received with three cheers, and before I left the 'Molly' every man-jack of them had disappeared under the table. Dan himself, however, kept tolerably sober, and promised, on account of his friendship for One-eyed Dick, to have the whole kit safe at Phil Doolan's by twelve o'clock next night, and with this assurance I made my exit from the premises, and steered for the 'George and Dragon.'

"The lieutenant agreed with me in thinking that it would cause too much uproar to attack the 'Molly Bawn.' He congratulated me on my success in laying a trap for the people, and promising to meet me at the Cove, he ordered a car, and drove off in the direction of the *Norfolk's* boat. Early next morning I started to reconnoitre the ground and organize my 'plan of operations. I found Phil Doolan's mansion to be a mud-built tenement, larger, and standing apart from, the houses that then constituted the village. It was ostensibly a sailor's lodging-house and tavern for wayfarers, but, like the 'Molly Bawn,' was in reality a rendezvous of smugglers, occasionally patronized by fugitive poachers and patriots. It was known to its familiars as 'The Crib,' but was registered by the authorities as the 'Father Mahony,' who was represented on the sign-post by a full-length portrait of James the Second. What gave me most satisfaction was to observe that the building was conveniently situated for a sack.

"When night set in I marched the *Norfolk's* men in

close order, and as secretly as possible, to the Cove. Approaching Phil Doolan's in one direction, I could just catch a glimpse of the red coats of a file of marines advancing in another, with the lieutenant at their head, and, exactly as twelve o'clock struck on the parish clock, the 'Father Mahony' was surrounded on all sides by armed men. Two or three lanterns were now lit, and dispositions made to close up every avenue of escape.

"'There he is!' cried Willis, interrupting himself, and staring into the air.

"Who?" inquired Jack — "Phil Doolan?"

"No — Bill Stubbs, late of the *Nelson*."

"Where?"

"That squat, broad-shouldered man there, bracing the maintops."

"Yes, now that you point him out, I think I have seen him before," said Fritz.

"Holloa, Bill," cried Jack.

"You see," said Willis, "he turned his head."

"How d'ye do, Bill?" added Jack.

"Are you speaking to me, sir?" inquired the sailor.

"Yes, Bill."

"Then was your honor present when I was christened? I appear to have forgotten my name for the last six-and thirty years."

"No use, you see," said Willis; "he is too old a bird to be caught by any of these dodges. But I have lost the thread of my discourse."

"You had surrounded the cabin, and were lighting lamps."

"Half a dozen men were stationed at the door, pistol in hand, ready to rush in as soon as it opened. The lieutenant and I went forward and knocked, but no one answered. We knocked again, louder than before, but still no answer.

"'Open the door, in the King's name!' thundered the lieutenant. Silence, as before.

"Calling to the marines, he ordered them to root up Phil Doolan's sign-post, and use it as a battering ram against the door. The first blow of this machine nearly

25

brought the house down, and a cracked voice was heard calling on the saints inside.

"'Blessed St. Patrick!' croaked the voice, 'whativer are ye kicking up such a shindy out there for? Whativer d'ye want wid an old woman, and niver a livin' sowl in the house 'cept meself and Kathleen in her coffin?'

"'Kathleen is dead, then?' said the lieutenant with a grin.

"'Save yer honor's presence, she's off to glory, an' as dead as a herrin' replied the voice.

"'Really!' said the lieutenant, 'and where is Phil Doolan?'

"'Och, yer honor? he's gone to get some potheen for the wake.'

"'Well,' said the lieutenant, 'I should like to take a share in waking the defunct—what's her name?'

"'Kathleen, yer honor.'

"'Well, just let us in to take a last look at the worthy creature.'

"The door then creaked on its rusty hinges, and we entered. Not a soul, however, was to be seen anywhere, save and except the old woman herself. The coffin containing the remains of Kathleen, resting on two stools, stood in the middle of the floor, with a plate of salt as usual on the lid. I fairly thought I had been done, and looked upon myself as the laughing stock of the entire fleet."

"So far," remarked Jack, "you story has been all right, but the last episode was rather negligently handled."

"How?" inquired Willis.

"Why, you did not make enough of the coffin scene; your description is too meagre. You should have said, that the wind blew without in fierce gusts, the weathercocks screeched on the roofs, and caused you to dread that the ghost of the defunct was coming down the chimney; large flakes of snow were rushing through the half-open door; a solitary rushlight dimly lit up the chamber, and cast frightful shadows upon the wall."

"Well; but the night was fine, and there was not a breath of wind."

"What about that? A little wind, more or less, a weathercock or so, some drops of rain, or a few flakes of snow, do not materially detract from the truth, whilst they heighten the color of the picture."

"And if some lightning tearing through the clouds were added?"

"Yes, that would most undoubtedly increase the effect; but go on with your story."

"I knew Phil to be an artful dodger, and was determined not to be foiled by a mere trick, so I laid hold of a lantern and closely examined the walls and flooring. My investigation was successful, for just under the coffin I detected traces of a trap-door."

"'Well, my good woman, what have you got down there?" inquired the lieutenant.

"'Is it under-ground, ye mane, yer honor? divil a hail's there, if it isn't the rats.'

"'Well, just remove the coffin a little aside; we shall see if we cannot pepper some of the rats for you.'

"Here the old woman appealed to a vast number of saints, and protested against Kathleen's remains being disturbed. The lieutenant, however, grew tired of this farce, and ordered the coffin to be shifted. A sailor accordingly laid hold of each end.

"'Blazes!' said one, 'here is a body that weighs.'

"'Perhaps,' said the other, 'the coffin is lined with lead.'

"The trap-door was drawn up, and the lieutenant, pistol in hand, descended alone.

"'Now, my lads,' said he, addressing some invisible personages, 'we know you are here, and I call upon you to yield in the King's name — resistance is useless, the house is surrounded, and we are in force, so you had better give in without more ado.'

"No answer was returned to this exordium; but we heard the murmuring of muffled voices, as if the rapscallions were deliberating. I now descended with my lamp, followed by some of the seamen, and beheld my friends of the night before either stretched on the ground or propped up against the walls, like a lot of mummies in an Egyptian tomb.

"They were handcuffed one by one, pushed or hauled up the stairs, and then tied to one another in a line. When we had secured the whole lot of them in this way —

"'Lieutenant,' said I, winking, 'will you permit me to send a ball into that coffin?'

"'Please yourself about that, young man,' said he.

"Here the old woman recommenced howling again, and called upon all the saints in the calendar to punish me for my sacrilegious design.

"'Shoot a dead body,' said I, 'where's the harm?' Besides, what is that salt there for?'

"'To keep away evil spirits,' was the reply.

"'Very well,' said I, 'my pistol will scare them away as well.' Then, cocking it with a loud clink, I presented it slowly at the coffin."

"The lid all at once flew off — the salt was thrown on the ground with a crash — the defunct suddenly returned from the other world in perfect health, and sat half upright in his bier. I did not recognize the individual at first, but, on closer inspection, found him to be my communicative companion of the preceding night — the horse-stealer of the 'Molly Bawn;' and, being a stout young fellow, he was harnessed to the others, and we commenced our march to the boats."

"You do not appear to have had much trouble in effecting the capture," remarked Fritz.

"No; the men were unarmed, and were nearly all intoxicated. You never saw such a troop; scarcely one of them could walk straight; they assumed all sorts of figures; the file of prisoners was just like a bar of music, it was a string of quavers, crotchets, and zig-zags. Luckily, it was late at night, else we might have had the village about our ears, and, instead of flakes of snow and screeching weathercocks, we might have had a shower of dead cats and rotten eggs. Probably a rescue might have been attempted; at all events, we might have calculated on a volley of brickbats on our way to the boats. There would have been no end of commotion, uproar, confusion, and hubbub, possibly smashed noses, blackened eyes, broken heads——"

"Holloa, Willis!"

"You said just now that a little colouring was necessary."

"Certainly ; but the privilege ought not to be abused. Besides, broken heads and smashed faces are the realities, and not the accessories of the picture."

"Oh, I see. If it is night, the moon should be introduced ; and if it is day, the sun — and so on?"

"Of course ; and, if the circumstances are of a pleasing nature, you must leave horrors and terrors on your pallette; change gusts into zephyrs, snow into roses and violets, and the weathercocks into golden vanes glittering in the sunshine."

"I understand."

"You want to color a popular outbreak, do you not?"

"Yes."

"Then you should introduce a tempest howling, the waves roaring, the lightning flashing, and discord raging in the air as well as on the earth."

"Well, to continue my story. Although it was midnight, the disturbance began to wake up the villagers, and a crowd was collecting, so we hurried off our prisoners to the boats as speedily as we could. Some five and twenty able bodied men were thus added to his Majesty's fleet. The object of our visit to the Irish coast was accomplished, and the *Norfolk* continued her voyage to the West Indies. Now you know what is meant by the word *pressed,* and likewise the nautical signification of the word *press-gang.*"

"And you say that Bill Stubbs has been trapped on board this ship by such means?"

"Yes, at New Orleans."

"According to your story, then, that does not say very much in his favor?"

"No, not a great deal; still, that proves nothing — the fact of his calling himself Bob is a worse feature. A man does not generally change his name without having good, or rather bad, reasons for it."

"What appears to me," remarked Fritz, "as the most singular feature of your press-gang adventure is, that you are alive to tell it."

"Why so?"

" Because I think it ought to end thus : ' The victims of the press-gang strangled Willis a few days after.' "

" Aye, aye, but you do not know what a sailor is ; our recruits had not been a fortnight at sea before they entirely forgot the trick I had played them."

Just as Willis concluded his narrative, the man at the mast-head called out, " Sail ho !"

" Where away ? " bawled the captain.

" Right a-head," replied the voice.

The *Hoboken* had hitherto pursued her voyage uninterruptedly, and the Yankee captain now prepared to signalize himself by a capture.

CHAPTER XXIV.

THE captain of the *Hoboken* was rather pleased than otherwise when the lookout reported the strange sail to show English colors. He looked rather glum, however, half an hour afterwards, when the same voice bawled that she was a bull-dog looking craft, schooner-rigged, and pierced for sixteen guns. The Yankee had hoped to fall in with a fat West Indiaman, instead of which he had now to deal with a man-of-war, carrying, perhaps, a larger weight of metal than himself.

The heads of the two ships were standing in towards each other, there was no wind to speak of, but every hour lessened the distance that separated the antagonists.

"Pilot," said the captain, addressing Willis, "be kind enough to let me know what you think of that craft."

"I think," said Willis, taking the telescope, "I have had my eyes on her before. Aye, aye, just as I thought. An old tub of a Spaniard converted into an English cruiser, and commanded by Commodore Truncheon, I shouldn't wonder. She has caught a Tartar this time, however. Nothing of a sailer. If a breeze springs up, you may easily give her the slip, if you like, captain."

"Give her the slip! No, not if I can help it. My cruise hitherto has not been very successful, and I must send her into New York as a prize. Mr. Brill," added he, addressing the officer next in command, "prepare for action."

In an instant all was commotion and bustle on deck. Half an hour after, the captain, now in full uniform, took a hasty glance at the position of his crew. A portion of the men were stationed at the guns, with lighted matches.

Others were engaged in heating shot, and preparing other instruments of destruction. Jack and Fritz, armed with muskets, were ready to act as sharp-shooters as soon as the enemy came within range, and Willis was standing beside them, with his hands in his pockets, quietly smoking his pipe.

"What, Pilot!" exclaimed the captain in passing, "don't you intend to take part in the skirmish?"

"I am much your debtor, captain, but I cannot do that."

"And these young men?"

"They are not Englishmen, and your kindness to them entitles you to claim their assistance. I am sorry that honor and duty prevent me giving you mine."

"No matter, captain," said Fritz, "my brother and myself will do duty for three."

"Then, Pilot, you had better go below."

"With your permission, captain, I would rather stay and look on."

"But what is the use of exposing yourself here?"

"It is an idea of mine, captain. But I shall remain perfectly neutral during the engagement."

"As you like then, Pilot, as you like," said the captain, as he resumed his place on the quarter-deck.

At this moment a cannon ball whistled through the air.

"Good," said Willis; "the commodore gives the signal."

"That shot," observed Jack, "passed at no great distance from your head, Willis. You had better take a musket in self-defence. Besides, that ship is English, and you are a Scotchman."

"The ship is a Spaniard by birth," replied Willis, "and it is pretty well time it was converted into firewood, for the matter of that. But it is the flag, my boy — *that* is neither Spanish nor English."

"What is it, then?" inquired Fritz.

"It is the union-jack, Master Fritz. It is the ensign of Scotland, England, and Ireland united under one bonnet; and as such, it is as sacred in my eyes as if it bore the cross of St. Andrew."

Musket balls were now rattling pretty freely amongst the shrouds. The young men levelled their muskets and fired.

Soon after, the two ships were abreast of each other, and almost at the same instant both discharged a deadly broadside. The conflict became general. The crashing of the wood-work and the roaring of the guns was deafening. A thick smoke enveloped the two vessels, so that nothing could be seen of the one from the other; still the firing and crashing went on. The sails were torn to shreds, the deck was encumbered with fragments of timber; men were now and then falling, either killed or wounded, and a fatigue party was constantly engaged in removing the bodies. There are people who consider such a spectacle magnificent; but that is only because they have never witnessed its horrors.

Already many immortal souls had returned to their Maker; many sons had become orphans, and many wives had been deprived of their husbands; but as yet there was nothing to indicate on which side victory was to be declared. Soon, however, a cry of fire was raised, which caused great confusion; and another cry, announcing that the captain had fallen, increased the disorder.

A ball crashed through the taffrail, near where Jack and Fritz were standing; it passed between them, but they were both severely wounded by the splinters, and were conveyed by Willis to the cockpit. The doctor, seeing his old friend Jack handed down the ladder, hastened towards him and tore out a piece of wood from the fleshy part of his arm. He next turned to Fritz, who had received a severe flesh-wound on the shoulder. When both wounds were bandaged, he left the care of the young men to Willis, who had escaped with a few scratches, which, however, were bleeding pretty freely — to these he did not pay the slightest attention.

"How stands the contest?" inquired Fritz in a weak voice.

"The *Hoboken* is done for," replied Willis; "the commodore was preparing to board when we left the deck; but it does not make much difference; we shall go to England instead of America, that is all."

"God's will be done," said Fritz.

Just then Bill Stubbs was swung down in a hammock;

both his legs had been shot off by a cannon ball. The surgeon could only now attend to a tithe of his patients, so numerous had the wounded become. A glance at the new comer satisfied him that he was beyond all human skill, and he directed his attention to the cases that promised some hopes of recovery. Willis, seeing that his old comrade was abandoned to die almost uncared for, staunched his wounds as well as he could, fetched him a panniken of water, and performed a number of other little acts of kindness and good will. This he did, less with a view of obtaining an explanation from him at a moment when no man lies, than to mitigate the pangs of his last convulsions. For an instant the old mariner's body appeared re-animated with life. His eyes were fixed upon Willis with an ineffable expression of recognition and regret. He convulsively grasped the Pilot's hand and pressed it to his breast, and his lips parted as if to speak. Willis bent his ear to the mouth of the dying man, but all that followed was an expiring sigh. His earthly career was ended.

The hardy sailor who is supposed never to shed a tear, then wiped the corner of his eyes. Next he turned to the children of his adoption, whose pale faces indicated the amount of blood they had shed, and whose wounds, if he could have transferred them to himself, would have less pained his powerful muscles than they now grieved his excellent heart.

A party of boarders from the enemy had taken possession of the ship. Willis reported himself to the officer in command, and at his request, Fritz and Jack, together with the cargo of the pinnace, were conveyed on board the victorious schooner. Shortly after the *Hoboken* was despatched to Bermuda as a prize, with the prisoners, the wounded, and the dying.

The old tub that had gained this victory was named the *Arzobispo*, having, as Willis supposed, been captured in the Spanish Main. It was under the command of Commodore Truncheon, better known in the fleet by the *soubriquet* of Old Flyblow.

The *Arzobispo*, though old and clumsy, was a stout-built

craft; and so thick was its hide, that the broadsides of the Yankee had done the hull no damage to speak of. The superstructure, however, was completely shattered; the masts and rigging hung like sweeps over the sides; and, to the unpractised eye, the ship was a complete wreck. A few days, however, sufficed to put everything to rights again so far as regards external appearance; but how this impromptu carpentry would stand a storm was another question.

The commodore was on his way to Europe when he fell in with the Yankee, and, notwithstanding the disabled condition of the ship, he resolved to continue his voyage. Some of the officers expostulated with him on the hazard of crossing the Atlantic in so shaky a trim. He only got red in the face, and said that he had crossed the herring-pond hundreds of times in crafts not half so seaworthy. He was like the

> Froggy who would a wooing go,
> Whether his mother would let him or no.

The consequences of this defiance of advice were fatal to Old Flyblow; for, a week or two after his victory, he was pounced upon by the French corvette, *Boudeuse*, which was fresh, heavily armed, and well manned. The commodore's jury masts were knocked to pieces by the first broadside, his flag went by the board, and he was completely at the enemy's mercy. Willis lent a hand this time with a good will; but it was of no use, the wreck would not obey the helm, and the corvette hovered about, firing broadsides, and sending in discharges of musketry, when and where she liked. It was only when the commodore saw clearly that there was neither mast nor sail enough to yaw the ship, that he waved his cocked hat in token of surrender.

Fritz and Jack were still confined below with their wounds, when Willis brought them word that they would have to shift themselves and their cargo once more. The captain received them on board the *Boudeuse* with marked courtesy, and informed them that he was bound direct for Havre de Grace.

"It seems, then," said the Pilot, "that neither America nor England is to be our destination after all. But never mind, there are no lack of surgeons amongst the *mounseers.*"

"If we go on this way much longer," said Jack, sighing, "we shall be carried round the world without arriving anywhere. Alas, my poor mother!"

CHAPTER XXV.

AT first the three adventurers were regarded as prisoners of war; when, however, their entire history came to be known, and **their** extraordinary migrations from ship to ship authenticated, **they were** looked upon as guests, and treated as friends.

"I thought I had only obtained possession of n English cruiser," said the captain; "but I find I have also acquired the right of being useful to you."

The commander of the *Boudeuse* was a very different **sort** of a person from Commodore Truncheon; t e former treated his men as if every one o them had a itle and great influence at the Admiralty, whilst the latte swore at his crew as if the word of command could not b understood without a supplementary oath The English commodore might be the better sailor of the two, but certainly **the** French captain carried off the palm as regards politeness, urbanity, and gentlemanly bearing.

The wounds of Fritz and Jack were healing rapidly under the skilful treatment of the French surgeon, and, with a lift from Willis, they were able to w lk a portion of the day on deck. With reviving health, heir cheerful hopes of the future returned, their dorman spirits were re-awakened, and their minds regained th ir wonted animation.

"The corvette spins along admirably, said the Pilot, "and is steering straight for the Bay of Biscay."

"Ah!" said Jack, sighing, "it is very asy to steer for a place, but it is not quite so easy to get here. I am sick

26

of your friend the sea, Willis; and would give my largest
pearl for a glimpse of a town, a village, or even a street.”

“If you want to see a street in all its glory, Master
Jack, you must try and get the captain to alter his course
for Delhi.”

“But I should think, Willis, that there is nothing in the
street-scenery of Delhi to compare with the Boulevards of
Paris, Regent-street in London, or the Broadway of New
York.”

“Beg your pardon there, Master Jack; I know every
shop window in Regent-street; I have often been nearly
run over in the Broadway, and can easily imagine the turn
out on the Boulevards; but they are solitudes in comparison with an Indian street.”

“How so, Willis?”

“Well, it is not that there are more inhabitants, nor on
account of the traffic, for no streets in the world will beat
those of London in that respect—it is because the people
live, move, and have their being in the streets; they eat,
drink, and sleep in the streets; they sing, dance, and pray
in the streets; conventions, treaties, and alliances are
concluded in the streets; in short, the street is the Indians’
home, his club, and his temple. In Europe, transactions
are negotiated quietly; in India, nothing can be done
without roaring, screaming, and bawling.”

“There must be plenty of deaf people there,” observed
Jack.

“Possibly; but there are no dumb people. Added to
the endless vociferations of the human voice, there is an
eternal barking of dogs, elephants snorting, cows lowing,
and myriads of pigs grunting. Then there is the thump,
thump of the tam-tam, the whistling of fifes, and the
screeching of a horrible instrument resembling a fiddle,
which can only be compared with the Belzebub music of
Hawai. If, amongst these discordant sounds, you throw
in a cloud of mosquitoes and a hurricane of dust, you will
have a tolerable idea of an Indian street.”

“There may be animation and life enough, Willis, but I
should prefer the monotony of Regent-street for all that.
Would you like to air yourself in Paris a bit?”

"Yes, but not just now; the less my countrymen see of France, under present circumstances, the better."

"What is England and France always fighting about, Willis?"

"Well, I believe the cause this time to be a shindy the *mounseers* got up amongst themselves in 1788. They first cut off the head of their king, and then commenced to cut one another's throats, and England interfered."

"That," observed Fritz, "may be the immediate origin of the present war [1812]. But for the cause of the animosity existing between the two nations, you must, I suspect, go back as far as the eleventh century, to the time of William, Duke of Normandy."

"What had he-to do with it?"

"A great deal. He claimed a right, real or pretended, to the English throne. He crossed the Channel, and, in 1066, defeated Harold, King of England, at the battle of Hastings."

"Both William and Harold were originally Danes, were they not?" inquired Jack.

"Yes; I think Rollo, William's grandfather, was a Norman adventurer, or sea-king, as these marauders were sometimes called. William, after the victory of Hastings, proclaimed himself King of England and Duke of Normandy, and assumed the designation of William the Conqueror."

"Then how did France get mixed up in the affair?" inquired Willis.

"William's grandfather, when he seized the dukedom of Normandy, became virtually a vassal of the King of France, though it is doubtful whether he ever took the trouble to recognize the suzerainty of the throne. As sovereign, however, the King of France claimed the right of homage, which consisted, according to feudal usage, in the vassal advancing, bare-headed, without sword or spurs, and kneeling at the foot of the throne."

"Was this right ever enforced?"

"Yes, in one case at least. John Lackland—or, as the French called him, John Sans Terre—having assassinated his nephew Arthur, Duke of Brittany, in order to obtain possession of his lands, was summoned by Philip Augustus, King of France, to justify his crime. John did not obey the summons, was declared guilty of felony, and Philip took possession of Normandy. Thus the first step to hostilities was laid down."

"The English having lost Normandy, the vassalage ceased."

"Yes, so far as regards Normandy; but, in the meantime, Louis le Jeune, King of France, unfortunately divorced his wife, Elenor of Aquitaine, who afterwards married an English prince, and added Guienne, another French dukedom to the English crown."

"So another vassalage sprung up."

"Exactly. All the French King insisted upon was the homage; but Edward III. of England, instead of bending his knee to Philip of Valois, argued with himself in this way: 'If I were King of England and France as well, the claim of homage for the dukedom of Guienne would be extinguished.'"

"Rather cool that," said Jack, laughing.

"'We shall then,' Edward said to himself, 'be our own sovereign, and do homage to ourself, which would save a deal of bother.'"

"Well, he was right there, at least," remarked the Pilot.

"The King of France, however, entertained a different view of the subject. Hence arose an endless succession of sieges, battles, conquests, defeats, exterminations, and hatreds, which, no doubt, gave rise to the ill-feeling that exists at present between England and France. It is curious, at the same time, to observe what mischief individual acts may occasion. If William of Normandy had remained contented with his dukedom, and Louis le Jeune had not divorced his wife, France would not have lost the disastrous battles of Agincourt and Poitiers."

"Nor gained the brilliant victory of Bovines," suggested Jack.

"Certainly not; but she would have been spared the indignity of having one of her kings marched through the streets of London as a prisoner."

"True; but, on the other hand, the captured monarch would not have had an opportunity of illustrating the laws of honor in his own person. He returned loyally to England and resumed his chains, when he found that the enormous sum demanded by England for his ransom would impoverish his people: otherwise he could not have given birth to the maxim, 'That though good faith be banished from all the world beside, it ought still to be found in the hearts of kings.'"

"One of the kings of Scotland," remarked Willis, "was placed in a similar position. The Scottish army had been cut to pieces at the battle of Flodden, the king was captured in his harness, conveyed to London, and the people had to pay a great deal more to obtain his freedom than he was worth. But, before that, the Scotch nearly caught one of the Edwards. This time the English army had been cut to pieces; but the king did not wait to be captured, he took to his heels, or rather to his horse's hoofs. He was beautifully mounted, and followed by half a dozen Scottish troopers; away he went, over hill and dale, ditch and river. Dick Turpin's ride from London to York was nothing to it. The king proved himself to be a first-rate horseman, for, after being chased this way over half the country, he succeeded in baffling his pursuers. All these escapades between England and Scotland are, however, forgotten now, or at least ought to be; there are, doubtless, a few thick-headed persons in both sections of the empire who delight in keeping alive old prejudices, but they will die out in time."

"It seems, however, they have not died away yet," said Fritz, "in so far as regards France and England, since the two countries are at war again. But, as I observed before, had it not been for the ambition of William and the anti-connubial propensities of John, the English would never have been masters of Paris, and a great part of France under Charles VI."

"Still, in that case," persisted Jack, "Charles VII. would not have had the opportunity of liberating his country."

26*

"Then," continued Fritz, "history would not have had to record the shameless deeds of Isabella of Bavaria."

"Nor chronicle the brilliant achievements of Joan of Arc," added Jack.

"Any how," observed Willis, "the mounseers are a curious people. I have heard it remarked that they are occupied all day long in getting themselves into scrapes, and that Providence busies herself all night in getting them out again."

By chatting in this way, Fritz, his brother, and the Pilot contrived to relieve the monotony of the voyage, and to pass away the time pleasantly enough. Each contributed his quota to the common fund; Fritz his judgment, Jack his humor. and Willis his practical experience, strong good sense, and vigorous, though untutored under·standing. A portion of Jack's time was passed with the surgeon, between whom a great intimacy had sprung up. Time did not, therefore, hang heavily on the hands of the young men; for even during the night their thoughts were busy forming projects, or in embroidering the canvas of the future with those fairy designs which youth alone can create.

One morning Willis arrived on deck, pale, and with an air of fatigue and lassitude altogether unusual. He gazed anxiously into every nook and cranny of the ship.

"Whatever is the matter, Willis?" inquired Jack. "Have you seen the Flying Dutchman?"

"No, Master Jack," said he in a forlorn tone; "but I have either seen the captain or his ghost."

"What! the captain of the *Hoboken?*"

"No; the captain of the *Nelson.*"

"In a dream?"

"No, my eyes were as wide open as they are now; h· looked into my cabin, and spoke to me."

"Impossible, Willis."

"I assure you it is the case though, impossible or not."

"Where is he then?" exclaimed both the young men, starting.

"That I know not; I have looked for him everywhere."

"What did he say to you?"

"At first he said, How d'ye do, Willis?"

"Naturally; and what then?"

"He asked me what I thought of the cloud that was gathering in the south-west."

"Imagination, Willis."

"But look there, you can see a storm is gathering in that quarter."

"The nightmare, Willis. But what did you say to him?"

"I could not answer at the moment; my tongue clove to the roof of my mouth, and I rose to take hold of his hand."

"Then he disappeared, did he not?"

"Yes, Master Jack."

"I thought so."

"But I heard the door of my cabin shut behind him, as distinctly as I now hear the waves breaking on the sides of the corvette at this moment."

"You ought to have run after him."

"I did so."

"Well, did you catch him?"

"No; I was stopped by the watch, for I had nothing on me but my shirt; the officers stared, the sailors laughed, and the doctor felt my pulse. But, for all that, I am satisfied there is a mystery somewhere."

"But, Willis, the thing is altogether improbable."

"Well, look here; Captain Littlestone is either dead or alive, is he not?"

"Yes," replied Jack, "there can be no medium between these hypotheses."

"Then all I can say is this, that as sure as I am a living sinner, I have seen him if he is alive, and, if he is dead, I have seen his ghost."

"You believe in visitations from the other world then, Willis?"

"I cannot discredit the evidences of my own senses, can I?"

"No, certainly not."

"Besides, this brings to my recollection a similar circumstance that happened to an old comrade of mine. Sam Walker is as fine a fellow as ever lived, he sailed with me on board the *Norfolk*, and I know him to be incapable of telling a falsehood. Though his name is Sam Walker, we used to call him ' Hot Codlins.' "

" Why, Willis?"

" Because he had an old woman with a child tatooed on his arm, instead of an anchor, as is usual in the navy."

" A portrait of *Notre Dame de Bon Lecours*, I shouldn't wonder," said Jack ; " but what had that to do with hot codlins : a codlin is a fish, is it not? "

" I will explain that another time," said Willis, the shadow of a smile passing over his pale features. " The short and the long of the story is, that Sam once saw a ghost."

" Well, tell us all about it, Willis."

" But I am afraid you will not believe the story if I do."

" On the contrary, I promise to believe it in advance."

" Very well, Master Jack. Did you ever see a wind-mill ? "

" No, but I know what sort of things they are from de-scription."

" There are none in Scotland," continued Willis ; " at least I never saw one there."

" How do they manage to grind their corn then ? There should be oats in the land o' cakes, at all events," said Jack, with a smile.

" Well, in countries that have plenty of water, they can dispense with mills on land. Though there are no wind-mills in Scotland, there are some in the county of Durham, on the borders of England, for it appears my mate Sam was born in one of them. His father and mother died when he was very young, and he, conjointly with the rats, was left sole owner and occupant of the mill. Some of the neighboring villagers, seeing the poor boy left in this forlorn condition, got him into a charity school, whence he was bound apprentice to a shipmaster engaged in the coal trade, by whom he was sent to sea. The ship young Sam sailed in was wrecked on the coast of France, and he fell into the hands of a fisherman, who put the mark on his arm we used to joke him about."

" I thought so," said Jack ; " the mark in question rep-resents the patron saint of French sailors."

" After a variety of ups and downs, Sam found himself

rated as a first-class seaman on board a British man-of-war. He served with myself on board the *Norfolk*, and was wounded at the battle of Trafalgar [1806], which, I dare say, you have heard of."

"Yes, Willis, it was there that your Admiral Nelson covered himself with immortal renown."

"There and elsewhere, Master Fritz."

"It cost him his life, however, Willis, and likewise shortened those of the French Admiral Villeneuve and the Spanish Admiral Gravina; that, you must admit, is too many eggs for one omelet."

"As you once said yourself, great victories are not won without loss, and the battle of Trafalgar was no exception to the rule. Sam, having been wounded, was sent to the hospital, and when his wound was healed, he was allowed leave of absence to recruit his strength, so he thought he would take a run to Durham and see how it fared with the paternal windmill. Time had, of course, wrought many changes both outside and in, but it still remained perched grimly on its pedestal, but now entirely abandoned to the bats and owls. The sails were gone, and the woodwork was slowly crumbling away; but the basement being of hewn granite, it was still in a tolerable state of preservation. The place, however, was said to be haunted; exactly at twelve o'clock at night dismal howls were heard by the villagers to issue from the mill. According to the blacksmith, who was a great authority in such matters, Sam's father was a very avaricious old fellow, and had hid his money somewhere about the building; and you know, Master Jack, that when a man dies and leaves his money concealed, there is no rest for him in his grave till it is discovered."

"I really was not aware of it before," replied Jack; "but I am delighted to hear it."

"When Sam arrived, nobody disputed his title to the property, except the ghost; but Sam had seen a good deal of hard service, and declared that he would not be choused out of his patrimony for all the ghosts in the parish; and, in spite of the persuasions of the villagers, resolved to take up his abode there forthwith. Sam accordingly laid in a supply of stores, including a month's supply of tobacco and rum. He first made the place water-tight, then made a fire sufficient to roast an ox, and when night arrived made a jorum of grog, a little stiff, to keep away the damp. This done, he lit his pipe, and began to cook a steak for his supper. The old mill, for the first time since the decease of the former proprietor, was filled with the savory odor of roast beef."

"And there are worse odors than that," remarked Jack.

"Whilst the steak was frizzling, he took a swig at the grog; and, thinking one side was done, he gave the gridiron a twist, which sent the steak a little way up the chimney, and, strange to say, it never came down again.

"'Ten thousand What's-a-names,' cried Sam, 'where's my steak?'

"No answer was vouchsafed to this query; he looked up the chimney, and could see no one."

"The steak had really disappeared then?" said Jack, inquiringly.

"Yes, not a fragment remained; but he had more beef, so he cut off another; and, as his head had got a little muddled with the grog, he thought it just possible that he might have capsized the gridiron into the fire, so he quietly recommenced the operation."

"And the second steak disappeared like the first?"

"Yes, Master Fritz, with this difference — there was a dead man's thigh-bone in its place."

"An awkward transformation for a hungry man," said Jack.

"'Here's a go!' cried Sam, like to burst his sides with laughing, 'they expect to frighten me with bones, do they? they've got the wrong man — been played too many tricks of that kind at sea to be scared by that sort of thing. Ha, ha, ha! capital joke though.'"

"Your friend Sam must have been a merry fellow, Willis."

"Yes, but he was hungry, and wanted his supper; so he continued supplying the gridiron with steaks as long as the beef lasted, but only obtained human shin-bones, clavicles and tibias.

"'Never mind,' said Sam to himself, 'they will tire of this game in course of time.'

"When the beef was done, he kept up a supply of rashers of bacon, and threw the bones as they appeared in a corner, consoling himself in the meantime with his pipe and his grog."

"He must have been both patient and persevering," remarked Jack.

"This went on till a skull appeared on the gridiron."

"A singular object to sup upon," observed Jack.

"'I wonder what the deuce will come next,' said Sam to himself, throwing the skull amongst the rest of the bones.

"The next time, however, he took the gridiron off the fire, there was his last rasher done to a turn.

"'Now,' said Sam, 'I am going to have peace and quietness at last.'

"He sat down then very comfortably, and kept eating and drinking, and drinking and smoking, till the village clock struck twelve."

"Good!" cried Jack. "You may come in now, ladies and gentlemen; the performance is just a-going to begin."

"Sam heard a succession of crack cracks amongst the bones, and turning round he beheld a frightful-looking spectre, pointing with its finger to the door."

"Was it wrapped up in a white sheet?" inquired Jack.

"Yes, I rather think it was."

"Very well, then, I believe the story; for spectres are invariably wrapped up in white sheets."

"The bones, instead of remaining quietly piled up in the corner, had joined themselves together — the leg bones to the feet, the ribs to the back-bone — and the skull had stuck itself on the top. Where the flesh came from, Sam could not tell; but he strongly suspected that his own steaks and bacon had something to do with it. But, be that as it may, there was not half enough of fat to cover the bones, and the figure was dreadfully thin. Sam stared at first in astonishment, and began to doubt whether he saw aright. When, however, he beheld the figure move, there could be no mistake, and he knew at once that it was a ghost. Anybody else would have been frightened

out of their senses, but Sam took the matter philososophi-
cally and went on with his supper.

"'How d'ye do, old fellow?' he said to the spectre.
'Will you have a mouthful of grog to warm your inside?
Sit down, and be sociable.'

"The spectre did not make any reply, but continued
making a sign for Sam to follow.

"'If you prefer to stand and keep beckoning there till
to-morrow you may, but, if I were in your place, I would
come nearer the fire,' said Sam; 'you may catch cold
standing there without your shirt, you know.'

"The same silence and the same gesture continued on
the part of the ghost, and Sam, seeing that his words produced no effect, recommenced eating."

"There is one thing," remarked Jack, "more astonishing about your friend Sam than his coolness, and that is
his appetite."

"The spectre did not appear satisfied with the state of
affairs, for it assumed a threatening attitude and strode
towards the fire-place.

"'Avast heaving, old fellow,' cried Sam, 'there is one
thing I have got to say, which is this here: you may
stand and hoist signals there as long as ever you like; but
if you touch me, then look out for squalls, that's all.'

"The 'old fellow,' however, paid no attention to this
caution. He strode right up to the fire-place, and, whilst
pointing to the door with one hand, grasped Sam's arm
with the other. Sam started up, shook off the hand that
held him, and pitched into the spectre right and left.
But, strange to say, his hands went right through its bones
and all, just as if it had been made of the hydrogen gas
you spoke of the other day. Sam saw that it was no use
laying about him in this fashion, for the spectre stood
grinning at him all the time, so he gave it up.

"'I wish,' said he, 'you would be off, and go to bed,
and not keep bothering there.'

"Still the spectre maintained the same posture, and
kept pertinaciously pointing to the door.

"'Well,' said Sam, 'since you insist upon it, let us see
what there is outside. Go a-head, I will follow.'

"The spectre led him into what used to be the garden

of the mill, but the enclosure was now overgrown with rank and poisonous weeds. There was a path running through it paved with flagstones; the spectre pointed with its finger to one of them. Sam stooped down, and, much to his astonishment, raised it with ease. Beneath there was an iron chest, the lid of which he also opened, and saw that it was filled with old spade guineas and Spanish dollars.

"'You behold that treasure!' said the spectre, in a hollow voice.

"'Ha, ha, old fellow! you can speak, can you? Now we shall understand each other. Yes, I see a box, filled with what looks very like gold and silver coins.'

"'I placed that treasure there before my death,' added the spectre.

"'Ah, so! then you are dead?' said Sam.

"'One half of that money I wish you to give to the poor, and the other half you may keep to yourself, if you choose.'

"'Golley!' said Sam, 'you are not much of a swab after all, though you look as thin as a purser's clerk. Give us a shake of your paw, my hearty.'

"Here Sam, somehow or other, stumbled over the lamp, and when he got up again the spectre had vanished. He laid hold of the chest, however, and groped his way back to the mill. When safe inside, he made a stiff jorum of grog, and then fell comfortably asleep. That night he dreamt that he was eating gold and silver, that he was his own captain, that the cat-o'-nine tails was entirely abolished in the navy, and that his ship, instead of sailing in salt water was floating in rum. When he awoke, the sun was streaming through all the nooks and crannies of the old mill. All the marks of the preceding night's adventures were there—the gridiron, the empty rum jar, the the table overturned in the *mélée* with the ghost—but the chest of money was gone."

"And what did Sam conclude from that incident?" inquired Fritz.

"Well, he supposed that he had slept rather long, and

that somebody had come in before he was up and had walked off with the box."

"If I had been in his place," continued Fritz, "I should have said to myself that the mind often gives birth to strange fancies, particularly after a heavy supper, and that I had muddled my brain with rum ; consequently, that all the things I imagined I had seen were only the chimeras of a dream."

"But that could not be, Master Fritz, for two reasons ; the first, that the mark of the ghost's hand remained on his arm."

"Very likely burnt it when he grilled the bacon."

"The second, that the ghost was no more seen or heard of in the mill."

"That proof is a poser for you, brother, I think," said Jack.

"Did you heave that sigh just now, Master Fritz?" inquired Willis, in a low tone.

"It was not I," said Fritz, looking at his brother.

"Nor I," said Jack, looking at Willis.

"Nor I," said Willis, looking behind him.

CHAPTER XXVI.

THE corvette, notwitstanding the multitude of British cruisers scattered about the ocean, and the other dangers that beset her, held on the even tenor of her way. A gale sprung up now and then, but they only tended to give a filip to the common-place incidents recorded in the log. This quietude was not, however, enjoyed by all the persons on board. Willis was a prey to violent emotions; and so it often happens, in the midst of the profoundest calm, storms often rage in the heart of man.

Whether in reality or in a dream, Willis declared that Captain Littlestone paid him a visit every night, and invariably asked him precisely the same questions. On these occasions, Willis asserted that he distinctly heard the door open and shut whilst a shadow glided through. That he might once, or even twice, have been the dupe of his own imagination, is probable enough; but a healthy mind does not permit a delusion to be indefinitely prolonged — it struggles with the hallucination, and eventually shakes it off; providing always the mind has a shadow, and not a reality, to deal with, and that the patient is not a monomaniac. The dilemma was consequently reduced to this position — either Willis was mad, or Captain Littlestone was on board the *Boudeuse*.

In all other respects, Willis was perfectly sane. He himself searched every corner of the ship, but without other result than a confirmation of his own impression that there were no officers on board other than those of the corvette; and yet, notwithstanding his own conviction in daylight, he still continued to assert the reality of his interviews with Captain Littlestone during the night. The Italians say, *La speranza è il sogno d'an uomo svegliato.* Was Willis also dreaming with his eyes open? Might not the wish be father to the thought, and the thought produce the fancy? There is only one other supposition to be hazarded — could it be possible, in spite of all his researches, that Willis did see what he maintained with so much pertinacity he had seen?

These questions are too astute to admit of answers without due consideration and reflection; therefore, with the reader's permission, we shall leave the replies over for the present.

On the 12th June a voice from the mast-head called "Land ahoy!" much to the delight of the voyagers. The land in question was the island of St. Helena. This sea-girt rock had not at that time become classic ground. It had not yet become the prison and mausoleum of Napoleon the Great. The petulant squabbles between Sir Hudson Lowe and his illustrious prisoner had not been heard of. Little wotted then the proud ruler of France the fate that awaited him, for, when the *Boudeuse* touched at the island, all Europe, with the single exception of England, was kneeling at his feet.

On the 30th the Island of Ascension was reached. Here, in accordance with a usage peculiar to French sailors, a bottle, containing a short abstract of the ship's log, was committed to the deep. Willis thought this ceremony, under existing circumstances, would have been better observed in the breach than the observance, for, said he, if a British cruiser picked up that bottle within twenty-four hours, she stood a chance of picking up the *Boudeuse* as well.

On the 15th July the peak of Teneriffe hove in sight. This remarkable basaltic rock rises to the extraordinary height of three thousand eight hundred yards above the level of the sea; it is consequently seen at a considerable distance, and constitutes a valuable landmark for navigators in these seas. Six weeks later the *Boudeuse* dropped anchor in the Havre roads.

Here the three adventurers had to encounter by far the
greatest misfortune that had as yet befallen them. The
continental system of Napoleon was then in force. The
importation of everything English or Indian was strictly
prohibited. The cargo the young men had brought with
them from New Switzerland, which already had escaped
so many perils, was, therefore, declared contraband, and
seized by the French *fisc* — an institution that rarely permitted such a prize to quit its rapacious grasp.

Behold now our poor friends, Fritz and Jack, in a
strange land, deprived at once of their fortune and their
chance of returning home — the two beacons that had
cheered them on their way! All their bright hopes of the
future were thus annihilated at one fell swoop. Their
fortitude almost gave way under the severity of this blow;
the excess of their distress alone saved them. Grief
requires leisure to give itself free vent; but when we are
compelled, by absolute necessity, to earn our daily bread,
we cannot find time for tears; and such was the case with
Willis and his two friends; they were here without a
friend and without resources of any kind whatever.

If they had only known Greek and Latin; if they had
only been half doctors or three-quarter barristers, or if
even they had been doctors and lawyers complete, it
would have sorely puzzled their skill to have raised a
single sous in hard cash. Fortunately, however, whilst
cultivating their minds, they had acquired the art of handling a saw and wielding a hammer. The blouse of the
workman, consequently, fitted them as well as the gown
of the student, and they set themselves manfully to earn a
living by the sweat of their brow. They were carpenters
and blacksmiths by turns, regulating their occupations by
the grand doctrines of supply and demand.

Jack alone of the three was defective in steadiness; he
only joined Willis and his brother at mid-day. What he
did with himself during the forenoon was a profound
mystery. He rose before daybreak, and disappeared no
one knew where, or for what purpose. His companions in
adversity endeavored in vain to discover his secret; he
was determined to conceal his movements, and succeeded

in baffling their curiosity. To judge, however, by the ardor with which he worked, he was engaged in some one of those schemes that are termed follies before success, but which, after success, are universally acknowledged to be brilliant and praiseworthy instances of industrial enterprise.

If, after a hard day's work, when assembled together in the little room that served them for parlor, kitchen, and hall, the power of regret vanquished fatigue, and sadness drove away sleep, then Jack, who compared himself to Peter the Great, when a voluntary exile in the shipyards of Saardam, would endeavor to infuse a little mirth into the lugubrious party. If all his efforts to make them merry failed, all three would join together in a humble prayer to their Heavenly Father, who bestowed resignation upon them instead.

If Willis and his two friends were not accumulating wealth, at all events they were earning the bread they ate honestly and worthily. They had all three laid their shoulders vigorously to the wheel and kept it jogging along marvellously for a month. By that time, a detailed report of the seizure of their property had been placed before the director of the Domaine Extraordinaire, who was the sovereign authority in all matters pertaining to the exchequer of the empire. He saw at once that this capture was extremely harsh, and probably thought that, if it became known, it would raise a storm of indignation about the ears of his department. Here were two young men— Moseses, as it were, saved from the bulrushes. Lost in the desert from the period of their birth, and ignorant of the dissensions then raging in Europe, they were unquestionably beyond the ordinary operation of the law. This will never do, he probably said to himself; the civilization which these two young men have come through so many perils to seek ought not to appear to them, the moment they arrived in Europe, in the form of spoliation and barbarism.

The name of this *extraordinary* director of Domaine Extraordinaire was M. de la Boullerie, and, when we fall in with the name of a really good-hearted man, we delight to record it. He felt that the two young men had been

hardly dealt with, but he had not the power to order a
restitution of the property, now that the seizure had been
made, and sundry perquisities, of course, deducted by the
excise officials. Accordingly, he referred the matter to the
Emperor, who commanded the goods to be immediately
restored intact. Napoleon, at the same time, praised the
functionary we have named for calling his attention to the
merits of the case, and thanked him for such an opportunity of repairing an injustice.*

There are many such instances of generosity as the
foregoing in the career of the great Emperor — mild rays
of the sun in the midst of thunderstorms; sweet flowers
blowing here and there, in the bosom of the gigantic projects of his life — which many will esteem more highly
than his miracles of strategy and the renown of his battles.
As nothing that tends to elevate the soul is out of place
in this volume, we may be permitted to insert one or two
of these anecdotes.

In 1806, Napoleon was at Potsdam. The Prussians
were humbled to the dust, and the outrage of Rossbach
had been fearfully avenged. A letter was intercepted, in
which Prince Laatsfeld, civil governor of Berlin, secretly
informed the enemy of all the dispositions of the French
army. The crime was palpable, capital, and unpardonable. There was nothing between the life and death of
the prince, except the time to load half a dozen muskets,
point them to his breast, and cry — Fire. The princess
flew to the palace, threw herself at the feet of the Emperor,
beseeched, implored, and seemed almost heart-broken.
"Madam," said Napoleon, "this letter is the only proof
that exists of your husband's guilt. Throw it into the
fire." The fatal paper blazed, crisped, passed from blue
to yellow, and the treachery of Prince Laatsfeld was
reduced to ashes.

Another time, a young man, named Von der Sulhn,
journeyed from Dresden to Paris; unless you are told, you
could scarcely imagine for what purpose. There are

* This circumstance is historical, and will be found at length in
the Memoirs of Napoleon, by Amédée Goubard.

people who travel for amusement, for business, for a
change of air, or merely to be able to say they have been
at such and such a place. Some go abroad for instruction,
others, perhaps, with no other object in view than to eat
frogs in Paris, bouillabaisse at Marseilles, a polenta at
Milan, macaroni at Naples, an olla podrida in Spain, or
conscoussou in Africa. Von der Sulhn travelled to assas-
sinate the Emperor. Like Scævola and Brutus, he, no
doubt, imagined the crime would hand down his name to
posterity. In youth, all of us have erred in judgment
more or less. Sulhn thought the Emperor ought to be
slain. Unfortunately for him, the Duke of Rovigo, the
then minister of police, entertained a different opinion.
He thought, in point of fact, that the Emperor ought not
to be killed: hence it was that the young Saxon found
himself in chains, and that the Duke went to ask the
Emperor what he should do with him. We ought, however, to mention that the young man, in his character of
an enlightened German, testified his regret that he had not
succeeded in carrying out his project, and protested that,
in the event of regaining his liberty, he would renew
the attempt. "Never mind," said the Emperor to the
duke, "the young man's age is his excuse. Do not make
the affair public, for, if it is bruited about, I must punish
the headstrong youth, which I have no wish to do. I
should be sorry to plunge a worthy family into grief by
immolating such a scapegrace. Send him to Vincennes
give him some books to read, and write to his mother."
In 1814, the young man obtained his liberty, his family,
and his Germany, and it is to be hoped that he afterwards
became a respectable pater-familias, a sort of Aulic coun-
cillor, and that, during the troublesome times in the land
of Sauerkraut, he was before, and not behind, the barri-
cades of his darling patria. If he be dead, it is to be
supposed that, instead of lying a headless trunk ignomin-
iously in a ditch, or in the unconsecrated cemetery of Cla-
mort, he is reposing entire in the paternal tomb.

On the 15th of March, 1815, the Emperor landed at
Cannes — he had returned from the island of Elba. On
the beach he was joined by one man, at Antibes by a com-

pany, at Digne by a battalion, at Gap by a regiment (that of Labedoyere), at Grenoble by an army. The hearts of the soldiers of France went to him like steel to the loadstone—first a drop, and then a torrent; the Empire, like a snowball, increased as it progressed. At Lyons, the Count of Artois, the setting sun, is obliged to go out of one gate the moment that Napoleon, the rising sun, comes in at another. Smiles, orations, triumphal arches, and even the discourses that had been prepared to welcome the Bourbons, were used to congratulate their successor on his return. Cockades and flags were altered to suit the occasion, by inserting a stripe of red here and another of blue there. One national guard, but only one, remained faithful to the Bourbons; he would neither alter his cockade nor his colors, and remained true to his patrons in the hour of disaster. Everybody asked, what would the Emperor do with him? Would he be imprisoned or banished? Neither; the Emperor sent him a cross of the order of merit! It is, no doubt, grand to have overthrown the brilliant army of Murad Bey in Egypt; to have vanquished Melas, Wurmser, and Davidowich in Italy; Bragation, Kutusoff, and Barclay de Tolly in Russia; Mack in Germany; and thus to have reduced the entire continent of Europe to subjection. But it appears to us that a still greater feat was the victory he gained over himself, when, in the midst of the fever excited by his return, and the animosity of parties, he gave this cross to the solitary adherent of misfortune. Having made these slight digressions into the future, it is proper that we should return to our story.

The mysterious roads of Providence do not always lead to the places they seem to go; it often happens that, when we expect to be swallowed up by the breakers that surround us, we are wafted into a harbor, and that we encounter success where we only anticipated disappointment. The rigorous enactments of the continental system, that the other day had ruined the two brothers, became all at once the source of unlooked-for wealth; for, on account of the scarcity of colonial produce, a scarcity dating from the prohibitory laws promulgated in 1807, the merchandise of the young men had more than quadrupled in value.

From the grade of hard-working mechanics they were suddenly promoted to the rank of wealthy merchants. They consequently abandoned the laborious employments that for a month had enabled them to live, and to keep despair and misery at bay. Willis, greatly to his inconvenience, found himself transformed into a gentleman at large, which caused him to make some material alterations in the manipulation and quality of his pipes.

Fritz busied himself in collecting in, the by no means inconsiderable sums, which their property realised. He did not value the gold for its glitter or its sound, he valued it only as a means of enabling himself and his brother to return promptly to their ocean home. Jack undertook the task of finding a scalpel to save his mother—doubtless a difficult task; for how was he to induce a surgeon of standing to abandon his connexion, his family, and his fame, and to undertake a perilous voyage to the antipodes, for the purpose of performing an operation in a desert, where there were neither newspapers to proclaim it, academicians to discuss it, nor ribbons to reward it? As for the gentlemen of the dentist and barber school, like Drs. Sangrado and Fontanarose of Figaro, the remedy was even worse by a great deal than the disease. But, as we have said, Jack promised to find a surgeon, and the research was so arduous, that he was scarcely ever seen during the day by either Willis or his brother.

To Willis was confided the office of chartering a ship for the homeward voyage, and there were not a few obstacles to overcome in order to accomplish this. French shipmasters at that time engaged in very little legitimate business; they embarked their capital in privateering, preferring to capture the merchantmen of England to risking their own. One morning, Willis started as usual in search of a ship, but soon returned to the inn where they had established their head-quarters in a state of bewilderment; he threw himself into a chair, and, before he could utter a word, had to fill his pipe and light it.

"Well," said he, "I am completely and totally flabbergasted."

"What about?" inquired the two brothers.

"You could not guess, for the life of you, what has happened."

"Perhaps not, Willis, and would therefore prefer you to tell us at once what it is."

"After this," continued Willis, "no one need tell me that there are no miracles now-a-days."

"Then you have stumbled upon a miracle, have you, Willis?"

"I should think so. That they do not happen every day, I can admit; but I have a proof that they do come about sometimes."

"Very probably, Willis."

"It is my opinion that Providence often leads us about by the hands, just as little children are taken to school, lest they should be tempted to play truant by the way."

"Not unlikely, Willis; but the miracle!"

"I was going along quietly, not thinking I was being led anywhere in particular, when, all at once, I was hove up by —— If a bullet had hit me right in the breast, I could not have been more staggered."

"Whatever hove you up then, Willis?"

"I was hove up by the sloop."

"What sloop?"

"The *Nelson*."

"Was it taking a walk, Willis?" inquired Jack.

"Have you been to sea since we saw you last?" asked Fritz.

"If I had fallen in with the craft at sea, Master Fritz, I should not have been half so much astonished. The sea is the natural element of ships; we do not find gudgeons in corn fields, nor shoot hares on the ocean. But it was on land that I hailed the *Nelson*."

"Was it going round the corner of a street that you stumbled upon it, Willis?" inquired Jack.

"Not exactly; but to make a long story short——"

"When you talk of cutting anything short, we are in for a yarn," said Jack.

" And you are sure to interrupt him in the middle of it," said Fritz.

" Well, in two words," said Willis, knocking the ashes out of his pipe, " I was cruising about the shipyards, looking if there was a condemned craft likely to suit us — some of them had gun-shot wounds in their timbers, others had been slewed up **by a shoal** — and, to cut the **matter** short ———"

" Another **yarn**," suggested Jack.

" I luffed up beside the hull **of** a cutter-looking **craft** that had **been** completely gutted. But, changed and dilapidated as that hull is, I recognized it at once to be **that** of the *Nelson*. Now do you believe in miracles?"

" **But are you sure**, Willis?"

" Suppose you met Ernest or Frank in the street tomorrow, pale, meagre, and in rags, would you recognize them?"

" Most assuredly."

" Well, by the same token, sailors can always recognize a ship they have sailed in. They know the form of every plank and the line of every bend. There are hundreds of marks that get spliced in the memory, and are never forgotten. But in the present case there is no room for any doubt, a portion of the figure head is still extant, and the word *Nelson* can be made out without spectacles."

" But how did it get there?"

" You know, Master Fritz, it could not have told **me**, even if I had taken the trouble to inquire."

" Very true, Willis."

" I was determined, however, to find it out some other way, so I steered for a café near **the** harbor, where the pilots and long-shore captains go to play at dominoes. I was in hopes of picking up some stray waif of information, and, sooth to say, I was not altogether disappointed."

" Another meeting, I'll be bound," said Jack.

" My falling in with the *Nelson* astonished you, did it not?"

" Rather."

" Then I'll bet my best pipe that this one will surprise

you still more.   You recollect my comrade, Bill, *alias* Bob, of the *Hoboken?*"

" Yes, perfectly."

" Then I met him."

" What! the man who had both his legs shot off, and died in consequence of his wounds?" inquired Jack.

" The same."

" And that was afterwards thrown overboard with a twenty-four pound shot tied to his feet!" exclaimed Fritz.

" The same."

At this astonishing assertion the young men regarded Willis with an air of apprehension.

" You think I am mad, no doubt, do you not?"

" Whatever can we think, Willis?"

" I admit that my statement looks very like it at first sight, but still you are wrong, as you will see by-and-by. I could scarcely believe my eyes when I saw him. 'Is that you, Bill Stubbs,' says I, 'at last?'

" ' Lor love ye!' says he, 'is that you, Pilot?'

" He then took hold of my hand, and gave it such a shake as almost wrenched it off.

" ' Where in all the earth did you hail from?' he said. 'I thought you were dead and gone?'

" ' And I thought you were the same,' said I, 'and no mistake.'

" ' Alive and hearty though, as you see, Pilot; only a little at sea amongst the *mounseers.*'

" ' But what about the *Hoboken?*' says I.

" ' What *Hoboken?*' says he.

" ' Were you not aboard a Yanke cruiser some months back?'

" ' Never was aboard a Yankee in all my life,' says Bill.

" And no more he was, for he never left the *Nelson* till she was high and dry in Havre dock-yard; so, the short and the long of it is, that I must have been wrong in that instance."

" So I should think," remarked Fritz.

" Yet the resemblance was very remarkable; the only

difference was a carbuncle on the nose, which the real Bill has and the other has not, but which I had forgotten."

"Like Cicero," remarked Jack.

"Another Admiral?" inquired Willis, drily.

"No, he was only an orator."

"Bill soon satisfied me that he was the very identical William Stubbs, and that the other was only a very good imitation."

"He did not receive you with a punch in the ribs, at all events, like the apocryphal Bill," remarked Jack.

"No; but what is more to the purpose, he told me that, after having struggled with the terrible tempest off New Switzerland — which you recollect — the *Nelson* found herself at such a distance, that Captain Littlestone resolved to proceed on his voyage, and to return again as speedily as possible.

"'We arrived at the Cape all right,' added Bill, 'landed the New Switzerland cargo, and sailed again with the Rev. Mr. Wolston on board. A few days after leaving the Cape, we were pounced upon by a French frigate; the *Nelson*, with its crew, was sent off as a prize to Havre, and here I have been ever since,' said Bill, ' a prisoner at large, allowed to pick up a living as I can amongst the shipping.'"

"And the remainder of the crew?" inquired Fritz.

"Are all here prisoners of war."

"And the Rev. Mr. Wolston and the captain?"

"Are prisoners on parole."

"Where?"

"Here."

"What! in Havre?"

"Yes, close at hand, in the Hotel d'Espagne."

"And we sitting here," cried Jack, snatching up his hat and rushing down stairs four steps at a time.

Willis and Fritz followed as fast as they could.

When they all three reached the bottom of the stairs.

"If Captain Littlestone is here, Willis," said Jack, "he could not have been on board the *Boudeuse*."

"That is true, Master Jack."

" In that case, Great Rono, you must have been dreaming in the corvette as well as in the Yankee."

" No," insisted Willis, " it was no dream, I am certain of that."

" Explain the riddle, then."

" I cannot do that just at present, but it may be cleared up by-and-by, like all the mysteries and miracles that surround us."

CHAPTER XXVII.

CAPTAIN LITTLESTONE IS FOUND, AND THE REV. MR. WOLSTON IS
SEEN FOR THE FIRST TIME.

JACK, on arriving at the hotel, ascertained the number
of the room in which Captain Littlestone was located.
In his hurry to see his old friend, the young man did not
stop to knock at the door, but entered without ceremony,
with Fritz and Willis at his heels. They found themselves in the presence of two gentlemen, one of whom sat
with his face buried in his hands, the other was reading
what appeared to be a small bible.

The latter was a young man seemingly of about twenty-
four or twenty-five years of age. He had a mild but noble bearing, and his aspect denoted habitual meditation.
His eyes were remarkably piercing and expressive; in
short, he was one of those men at whom we are led involuntarily to cast a glance of respect, without very well
knowing why; perhaps it might be owing to the gravity
of his demeanour, perhaps to the peculiar decorum of his
deportment, or perhaps to the scrupulous propriety of his
dress. He raised his eyes from the book he held in his
hand, and gazed tranquilly at the three figures who had so
abruptly interrupted his reveries.

" May I inquire," said he, " to what we owe this in-
trusion on our privacy, gentlemen ? "

" We have to apologise for our rudeness," said Fritz;
" but are you not the Rev. Mr. Wolston ? "

" My name is Charles Wolston, and I am a minister of
the gospel, and missionary of the church."

" Then, sir," continued Fritz, " I am the bearer of a
message from your father."

" From my father ! " exclaimed the missionary, starting
up ; " you come then from the Pacific Ocean ? "

Here the second gentleman raised his head, and looked as if he had just awakened from a dream. He gazed at the speakers with a puzzled air.

"Do you know me, captain?" said Willis.

Littlestone, for it was he, continued to gaze in mute astonishment, as if the events of the past had been defiling through his memory; and he probably thought that the figures before him were mere phantom creations of his brain.

"Willis! can it be possible?" he exclaimed, taking at the same time the Pilot's proffered hand.

"Yes, captain, as you see."

"And the two young Beckers, as I live!" cried Littlestone.

"Yes," said Jack, "and delighted to find you at last."

Littlestone then shook them all heartily by the hand.

"It is but a poor welcome that I, a prisoner in the enemy's country, can give you to Europe; still I am truly overjoyed to see you. But where have you all come from?"

"From New Switzerland," replied Jack.

"But how?"

"By sea."

"That, of course; and I presume another ship anchored in Safety Bay?"

"No, captain. Seeing you did not return to us, we embarked in the pinnace and came in search of you."

"Your pinnace was but indifferently calculated to weather a gale, keeping out of view the other dangers incidental to such a voyage."

"True, captain; but my brother and I, with Willis for a pilot and Providence for a guardian, ventured to brave these perils; and here we are, as you see."

"And your mother consented to such a dangerous proceeding, did she?"

"It was for her, and yet against her will, that we embarked on the voyage."

"I do not understand."

"For her, because, when we left, she was dying."

"Dying, say you?"

28*

" Yes, and our object in coming to Europe was chiefly to obtain surgical aid."

" And have you found a surgeon ? "

" Not yet, but we are in hopes of finding one."

" If money is wanted, besides the value of the cargo I landed for you at the Cape, you may command my purse."

" A thousand thanks, captain, but the merchandise we have here is likely to be sufficient for our purpose. Unfortunately, gold is not the only thing that is requisite."

" What, then ? "

" In the first place, a disinterested love of humanity is needful ; there are few men of science and skill who would not risk more than they would gain by accepting any offer we can make. It is not easy to find the heart of a son in the body of a physician."

" What, then, will you do, my poor friend ? "

" That is my secret, captain."

During this conversation, the missionary had put a thousand questions to Willis and Fritz relative to his father, mother, and sisters, and a smile now and then lit up his features as Fritz related some of the family mishaps.

" You must have undergone some hardships in your voyage from the antipodes to Havre de Grace," said Littlestone to Jack, " notwithstanding the skill of my friend the Pilot."

" Yes, captain, a few," replied Jack. " I myself made a narrow escape from being killed and eaten by a couple of savages."

" And how did you escape ? "

" Providence interfered at the critical moment."

" Well, so I should imagine."

" Our friend the Pilot was more fortunate ; he was abducted by the natives of Hawai ; but, instead of converting him into mincemeat, they transformed him into a divinity, bore him along in triumph to a temple, where he was perfumed with incense, and had sacrifices offered up to him."

" Willis must have felt himself highly honored," said the captain, smiling.

" These fine things did not, however, last long, for next day they were wound up with a cloud of arrows."

" And another interposition of Providence?"

" Yes, none of the arrows were winged with death."

" After that," remarked Willis, "we fell in with a Yankee cruiser, were taken on board, and carried into the latitude of the Bahamas. where we fell in with Old Flyblow, who, after a tough set-to, sent the Yankee a prize to Bermuda, and took us on board as passengers."

" And," added Jack, "whilst we were under protection of the American flag, Willis fell in with a certain Bill Stubbs, who was shot in the fight and died of his wounds. This trifling accident did not, however, prevent Willis falling in with him alive in Havre."

" You still seem to delight in paradoxes, Master Jack," said the captain.

" The English cruiser," continued Jack, "was afterwards captured by a French corvette, on which it appears you were on board *incognito*."

" What! I on board?"

" Yes; ask Willis."

" If you were not, captain, how could you come to my cabin every night and ask me questions?" inquired the latter.

At this point, a shade of anxiety crossed Littlestone's features; he turned and looked at the missionary — the missionary looked at Fritz — Fritz stared at his brother — Jack gazed at Willis — and Willis, with a puzzled air, regarded everybody in turn.

" At last," continued Jack, "after experiencing a variety of both good and bad fortune, sometimes vanquished and sometimes the victors, first wounded, then cured, we arrived here in Havre, where, for a time, we were plunged into the deepest poverty; we were blacksmiths and carpenters by turns, and thought ourselves fortunate when we had a chair to mend or a horse to shoe."

" The workings of Providence," said the missionary, " are very mysterious, and, perhaps, you will allow me to illustrate this fact by drawing a comparison. A ship is at the mercy of the waves; it sways, like a drunken man, sometimes one way and sometimes another. All on board are in commotion, some are hurrying down the hatchways, and others are hurrying up. The sailors are twisting the sails about in every possible direction. Some of the men are closing up the port-holes, others are working at the pumps. The officers are issuing a multiplicity of orders at once, the boatswain is constantly sounding his whistle. There is no appearance of order, confusion seems to reign triumphant, and there is every reason to believe that the commands are issued at random."

"I have often wondered," said Jack, "how so many directions issued on ship board in a gale at one and the same moment could possibly be obeyed."

" Let us descend, however, to the captain's cabin," continued the missionary. "He is alone, collected, thoughtful, and tranquil, his eye fixed upon a chart. Now he observes the position of the sun, and marks the meridian ; then he examines the compass, and notes the polary deviation. On all sides are sextants, quadrants, and chronometers. He quietly issues an order, which is echoed and repeated above, and thus augments the babel on deck."

" A single order," remarked Willis, "often gives rise to changes in twenty different directions."

" On deck," continued the missionary, " the crew appear completely disorganized. In the captain's cabin, you find that all this apparent confusion is the result of calculation, and is essential to the safety of the ship."

" Still," said Jack, " it is difficult to see how this result is effected by disorder."

" True ; and, therefore, we must rely upon the skill of the captain ; we behold nothing but uproar, but we know that all is governed by the most perfect discipline. So it is with the world ; society is a ship, men and their passions are the mast, sails, rigging, the anchors, quadrants, and sextants of Providence. We understand nothing of the combined action of these instruments; we tremble at every shock, and fear that every whirlwind is destined to sweep us away. But let us penetrate into the chamber of the Great Ruler. He issues his commands tranquilly; we see that He is watching over our safety; and whatever happens, our hearts beat with confidence, and our minds are at rest."

"Therefore," added Littlestone, "we are resigned to our fate as prisoners of war; but still we hope."

"And not without good reason," said Willis; "for it will go hard with me if I do not realize your hopes, and that very shortly too."

"I do not see very well how our hopes of liberty can be realized till peace is proclaimed."

"Peace!" exclaimed Willis. "Yes, in another twenty years or so, perhaps; to wait for such an unlikely event will never do; my young friend, Master Jack Becker, is in a hurry, and we must all leave this place within a month at latest."

"You mean us, then, to make our escape, Willis; but that is impossible."

"I have an idea that it is not impossible, captain; the cargo Masters Fritz and Jack have here will realize a large sum; the pearls, saffron, and cochineal, are bringing their weight in gold. I shall be able to charter or buy a ship with the proceeds, and some dark night we shall all embark; and if a surgeon is not willing to come of his own accord, I shall press the best one in the place: it won't be the first time I have done such a thing, with much less excuse."

"One will be willing," said Jack; "so you need not introduce One-eyed Dick's schooner here, Willis."

"So far so good, then; it only remains for us to smuggle the captain, the missionary, and the crew of the *Nelson* on board."

"But we are prisoners," said Littlestone.

"I know that well enough; if you were not prisoners, of course there would be no difficulty."

"Recollect, Willis, we are not only prisoners, but we are on parole."

"True," said Willis, scratching his ear, "I did not think of that."

"The situation," remarked Jack, "is something like that of Louis XIV. at the famous passage of the Rhine, of whom Boileau said: 'His grandeur tied him to the banks.' Had you been only a common sailor, captain, a parole would not have stood in the way of your escape."

"But," said Willis, "the parole can be given up, can it not ?"

"Not without a reasonable excuse," replied the captain.

"Well," continued Willis, "you can go with the minister to the Maritime Prefect, and say: 'Sir, you know that everyone's country is dear to one's heart, and you will not be astonished to hear that myself and friend have an ardent desire to return to ours. This desire on our part is so great, that some day we may be tempted to fly, and, consequently, forfeit our honor; for, after all, there are only a few miles of sea between us and our homes. We ought not to trust to our strength when we know we are weak. Do us, therefore, the favor to withdraw our parole; we prefer to take up our abode in a prison, so that, if we can escape, we may do so with our honor intact.'

"And suppose this favor granted, we shall be securely shut up in a dungeon. I scarcely think that would alter our position for the better, or render our escape practicable."

"You will, at all events, be free to try, will you not ?"

"That is a self-evident proposition, Willis, and, so far as that goes, I have no objection to adopt the alternative of prison fare. What say you, minister?"

"As for myself," replied the missionary, "a little additional hardship may do me good, for the Scriptures say: Suffering purifieth the soul."

"We shall, therefore, resign our paroles, Willis; but bear in mind that it is much easier to get into prison than to get out."

"Leave the getting out to me, captain; where there's a will there's always a way."

"Do you think," whispered the captain to Fritz, "that Willis is all right in his upper story?"

Fritz shook his head, which, in the ordinary acceptation of the sign, means, I really do not know.

CAAPTER XXVIII.

THREE weeks after the events narrated in the foregoing
chapter, the thrice-rescued produce of Oceania had been
converted into the current coin of the empire.

The greater portion of the proceeds was placed at the
disposal of Willis, to facilitate him in procuring the means
of returning to New Switzerland. He — like connoisseurs
who buy up seemingly worthless pictures, because they
have detected, or fancy they have detected, some masterly
touches rarely found on modern canvas — had bought, not
a ship, but the remains of what had once been one. This
he obtained for almost nothing, but he knew the value of
his purchase. The carcass was refitted under his own eye,
and, when it left the ship-yard, looked as if it had been
launched for the first time. The timbers were old; but
the cabins and all the internal fittings were new; a few
sheets of copper and the paint-brush accomplished the
rest. When the mast was fitted in, and the new sails bent,
the little sloop looked as jaunty as a nautilus, and, according to Willis himself, was the smartest little craft that
ever hoisted a union-jack.

Whether the captain and the missionary still entertained
the belief that the Pilot's wits had gone a wool-gathering
or not, certain it is that they had followed his instructions,
in so far as to relinquish their parole, and thus to lose their
personal liberty. They were both securely locked up in
one of the rooms or cells of the old palace or castle of
Francois I., which was then, and perhaps is still, used as
the state prison of Havre de Grace. This fortalice chiefly
consists of a battlemented round tower, supported by strong

CONCLUSION.

THREE months after leaving the Cape, the coast of New Switzerland was telegraphed from the mast head by Bill Stubbs. A gun was immediately fired, and towards evening the *Nelson* entered Safety Bay. Fritz, Jack, Captain Littlestone, the missionary, and Willis, were all standing on deck, eagerly scanning the shore.

"There is father!" cried Jack, "armed with a telescope; and now I see Frank and Mrs. Wolston."

"There comes Mr. Wolston and Master Ernest," cried Willis, "as usual, a little behind."

"But I see nothing of my mother and the young ladies!" said Fritz.

"Very odd," said Captain Littlestone, sweeping the horizon with his glass "I can see nothing of them either."

A horrible apprehension here glided into the hearts of the young men. They knew well that, had their mother been able, she would have been the first to welcome them home. Perhaps, under the inspiration of despair, their lips were opening to deny the mercy of that Providence which had hitherto so remarkably befriended them, when at a great distance, and scarcely perceptible to the naked eye, they descried three figures advancing slowly towards the shore.

One of these forms was Mrs. Becker, who was leaning upon the arms of Mary and Sophia Wolston.

"God be thanked, we are still in time," cried Fritz and Jack.

A loud cheer, led by Willis, then rent the air. Half an hour after, the two young men leaped on shore; they did not stay to shake hands with their father and brothers, but ran on to where their mother stood. It was a long time before they could utter a syllable; the greeting of the mother and her children was too affectionate to be expressed in words.

Next morning, at daybreak, preparations for a serious operation were made in Mrs. Becker's room. The entire colony was in a state of intense excitement, and an air of anxiety was imprinted on every countenance. In the room itself the wing of a fly could have been heard, so breathless was the silence that prevailed. The patient's eyes had been bandaged, under pretext of concealing from her sight the surgical instruments and preparations for the operation. The real design, however, was to hide the operator, whom Mrs. Becker supposed to be an expert practitioner from Europe; for it was not thought advisable that a mother's anxieties should be superadded to the patient's sufferings.

At the moment of trial the few persons present had sunk on their knees; Jack alone remained standing at the bedside of his mother. The Jack of the past had entirely disappeared; he was somewhat pale, very grave, but collected, firm, and resolute. It was, perhaps, the first instance on record of a son being called upon to lacerate the body of his mother. But the moment that God imposed such a task upon one of His creatures, it is God himself that becomes the operator.

When, some days after, Mrs. Becker — calm, radiant, and saved — requested to see and thank her deliverer, it was Jack who presented himself. If she had known this sooner, it would, most undoubtedly, have augmented her terror, and increased the fever. As it was, it redoubled her thankfulness, and hastened her recovery.

Frank and Ernest embarked on board the *Nelson* when she returned to New Switzerland on her way to Europe. Two years afterwards, the former returned in the capacity of a minister of the Church of England, bringing with him a sufficient number of men, women, and children to furnish a respectable congregation; and it was rumored, though with what degree of truth I will not venture to say, that one of the young lady passengers in the ship was his destined bride. Ernest remained some years in Europe, partly to consolidate relations between the colony and the mother country, and partly with a view to realize his pet project of establishing an observatory in New Switzerland.

Willis, instead of being suspended at the yard-arm as he had insisted on prognosticating, received his lieutenancy in due course, accompanied by a highly flattering letter from the Lords of the Admiralty, thanking him, in the name of the captain and crew of the *Nelson*, for his exertions in their behalf. As soon, however, as peace was proclaimed, he retired on half-pay, and, with his wife and daughter, emigrated to Oceania. He assumed his old post of admiral on Shark's Island, where a commodious house had been erected. We must premise, at the same time, that to his honorary duties as admiral, conjoined the humbler, but not less useful, offices of lighthouse keeper, manager of the fisheries, and harbor-master.

As a country grows rich, and advances in prosperity, it rarely, if ever, happens that the sum of human life becomes happier or better. It is, therefore, not without regret we learn that gold has been discovered in a land so highly favored by nature in other respects; for, if such be the case, then adieu to the peace and tranquillity its inhabitants have hitherto enjoyed. The colony will soon be overrun with Chinamen, American adventurers, and ticket-of-leave convicts. Farewell to the kindliness and hospitality of the community, for they will inevitably be deluged with the refuse of the old, and also, alas! of the new world.

THE END.